About the Author

Pat was born in the 'Black Country' of the West Midlands and still resides there. She studied psychology and still finds people and their stories fascinating. A more recent interest in family trees and ancestry provided the spark for the Ellie Black novels. When not writing she can be found indulging her other passion of horses and the countryside.

Fire and Stone

Pat Daniel

Fire and Stone

Olympia Publishers
London

www.olympiapublishers.com
OLYMPIA PAPERBACK EDITION

Copyright ©Pat Daniel 2024

The right of Pat Daniel to be identified as author of
this work has been asserted in accordance with sections 77 and 78 of
the Copyright, Designs and Patents Act 1988.

All Rights Reserved

No reproduction, copy or transmission of this publication
may be made without written permission.
No paragraph of this publication may be reproduced,
copied or transmitted save with the written permission of the publisher,
or in accordance with the provisions
of the Copyright Act 1956 (as amended).

Any person who commits any unauthorised act in relation to
this publication may be liable to criminal
prosecution and civil claims for damage.

A CIP catalogue record for this title is
available from the British Library.

ISBN: 978-1-80074-399-1

This is a work of fiction.
Names, characters, places and incidents originate from the writer's
imagination. Any resemblance to actual persons, living or dead, is
purely coincidental.

First Published in 2024

Olympia Publishers
Tallis House
2 Tallis Street
London
EC4Y 0AB

Printed in Great Britain

CHAPTER ONE

Only half a year ago Eleanor Black had been a librarian in London but life had taken one of its inimitable turns and the path which had seemed to be prescribed changed dramatically. She had always thought she didn't have any family and was alone in the world except for her adoptive parents. They had been much loved and were now sadly dead but had bought her up to make her own way in the world. After a chance moment of being in the wrong place at the wrong time she had found out she had a twin. This knowledge came to Ellie after she had been kidnapped, shot at, and generally had her life messed about with by Mr. A. Morgan, one of the richest men in Christendom. She had always seemed to manage to crop up in his life without even trying, and their paths and swords had crossed with a vengeance. Alistair, as that was his name, had tried to force Ellie to stay with him but she was having none, until he had used some sort of supernatural legacy to bind her to him. He had always asserted that until he had met his twin, Ellie, his life hadn't been complete. He wasn't an ungenerous man and Ellie had enjoyed the privileged lifestyle of being a 'Morgan' if not in name but in lineage. The legacy of the powers passed down through the Morgan line had become apparent to them both and Alistair hadn't been able to resist using them to his own advantage. Ellie had been horrified by this and couldn't believe that such powers existed on Earth. The showdown had come at Alistair's French Chateau when she had challenged him to prove what he said he could do. Basically, he had to put his money, lots of it, where his mouth was. He was unable to back down from such a challenge and had summoned an entity which had nearly destroyed them both. It had been sent back to Hell on this occasion but had reduced the chateau to rubble in the process.

Ellie was engaged to be married to Rory McGovern and had felt her life had been mapped out, and this had made her feel safe and secure. He was a good guy, never going to set the world on fire, but Ellie had tried desperately to keep him out of the Morgan machinations to protect him but failed. He was still marooned in a lonely farmhouse in Northern England whilst Ellie was now sipping tea in a room with a log fire to keep the chill at bay in Italy in January. There was a problem that she kept pondering as she had slipped seamlessly into a life of plenty, where every whim was catered for and she couldn't begin to imagine going back to what she had before. The flat in London had been her haven and home but seemed mean, small and cramped now. All her memories of it were coloured grey and she honestly didn't want to go back there and scrape her living wondering where the next rent money was coming from.

When Ellie allowed those thoughts to surface and she dissected them she always berated herself and thought how shallow she had become. So, unable to deal with them, she tied them up and put them away until she could think of a solution. One obvious one was to bring Rory over to Italy and resume their engagement. This kept popping into her mind but she didn't think things would be the same. She had moved on now and what she had craved before wasn't what she wanted now. Rory, bless him, was his own man and she couldn't see him fitting in here at all. Maybe, she told herself sternly, that she shouldn't second guess what people think or do as they can surprise you every time. But she mentally closed the drawer on that thought and put it away for later.

Part of Ellie's 'moving on' or rather going with the flow had been when she had been rescued on a few occasions by a team of operatives who were employed by the Government. Ellie understood that they were part of a Security Force that worked mainly undercover and their collective skills were an effective shadow task force. They were, at the present time, trying to get back a collection of manuscripts and books that Alistair had basically stolen and sold to the highest bidders. Ellie had become part of this team and had even signed the Official Secrets Act! Her main job at the moment was to keep Alistair from reverting to his old persona of a mob boss and recover what they could of the priceless collection. That is why the team and Ellie were sitting in the room in Italy. Earlier in January, Ellie and Alistair had accepted an invitation from another super rich 'A' lister. He was called Kahlid Dehbi and lived in Morocco. They had joined his house party and Ellie was to be the inside woman for the team. He had been one of the participants at the 'auction' in England and had bought one of the priceless books. After gaining access to the vast book collection of Kahlid's, she had managed to steal one of them with the help of her maid, Maria.

The whole experience had unlocked another part of her and she looked back on the experience as an adventure. It had been really scary in parts but Ellie had realized she thrived on the adrenaline rush and would have hated to give that up and slide back into anonymity. That was another reason why she couldn't see how Rory would fit in with her new lifestyle. Maybe she was prejudging and ascribing traits that she was unaware of. How did she know how Rory really functioned? Ellie had found another part of herself and maybe Rory should be given the chance to do the same. She was in turmoil about it every time she thought about it but knew she would have to do something soon.

But right now, she was sitting holding a cup and saucer hearing the exploits of Jack and Phil who had been captured by bandits in the desert and had saved the day at the end. Nigel and Robert were there with Claire who had just dropped the bombshell, 'You stole the wrong book.'

Ellie was aghast and her cup clattered into her saucer. 'What do mean the wrong book? It was the illuminated manuscript that was sold at the auction.'

'No, it wasn't,' said Claire gently, 'it was, in fact, one that had disappeared many years earlier from Scotland. I agree that it was originally stolen and should be returned, but that doesn't solve the immediate problem of where the British Library codex has gone.'

Ellie was dumbfounded and mortified at Claire's words. After all she and the team had gone through and she had let them down by stealing the wrong book. 'I was sure that was the one. It had the drawings of the mythical sea creatures on the title cover.' Ellie put down her cup and covered her face with her hands.

Claire reached across and put her hand on Ellie's arm. 'Don't feel too bad about it, as the Scottish Archives were overjoyed to get it back, but you're going to have to do some serious homework next time to get the right one. You could have stolen a book that was bought by legitimate means and that would mean we would have to return it. A lot of messy explanations would be in order then and I don't think it would go down too well with our bosses.'

Ellie faced Claire. 'You mean there's going to be a next time? I seriously can't go back to Khalid's place as I don't think he would let me into the vault again. I think he had his suspicions the first time round and also Alistair wouldn't have anything to do with the theft as he had too much to lose. If he was implicated, I don't think we would get any invitations anywhere and I couldn't get access to anything again.'

Jack stopped gazing out of the window and said, 'I think you're right, Ellie, we need you to get invitations to Alistair's friends and I can see why he doesn't want to mess that up as someone would probably see that he had an unfortunate accident or something. He doesn't play with the good guys and can't be tied into any thefts. These so called friends of his are just as rich and powerful as he is and their friendships are probably only skin deep.'

Nigel added to this. 'Yes, I agree. The thing to remember is that we can only do so much from the outside as these houses are so well guarded and fortified, we really do need you on the inside to know what's happening. It's unlikely we could get in and out again without being spotted, or having to wait a long time to get someone set up as a servant.'

Ellie felt a bit better and nodded at the comments. She vowed to do her homework properly next time and not make such a glaring rookie mistake again. 'Well I feel a bit better now but I still can't believe I did that. I suppose we'll have to wait till the next invitation and see who it is. We have got the list of who bought what and I'll do my homework properly next time,' she promised.

Robert looked at Ellie and said, 'We have got a bit more news for you. It seems that the Government took pity on Rory and his minder John and flew them by helicopter to London. Rory is now back in his flat and is, sadly, not a happy man.' He added, 'Maybe you should give him a ring and sort things out as we don't want him going off half-cocked to the press or anything.'

Ellie's past life jumped up and bit her firmly. 'I'll do that straight away,' she mumbled. She wondered what on earth she could say that would make things right with him but she had to try as there seemed to be an awful lot riding on it.

A cool draught made Ellie shiver as the door was opened and Alistair, her twin, came in. 'Good, I see that tea has been served, may I join you?' Everyone shuffled up and Alistair sat down and poured himself some tea. 'I'm glad you could join us and want to know how everything went. Ellie has told me her story, how she stole the book, and I am amazed at her bravery, as Khalid is not someone I would personally mess about with. It appears that he doesn't suspect her as I've been in contact and made enquiries about the aftermath of the theft. I've had to live up to my past persona.' He cocked an eyebrow at this. 'And I have promised to look about for him for a replacement. I do assure you I've got no intention of stealing one for him but sometimes these things come on the market.' He took a sip of tea. 'I do have lots of contacts still and I intend to keep them. Wheels within wheels you know how it works.'

Phil said, 'I'm sure we do Alistair, and I thank you for allowing us to stay here for a few days while we sort out where we go next. I don't know if you've had any other invitations from persons of interest?' Phil was fishing.

'Actually, I do,' said Alistair. 'In about a week or so we could go to St. Lucia and see my old friend Fortune. He's got lots of those resorts where the rich can hideaway and recuperate from the stresses of life in the fast lane. They do all the usual spa stuff and I must admit they're very good. I don't even need to take my chef.'

Ellie rolled her eyes and looked at the others. 'Alistair you can't be serious that you need your own chef to serve you up tonic water or some soup? Be real!'

'But I am being real, Ellie.' Alistair turned to face her. 'Imagine if someone wanted me out of the way. The easiest thing in the world would be to slip me some poison in my food. Then bingo, Alistair is no more and my companies and holdings would be ravaged to shreds, probably you with them,' he added darkly.

'I suppose I never thought of it that way,' said Ellie.

'You can never be too careful,' said Alistair meaningfully. 'Anyway, Fortune has asked us to go over for a bit of winter sun. He couldn't get to Khalid's house party and I suspect he wants to meet you "in the flesh" so to speak. He bought a bit of the Staffs hoard and also a book of something or other. I have the list so you'll know what you're looking for.' Alistair looked at the assembled group. 'But I must stress, as I told Ellie before, I'm not going to steal the things myself. I'll help but I won't get my hands dirty. The trail will never lead back to me, are we clear?'

'Yep, you told me that before,' said Ellie, 'but I'm not particularly happy about Maria being involved again. She was absolutely marvelous last time, and I'm not sure I could have done it without her, but I can't take the risk again.' Ellie looked at the others, unsure at what their reaction might be.

Phil broke the silence. 'What about if Claire goes as your maid, then Maria will be safe and in the clear?'

Claire sat up straight. 'I suppose I could, but I'll have to stay here from now on and take up the duties and learn from Maria, things like how hot Madame's bath should be etc.,' she added, laughing.

Ellie laughed out loud with her. 'Sorry but you're going to be a terrible maid, Claire. I suppose I'll just have to put up with it. You just can't get the staff these days, but it could work to our advantage as I won't be going in with a half-formed plan like last time. You'll be there to do better reconnaissance and we'll have a bit more time than before. We can also plan how to get the stuff out rather than Maria just chucking it over a wall and me praying.'

Alistair turned to Phil. 'Is there any news on what the Government wants to do with me? I know if I set foot back in England I'll be roasted alive by the press at the instigation of the Whitehall mandarins. It'll be a trial by media with all the trimmings. My legal team is earning their keep at the moment and issuing suit and countersuit like confetti to keep everyone tied up in paper, but it won't last forever. Also, there's the small matter of what happened in France. One of their historic chateaux was destroyed and there was an unexplained death on their soil. Is there any news on that one?'

'Well, I certainly wouldn't go back to France in a hurry if I were you,' said Phil. 'The powers that be in France were glad to see the back of us and I'd let a sleeping *chien* lie if I were you. As to England, well, I'd just stay away for the moment and we'll keep working on some sort of amnesty if we can. To be honest I haven't heard anything definite yet, but I'll let you know the moment I do.'

Alistair looked as if the news wasn't what he wanted to hear but said nothing. He couldn't push the point as besides his legal team these people were the only link he had to England. They were his only real hope of getting back there and fighting off any extradition orders that may come flying his way.

Ellie broke the silence. 'You remember that I was engaged.' She held up her hand and waved the ring at Alistair. 'Well, it seems Rory has been rescued from his snowbound farmhouse and I've decided to invite him here.' As soon as the words left her mouth she cringed. What had made her say that! She knew she had to do something, and soon, but to have him here would probably really set the cat among the pigeons. It could be a 'make or break' situation and Ellie wasn't going to look forward to it one bit. She remembered the last conversation she had on the telephone on Christmas morning and her stomach knotted up, but he was worth more to her than that. If it really was going to break them up then it shouldn't be by phone or text, it should be face to face like adults. In truth she knew that Rory was going to have to adopt her new lifestyle as she wasn't going to give it up now and she didn't know if that was going to be possible.

'Whatever you want to do Ellie,' said Alistair, 'but he isn't going to have any part of my companies or be involved in any way.'

'You've never even met the guy,' said Ellie, astonished at the sweeping statement.

'Don't need to,' said Alistair, 'if he were your one and only true love you would have moved Heaven and Earth to be with him by now. You haven't. I can also see a small family trait in you that pushes you to get what you want. I have that also but I haven't seen it with regards to Rory, so invite him by all means and I'll make him welcome. I will even order the jet for him from London but tread carefully sister,' he admonished.

Ellie was silent. All that Alistair had said was true and she hadn't moved mountains to be with Rory since last year. Maybe she should have kept her mouth shut in the first place, but what was done, was done, and she couldn't take it back. It really was making or break time now.

Claire rose. 'I suppose I better get started with Maria and sort out what my duties are going to be.'

Phil said, 'We'll have a meeting tomorrow now we know we're going to be in St Lucia. I'll check out this guy Fortune and see if we can get a plan of his house.' He also rose to leave.

Alistair stood with him. 'I've arranged some rooms for you all and dinner will be at eight, so we can meet down in the Drawing Room for drinks before we go in. I hope you will be comfortable but please ask if there's anything you need.' He bowed slightly then left.

Ellie said, 'It will be black tie tonight for all you gents, just ask the servants if you've forgotten to pack the kit.' Ellie turned to Claire. 'We are reasonably about the same size so if you want to have a ferret through my wardrobes feel free, Maria will give you a hand. She's also aces at the hair and make-up so let her loose if you want to. I'll be up in a moment.' Ellie paced up and down after they had gone and decided there and then she would have to break the silence between herself and Rory now. She went to the desk and opened a laptop and sat down. She would send him an e-mail, at least if she wrote everything down then they wouldn't end up in a slanging match on the phone. She flexed her fingers and typed in his address then paused. How did you start a letter like this? After the initial, 'Hi, Rory', the words eventually began to flow. She typed furiously and all the bewilderment at her situation came tumbling out, she wrote from her heart and while she hoped he would understand that her circumstances had changed dramatically, she still wanted to see him again. She tentatively offered the invite to the castle and said that she really hoped he would take it up. Eventually she ran out of steam and the words dried up. She sat and was going to read it through but decided not to as she would probably change everything about and it would sound stilted and not what she really wanted to say. Shutting her eyes, she pressed 'send'. A big sigh of relief escaped her as she had now grasped the nettle that had been overshadowing her since all this had begun. She would check for a reply tomorrow as now she had to change and play the part of the hostess. Ellie felt as if a great weight had been lifted as she walked up to her room.

Maria stood in the centre of the room and Claire was sitting at the dressing table. Maria said, as soon as Ellie walked in, 'I am not happy that Claire is now going to be your maid.' Ellie caught Claire's glance through the mirror on the dressing table. 'I was not good enough for you last time?' Maria was still standing stiffly with her arms folded. 'I do all that for you and now you want to replace me?'

'No, no, Maria,' said Ellie and she guided Maria to a chair where she sat down with a huff. 'We're all going to St. Lucia soon and Claire here is part of a team with the British Government and will have to go in undercover. We have to get her into the house on St. Lucia and I can't think of any way to do it. So, she will have to be a maid with you, is that all right?' Ellie looked at Claire for back-up.

Claire twisted round on the chair. 'Yes, Maria, we need you desperately, we wouldn't think of leaving you behind, it's just that Ellie will have to have two maids from now on. Anyway, I can't do hair and make-up like you can, and I couldn't possibly learn in so short a time. You have to be there for me so I don't make any mistakes that could give me away. Will you do that for us?'

Maria was only slightly mollified and said, 'Only if it's what Miss Ellie wants. I was good last time and got the book over the wall for you.'

'Yes, Maria, you were a star, you came up with a plan and it worked,' said Ellie enthusiastically. 'Without you I'd never have done it and I'm eternally grateful. It's just that we may need a bit more help with this one and we need Claire on the inside with us.

Are you up for it?'

'OK, I'll show Miss Claire all that she needs to know,' said Maria, relaxing a bit. 'But I don't want anything to happen to you as you have done a lot for me.' Maria looked meaningfully at Claire when she said this.

'Absolutely, Maria,' said Ellie, glad at last that Maria was on their side. 'Your part in this is to perhaps carry messages, prop Claire up when she looks as if she's doing something wrong, and help me when I get stuck like last time.'

Maria smiled at this. 'I did help you when you got stuck, didn't I?'

'So that's what I need you to do again, Maria,' said Ellie, relieved. 'Thank you for doing this as I couldn't do it alone.'

'No thanks necessary,' said Maria, standing up. 'Now you both dress for dinner. I have picked out your gown for tonight, Miss Ellie and for Miss Claire.' She walked to the walk-in closet. 'Maybe this one, or this one?' She held out two for inspection.

Claire walked over and took both dresses. 'My God, these are top designer dresses from this year's collection.' She held them up one by one in front of her by the full length mirror.

'Yes,' said Maria, not batting an eyelash, 'either will suit you perfectly for tonight. Perhaps the gold and black one is the most suitable, but please try them on first.'

Ellie said, 'Maybe you'd like to stay with me to get changed? Then you can see what Maria actually does.' Ellie looked at Maria to check this out.

'Of course, I'll do both your hair and make-up and then you can go down together looking a million dollars.' Maria smiled at this as she was in her element making women look beautiful.

An hour later both new women stood and admired themselves in the mirror.

'Oh my God! Maria is a miracle worker,' said Claire twisting from side to side. 'I never thought I could look this good. Wait till the others see me now.' As she smoothed the dress down over her hips, Ellie just smiled as she had been at the receiving end of Maria's ministrations before and knew she was indeed a 'miracle worker'.

They gracefully walked down to the Drawing Room and were met by a footman with cocktails. Ellie had her favourite Peach Bellini and Claire joined her with a tall frosted glass. The men walked in and were so smart that Claire almost didn't recognize them. They joined the ladies and everyone stood about on their best behaviour making small talk.

'You both look fabulous,' said Phil, looking at Claire in particular. Jack had been a guest of Alistair's before so this was nothing new and he wandered about looking at the paintings and sculptures that adorned the room. Both Nigel and Robert both appeared to be a mite uncomfortable in their outfits and didn't wear them with ease. Robert in particular ran his finger round his collar a few times as if to try and unleash it. Alistair came in and took his customary glass of tonic water and joined the group.

Ever the good host, he enquired, 'I hope everything was to your satisfaction and you had everything you needed?' Everyone nodded and he turned to Claire and Ellie. 'You're looking astoundingly beautiful tonight, Ellie, as I've said before you seem to have bagged all the good genes on that front. Also, Claire, I do admire that dress and you should wear your hair like that again, why hide such a graceful swan neck such as yours?' Claire actually nearly blushed as Ellie rolled her eyes.

'You're such a charmer when you try, Alistair, give it a rest tonight though,' said Ellie, waving an empty glass.

Dinner was a hit with everyone and Alistair had obviously

given instructions to the chef to pull out all the stops. The guys loosened their ties and as the wine flowed, they regaled each other with banter and made light of the sticky situations they had found themselves in on past adventures. The camels still held pride of place though and Alistair couldn't believe the trials and tribulations Phil and Jack had been through in the desert.

'I'll fill you all in on the aftermath of that one if you like,' said Phil. 'It appears that camels have a homing instinct and they just wandered back to where we got them from. It seems the boy, who is named Ali, by the way, knew this all the time. He had told me to just let them go and they would go back. His help was beyond anything we could have hoped for and he was definitely one of the good guys. He was a skinny little runt but it appears he was thirteen years old and I arranged for him to get a scholarship to the school in Béchar. We couldn't give him goods as the tribe would have just taken them away and he wanted to learn how to fly rockets to the moon. I hope he does but we've paid for his education until he's eighteen. If he works hard who knows?'

'I hope he still has my watch,' said Jack, looking at his empty wrist. 'It was all we had at the time to pay him with and he seemed to like it. As Phil said, we would have been totally lost without him.'

When everyone had finished, they all retired back to the Drawing Room and Robert found a pack of cards on a side table. He flicked them and did a master shuffle. 'Anyone fancy a game?'

'Not with you,' said Nigel, 'you always beat me and it gets quite boring after a time.'

'How about I show you some card tricks then,' he said and pulled a card table over. He then proceeded to astound everyone with his apparent second sight on how the cards would fall. Even Alistair was amused and gave Robert his full attention.

Claire was also mesmerized and said, 'You've got hidden talents, Robert, remind me never to play cards with you ever.'

'It's easy really,' said Robert, 'all I've got to do is keep your attention focused where I want it then do something with the other hand that you think you don't see. Look.' He shuffled the deck then showed them a simple trick of making a card disappear. 'See you're all watching here.' He held up the cards. 'While my right hand is doing this.' In the blink of an eye a card disappeared.

'Well, that's a skill I didn't know you had, Robert,' said Phil, 'it could come in useful in the future.' He looked round at the others and they all nodded.

'You could teach me how to do that as I'm the one who has to steal things,' said Ellie, still amazed at what she had seen.

'Me as well,' said Claire, 'as I'm going to be in the thick of it soon.'

'Yep, will do, anytime you like, it's easy but you do need to practice to get the whole thing to flow seamlessly.' Robert flicked the cards experimentally. 'Anyone for poker?'

A resounding 'No' came from everyone.

Jack turned to Alistair, 'How's the hand, Alistair? I know you had a big problem in France and we were all worried about you.' He was referring to the destruction of the Chateau of the Birds when Alistair had summoned some supernatural being and had his fingers burnt off in the process. Ellie shot Jack a glance as if to say it was still quite a delicate subject. Jack ploughed on, 'I notice that you have a glove on but I hope everything healed up well. It doesn't seem to bother you much.'

'I wear the glove.' Alistair waved his hand covered with the fine ostrich skin glove. It was nearly flesh coloured and it wasn't really apparent that he had lost the end digits of his left hand– 'so that the scars don't offend anyone. It seems that they will all be properly healed in a month or two but there is no pain and I'll be having some skin grafts to tidy it all up in a month or two.'

Jack said, 'What are you going to do about the chateau? It was razed to the ground and there was nothing left at all. Are you going to rebuild it?'

'No, I haven't got any plans to do that at the moment and I agree with Ellie that it should be left as it is, just a heap of charred stone. All the staff have been found other jobs and I'll look about eventually, with Ellie of course, to find another one when the heat dies down in France.'

Ellie breathed a sigh of relief and nodded. 'I couldn't go back to that place again after what happened, even if you did rebuild it from scratch. Knowing what lies under there with that huge bird from Hell lurking about – I just couldn't do it. Let's just go somewhere new.' She looked at Alistair pleading with her eyes.

'Yes, I understand how you feel, Ellie, I don't think I could go there either,' said Alistair, 'we nearly lost so much that night.'

'We sure did,' said Jack, remembering how close they had come to losing their souls to fulfill the ancient contract.

'Did you know "Ucello" means birds or wildfowl?' said Nigel absently. 'That's the name of this castle isn't it?'

The room fell silent.

'I know that our father used to like this place a lot, but it's not somewhere I've been much,' said Alistair. 'Do you think there could be a link with the past here as well?'

'Well, there's a bird, a very big nasty one at the Chateau of the Birds, Jack and Ellie nearly got taken to Hell by a big bird, Jack and Rory saw a big bird at the farmhouse, and this place is called after the birds?'

'What's this thing with our father and all these birds?' said Ellie, suddenly uncomfortable.

'I've no idea,' said Alistair, lying. He had used the Grimoire book to put his spirit into a huge griffin and find Ellie when she had gone to the supposed 'safe house'.

'I saw a huge bird today wheeling round over the castle when we arrived,' said Jack.

'That's probably just one of the local bird populations,' said Nigel knowingly.

'Yep, I suppose so, but it was a huge beast even though it was really high up,' said Jack.

'Let's all search the castle tomorrow as we have nothing better to do then everyone's mind will be put at rest,' said Alistair. 'I'll find someone to give us all a guided tour as I don't know much about it myself. We'll search every nook and cranny and see if there are any secrets here.'

'Yes, please,' said Ellie and she wondered how she was going to sleep tonight knowing there could be another secret cavern underneath the castle with all manner of hideous things down there. She looked at Jack and he nodded as if it was what he was thinking as well. They didn't want to be nearly dragged off to Hell again.

CHAPTER TWO

The next day Ellie woke up refreshed. She had been spooked by all the talk of birds last night and was convinced she wouldn't sleep at all. The coincidences, if that was what they were, would be all laid to rest today as they were going to search the castle from top to bottom. Ellie still wasn't one hundred per cent sure that Alistair was being totally honest when he said that he didn't know about the 'bird' connection, but she had to take his word for it. Also she had sent the e-mail to Rory and would probably get a reply today. That would be the make or break situation she was quietly dreading either way. If he came there would undoubtedly be recriminations, or if he didn't come then it was all over, end, finito. She was still very ambivalent about her feelings as Rory was a good guy but she wasn't sure if he would like the new lifestyle and she wasn't going to give it up now. Well, the e-mail would say it all!

Everyone met at the breakfast table and Phil said, 'Let's get to business first before we go bird hunting. I think Alistair has accepted the invitation from Fortune?' He looked across at Alistair who nodded. 'I hope Nigel and Robert are onto the plans of the house?' They nodded. He looked across at Claire, 'Claire, how's it going with being a maid?'

She replied, 'Well, Maria didn't like the idea much but she's okay now and I think I'll get the hang of it before we go. Maria will have to go with us as I can't do hair and make-up like she can but I don't think it'll be unusual for Ellie to travel with two maids will it?' She looked at Alistair.

'No, certainly not,' said Alistair, 'I'll just tell Fortune how many staff I have and he'll put them up. It's not unusual at all. Some people take one or two chefs with them or even a dog handler if they travel with a pet, it's no problem at all.'

Everyone swapped glances at this as it was really out of their realm of understanding how the really rich people lived.

'So,' said Phil, 'are we really going to have a top to toe look at this castle of yours before we have to leave tomorrow? It really is a fascinating place and there's so much history here, you can almost feel it.'

'Don't say that,' said Ellie, 'this place is beginning to give me the creeps a bit. I don't want to find any more bird things. The last time was enough!'

'Point taken, Ellie,' said Jack, 'I don't want to meet that thing again. It scared the hell out of me, literally!'

Alistair said, 'I've called up one of the local historians and he appears to be the man to ask about the Castle. He's even written a book about it apparently. He's asked before if he could look round and I gave him the run of the place so he's the one that will know all its secrets. He should be here shortly and I'll join you for the tour. Ellie has asked me before about the history of the place and I must admit I haven't taken much interest in that side as I haven't visited since I was a boy. But it should be interesting.' At that point a little hunched figure was shown into the breakfast room by a footman and he was invited to sit down and share some breakfast. 'This is Mr. Salieri who is our guide for today. Thank you for taking the time to show the Castle secrets to my guests, I'm sure it will be most enlightening.'

Mr. Salieri appeared to be a little in awe of Alistair and mumbled his thanks at being allowed to roam the castle for information for his book. He had a sheaf of papers and said, 'I have bought these for you to read should you wish at a later date as it goes into more depth than I can reasonably give in a few hours. Please keep them for your library should anyone else be interested.' He offered the papers across and Ellie rose and took them, thanking the man for all thoughtfulness.

'Is there anything you are particularly interested in as a full historical tour of your home would take days not just a few hours?' Mr. Salieri looked round at the group.

'Well, there is actually.' Ellie looked round at everyone. 'We've been discussing if there are any secret passages or rooms, or even unexplored parts of the castle. Alistair may want to do some more restoration in the future and it would be helpful to know so nothing gets destroyed inadvertently in the future.' Ellie looked at the historian hopefully.

'Now, funny you should say that as there are obviously secret passages that allowed people to go to and from the castle unobserved. There are a few still in existence but they are reached by trapdoors and are very dirty places to explore. We can go down them if you want to but you will need flashlights and walking boots as they can get very wet from the ground water. There are also the usual secret passages from room to room, these allowed secret assignations between lovers.' Mr. Salieri's face took on a distant dreamy look as if he wished he could be transported back to the age of chivalry. 'It's quite possible that there are more as yet undiscovered as this is something I have not explored fully, but will in the future with your kind permission, Mr. Morgan.' Mr. Salieri looked at Alistair who nodded his permission.

The little man stood and went to a bookcase that stretched from the floor to the beginning of the vaulted roof. 'Now, here is a perfectly ordinary bookcase that has stood here for many hundreds of years, but it is not all as it seems.' He touched a piece of panelling and the bookcase moved about six inches from the wall on the one side. 'The mechanism is obviously very old, but it still works if you could give me a hand?' Robert and Nigel were there first and gently eased the bookcase away from the wall and it swung open like a door. 'We will need some torches.' Mr. Salieri looked at Alistair who rang the bell for a footman.

Ellie and the others felt their jaws drop as the little man performed what seemed to be a conjuring trick. The door had been there for hundreds of years and no one except this man had known. 'Wow!' was all that Ellie could manage.

The flashlights were brought and they all set off down the tunnel. 'Where does it go?' said Phil.

Mr. Salieri had them in the palm of his hand now and was playing the moment for all it was worth. He tapped his nose with his finger and said, 'We shall see, we shall see soon.' He led them through the cobwebby passage until they came to a dead end but Mr. Salieri gently eased a lever set in the wall and a door creaked open. They stepped out into Phil's suite by a door covered by a large painting of some idyllic rural scene.

'This is going to be my quick route down to breakfast in the future,' said Phil and watched as the picture swung back into place and the lever clicked shut. 'So how does it open this side?' said Phil, prodding the mouldings on the picture frame. Mr. Salieri stepped forward and pushed a rose carving by the fireplace and Phil heard the lock click open once more. 'How on earth did you find that out?' asked Phil, fascinated.

'I found out by doing lots of research and delving into books and papers in the archives. It was mentioned in some letters I came across and they mentioned a rose. This is the only rose carving I could find in the room so I put two and two together and tried it out. The rest, as they say, is history.' Mr. Salieri smiled and appeared to be well pleased at the impression he had made. 'So, follow me.' He beckoned them into the hall. He walked along staring at the paintings and stopped in front of a huge one of some rather large ladies disporting themselves in a Roman pool. 'Now here we have a rather grand work of some note.' He gestured at the oil. 'Again it hides a secret.' He stepped forward and performed the magic of making the painting swing back exposing a doorway.

Robert said, 'This guy is really worth the money, Alistair, he's amazing.'

'I never had any idea this was all here. I suppose that castles of this age have been through a lot of transformations but I'm as amazed as you are,' Alistair replied.

They all stared down the dark passage that wound into inky blackness. A footman came hurrying along the corridor and gained Alistair's attention, he gave him a folded note. Alistair glanced at it and said, 'I'm so sorry that I have to leave you now, but please continue and I'll hear all your exploits at lunchtime.' Alistair smiled and left them.

'Come on then,' said Nigel, 'I can't wait to see where this one comes out,' and he played his torch off the stone walls.

Mr. Salieri again led the way and they came out in Ellie's suite. The doorway was in her walk-in closet and as they came into the room Maria nearly fainted. She jumped like a startled horse and just stared at them clutching a pile of towels to her chest. 'Where did you come from? Miss Ellie, you're all dirty with cobwebs.' Maria used a towel to wipe some from Ellie's hair.

'There's a secret passage that comes out here and Mr. Salieri is showing us some more of them. It's really great fun and no-one knows they are here.' Ellie was smiling broadly and said, 'I can't wait for the next one, if there is one?' she turned to Mr. Salieri.

'Oh yes, there are many and there may not be time to show them all, but in the papers, I've left you are some maps of the castle throughout the ages and the instructions of how to get into the secret places I've found.'

Everyone murmured their appreciation as this was turning out to be a really good morning and Ellie's fears of finding a secret cave dedicated to the occult were rapidly receding. There were many more rooms and passages that were concealed, some so obvious that it was a surprise how they had been ignored in the past. It was getting towards lunchtime and Mr. Salieri had begun to look at his watch. 'I have to go soon as I have a lecture to give at the University this afternoon but I would be pleased to come back again if you wish?'

'Oh, please do,' said Ellie as they began to go down to their starting point in the Breakfast Room.

'I will leave you with this puzzle I can't solve,' said Mr. Salieri. He began to shuffle through his papers. 'Here.' He jabbed his finger at a hand-drawn map. 'I have measured the rooms and the corridors but they do not match up. The measurements are wrong but I have checked them again and again. There appears to be another room here but I cannot find a way in. I leave you with the puzzle.' With their thanks he bowed and left.

Ellie's heart sank down to her shoes. This could mean another occult meeting place and she really didn't want Alistair to know about it. She still wasn't absolutely sure that he wouldn't dabble with it again. The temptation could be just too strong for him even though he'd got his fingers burnt off literally last time. She grabbed Jack's arm and dragged him to one side. 'You heard what Mr. Salieri just said about another hidden room. Well, I don't trust Alistair not to play at witches and warlocks again if it's what I think it might be. I'm sure you agree with that so let's just hide all this information and tell the others not to talk about it.'

Jack knit his brows. 'I do agree with you, it's just too dangerous and I certainly don't want another experience like that again. It could put you in danger again as the bird thing wanted you first then Alistair. Let's tell the others now.' He moved back to the table but the salon door opened and in strode Alistair.

'I hope you enjoyed the tour and creeping about secret passages. I would have liked to join you but something came up I couldn't put off. So was our local historian any good?'

'Bloody marvellous,' said Claire. 'He had so many stories about this place and we scared Maria nearly to death by popping out of the closet in Ellie's room. It was certainly an experience I won't forget in a hurry.'

Ellie started to gather the papers together. 'He's left all this stuff for us to ponder later, I'll just put them together in the Library so we can pore over them later,' she said the word 'later' meaningfully.

'Yes,' said Jack, 'I think we all need to change for lunch as we're still all covered in cobwebs.' He pulled one from Claire's hair trying to change the subject. 'Look at the time! We'll have to hurry if we want to shower and pack before lunchtime. We're going back to England this afternoon aren't we?'

'Yes, I suppose so,' said Robert.

'Also, we've still got to firm up the travel plans for St. Lucia and get a few ideas in place for when we get there,' said Jack as Ellie roughly gathered all the papers up and tucked them firmly under her arm.

'So, I reckon we've got about forty-five minutes then we'll meet up and have a discussion about what we're going to do,' said Phil. He looked at Alistair. 'I hope you can join us as I would like you to be in the loop with this?'

Alistair nodded. 'Yes, I think I'd better be as my reputation and also possibly my life is at stake with this plan. The last one worked, after a fashion, but I don't want myself or Ellie in any jeopardy whatsoever.'

'You're beginning to sound like a mother hen, Alistair,' said Ellie. 'I won't remind you again but if you hadn't stolen those books in the first place, and nearly got Claire killed in the process, then we wouldn't be in this mess now.'

'Touché,' Alistair remarked to her receding back.

Ellie attempted to look indignant as she swept out of the room but the important thing was that she'd got the papers under her arm. She went directly to the Library and deposited them on a reading desk and rifled through them until she found the plan with all the measurements on that Mr. Salieri had pointed out. She folded it up as small as she could and tucked it down her bra before going up to her room. What she was going to do with it she didn't know, she'd just hide it for now and decide later.

Lunchtime turned out to be an intensive planning meeting with the food as a secondary item. It was all in place that Claire would go with Maria on a scheduled flight the day after tomorrow. Phil, Robert, Nigel and Jack would go as tourists in Economy class on the same flight. The jet would take Alistair and Ellie in two days' time so the staff could be in place with the luggage sorted when they got there. Carter, Alistair's manservant, would go on the flight with Alistair.

Ellie dropped a bombshell at lunchtime. 'I've sent Rory an e-mail and invited him here but I don't know if he's replied yet,

I haven't checked.' The room fell silent.

'You do pick your moments,' said Alistair. 'We're all supposed to be going to a house party in the Caribbean and suddenly an ex-boyfriend is going to turn up.'

'Rory is not an ex-boyfriend,' said Ellie indignantly. 'He's my fiancé and I'm still engaged, remember.' She held up her hand. 'Anyway, I don't know if he'll visit at all. I'll have to check and see if he's replied.'

Alistair beckoned to a footman who fetched a laptop. 'Well do it now and put us all out of our misery, please.' He placed the laptop in front of Ellie.

Ellie felt all eyes on her. This wasn't how she wanted to read the e-mail if there was one. She wanted to do it quietly on her own, not as the centre of attention. She typed in the code for her e-mails and one popped up. It was from Rory and she opened it. She angled the screen away from everyone and read it. It was a short one and Rory hadn't revealed much about his feelings but had accepted the offer to stay.

'Well, it looks like he's coming,' said Ellie, shutting the laptop with a snap.

'You better sort out your love life PDQ or else he'll be coming to St. Lucia with us,' said Alistair, exasperated.

'My "love life" as you put it has nothing whatsoever to do with you, Alistair, and if I want to take Rory with me to St. Lucia then I bloody well will.' Ellie glared at Alistair.

Everyone began to make banal conversation to ease the tension in the room. Claire was the first one brave enough to address Alistair directly. 'I'm the one that will be there in the house with you so I can always keep Rory out of any trouble if needs be. I don't suppose another surprise guest will be any problem to Fortune, will it?'

Alistair was still seething. 'Let's just wait and see what happens when he comes and then I'll make the arrangements.'

Ellie was quick to pick this up. 'What do you mean, let's just wait and see what happens? You're intending to be as obnoxious as possible to Rory so he won't want to come. That's it isn't it? That's your little plan. God! You're so devious sometimes, Alistair, but you're transparent to me. Don't even think about it, he's going to be a guest here and treated like one at all times. Do I make myself crystal clear on this issue? Rory is not an ex-boyfriend he is my fiancé and may well end up as your brother-in-law, so tread carefully, Alistair, very carefully. I'm not hungry any more I think I'll go to the rifle range and shoot something.' She stared pointedly at Alistair, threw her napkin on the table and left the room.

'Wow,' mouthed Robert as Ellie left.

'Well, I can't follow that,' said Phil and looked round at the others. 'I have to thank you again, Alistair, for all your help with this and having us here has been great fun, but we do need to make tracks now. I'll make sure that all your co-operation is noted in London with the right people and we will be in contact as soon as all the plans are finalized and in place.' He pushed back his chair and Alistair rose at the same time. Both men shook hands and Phil bade him farewell.

Claire said, 'If it's all right with you, Alistair, I think I'll just stay here till we go. I do need to have some more lessons from Maria and I can have a chat with Ellie and see how the land lies with her and Rory. She may confide in me where she maybe wouldn't with you. You know just "girl to girl" talk.'

Alistair looked at Claire. 'Yes, please do this "girl to girl" stuff with her when he comes. I've got nothing against the man but he's not, shall we say, what I would have picked for my sister.'

'I don't think picking has got anything to do with it Alistair,' said Claire evenly, 'my job will be to smooth the path so our operation can go ahead smoothly, nothing more. I don't want Ellie in an emotional turmoil when she has to play her part. Her emotions are hers to deal with alone but rest assured I'll have no compunction about removing Rory from the playing field if I have to.'

Alistair looked at Claire with renewed respect. She was a woman with a total focus on the task in hand and he could understand that. The emotional vagaries of women were beyond his grasp and he didn't have much time for them but Claire could certainly smooth that stony path. He knew, without a doubt, that to interfere could cause an enormous rift between himself and Ellie and she was still the catalyst that seemed to give him power.

'I'll go and check out the rifle range and see what she's shooting at then,' said Claire, taking her leave.

Ellie stood with her arms out and was totally focused on the moving target before her. She had played with the computer holographic image and it was Alistair she was shooting at. He popped out from behind doors and appeared at windows in the run-down streets she had picked as background. Her aim wasn't perfect yet but she had caused him a lot of damage and it felt good. She didn't hear Claire come in until a light lit up on her station and she knew there was another in the room. Ellie carefully ejected the magazine and put down the Glock. She removed her ear muffs and turned to face Claire.

'So, what's he said to you then? Has he sent you down here to smooth my ruffled feathers?'

'No, not at all,' Claire answered. 'I actually told him that it was totally your business how you conducted your private life and he shouldn't interfere.'

'Well, well done you. I am actually sick of him trying to control everything I do.' Ellie was still seething.

I will say though; your timing wasn't superb was it? Anyway, what's done is done and we have to go with it. It's more than likely that Rory will be coming to St. Lucia and you will have to stay totally focused on the task in hand. Make no doubts about it I will lock him in a broom cupboard or something if he threatens to compromise the operation. It'll be up to you to see that he doesn't. I don't know what you'll tell him, but if you want my advice, I'd keep it to a minimum if I were you. The less he knows, the less he can tell anyone else and these people don't play by any rules.'

Ellie nodded, 'I see where you're coming from and I have to apologize that I haven't thought the whole thing through properly. I'm sure Rory can be trusted though, but I did try my best to keep him out of it at the beginning, all it did was alienate him and drove him away from me. I've got to try and build some sort of a bridge as I'm sure he thinks I don't love him anymore and have forgotten him.' Ellie wiped away a tear that had suddenly started in the corner of her eye.

'Come on, Ellie, let's put the guns away and have a quiet chat with some tea as you have an e-mail to send to him and he'll be here tomorrow. Then you can sort everything out. Don't worry about Alistair as I'm sure he's got the picture now and won't interfere.'

'If he does, I'll bloody kill him and feed him to that bird thing,' said Ellie through gritted teeth.

Ellie spent the next hour composing and recomposing the e-mail she was going to send to Rory. Nothing seemed quite right and she could pick flies out of every sentence. In the end she just opened the laptop and typed out the travel arrangements for the next morning. It was terse but she couldn't think of what else to put. She did end it with 'I love you' and some kisses in the vain hope it would give the right impression. It was a poor attempt at bridge building by anyone's standards but she just couldn't think of what else to put.

Ellie had a tray sent up to her room that evening and rebuffed Claire's attempts at getting her to talk. Even Maria got nowhere and Ellie was eventually left alone with the television for company. When she was getting changed for bed she saw the folded piece of paper fall out of her bra. It was the map with the dimensions of the rooms and corridor drawn by Mr. Salieri. Ellie smoothed it flat and had a better look at it. He was right, the measurements didn't add up at all. There was another room tucked away in there but as he had said, he couldn't find the way in. Ellie debated what to do with the piece of paper. Maybe she should just burn it there and then and let the past fade away, but she had to admit that it was intriguing. So, she carefully folded it again and cast about the room for where to hide it. There was a small safe in the closet and only she had the code, so she placed the map in there for a future time.

All night Ellie tossed and turned and when all hope of sleep had passed, she got up and showered. Rory was arriving this morning and Ellie was on serious tenterhooks as to how the meeting would go. She had received an equally terse reply confirming that he would be coming by the jet and would be there at about eleven o'clock. Ellie knew she only had a day before they went to St. Lucia and cursed her own impulsiveness and bad planning. At breakfast the conversation was strained to say the least. All Ellie could manage was a 'get lost' to Alistair and an 'um' to Claire. She ate little and then paced from room to room unable to settle to anything.

Rory turned up on time and Ellie was on the main steps to greet him. Both Claire and Alistair had made themselves scarce and Ellie thought she was going to be sick as the big car crunched across the gravel and drew to a halt. She started down the steps as the chauffeur went around to open the door for Rory.

'Well, hi there, I hope you had a good journey,' she opened lamely as Rory just stood there and took in the lavish surroundings. Ellie reached out and took Rory's hand and led him up the steps. 'I've been waiting for this moment forever and I can't wait for us to be together again.' Even to Ellie's ears this all sounded insincere and Rory still hadn't said anything. 'I've asked for a bit of brunch to be laid out as I don't know if they've given you anything on the plane.' Again, she knew she was lying as there would have been anything he'd wanted on the flight. She took his hand. 'At least let's go and get a cup of coffee.' She led him to the Breakfast Room and there was a table laid with a snowy cloth and she signalled the footman for fresh coffee. 'Sit there and it'll be along in a minute,' she tailed off not really knowing how to get the conversation started.

'You're not coming back are you?' Were Rory's first words. 'You won't leave all this for London and me.' He looked her full in the eye. 'I mean, how could you give all this up for what I can offer?' He waved his arm around the room taking in all the antiques and the footman hovering with the coffee pot.

'Rory, let's just have some coffee first.' Ellie poured the coffee and signalled that the footman should leave them alone. 'Rory.' Ellie reached across and held his hand. 'It's not about what I've got or haven't got. A few months ago, I had you and that was all that mattered. It still does. People are more important than things and I've still got your ring on my finger and you are still my fiancé. But things have changed for me. I got embroiled in the thefts and found my twin brother. I know he can be an absolute shit at times but he's still my brother and the only family I'll ever have. With him comes all this and I still want to be part of both worlds.' Ellie looked at Rory and pleaded with her eyes for him to understand. She felt shallow to want all the wealth and trappings of a jet set high life but if she gave them all up then she knew it would become a source of discontent between her and Rory. It would probably mar the relationship and Rory would always feel inadequate in what he could provide for her and would see through the façade eventually.

Rory took a sip of coffee. 'So, what you're saying is, that you want all this and me as well?'

Ellie couldn't answer so blunt a question with a plain 'yes' so she crumbled some croissant between her fingers.

'So where would I fit into all this? Would I just trail round after you? I need a job, Ellie; I need a purpose in life. I know I'm just the "tech" guy at the local college but I've got that, I've worked for it and I'm proud of what I've done on my own.' Rory reached across and tilted Ellie's chin so she had to look at him. 'Do you understand?'

Ellie replied in a small voice, 'I don't know, Rory, I really don't know.' A small tear started at the corner of her eye. 'I don't know what's happened to me in the last few months and I'm still trying to get my head round it right now. There's a lot more to tell you and I know I still love you and want to be with you. I don't think we can sort all this out in a few minutes over a coffee but believe me when I say that I do love you and you are everything to me.' Ellie stood and went around the table to Rory and he rose and embraced her as if he'd never let her go again. Ellie was full on crying onto Rory's shoulder and realized how much she had missed his arms around her shutting out the world. She felt safe and secure and above all loved to the very core of her being. All the trauma she had gone through, all the hurt and soul searching she had done since the very beginning was released and she cried it out.

'Steady up,' said Rory picking up a napkin and drying her eyes. 'I think we've got a lot to talk about but how about you show me round this castle of yours and we'll take it all step by step.' Rory took her hand and Ellie clasped it tightly never wanting to let it go. She pushed the big question of St. Lucia to the back of her mind.

CHAPTER THREE

Back in London, Jack, Nigel and Phil were making the arrangements to travel out. Their flights were booked and they had got places at the resort which Fortune owned. It was one of many on the island but it was the nearest one to his main residence. They were to board early the next day and fly to Hewanorra at the southern end of the island. The resort was right up the top on the Caribbean side so it was a sheltered haven for the super rich. They wouldn't be bothered by the Atlantic gusts but would be in a sheltered cove near to where Admiral Rodney had made the first landings. Jack was secretly very excited about this as he had never travelled so far in his life and to visit such a verdant, luxurious place was beyond his wildest dreams. He kept thinking he was a lottery winner and even went out and bought some new clothes suitable for such a grand resort. They all had cover stories of being dotcom millionaires out to play for a week or so and soak up some sunshine. Their work kept them busy but they had decided to meet up for a week of relaxation. Jack and the others were going Virgin First Class and even that experience was one to be savoured for Jack. To be looked after to the nth degree for eight whole hours was bliss. Better than traipsing round the desert on a camel in anybody's language. Phil had come up with various different scenarios for their cover but travelling salesmen and the like wouldn't have even got them into the resort at all. They needed to splash the cash around.

Maria and Claire were to fly out that evening with the luggage and Ellie had a 'stand-in maid' till she left the next day.

Ellie and Rory wandered round the castle hand in hand. She felt she would never let him go again and decided to broach the subject of St. Lucia there and then. Screwing up her courage she said, 'You know there's something else I wanted to tell you, well, there's a little trip I want us to take. Just for a few days and I think you'll like it a lot.'

'Where?' said Rory suspiciously.

'Well we're going to St. Lucia tomorrow,' Ellie rushed on, 'and I want you to come with me as it'll only be for a few days and it's a beautiful place we're going to. So I dearly want you to come with me and I hope you'll say yes, please Rory.'

'Are you out of your mind? What else aren't you telling me Ellie? I'm here to try and salvage our relationship and now you spring this on me. This is just what I mean, like I said earlier, am I just going to be trailing round after you? What do you want me for?'

'Oh, Rory, it's not like that at all. It's me and my bad planning and Alistair and I have already accepted this invitation. I wanted to see you so desperately that I didn't think it through. I didn't want not seeing you to drag on another week as I've already hurt you enough. I tried to keep you out of all the bad stuff that was going on as I didn't want you to get sucked into all my problems with Alistair. That's now sorted, I think.' Ellie ended and looked at Rory hopefully.

'So, leaving me marooned in the North in a blizzard and flying off handcuffed to Jack wasn't anything to do with it at all?'

'You know I didn't handcuff myself to Jack, he did it to me and I had to go and confront Alistair as all the kidnapping and the guns wouldn't have gone away would it? It would have just got worse and worse. Now things are more on an even keel and I'm in no danger.' Ellie's thoughts flitted back briefly to the cavern in

France with the beast from Hell. 'Perhaps we can pick up where we left off.'

'This certainly isn't the same playing field we're on now and you seem to keep changing the goal posts.' Rory grasped both of Ellie's hands and looked into her eyes. 'You have got to promise to talk to me and let me know what's going on in future. I can't keep being in the dark like this and if we're going to make a go of us then there can't be secrets. Well, not huge "elephant in the room" type secrets like you seem to have. Please, Ellie, promise me?'

Ellie looked back at Rory and knew everything he had said was true. They would never be an item if she didn't include him totally in her life at her side. 'OK, Rory, if I tell you everything, no holds barred, will you come with me?'

'I'll think about it,' said Rory noncommittally.

'OK it's nearly time to get changed for dinner and I've made sure you're in the adjoining room to mine. We'll have dinner and you can chat to Alistair.' Ellie mentally crossed her fingers. 'Then tonight when we're alone I'll tell you absolutely everything. I promise, faithfully, cross my heart.' Ellie took Rory to his room and opened the adjoining door. She showed him where his luggage had been stored and the black tie suit laid out for him was for tonight. She explained that they always changed for dinner which would be served at eight o'clock. They had about three quarters of an hour to shower and change before the pre-dinner drinks. Ellie would go down with him to meet Alistair then.

'Is it always so formal?' said Rory, eyeing the suit. 'Do you do this all the time?'

'Yes, Alistair likes to get changed for dinner as there may be a few guests. I've also got used to it and it's a chance to get a bit dressed up. Just pretend it's an occasion and it's our special night after so long.' As soon as the words left Ellie's mouth, she realized she'd said the wrong thing. It wasn't any good trying to put it right as she'd probably dig an even deeper hole so she quickly kissed Rory on the cheek and said, 'See you in a bit then, just come in when you're ready,' and left with alacrity.

Rory came into Ellie's room just as the maid was pinning up the last tendrils of hair. Ellie's dress was a shimmering peacock blue and grey creation that bought out the colours of her amazing eyes. The soft grey irises picked up the colours in the dress and turned them a smoky blue with the gold flecks accentuated. Her make-up was understated and showed off her flawless complexion. Rory stood there in his black tie evening dress and all he could manage was, 'Wow.'

'Well, "wow" to you as well. Rory you look magnificent. I've never seen you in black tie before and I have to say it suits you well. Shall we go down to dinner?' Ellie offered him her arm and they walked down the huge staircase to the palatial Drawing Room.

Alistair was already there with a drink in his hand leaning negligently on the fireplace. He straightened up, put his drink down and offered a hand to Rory. 'Ellie you look magnificent as usual and this must be Rory, so pleased to meet you.' He shook Rory's hand and made a small bow. Rory returned the firm grasp and muttered the same greeting without the bow.

'So, Rory, what would you like to drink, maybe some champagne, wine, gin and tonic? Just name your poison,' said Alistair, signalling a footman.

'I'd like a G and T please, no ice,' said Rory and looked at Ellie.

Ellie just shrugged and said, 'The usual,' meaning her peach

Bellini. She shot a glance at Alistair who smiled back urbanely.

'So, Rory, have you decided to come to St. Lucia with us tomorrow?'

Ellie could have killed Alistair there and then for jumping the gun and undoing all the soul searching and preparation she'd been doing. 'Rory's not decided yet,' she answered for him. 'I'm sure he'll make his own mind up in his own time.' This effectively closed the question down and she turned to Rory. 'We've been touring the castle and I've shown him the entrance to a couple of the secret passages. We may explore those at some point. What have you been doing all day, Alistair? I haven't seen you since breakfast.'

'Well, you know how it is, work, work, and more work. I'm looking forward to a bit of a break and a little sunshine. I mean proper sunshine by an outdoor pool,' said Alistair turning the conversation back to St. Lucia again. 'The place we're going to is owned by a good friend of mine, Fortune is his name and it's fortune by nature as well. He's been a lucky man and I'm going to enjoy our few days there to catch up on old times,' said Alistair blandly. Alistair was baiting Rory and Ellie couldn't stop him so she gave up and sipped her drink. 'We've got another couple joining us for dinner tonight, Ellie. I thought you'd be interested to meet the curator of the local museum and his wife. The museum is quite interesting; right up your street, in fact, got a good collection of old books and manuscripts.'

Ellie downed her drink in one and signalled for another. She threw caution to the winds and said, 'I know what you're doing, Alistair, you've set out to make Rory feel uncomfortable with your hidden agendas. Well, it won't work and you might as well stop it now as Rory and I will go and have dinner served in our room if you don't.'

'What have I said,' said Alistair feigning surprise. 'I most humbly beg your forgiveness, Rory, if I've made you feel uncomfortable, but I'm sure that's not the case. It's just my sister is sometimes a little hypersensitive and reads things into words that are not there.'

Rory was, in fact, feeling most uncomfortable at this point and could feel the undercurrents in the conversation swirling round him. He felt left out again and looked at Ellie. Her brows were knitted and she was glaring at Alistair. She pointedly turned her shoulder against her twin and said to Rory, 'Just ignore him, he's being an arse and trying to stir things up between us. As I said before you'll make your own mind up about St. Lucia, we'll discuss it later,' she added, pointedly, indicating the conversation was well and truly closed.

The footman ushered in the dinner guests and introductions were made all round and the couple, Signor Fratelli and his wife, were given their chosen drinks. They proved to be an amusing couple and the dinner party began to gel. Ellie had a fleeting chance to discuss with the curator the collection of books and was offered a guided tour at her own convenience and was anxious not to let the opportunity slip, even though it could have been made out of politeness. The party went into dinner and besides a few digs at Rory everything went well. Ellie fended these off and she noted that Rory was a big hit with Signora Fratelli who had begun to drink a little too much and was fluttering her eyelashes and beginning to behave like a schoolgirl.

Oh, well, thought Ellie, *things could be worse*, and turned her attention to Alistair and the Signor. He was angling for a look at the Library and Ellie jumped in and said she would be pleased to show him round when the others sat for their coffees and brandy after the meal. She wasn't sure about leaving Alistair and

Rory together but with all the hand patting and napkin waving that was going on with Signora Fratelli she thought they'd be safe enough. As everyone rose, she led Signor Fratelli to the library. Again, as with the chateau in France it was stuffed with rare books and would be a delight for the museum curator. He settled himself down in a chair by a reading desk and Ellie switched the reading light on.

'Signor, I know a little about the books here but I don't have an extensive knowledge yet. Is there anything you are particularly interested in?' said Ellie.

'There is something I would like to see again if I could,' said the Signor.

'Again?' Ellie queried.

'Yes, I was a great friend of your father's and although you didn't know him at all, he loved this collection. We used to sit here and peruse the manuscripts together. He had a wonderful knowledge about this castle and all its secrets. There was one particular book.' The Signor stood and scanned the shelves. 'Yes, here it is,' he said, indicating a massive tome bound in faded red leather. 'This is the one.'

'Let me help you,' said Ellie and lifted the book down. It was certainly a weighty piece of work and they carried it carefully to the table. The leather creaked as they opened it.

'Yes, this is it,' exclaimed Signor Fratelli as if finding an old friend after many years. 'It's a history of the castle written many hundreds of years ago. It tells of the intrigue and the wars that were fought over its possession. Many people wanted this Castle of the Birds.'

Ellie's blood ran cold, 'What did you say, this place is called the Castle of the Birds?'

'Why yes, didn't you know?' enquired Signor Fratelli.

'There are many legends associated with the site right back to before the Dark Ages. There was supposed to be a great bird that built its nest here, look here's an engraving.' Signor Fratelli turned to the front sheet and there was a picture of the beast from the chateau in France. It seemed to be looking straight at Ellie and its cruel, curved beak held a hint of a smile.

'But it's only a legend,' said Ellie half to herself.

'Of course, it is, but there was a cult that sprang up and the followers did all sorts of ritualistic things to gain the power from the bird.'

'What sort of things?' said Ellie bleakly, although she already knew the answer.

'Oh, it was said that great power would flow to the followers from the bird. They would be given everything they wanted on Earth but their souls would be forfeit on their death. The bird would claim them and fly them down to Hell. Maybe it was worth it for the cult as a lot of people who lived here became very rich and powerful. See, here are some of the family trees of the people. Your father and I would sit and trace them back for generations. I think if I remember rightly, he was descended from one of the families of the fourteenth century. That makes you a descendant as well,' said Signor Fratelli, having a revelation. 'It's good that a castle of this antiquity has been with one family for so many generations. I hope it continues and perhaps when you have more time I could show you the work your father and I did on the genealogy?'

Ellie could barely comprehend what Signor Fratelli was telling her. She was a descendant of some blood thirsty Borgia type dynasty that ruled the countryside with a rod of iron. Vlad the Impaler would seem like a pussy cat compared to this lot. Also, they drew their power from a great bird from Hell and Ellie knew this wasn't fiction. She'd seen it and knew the power it had. It had been thwarted last time and Alistair had lost some of his fingers in that meeting. Ellie knew it wasn't a happy bird and would do all it could do to claim the bargain written on the scroll. It was going to try to have her soul and she knew at that point she would fight it till her last breath, if that was what it took. Composing herself she smiled at Signor Fratelli, 'I would like that very much but perhaps we should now join the others again. Alistair and I are going on a short holiday but when we get back, I will be sure to contact you and make arrangements for you to visit us again. It's the least we could do when you've promised me a guided tour of your museum. I'll be looking forward to that very much on my return.' Ellie practically heaved Signor Fratelli out of his chair and propelled him to the Drawing Room where the others were chatting over glasses of brandy and cups of coffee.

It was quite an amusing picture in the salon as Rory was crammed up the side of a sofa and Signora Fratelli was practically sitting on his lap. Ellie would have laughed out loud if she didn't have other things on her mind. Alistair was sitting nonchalantly swirling a brandy glass and a small smile of amusement played round his lips.

'Ah, here you both are, I'll call for some fresh coffee,' Alistair said as Ellie and the Signor walked in. 'I hope you had a sufficient time to have a good look at the library Signor Fratelli?'

'Why yes, thank you very much. I was telling your sister that I was a great friend of your fathers and we used to sit for hours poring over his collection. I am very grateful to be able to have another look,' said Signor Fratelli politely.

'Yes, Signor Fratelli has shown me a book about the history of this castle and it appears we're both descended from some bloodthirsty clan that lived here six hundred or so years ago. Nice to keep it in the family if you like that sort of thing,' said Ellie accepting a fresh coffee. She decided at that point to keep the knowledge of the name of the castle to herself for the time being. It could be the catalyst that set Alistair off on one of his explorations for power through the occult again. Ellie didn't know him well enough to trust him not to break the promise he had made to her. He seemed to be on the straight and narrow at the moment but that could all fall apart instantly if he hadn't got the strength of will to resist it. She just didn't know.

Ellie turned her attention to Signora Fratelli. 'I hope you enjoyed the dinner, it'll be so nice to make some friends round here as we don't really know anyone yet.' Ellie shot a meaningful glance at Alistair. 'I've extended an invitation for your husband to visit again and I hope you have the time to accompany him. It would be nice to have another female to chat to.'

'Ah, yes,' sighed Signora Fratelli, 'these men, when they get together all else goes out of the door. Is that how you say it?'

'I understand totally and it would be nice just to sit over a coffee and chat sometime,' said Ellie and Alistair raised an eyebrow at this as he couldn't begin to imagine what Ellie and the Signora could possibly talk about for more than two minutes.

'When Luigi used to come to the castle before when your father was alive.' The Signora crossed herself. 'He used to be here for whole nights sometimes and all he could talk about when he got back was the birds and the books. I have no interest in birds or books but I do know some nice places to visit,' she looked expectantly at Ellie.

'I'm sure we could fix something up when I get back, sadly I'm away for a few days visiting friends but I'll contact you on our return, 'said Ellie.

Signor Fratelli put his coffee cup down and rose. 'We really must be getting back now and I thank you both for the wonderful meal and hope to see you again soon.' He got his wife, none too gently, by the elbow and prised her off the sofa. 'Come along my dear, we have taken up too much time from these good people already, let's get you home.' Signora Fratelli walked unsteadily to the door and Rory breathed a sigh of relief. They all rose to see the guests out and Rory quietly held Ellie's hand behind her back as they waved them goodbye from the main door.

Alistair sat back in his chair in the Drawing Room and picked up the brandy glass again and began swirling the contents. Ellie knew he wouldn't drink it but kept up the façade of enjoying a post dinner drink. 'You did well there, Rory, I really thought she was going to eat you and spit the bones out later. It was most amusing to watch you fending her off.'

Rory loosened his tie and sat back. 'Yep, she was a bit forward and kept touching me. Did you know she had her hand on my leg under the table and kept squeezing my knee?'

Ellie snorted. 'She was quite a good-looking woman though, yours for the asking, Rory.'

'Shut up,' said Rory reddening, 'she was a harpy and I'm not going to sit by her next time, that's for sure.'

Ellie and Alistair exchanged a glance and Alistair said, 'So there could be a next time then, Rory?'

'You know what I mean,' said Rory, blustering.

'Come on, admit it,' said Alistair, 'you enjoyed the dinner and some of the attentions of the Signora. You'd quite like to live this life if the truth be told.'

'Yes, I'll admit the dinner was wonderful and it's nice to experience how the other half lives for once and not have to worry about the gas bill and things like that, but like I said to

Ellie I have to "do" something with my life and not just trail round from dinner to dinner in Ellie's wake.' Rory stared at his cup.

'Well, you've got until tomorrow morning to sort it out as we're off to St. Lucia,' said Alistair with finality. 'So do your soul searching tonight and see if you can forego my sister in a bikini with sun, sand and sea.'

'Alistair!' said Ellie, 'that was totally uncalled for. We'll sort out what needs to be sorted in our own good time. I've had enough of you tonight and I think the conversation is just going to be about me and Rory. So, I'm off to bed and I'll leave you two to your own devices.' Ellie put her cup down with a clatter and left.

'Actually,' said Rory, 'I'm bushed and it's been a big day for me so I think I'll go up as well. I'll let you know at breakfast what we plan to do,' said Rory and left the room quickly, forestalling any further comment from Alistair.

Alistair sat and looked at the flickering fire. He'd enjoyed baiting Ellie and Rory and it had provided amusement during a very dull dinner. Rory wasn't a great raconteur or conversationalist and he couldn't see what Ellie saw in him, but he couldn't push it too far as he knew Ellie would run off into the sunset with Rory. He needed Ellie, she was still his other half and he had been though many conversations with her about it. She couldn't seem to grasp what he meant. Whilst he had been with her everything had turned to gold with his businesses and enterprises, it was as if she was his lucky charm and he couldn't let her go. Also, she had turned out to be a good hostess and he needed that as a foil to his own personality. She had wit and charm naturally, whereas he could turn it on and off like a tap when he needed it. The small problem of the stolen manuscripts appeared to be resolving itself well and he had a mountain of invitations to various house parties to work through. Everyone wanted to meet Ellie, his long lost twin, and as she was beautiful and clever he could spend a lot of time networking for his own ends. Social media had played its part and he had milked it to its full advantage. Okay, he was using her to his own ends but so what? She got what she wanted out of the relationship. One thing had piqued his interest tonight at the dinner. Signor Fratelli had come back into the Drawing Room smiling like a cat that had got the cream. He'd been a long standing friend of their fathers and had spent many hours with the books in the Library.

Alistair decided to go and have a look at what they had been perusing and wandered down to the Library. There was the great tome open at the page showing all the genealogy of the family tree. It seems they did go back a long way and this castle had been in the family for many a generation. So, he mused it was called the Castle of the Birds, the chateau in France had got the same name, strange or just a coincidence? Alistair didn't think so. He had harnessed the power of the beast in France and he had enjoyed the abilities it gave him. Their father had harnessed the same power as his father had done before him and it had led them to great wealth and riches. Alistair was by no means poor but the flaw in his character was greed and when he had something he always wanted more. That was partly why he didn't eat or drink to excess as he knew it would overtake him and he would turn into an obese drunk. Much always wanted more where Alistair was concerned. He placed his hand on the book and felt the familiar tingle as its power revealed itself. This wasn't a Grimoire, or spell book, that he had used earlier, just a history of the castle, but it still had some power. Alistair vowed that he would uncover the legacy his father had left them but would control it better this time and make it work for him.

Ellie and Rory were snuggled up in the dark and Ellie was just enjoying Rory's arms around her again. It was warm and comfortable and all the misgivings Ellie had felt were washed away by the tide of emotion that she felt.

'Rory, I hate to ask this now, but what are you going to do tomorrow? Are you going back to London or going to St. Lucia with me for a few days?'

'What do you want, Ellie?' said Rory drowsily.

'I know what I want, but is it what you want?' Ellie leaned on one elbow and looked at the contour of Rory's jaw line. She traced her finger down the line and into the hollow of his neck.

'I know I want to be with you, but I'm not sure this is the life that I want, I'm just not sure. It's all new to me and I still feel that you've messed me about in the past. You went off with Jack and I got left up north and was worried sick. Then you called on Christmas day and I'd never heard from you till then and I was convinced it was over between us.' Rory propped himself on his elbow and faced Ellie. 'I'll bet there's another agenda for going to St. Lucia isn't there?'

Ellie dropped her eyes. 'Yes there is. I'm going to St. Lucia to try and get another one of the stolen books back. When Alistair stole those books, he auctioned them off to the highest bidders and it's a priceless collection. It can't be replaced and Alistair is stuck in Italy now because he can't go back to England as he'll end up in jail. He's got to try and get them back and I'm the one to help him. He can't just buy them back as these people are his friends and he'll be sunk without a trace if they get wind of what he's trying to do. So, with the help of Claire, Phil and the others we're trying to put things right. You do understand, don't you?'

Rory was silent as if processing all the information.

'Please say you'll come with me Rory. I know you'll help me and I need you.'

'You didn't seem to need me in the past,' said Rory, sulkily.

'I know it seemed like that Rory but I *did* need you and I only did my best to keep you out of it all because I was scared. I didn't want you dragged into it and I couldn't bear it if anything happened to you.' Ellie's eyes pleaded with Rory.

'So, when you came to the farmhouse all battered and bruised and when you'd been kidnapped and tied up, and all the shooting started at the farm that was all because you hadn't told me the truth?' Rory's tone was accusing.

'Yes, I'm afraid it was, Rory, and I'm really sorry about all that. I didn't know how things would turn out but like I said earlier, cross my heart, there won't be any more secrets now and I'm telling you all this because I really want to be with you.'

'I suppose someone has got to look out for you as you seem to attract trouble,' said Rory, slightly mollified. 'Anyway, a short holiday would be nice, I haven't had one for years.'

Ellie hugged Rory for all she was worth and was overjoyed that he'd said he would go with her. 'We'll only be away for about four or so days and it'll be lovely with you there. You'll enjoy it, I know you will. It'll be like a pre-honeymoon honeymoon if you know what I mean.' A little thought jabbed at her psyche and the scenario of what she had to do while she was there surfaced. She had to go through the whole business of stealing something that would be closely guarded and still appearing to be snowy white afterwards was a daunting thought. She'd done it once and made the abysmal mistake of stealing the wrong manuscript, Ellie thought that certainly wouldn't happen again. At least this time she would be better prepared and the whole team would be there to help her and she would have a glorious few days with Rory.

CHAPTER FOUR

Ellie breezed down to breakfast the next morning and helped herself to scrambled egg and toast. All was right with the world and Rory soon followed her and was pondering over the array of continental meats when Alistair came in.

'Good morning, Alistair, I hope you are well and happy this beautiful morning?' said Ellie with her cutlery poised to dive in.

'Umph,' was all that Alistair could manage. He sat with his plate empty and a footman hovered expectantly with the coffee pot.

'What's that supposed to mean, Alistair? We're off to a holiday paradise today and Rory has decided to come with us. That'll be nice, won't it?' Ellie adopted a tone you could use with a recalcitrant five-year-old.

'Looks like there's a bit of a crisis brewing in one of the chemical plants and the Bank is making lots of noise at the moment,' Alistair said flicking through his mail abstractedly. 'I should be in England now to sort this out.' He threw the mail across the table in frustration.

'If you don't come to St. Lucia, you're going to have a bit of a crisis in the rare books and manuscripts division as well,' said Ellie pointedly. 'You have hundreds of minions, just get your best person to hold the fort for a few days and you'll be back in charge again. Even better,' she added, 'take a few of them with you and set up shop over there under a palm tree. Banks do all their stuff by electronic transaction anyway and you'll be in a different time zone, so it could work to your advantage.'

'Sister, you are brilliant! Why didn't I think of that? I totally forgot the changes in the time zones; I'll arrange it right away and see you both on the plane.' Alistair grabbed a banana and was gone.

'Is he always like that?' said Rory sitting down with his plate.

'In a word, yes. Once he gets an idea, he's so totally focused he can forget to sleep or eat, but that's his problem, not mine. He didn't raise any objections to us going together and we've got a few hours before we go, so how about looking at some of the secret passages in the castle? We can play Dungeons and Dragons for real,' said Ellie.

'Sounds great,' said Rory with a mouthful of Parma ham.

'Maybe there's something you can help me with as I've got a map to a secret tunnel that no-one has managed to find yet. We could have a go at cracking the code and seeing where it goes if we find it,' Ellie said enticingly. She had to admit she was intrigued by Signor Fratelli's map even though it could spell great danger to her as she suspected her father had hidden his secret world down there. She had placed the map carefully in the safe in her room and hadn't destroyed it straight away, which said which way her thoughts were going.

Ellie started by showing Rory the passage from the Breakfast Room and he was intrigued by the mechanisms that opened the secret doors and how they had been carefully hidden. She retrieved the map from her safe and they went to the corridor and began pacing out the measurements on the diagram. 'Looks like Signor Fratelli was right, there is a discrepancy here,' said Ellie. 'There seems to be a passageway leading God knows where from this section of the hall.' She looked in puzzlement at Rory who was lifting up the paintings and examining the wood carvings round the doors.

'Going on what we've seen before there has to be a doorway in this ten metre section here.' Rory waved his arms. 'Can you see anything like a doorway cut into the tapestry or a big enough painting or sculpture that could move?'

'Let's do this methodically,' said Ellie. 'We'll start this end and work down.'

They stood side by side at the start of the section and looked at a rather depressing landscape picture.

'It's hung very high and even if it moved, I can't see how anyone could crawl through that space,' said Rory, wrinkling his lip.

'True,' said Ellie, 'but what about this?' She stood in front of a bust of someone with a laurel wreath on his head. 'The plinth is right up by the wall and could hide a passageway.'

They both stood in front of the sculpture and grasped the plinth and tried to swing it to one side. The bust wobbled alarmingly.

'Maybe we have to get Claudius off his stand and then it'll move,' said Ellie hopefully.

They both heaved the bust from the plinth and had another go. This time the large wooden plinth moved away from the wall but there was nothing behind it. No cuts in the wallpaper or any cracks or joins that could suggest a door. Claudius was replaced and they moved onto the next item which was a side table.

'At least this'll be easier to move,' said Rory, pulling the table away from the wall. Again, after a minute inspection of the wall, there was nothing. 'Is this worth it?' said Rory. 'We've only got about half an hour left before we get on the plane.'

'Just one more, please,' begged Ellie.

'Okay,' replied Rory and moved onto the next item which

was a huge floor to ceiling painting of some medieval guy with his foot on a dead stag.

'If I've got to live here for any length of time, I'm going to have to change the décor,' said Ellie with distaste, looking at the painting.

They tried to lift the painting off the wall but it wouldn't move. 'Perhaps this is it,' said Ellie excitedly. 'There has to be a knob or button to press to move it like the other entrances.'

They both got chairs and stood on them whilst examining the top of the frame. Rory said, 'Thinking about it logically, you wouldn't want to get a chair or a pair of steps every time you wanted to use the passage, would you?'

'No, you're right,' said Ellie, 'the lock would have to be at a sensible height to use.'

They both climbed down and began running their hands down the frame, prodding and pushing every likely bit of carving. 'I'm sure this is it Rory, we've just got to find it,' said Ellie.

'Why is this so important all of a sudden?' said Rory mystified.

'It's just another secret I'd like to unravel,' said Ellie glibly while continuing to work on the frame. Her hand felt a rose carving and suddenly she was sure it moved. She looked carefully and thought it wasn't quite in the same place as before. 'Hey, look at this Rory do you think this could be it? I'm sure I felt it move,' said Ellie excitedly.

Rory climbed down off his chair and bent down for a closer look. A deferential cough came from a footman who had appeared unnoticed behind them. 'Miss Morgan, your car is waiting.'

'Thank you, we'll be down directly,' said Ellie to the footman. 'Damn, damn and double damn,' she said to Rory.

'We'll have to leave it now till we get back, and we were so close.'

'Never mind,' said Rory, placating her, 'I'm sure it'll still be there when we get back. Come on we'll have to run.' He set off with Ellie holding tight to his hand and laughing.

The flight was on time although the driver had to negotiate the hairpin bends at breakneck speed and Ellie was left feeling rather sick by the time Naples came into view. At least there were no tedious check-ins and luggage traumas to deal with. This was the part Rory enjoyed the most as the car drew up by the jet and they embarked straight up the steps. Alistair was already ensconced and waved a hand at them in greeting and looked pointedly at his watch. He had taken the back half of the cabin with his PAs and they were deep in conference already, so Rory and Ellie chose to sit at the front and made themselves comfortable.

The flight was relatively uneventful and Ellie dozed a lot of the time and Rory played with the in-flight entertainment and found a lot of the games he used to play in London. He was happy shooting things and disappearing into far off lands as a warrior or a battle strategist. Alistair kept up the pressure on his team and by the time they landed at Hewanorra airport he had a smile on his face. A fifteen minute helicopter ride took them to the top of the island and landed near Fortune's resort where they would be staying. His house was at one end on a slight rise and overlooked the magnificent bay with its silver sand and palm trees.

Their host was there to greet them when they arrived at the resort. Fortune was an extremely tall guy and was dressed casually in a loose shirt and shorts. He embraced Alistair who looked slightly uncomfortable with this style of greeting and then he grabbed Ellie's hands and held her at arm's length. 'My man, you never said that your sister was such a beauty. Welcome to our small island and I hope you enjoy your stay here.'

'It's like a jewel in the ocean, it's just so beautiful,' said Ellie, taking in the deep blue ocean and the flower beds filled with strange tropical flowers.

'Everything the resort has to offer is yours. You can have a personal masseuse, dive on the reef and swim with the fishes, go sailing, everything you want to do is yours whenever you like,' said Fortune, expansively waving his arms. 'Just say the word and it's yours.'

'Well, yes,' said Ellie, not knowing quite how to respond to such largesse. 'I'd like you to meet Rory,' said Ellie grabbing Rory's arm and dragging him into the conversation. 'He's my fiancé and he's got a few days off so he thought he would join us.'

'I am devastated,' said Fortune pretending to wipe away a tear. 'You are already spoken for and here I was thinking I had met the girl of my dreams.'

A tall stunningly beautiful black woman materialized at Fortune's side. 'Don't let the old charmer fool you. I am Honey, Fortune's wife of many a long year.' She extended her hand in greeting. 'He's a fraud really and couldn't cope with more than one woman in his life.'

Ellie grasped her hand and smiled at Fortune. 'Sorry but your luck's out today. I'm Ellie and this is Alistair, my twin brother, and Rory, my fiancé,' she said, introducing the party. She looked round for the PAs that had accompanied them but they had made themselves scarce. 'I was just saying that this place is really a jewel and we are really grateful that you have given us the opportunity to visit it.'

Honey said, 'Don't worry about a thing. This party is for

Fortune's birthday and we just hope we can all give the old man a good time.'

'Surely not that old, and I'm sorry we didn't know it was for your birthday,' said Ellie.

'Yes, the old man is fifty soon and being as there is a zero on the end, we thought we would have a big party of all our old friends and make some new ones on the way. Don't even think about gifts as you being here is more than enough. If someone can give time then that's the greatest gift of all,' finished Honey sagely. Fortune nodded his agreement. 'I don't know if you are interested but we try and do lots for the people of the island and I can take you round and show you a few of the projects we're involved in, just in case you get bored here.'

'I'm sure that won't be the case,' said Ellie, 'but I would be interested in what you do as Alistair and I could perhaps replicate some of the projects back home. It's always nice to try and help others.' Ellie shot a glance at Alistair.

'Yes,' said Alistair, 'I'm sure my sister would be interested in what you do for the islanders and she may decide to set up some sort of foundation when we get back. We haven't got anything like that the moment,' said Alistair, smiling condescendingly at Ellie.

'With great wealth comes great responsibilities,' said Honey, pointedly looking straight at Alistair. He just nodded. 'We've set your assistants up in the Library so you can beaver away while we're having fun, although I can't imagine why you need to do that.' Honey shook her head and looked at Ellie. 'You just make sure he has some downtime in the pool, he'll look and feel better for it.'

Ellie warmed to the outspoken Honey there and then. She couldn't believe that Fortune and Honey were mixed up in drugs, mayhem and shady undercover dealings. She could be totally wrong but her gut said otherwise. 'I'd love to see what you do and maybe we could talk later but I'm sure you have loads to do but I will take you up on your offer, definitely,' said Ellie.

Fortune summoned a man in a white uniform who had been hovering at the edge of the group. 'Philip will take you up and show you your rooms and perhaps you'll meet us about six o'clock for drinks by the beach. It'll be a bit cooler then, not by much, but you'll meet the rest of the guests and maybe meet some more old friends,' said Fortune, blowing a kiss to Ellie before being dragged away by Honey with mock disgust.

Philip took them up to their suites and they were all on the second floor each with a balcony overlooking the sea. When Ellie got into her room, she found Maria and Claire waiting for her.

'What a fabulous place,' said Claire. 'Just imagine living here with all this sea and sand.' Ellie went and stood on the balcony and gazed appreciatively at the vista. There were brightly coloured sailboats, jet skiers, boats with dive flags up, and a gentle breeze filled the sails of a three mast schooner on the horizon. 'It's a paradise and I'm glad to have come as your maid with Maria. It seems we don't have to keep in the shadows either and we can mingle freely with the other guests, so that'll be useful to us over the next few days,' said Claire, joining Ellie enjoying the view.

'I don't know if you've met Honey and Fortune,' said Ellie, 'but they don't seem the type of people to be mixed up in drugs and stuff like that at all. Honey's offered to take me and show me some of the work their foundations do to better the lives of the islanders. I know appearances can be deceptive but I just don't think they're that kind of people. I know they are uber- rich and make millions from all their resorts but they don't seem to be the usual type of greedy people.'

'I know what you mean,' said Claire, 'Maria and I have been chatting to some of the permanent staff here and they all say the same. Honey, especially, is always off doing some good work or other and Fortune just seems to go with the flow. He stumps up the cash for all her schemes but he appears to be happy to do it. I've also found out that his house, over there.' Claire pointed to the edge of the resort. 'Doesn't have any rare books or anything like that in it. It's just a normal house with ordinary books and magazines lying about. There aren't any great works of art there either, just local artists and local carvings and things like that. It's a bit of mystery really.'

Maria leaned on the balcony and agreed with what Claire had found out. She said everyone had said that Fortune and Honey weren't really interested in that sort of stuff at all and didn't give house room to antiques and the like. She couldn't understand why Fortune had paid a lot of money for a rare manuscript when he didn't have any real interest in things like that. She also informed Ellie that Claire had made contact with Phil, Nigel, Robert, and Jack and they were just down the road in some lodgings. There was going to be a street party that night and they were both going into town to enjoy the evening.

'That sounds like fun, Maria,' said Ellie, 'just go and enjoy yourself, and I'll see what I can find out tonight when I meet the other guests. We're all supposed to meet up as it gets dark about sixish and get together as a party for drinks. Please put something cool out for me as I don't think the humidity drops at all at night and I'll be a sweaty mess by seven!'

'It's all ready,' said Maria and pointed to an off-the-shoulder rainbow creation. 'I think you should have your hair up, it'll be cooler and I'll keep the make-up to a minimum so you don't have to worry about looking shiny.'

'Maria, I never worry about that anyway but the hair up would be a good idea as I feel like an oil slick already. I'll have a shower now and you can start and we'll chat about what we've got to do. I don't think Alistair is going to be of any help, as usual, as he's bought along an office full of people and clearly intends to work in between socializing. I don't think he was actually going to come and was going to back out at the last moment till I forced him to,' said Ellie, exasperated.

Ellie went and had a quick shower and sat in a robe in front of the dressing table. Claire perched on the bed and Maria began to dry her hair. 'I don't know what Fortune's done with the manuscript if it isn't in the house. How are we going to find out?' said Ellie.

'We've just got to keep doing what we normally do and keep asking questions I suppose,' said Claire, watching Maria weave her magic with Ellie's hair. 'You could take the opportunity Honey gave you and let her take you round some of the foundations and see if anything turns up there. Although I haven't got a clue until I see everyone else tonight.'

'At least I don't have to steal anything this time,' said Maria, pinning the last piece in place. 'It was awful in Morocco, I had to throw the book over the wall and we thought we were going to get caught. I think that horrible man would have killed us,' said Maria with a shudder.

'He was awful, I agree,' said Ellie. 'I hope I never have to meet him again. I'm sure he was eyeing me up for his harem.'

Claire looked at Ellie through the glass. 'The bad news is that I think he's been invited here.'

'Oh God, no! Please tell me that's not true, it's just a joke isn't it?' Ellie pleaded.

'Sad, but true I'm afraid,' said Claire. 'I sneaked a look at the guest list and he's there, large as life and twice as nasty. You'll just have to keep your wits about you and not let him get too close. Other than that, take up smoking and give him a blast of dog breath, that'll put him off.'

'Or garlic,' said Maria, 'always good.'

'Gee, guys, thanks a lot, that's just the type of advice I need right now,' said Ellie, rolling her eyes.

'There is one guy you could get to meet if you want to,' said Claire, 'he could be quite useful in the future. He's a Russian by the name of Valentin Andrei Salnikov. Apparently, he's big into everything we want stopped.'

'I really meet the nicest people through you, don't I?' said Ellie, grimacing at Claire. 'I'll try but can't promise anything. What's he looks like?' she asked.

'Everything a girl could want, tall, blondish, very handsome, a bit of a charmer really, but big into the sex slave business. Ships all his girls to the U.S, England, and now Australia we think. He's got most of the Russian government in his pocket so we wouldn't get very far if we went there. Any intelligence is good intelligence, so just do your best,' said Claire.

'Well I for one don't like this at all,' said Maria. 'Miss Ellie is not going to get mixed up with all these bad men again so I'm not going to the street party tonight. I'm going to stay here and look after her,' she said and folded her arms.

'Now, Maria,' said Ellie, 'don't get all worked up. I'll be fine as I'll have Rory at my side all evening. You go and have a good time and I'll tell you all about it later.' Ellie turned to Claire. 'You'd better have a word with Rory as he's going to go off half-cocked when I sidle up to some Russian brute named Valentin, particularly if he's handsome as well. Just tell him not to get all jealous and balls it up for me please. You'll probably have to sit him down and give him an abridged version of what I'm doing while we're here. I'll tell you now he won't like it.'

'Don't worry, I'll sort it,' said Claire with a grin. 'I'll probably have to lock him in a broom cupboard as I threatened before if he doesn't want to play his part. I'll tell him it's of national importance and he'll be watched all evening and if he doesn't play, he'll develop a mystery virus and have to leave immediately. That'll shut him up.'

'That's devious,' said Ellie, aghast at what Claire was going to say to Rory.

'Yep,' said Claire with a shrug.

Half an hour later and everyone was ready for drinks on the boardwalk by the beach. Rory knocked on Ellie's door and they went down together arm in arm. The night was magical and a thousand stars glittered for them overhead and frogs and cicadas sang in the foliage. There were huge candles lit all along the beach to light their way and the bar was already full with a soft steel band playing in the background.

'You look marvellous, Ellie,' said Rory, giving her a kiss. 'This place is certainly a honeymoon venue on my list.'

'You look good yourself,' said Ellie, taking in the relaxed dress code. 'Black tie would have been a bit much tonight and you would have melted.' She laughed. 'Let's just enjoy ourselves a bit and put England and Italy behind us for a few days, if we can,' she added.

'Your mate Claire did pay me a visit earlier,' said Rory, not sure how to broach the subject.

'Yes, she did say she'd pop along,' said Ellie, making light of what had probably been a fraught conversation.

'The way she put it seems as though you now work for MI

something or other and it's all cloak and dagger stuff from now on,' said Rory, fishing.

'Pretty much,' said Ellie, refusing to be drawn. 'Let's just enjoy tonight and if I'm talking to a tall Russian don't get all jealous as I'm just trying to find out some information, that's all. It's not a "honey trap" or anything like that as I'm sure he's got any number of women falling at his feet. In fact, hundreds of them and I'm not sure they want to.'

'Okay,' said Rory, 'I promise not to get jealous and I'll play my part as Claire said I would be on the next MediVac flight out if I didn't. I don't know if I like that woman or not,' he said, furrowing his brow.

'Don't worry about Claire,' said Ellie, smiling, 'she's on our side and if you're in a jam she's the one I would most like to ride to my rescue. She saved my life once and I trust her.'

They had reached the boardwalk and accepted drinks from the white-gloved waiters and surveyed the scene. There were big candles throwing a soft, warm glow and the sound of the sea was the background for the steel band. Suddenly a big cheer went up as Fortune and Honey arrived. Everyone began to sing Happy Birthday and clap Fortune on the shoulder as he went past. Ellie spotted Alistair on the far side of the room deep in conversation with a tall, blond guy who met the description of the Russian she was supposed to schmooze. Turning to Rory she said, 'I think that's him over there with Alistair, you know the Russian, Valentin something or other that I'm supposed to meet. Will you be okay here for a minute or two while I go and make his acquaintance? I won't be long just to get my face known to him.'

Rory looked at his fizzing drink. 'I suppose so, it's your job now isn't it?'

'That sounds a bit off, Rory, just mingle a bit till I get back.

I thought we had sorted out all this? I love you dearly but he may be put off if I'm attached by the hip. I promise I won't be long.' Ellie pecked Rory on the cheek and wended her way to Alistair.

'Hi, Alistair, isn't this a wonderful place?' said Ellie breezily when she reached them. She looked at Alistair pointedly to perform the introductions.

'This is my twin, Ellie, and this is Valentin one of my Russian comrades,' said Alistair with aplomb.

Ellie extended her hand. 'How lovely to meet you, Valentin, I'm sure "comrade" is not an acceptable form of greeting any more, although I know nothing about Russia at all. Maybe you could help me along in this?' She left the question hanging in the air.

Valentin hadn't let go of her hand yet but stared into her eyes. 'If I may say so, you have mesmeric eyes, so like your brother's, they are very unusual and I would very much like to tell you all about Mother Russia.'

'Yes, our eyes are a bit of a giveaway and that's what led Alistair to think we were related.' Ellie withdrew her hand. 'I'm just so interested in Russia and would love to hear about it first hand if you have the time on your holiday.'

'I'll always make the time for you, Ellie,' said Valentin and Ellie felt Alistair kick her ankle.

'Well, I mustn't keep you any longer,' said Ellie and pointed a finger at Valentin. 'But I will hold you to your promise,' and she sashayed away into the throng. Ellie let out the breath she'd been holding in and wended her way back to Rory who was deep in conversation with Honey.

'Honey's been telling me about what they do for the islanders and guess what?' said Rory. 'Did you know there are two Nobel Prize winners for Literature who come from St.

Lucia.'

'Yes, two,' said Honey, 'we believe that education is the key to all things and we encourage all our young people to go on to higher education. Many go the United States or England and continue at their great universities. My eldest son is studying to be an engineer in England at the moment,' she added proudly.

'Wow,' said Ellie, 'you must be so proud of him.'

Rory added, 'They do this by creating libraries and collections of art work so that the students can study these first hand.'

Ellie's interest was suddenly riveted. 'You have collections of books and works of art so that students can see them and study them here on the island?'

'Why, yes,' said Honey, amused, 'everything is here for them and that's what one of our foundations does. It provides the materials for students of the arts to study. They don't have to travel far to see these great things for themselves. I said we could show you round if you were interested?'

Ellie accepted with alacrity. 'I would be absolutely fascinated to see the work you do. I'm sure Rory would be as well and I hope you will have the time to show us something of what you do. It may be that we could replicate some of it back in Europe,' said Ellie, looking at Rory.

'Yes, it would be great to see what you do and also something of the island as well,' said Rory, following Ellie's lead.

'It's a date then,' said Honey, 'perhaps tomorrow, I'll catch you at breakfast, which won't be too early I promise, but I must tear my husband away from the cabaret singer which I see has just arrived.' She rolled her eyes. 'A pretty face and a short skirt and he's fallen.'

Ellie smiled as she knew that wasn't true but just a façade

that they kept up to keep Fortune's persona to the world intact. The marriage was as solid as the rock of Gibraltar and they had both met their soul mates. They were still so much in love after many years and Honey had mentioned an eldest son so there must be more children. Ellie hoped that when she married it would endure as theirs had, it had undergone changes over the years but the foundations were sound.

Ellie looked at Rory and wished on a sudden shooting star that they could be like Fortune and Honey in their abundant happiness. She raised her glass. 'To us,' she said and they sipped their drinks in toast.

The street party was in full swing when Maria and Claire arrived. The streets set aside were barred to traffic and were crammed with stalls selling every type of native food and drink, bands played and everyone was just out for a good time on a Friday night. There were pockets of dancing and their arms were grabbed by young men trying to drag them into the festivities. It was quite daunting for Maria and she kept close to Claire and was relieved when they saw the four men standing at the rendezvous point clutching some strange drink with bits of bark floating in them.

'Well you lot seem to have gone native very quickly,' said Claire, eyeing the flamboyant shirts and the weird drinks.

'Yeah, what a cool place,' said Nigel. 'The music is off the wall and everyone is so friendly. Check this out.' He offered Claire his drink.

'I think I'll pass on that one,' said Claire, 'I don't think my liver would stand it whatever it is.'

'It's okay, honestly,' said Nigel, 'they've got a sugar cane distillery up the road and it's some sort of rum mixed with banana. It's good,' he said, sipping his drink appreciatively. 'It costs next to nothing as well. I know the Queen's head is on the notes but believe me it's really cheap.'

'So,' said Phil, bringing the impromptu meeting to order, 'where are we right now?'

'Not very far,' said Claire, 'none of us can believe that this guy Fortune is mixed up in anything really bad. He comes across as clean, so clean, in fact, he squeaks.'

Jack said, 'Yep, that's exactly the picture we're getting as well. All he seems to do is follow his wife's lead and puts his money, of which there is a lot, into various good works for the benefit of the islanders. No-one seems to have a bad word to say about him or his wife.'

Maria said, 'I've been in his house with one of the other staffs and there's nothing there that looks old or antique at all, it's all local ethnic stuff, carvings, paintings and wall hangings etc. If there is a secret room or vault it's not there.'

'Well,' said Phil, 'we've just got to keep asking about and see what turns up, but now let's just party till dawn and have a good time, we deserve it.' Everyone agreed loudly and wholeheartedly.

CHAPTER FIVE

The party at the resort had begun in earnest and champagne was flowing like a river in full flood. The dinner had been magnificent and everything from crab flown in from Alaska to Japanese beef renowned for its sweetness had been prepared by French chefs and served by impeccable waiters. The party had again moved out under the stars and the band played tunes no-one could resist dancing to. A trolley had appeared, carefully weaving its way through the guests, carrying a huge cake made into the tear drop shape of the island resplendent with palm trees, sailing boats and fifty candles that fizzed like mini fireworks. Fortune was called forward and looked slightly abashed to be at the centre of attention again.

H raised his glass. 'Thank you so much my kind friends for all being here for this day. I will toast myself to the next fifty years.' He sipped his champagne and everyone shouted, 'Hear, hear,' and broke into a Happy Birthday serenade. He smiled and pulled Honey to his side. 'But most of all I would like you all to raise a glass to my beautiful wife who has made all this possible and for giving me three wonderful children. Without her to keep me on the straight and narrow I wouldn't be here now with you all. I was a bad boy.' He leered round at the women next to him. 'I got mixed up with the wrong people in my youth and she put me straight. She could see underneath my skin and knew there was something good trying to get out. She helped me when the going got tough and I would like to toast Honey for all the work she has put done in the past and all the wonderful work she continues to do on the island today. To Honey.' Fortune raised a glass and gave her a kiss.

'He's just an old softie really, 'said Honey, wiping away a little tear, 'but enjoy the party and here's to you all, as I said before, the old friends and to the new ones we will make tonight.'

Everyone raised their glasses yet again and the band struck up and Ellie felt a tap on her elbow and Valentin stood there and offered her his arm to go and dance. Ellie couldn't really refuse so she gave her glass to Rory and followed him onto the dance floor. He swept her up and was a very good dancer and Ellie was whirled round till she was quite breathless and exhilarated. A quieter number came on and the tempo lessened and she swayed in time to the music and her partner.

'So, Ellie, you are the long lost twin of Alistair. It must have been a bit of a surprise to you to find you had a brother,' said Valentin. 'I know I would be if I suddenly found a sister. I've known Alistair a long time and he and Max were very close. I must admit I dealt with Max more than I did with Alistair, we got on very well. The helicopter accident was a terrible tragedy.'

Ellie was a bit nonplussed as it was, she that had caused the demise of Max by kicking him out of the helicopter in the first place. She decided to play it cool. 'I only met Max for a few weeks before the accident and I didn't know him all that well. He was Alistair and my half brother, same father, different mothers.' Max had been a sadist and intent on Ellie's downfall and she had killed him because he would have killed her eventually. 'We don't really talk about Max,' she lied, 'as I think it's still quite painful for Alistair. So, you have flown here all the way from Russia to be at the party,' she said, trying to change the subject. 'What line of business are you in when you're at home?' she enquired politely. 'I always try to take an interest in Alistair's business dealings, two heads are often better than one, don't you think?'

'When it's a head a pretty as yours then it would always be a bonus to any man,' said Valentin gallantly.

'We are talking about my brother here,' said Ellie reprovingly. 'I never knew he had dealings in Russia though.'

'Yes, we have many things in Russia of interest to your brother and we have made some good deals in the past.' Valentin left it there refusing to be drawn further.

Ellie sensed she wasn't on a winner with this one, and decided to leave it alone as to probe further would arouse his suspicions. 'I hope we can meet again and I will look forward to the time when we can discuss things to our mutual benefit.' Ellie disentangled herself from Valentin and hoped she had sown the seeds of him thinking she was Alistair's business partner as well as twin. He led her back to Rory and left after kissing her hand.

'He kissed your hand,' said Rory, handing Ellie back her drink.

'Yep, that's what they do in Russia. Don't worry, Rory, he's not my type at all and I wouldn't trust him as far as I could throw him, and that's not very far at all,' Ellie said, and suddenly thought of how many people she could really trust in this world and there weren't very many at all. She could trust Rory with her life and this realization made her feel all warm. 'Come on, let's just dance and enjoy the night. We're here in St. Lucia and we may never be back, let's just go for the moment and sod tomorrow.' Ellie put her glass down and took Rory's from his hand and led him onto the dance floor. The band had begun to play a soft melody and Ellie put her head on Rory's shoulder and was lost.

The next day dawned and no-one saw the sun come up. Ellie

had gone to Rory's room last night and he was still snoring gently when she opened her eyes. Ellie pulled on a robe and wandered onto the balcony and watched the fishermen on the reef balancing precariously while flinging their nets. A few people were doing a stretch class on the beach as the tide went out and the day was cool. Staff were gently raking the sand to make it pristine for the guests and a few gardeners wandered about snipping the dead heads from the flowers. It was so quiet and she enjoyed just hearing the soft lisp of the surf on the white sand. She decided not to wake Rory and she went back to her own room and found Maria sorting out her clothes for the day.

'Hi, Maria, how did you get on last night, did you meet up with everyone?'

'We went into the town and everyone was there and we had a wonderful night. I danced to the bands and drank some rum and it is very good after the second glass,' said Maria, with a smile. 'I also talked a lot to Robert and he was telling me all about his job and his life in London, it sounds very exciting,' she said wistfully.

'I thought you had enough excitement at the last house party,' said Ellie, reminding her of the adrenaline-fuelled experience they had been through.

'Yes, but he is a very nice man and I had a nice time talking to him,' said Maria, wishing to close the subject.

'Oh,' said Ellie, 'so that's how the land lies then,' she said, teasing Maria who blushed. 'I'm sure you'll have lots of time to talk some more to Robert if you want to.' She left it as an unspoken question.

'Today,' said Maria, 'you can go with Miss Honey to see one of her foundation works after breakfast if you want to. I've had a message from her maid to say to meet her at breakfast and you can decide then,' said Maria, changing the subject entirely.

'That sounds like a good idea as we're only here for a few days and I'd like to chat with Honey some more if I can,' said Ellie and picked up some pale linen trousers and a cool top to wear. 'I'll go with the trousers as there's likely to be some big insects here that bite and I don't want to be covered in craters before lunchtime.'

Breakfast was a quiet affair and Ellie just got herself some bacon and the chef made her a two egg omelette with mushrooms and she settled herself down with a pot of tea. There were a few guests dotted about but the atmosphere was quiet and subdued. They were obviously nursing gargantuan hangovers and Ellie felt quite smug about deliberately not drinking too much in the heat and with the jet lag as well. Just as she was finishing her breakfast Honey breezed in and took the seat opposite Ellie.

'I had hoped you would be here,' she said and called for some Ceylon tea. 'I thought we could go and see a library I've set up as I've been doing my homework.' She tapped the side of her nose. 'I think you are interested in rare books and you used to work in a library before.'

'I'm impressed,' said Ellie. 'Yes, I did used to work with old books and manuscripts and I find them fascinating. If it's not too much trouble I'd love to see your collection.' Ellie's stomach did a flip as she thought she may get access to some sort of repository for manuscripts.

'No problem, we'll leave in about an hour if that's okay as I've just got a few things to sort out before we go. We don't want to leave it too late as you may find it a bit hot to be wandering about in the full sun. Anyway, you're on holiday and you can just lie by the pool or go sailing this afternoon.'

'It's very kind of you, Honey, and I do appreciate it, the party last night was amazing and I don't think I've ever been to one so lavish or so meaningful.' Ellie looked at Honey and was met with a steady stare.

'Yes, that silly old husband of mine got quite emotional but he seemed to enjoy it.'

'Enjoy it,' Ellie exclaimed, 'he seemed quite overwhelmed, and when the cake came in and he made that speech I don't think there was a dry eye in the house. You certainly know how to throw a Caribbean party, Honey, I'll have to take a few lessons from you.' Ellie laughed.

'Anyway, I thank you for that and I'm glad you enjoyed it as much as I did, but I have to go now and I will see you later,' said Honey, pushing back her chair and leaving Ellie sipping the last of her tea.

Ellie tried to be nonchalant as she strolled back to the room but she really wanted to run and grab the sat phone and let Phil know where she was going. Halfway back she realized that she didn't actually know where she was going and felt a complete idiot. All she knew was that she was going to a library but she didn't know where it was. She ran up the last few stairs and grabbing the phone she dialled the number she had committed to memory. At least she hadn't got that wrong as it was picked up on the second ring.

'Hi, is that Phil,' said Ellie breathlessly.

'Yes,' said Phil.

'I've got some news. I'm going with Honey this morning to see some books and manuscripts in a collection at a library, but I haven't managed to find out where I'm going exactly,' Ellie tailed off.

'No worries, when are you leaving?' said Phil.

'What do you mean, "no worries"? I don't know where I'm

going,' said Ellie, confused.

'We'll just put a tail on your car and follow you,' said Phil as if talking to a five-year-old.

'Oh, yeah, okay, never thought of that,' said Ellie, feeling stupid. 'I'm going in about an hour.'

'You may see us but don't recognize us if you do, okay?' said Phil, carefully.

'I won't even look in your direction,' said Ellie, tersely, annoyed at Phil's tone.

'See you there,' said Phil and hung up.

Ellie wandered into Rory's room as she was unable to keep still. He was sitting on the balcony drinking coffee and reading an English newspaper. He had his robe belted loosely and his feet on the balcony rail. 'This is certainly the life, Ellie. You think these sorts of places only exist in films and in books but I'm really here.' He looked at Ellie. 'You know what I'm going to do today? I'm going to get one of those guys to take me diving on the reef.'

'Diving, Rory, you must be insane,' said Ellie, 'I can't even remember you going to the swimming baths!'

'I talked to the guy who bought the coffee and he says that you can do the whole Dive Certificate here and I thought I'd give it a go. I don't know what the problem is,' he muttered.

'That's okay, Rory; I just had visions of you being eaten by a shark or drowning or something. I didn't know it was a proper course you were going to do. Have fun but I won't be joining you as I'm going with Honey to see one of the libraries she's set up this morning,' said Ellie.

'I'd rather have a go at diving than that anyway, just as well I wasn't invited,' said Rory, pointing out her lapse.

No Rory, I don't think you going would be a good idea, a)

you'd be bored sick, b) it comes under the banner of work and why I'm really here, and c), well I can't think of a c) at the moment but I'm sure there is one somewhere,' said Ellie in a tone that brooked no argument. 'Phil and the others are here already and are going to shadow me at the library to see if the manuscript we're after is there, so I'm only going to have a look. It'll be interesting for me anyway.' Ellie leaned over and gave Rory a meaningful kiss before sketching a wave and a 'See you later'.

A car was waiting for Ellie and Honey was hovering when she got down to the reception.

'Sorry, I'm not late am I?' Ellie asked, feeling guilty.

'No, I was just sorting out a few bits and pieces, but we're ready to go now if you are?' said Honey walking towards the car. 'We're going to the capital today but I thought we would take our time and you could see some of the island as we drive.'

'That'd be lovely,' said Ellie, wondering how a car tail would manage if they were ambling along some country road. They got in the car and Ellie immediately shivered, with the air conditioning on full, it seemed like a refrigerator after the climbing humidity and heat outside. Honey was an interesting companion and filled Ellie in with a lot of the history of the island, how it had gone back and forth from the French to the English many times. They passed banana plantations with all the long bunches of bananas bound up in blue sacks to ward off pests and the luxuriant foliage astounded Ellie as she could see fern leaves as big as herself. There were mountains in the distance covered in green cloaks and Honey explained that there were very few settlements on the Atlantic side of the island and not many roads. After about an hour they drove into Castries, the capital of the island. Here there were shops and markets in the busy town and everyone appeared to be bent on some errand or other. Ellie had completely forgotten about the car that was supposed to be following her and gave a guilty look out of the back window but saw nothing except a beat up delivery van. They drew up outside a long, low, one storey building that had a sign, 'Castries Free Library', emblazoned across the front. It was freshly painted in a lemon yellow and people were wandering in and out through the glass doors.

It was cool inside and Ellie was certainly not expecting what she saw. There were paintings on the walls and on easels, books were displayed in glass-fronted cabinets, people were sketching the paintings and others were poring over the books. The place was a hive of activity and there was a low hum of students discussing the attributes of authors or painters with their tutors.

'We like to encourage the arts and we also have theatre groups and workshops here in the evenings. There are book and poetry clubs and we keep this as a hub for the islanders to come and enjoy or take part if they wish. I believe that by encouraging the arts we can set free the imagination, and who knows where that will take us,' said Honey, smiling.

'There are certainly some major works here,' said Ellie, recognizing a Picasso parked next door to a Dali.

'We recognize that not everyone is interested in the Old Masters so we try and get something to provoke discussion.'

'How do you get the paintings?' Ellie couldn't resist asking. 'Surely you don't buy them all.'

'No, not all of them, but we do have a fine collection built up over the years. We have agreements with a lot of the major galleries around the world and they loan some to us occasionally.'

'But they seem to be on show with no security,' said Ellie, baffled. 'Anyone could come in and steal them.'

'Maybe they could but we've never had a problem,' said Honey, 'where would you take them to? There's nowhere to go on this small island where you could keep a secret like that. We have a British Justice system and also a jail up in the mountains. If anyone tries to escape from there they are shot before the rainforest claims them. It's a very difficult place to escape from, both the jail and the island, so we don't have a problem.' Honey shrugged her shoulders.

Out of the corner of her eye Ellie saw Phil admiring a Pissarro stood on an easel. He was ostensibly making some notes on a notepad and studying the painting from all angles.

'You also have books and manuscripts on display,' said Ellie moving closer to Phil so he could hear the conversation. There was a display case with some illuminated pages on display and a group of students were drawing the dragons and mythical beasts created by the monks long ago. She bent over the case and began looking closely at the pages. These weren't the ones she was after. She had done her homework thoroughly this time and had committed the documents to memory in the finest detail. Ellie was absolutely sure she wouldn't make the same mistake twice of stealing the wrong ones. She exclaimed at the quality of the work and admired the student's efforts to reproduce the jewel colours. She moved on to the next one and there it was in all its glory. The book was there nestling in pride of place open to show the painstaking work and it seemed to glow with a life of its own.

'That's a particularly fine piece,' said Ellie, bending down closer to get a better look and make absolutely sure it was the right one.

'One of our more recent acquisitions,' said Honey. 'We bought it from an auction. Well, strictly speaking we didn't but Valentin got it for us. He heard about it and did some telephone bidding and a courier bought it across. Have you met Valentin, he's a tall blond Russian? He's been across to see us many times and usually does something to help the Foundation.'

'It certainly is a very fine piece,' said Ellie and wondered what to do next. Technically speaking Fortune and Honey hadn't stolen the book and they hadn't actually bought it. It had been bought by Valentin and given as a gift to the Foundation, not to Honey and Fortune themselves. Ellie thought that this situation was certainly a tricky one. She moved on while she sorted out her thoughts.

Phil had heard the conversation as well and it was obvious that his thoughts were running along the same lines, as Ellie saw him bodily stiffen when he heard Honey say it belonged to the Foundation.

Honey said, 'We have no need of things like this to be kept in a vault. I do not need big jewels to feel beautiful or priceless possessions to feel rich. I am a very rich woman even if I had no money at all.'

Ellie turned and looked into the unlined face and said from her heart, 'I really envy you, Honey. I really do. You are perhaps the only person I've ever met that has found a deep inner peace.' She clasped Honey's hands in her own. 'I wish that everyone could be like you and not fall prey to greed and avarice, and they always seem to want more and more.'

'Yes, material things are nice to have but when someone just keeps buying or collecting it's almost as if there's a hole somewhere and they are trying to fill it up. If they began to give instead then that hole would heal quickly,' said Honey, 'but that's just my take on life and it wouldn't do if we were all the same. The world would probably grind to a halt.' She laughed.

OMG, thought Ellie; *this woman is a saint on earth. She*

believes what she says and lives it through as well. 'Those are wise thoughts,' said Ellie, 'I'm going to hold onto them and try and pay a little more thought to my life in the future, but you certainly have a wonderful collection and I can see everyone is using it to the full.'

'Yes,' replied Honey, 'I just hope it continues to grow and flourish and give people inspiration.'

'I'm sure it will,' said Ellie wholeheartedly.

'If we're done here we can get back for some lunch and you can relax this afternoon,' said Honey, meandering back to the door. 'If you're really interested in what the Foundation does I can show you something different tomorrow. We fund a small Convent in the hills and attached to it is a hospital. Perhaps you would like to see that?'

Ellie glanced at Phil and he was nodding as if to some comment from a student. 'Yes, that would be lovely and I'll look forward to it, 'said Ellie. They reached the door and the heat hit Ellie like a sledgehammer and she was grateful for the air conditioned interior of the car. It was a quiet ride back to the resort as Ellie was rather lost in her own thoughts. She mused over what Honey had said and how true it was that some people were just compulsively greedy. She thought of Alistair and how he spent his life in pursuit of money. Even on holiday he was sequestered in an office and his PAs were tapping keyboards sending money on circuitous routes round the world to make more. She knew he had a crisis with one of his businesses but even if it failed he would hardly be poor. She resolved to take a leaf out of Honey's book and make people, not money, her priority in the future. They got back in time for lunch and Ellie thanked Honey again for her time and hoped to meet her again at dinner, and, failing that, at breakfast the next morning. Honey accepted the thanks and drifted towards the dining room to check on lunch.

Ellie raced up to her room and found Claire sitting on the balcony. 'Have you heard what I found out this morning,' said Ellie, plonking herself down next to Claire.

'Yep, heard it all from Phil on the sat phone, it's certainly a turn up for the books as we didn't expect that at all. It seems as if Fortune and Honey really are squeaky clean after all. It's your mate Valentin that's the bad boy here,' said Claire, pouring Ellie an iced drink from a pitcher on the table.

'Hey, I don't like this "my mate" bit, 'said Ellie indignantly. 'Since when is he a friend of mine?'

'Well, seeing you pair on the dance floor last night, you seemed to hit it off from where I was standing,' said Claire teasing.

'I thought that was what I was supposed to do,' said Ellie, 'get to know him better.'

'Well, you certainly did that,' said Claire remorselessly.

'Oh, shut up,' said Ellie, suddenly realizing she was being teased. 'It appears that Valentin is indeed the bad boy. He bought the book then donated it to the Foundation, so where does that leave us?'

'I don't really know right now,' said Claire, 'we're going to have to have a meeting and sleep on this one. We're going to have to come up with a solution somehow, but I know we can't just waltz in and steal it like last time.'

'No, I don't want to do that at all,' said Ellie, thoughtfully sipping her drink. 'I'll have a think as well and see what I can come up with.' She leaned over conspiratorially. 'Did you know that Maria and Robert seem to have hit it off?'

'Yes, I got wind of that last night when they were dancing

cheek to cheek, and Robert is a very happy man today,' agreed Claire. 'It's about time he found someone to tear him out of his cyber world and ground him on planet Earth. I hope it works for them as I've grown to like Maria a lot.'

'It would be lovely if they could get together,' said Ellie, sighing romantically.

'Come on, get your head out of the little pink clouds and go down to lunch and cuddle up to Valentin if he's there,' said Claire, jerking her back to reality.

'Okay, I think I'll just change my top as I'm a bit hot and then I'll go and see if Rory's about. He's supposed to have gone diving this morning and I wonder how he got on with that. I never knew he even liked the sea,' said Ellie, getting up and stretching.

Rory wasn't in his room and Ellie gathered together a few bits and pieces in her beach bag as she wanted an afternoon under a palm tree. She wandered down to lunch and was amazed at the variety of foods available at the buffet. There was also a beach barbeque going on if guests wanted anything from roast suckling pig to fresh made pizzas. Torn with indecision she opted for the cool of the dining room with a buffet and a glass of chilled wine. It was cooler in the room even though it didn't have any walls, just lattice work open to the beach and gardens. There were trailing vines and flowers that flowed over it and tiny humming birds flitted about in among the foliage. She picked a table by the lattice and sat back to enjoy the view when she was joined by Alistair.

'Hello, brother, I haven't seen much of you lately; you should have come with me this morning and seen some of the work of the Foundation. It did give me some ideas for what we could do when we get back to Europe. Fortune and Honey are really lovely people, have you known them long?'

Alistair unrolled his napkin. 'Probably about fifteen years in total I suppose. One of the companies did some work on the island and I flew across and met them as they were footing the bill. We became friends and I've seen them off and on ever since then. They've never been to Europe though, I've invited them in the past but I don't think they've ever left the island.'

'That figures,' said Ellie, 'they seem very wrapped up with this place and I suppose if I lived here, I wouldn't want to leave it.'

'Sister,' said Alistair, 'you know you'd get bored with Paradise just as I would eventually.'

Ellie didn't think she would ever get bored on an island like this but said nothing. 'So, how's the work going? Are you ever going to take any time off at all,' she said, changing the subject? 'I really don't know much about you at all, I mean, do you like sailing, diving, tennis, or just a round of golf. I've never seen you play any sports at all,' she quizzed.

'I do like to keep fit,' said Alistair and Ellie took in his spare frame. 'I can play golf but I admit I find it boring knocking a ball into a hole. Other sports I've tried but there are usually time restrictions on them, and I haven't got a lot of that sometimes. So, I tend to go to the gym and all my houses have a gym with an instructor if I need them. I've already been to the gym today but it was before the sun was up. They've got a good one here and the instructor certainly put me through my paces.'

This was a revelation to Ellie as she didn't know there was a gym at Castle Uccello. Her mind drifted back to the hidden room she and Rory had been so close to discovering before they left for St. Lucia. How many more secrets did the castle hold for them to discover? 'Well, I'm impressed,' said Ellie, thinking how she'd let her own fitness training slip. 'My names' on a palm tree this afternoon and I'm going to lie underneath it,' she said emphatically. Changing the subject again she asked, 'How well do you know this guy Valentin as he seems to be a big buddy of yours? I mean,' she backtracked hastily, 'is he someone who I should get to know better for the future of the businesses? He seemed to have had dealings with you from way back.'

Alistair toyed with a piece of chicken as if trying to make up his mind as to how far to go with his explanation. 'Believe it or not, we were at school together and I've been a friend of Valentin a very long time.'

'Have you been to Russia then?' queried Ellie.

'Yes,' said Alistair, 'on many occasions but not so much in the winter as it's far too cold for me!'

'What's it like? I mean could we go as I've always wanted to see Russia,' said Ellie, playing along trying to get as much information about the Russian as she could. 'Is it really windswept steppes and fantastic palaces?' she added romantically.

'No, it's more nightclubs and factories,' said Alistair, smiling at Ellie's flight of fancy. 'But we could go as long as it's in the summer. You should get to know Valentin better as he's a major player in Russia at the moment, you know, oil and gold, things like that.'

'I'll certainly try for you,' said Ellie ingenuously as Alistair pushed back his chair. She hoped she had sown the seeds of an interest in Valentin with Alistair and she could go and see for herself what Valentin was really 'into'. She had the suspicion that it wasn't just 'night clubs and factories' but would be drugs, white slave trade, sex workers and the like in reality. She would have to tread carefully with Valentin but hoped she would have some sort of immunity as she was Alistair's twin and part of his business. If their friendship went back that far then hopefully, she would be granted a passport into the inner circle if she played her cards right. She stored this little piece of information away and would relay it later to Claire but now the sand and the surf were calling.

CHAPTER SIX

While Ellie lay and soaked up the glorious sunshine, Valentin and another man were deep in conversation behind the fitness centre and gym. It was a secluded area bounded by dense palms and foliage. They couldn't be seen either from the entrance or by any casual stroller. The body language was relaxed and they stood closely as friends might. Valentin had his hands in his pockets and was rocking slightly on his heels as he processed what the other man was telling him. 'So, you're saying that when Max died it wasn't a simple helicopter crash at all?' Valentin asked again as he couldn't really believe what he was hearing. 'You're telling me that Max died because Ellie killed him, and it was deliberate?'

The other man was Karl who was Alistair's new Chief of Security. Alistair hadn't told Ellie that Karl would be accompanying them to the island as he knew Ellie couldn't stand the man. Ellie and Karl had been introduced under less than ideal circumstances when he had been in charge of her abduction. Alistair's half brother Max had always worked very closely with Karl and Alistair had always preferred not to know what Karl had done. The only times he had come to Alistair's notice was when he had to 'clean up' after his half brother and Karl's overzealous ministrations. He knew Karl had a sadistic streak but he was very loyal and after the debacle at the French chateau Alistair had promoted him. Karl was well known to many of Alistair's friends and he had been gently groomed by them to pass on information as needed, unbeknown to Alistair. So, consequently Valentin was having a deep and meaningful conversation with Karl at that moment. Money would find its way into Karl's bank account and nothing would be said about it ever again.

'Yes, I saw it with my own eyes,' said Karl, 'the bitch kicked him out of the helicopter and he fell to his death. I know she hated Mr. Max and I wanted to get rid of her there and then but he wouldn't do it my way. She's trouble and a half and we'd be better off without her,' said Karl and a small muscle pulsed in his neck. He pulled out a packet of cigarettes and lit one after offering them to Valentin who declined. 'Mr. Alistair's not the same since that slag came on the scene; he used to work well with Mr. Max and they used to get things done together. Now he's changed and all the better parts of the business, like the drugs or the art stuff, for instance, have gone down the pan. He just doesn't seem interested at all. I mean, we're all going to lose money here.' Karl knew he had touched the right nerve with the Russian who removed his hands from his pockets and ran his fingers through his hair.

'I see what you mean Karl,' said Valentin thoughtfully, 'but perhaps this isn't the right place or time to restore the status quo.' He looked at Karl's puzzled expression. 'I mean to put things back how they were before,' he explained. 'It may be that we have to have a party, Russian style, like the good old days, back in Mother Russia. I have more control over things there and as you know, "accidents" do happen,' he added meaningfully. 'I will get to know this Ellie Black a bit better and see where the weak spots are, any information you have will be most gratefully received as usual, and rest assured you can always have a job with me if you want one,' said Valentin, nodding to Karl and strolling away deep in thought.

Oblivious to all this, Rory had made a point of finding Ellie when he still had all his dive gear with him and tried to pass off as the all action hero as he strode along the sand. In reality the sand was so hot it was burning the soles of his feet and the dive stuff was really heavy out of the water, but he nonchalantly sat on the lounger at her side.

'So how did it go?' said Ellie, squinting into the sun.

'Did all the basic stuff today and I think I've got the hang of it now. Got another few hours of training then it's the open water and the reef for me. You should try it, it's amazing,' said Rory enthusiastically.

'I'm impressed, but it's really not my thing,' said Ellie. 'I'd like to see the fish but I think a snorkel is about what I could manage, but don't let that stop you. We're here and you should take the opportunity when it comes along. I must admit I never thought it would be this good though,' she said, lazily watching two paddle boarders trying to do hand stands and failing. She reached out and took his hand. 'I do love you lots and want us to be happy but this is the honeymoon before the real honeymoon and we've got to decide what we both want before we marry. I know I'm being mean and greedy but I want all this as well as you.' She waved her hand expansively. 'Can I have everything Rory? That question is really up to you and you alone.' Ellie felt a complete arse for bring the subject up then but time was running out and in a few days, they would be on a plane again. She felt she had to know if Rory would stay with her or his pride would get the better of him and he would hightail it back to London without her. 'Today's Tuesday, I think, and we've got to go back on Thursday, so you need to do a bit of soul searching before then Rory.' She sat and faced him clasping both hands in hers. 'Whatever decision you come to I'll live with it, but that's not going to say I'll be happy,' said Ellie fervently.

Rory was taken slightly aback by this outpouring as he'd lost himself in the moment of going diving on a Caribbean island. He knew he'd have to make a decision soon but had been putting it off as he was enjoying himself to the full. What could be better than being with his beautiful fiancée in Paradise while all was right with the world. He deflected the massive question by saying, 'I'm going to have to get out of this wet suit soon as I'm cooking. I'll be "boil in the bag" Rory if I'm not careful.' He stood and heaved his dive gear onto his shoulder. 'See you later,' he said over his shoulder.

Ellie sighed and returned to her sunbathing and thought about men in general and why they couldn't seem to talk about what they really felt. She knew that he would have to tell her sooner or later so decided there and then to leave the subject alone and just see what happened. It was the easy way out but she knew that if she pushed him, he would just back off and it could all go the wrong way. Let fate or nature take its course and live with the consequences was all she could do right now.

Dinner was another delight that evening and the blond Russian was seated with them on a table for six. Every meal the place cards were set out and another set of dinner guests were mixed and matched. Ellie was glad to see that Alistair was there at the dinner and was in animated conversation with a tall blonde Swedish woman who was something to do with computers. She sat down and began the first course. Everyone seemed to be fully recovered from the excesses of the night before and Ellie was again careful about how much she had to drink. Valentin was on her right hand side on the round table and was an attentive companion. He kept trying to fill her glass up and she kept declining as graciously as she could. 'If I didn't know better Valentin, I would say you are trying to get me drunk?' Ellie said putting her hand over her glass. 'It won't work you know.' She arched her eyebrows. 'You know Alistair only drinks tonic water and I think there's something in the genes that doesn't let me drink too much as well.'

Valentin mentally crossed that off his list of weak spots in Ellie's character. There would be one and he would find it and dig it out. Even if he couldn't get rid of her for good it could be used as a lever in the future to discredit her and make her name mud. 'How right you are Ellie,' he said sententiously, 'we should all take a leaf out of your brother's book and be strong. In Russia, sadly, we are bought up on vodka and take it almost with our mother's milk.'

'If I went to Russia, I would certainly try it the Russian way but it's not something I've been desperate to try out here. I go more for the chilled fruit juices in this heat,' said Ellie, totally oblivious as to what he was doing.

'You will certainly have to come to my home country in the spring and we'll go to one of my dachas and we'll drink vodka by a log fire kept warm by furs of the bear and the wolf. We'll ride horses across the steppes to the forests and hunt the wild boar like the old times. I think you would like that Ellie Black.'

'It sounds amazing and I'm surprised as Alistair said it was all factories and things nowadays.'

'No, Ellie, there is still romance in the old ways and I preserve that wherever I can. I love the outdoors and the wild places, it's wonderful to ride and see no-one. To be at one with the nature, is that the right way to say it?' he enquired.

'That says it perfectly Valentin,' said Ellie, impressed that here was a man in touch with his feelings. 'I love the outdoors but I've never hunted for wild boar and I'm not sure I'd like that bit,' said Ellie, wondering if she could actually kill a pig. 'I have to be honest I can't say I've even seen one close to. I have ridden a horse though and it was an amazing experience and I'd like to do that again,' she added.

'So, we will ride horses in the Russian wilderness and just look at the wild boar in the forests. I can show you ice caves and if we go far north you may see the Northern Lights with their fantastic colours.' Valentin was laying it on thick but Ellie was entranced and her imagination was conjuring pictures of an untouched land where nature was king.

'Valentin, it sounds absolutely wonderful and I'd like to take you up on your offer but Alistair says he won't go there in the winter as he doesn't like it that cold.'

'No, he doesn't,' said Valentin, 'he has been before but goes into his shell like a snail. I will arrange it for when the day and the night are equal so you can see the glories of Russia. We will toast it now.' He poured some wine into Ellie's glass and raised his own. 'To Russia and all her riches.'

Ellie followed suit and raised her own glass and toasted his home not suspecting at all the plan Valentin was hatching at that very moment.

The evening progressed much as the night before with dancing and Ellie enjoyed the moonlit night close in Rory's arms. It was magical and a soft breeze took the edge off the heat and everything was just perfect for Ellie. She had spoken to Honey in passing and confirmed she would be at breakfast bright and early to go and see another of the Foundation's works in the morning. Rory had decided to forego that treat as he wanted to get back to his diving and would be out on the water nearly all day tomorrow.

Ellie chatted to Claire as she got ready for bed. 'I'll be up early tomorrow as I'm going to some hospital to see what goes on. I don't know if Phil and the others are going to tail me again but I'm just going for a look round and see what they do. I don't think that it's in any way involved with the books and manuscripts at all. It's up to you,' Ellie said dismissively, shrugging her shoulders.

'Probably not but I'll run it past them just in case they think it's worth a look. I'll leave you to it then and maybe see you tomorrow,' said Claire, closing the door.

Ellie went again to Rory's room and slept soundly to the tune of the surf and the cicadas.

She met Honey at breakfast and they went in an air-conditioned Land Rover this time. They headed into the interior of the island and many of the roads wound round the banana plantations. They were dirt roads and very unmade in parts and Ellie was bounced around like a pea in a can. This made conversation difficult and she wondered where on earth they were going as there were no signposts. Eventually they came to a long building that was set into a hillside. There was an obviously older part of wooden construction in the middle and two newly built wings stretched out from either side.

'Forgive me for saying but this seems a strange place to put a hospital Honey,' said Ellie. 'There doesn't even seem to be a village nearby and the only road is bumpy to say the least,' said Ellie, gazing about.

'Not really as there are many small villages dotted about the mountains and the people can't make the journey to Castries if they are ill. It's an Order of nuns that run it and they like the seclusion as well, so it suits everyone. Also, we take in some patients that can pay who want to be away from the public. They don't want the press by their bedsides and this place is so out of the way that they can recover in peace. It brings in quite a bit of money for the Foundation and we can invest in the best medical equipment there is. So, you will see a state of the art hospital that treats all the locals for free, and the rich make their own contributions in their own way,' said Honey.

'That's a very clever idea and I'm sure I'd never have thought of it,' said Ellie admiringly.

'I'm going to leave you for the morning as I have some errands to run and things to take to the most isolated villages, but I'll leave you in the capable hands of Sister Margaret who is expecting us,' said Honey. 'I hope that's okay with you?'

'Yes, perfectly,' said Ellie, gathering up her bag with her water and bug repellent.

They walked to the old wooden building and were met by a nun in full black habit. Ellie thought she must have been sweltering in the robes but there wasn't a trace of moisture on her face. She extended her hand and greeted them. 'Honey, so nice to see you again, and you must be our visitor. We're so glad you could make the trip and see what we do.'

'Thank you, Sister Margaret,' said Honey, 'but I'm going to leave Ellie with you as I've got some things to take to some other villages and I'll be back in a few hours. Is there anything you want me to take with me?' Honey enquired.

Sister Margaret replied that she didn't as all the prescriptions had already gone out that week and everything was accounted for. 'Just enjoy the trip, Honey, and we'll see you later,' Sister Margaret said, ushering Ellie into the old building. It was cool inside and Ellie sat down and Sister Margaret offered her some iced tea. When she was comfortable Sister Margaret said, 'I'll begin by telling you something of our Order. We have all taken vows to God of poverty and chastity and our Order began about two hundred years ago. We're a bit of splinter group as we're all trained as nurses and doctors and we found much work on the battlefields of Europe. We still are found where there is the carnage of war but we are small in number. All our Order is trained in Russia and that is our common language.'

'I did notice your accent,' said Ellie, 'but you must find this work very different to a battlefield,' she queried.

'Yes, there are many countries where wars are fought and we feel we are needed everywhere but we have to get the skills to treat people effectively somehow. So, we have a few of these hospitals where our newly trained sisters can hone up their skills before being sent to do Gods work elsewhere,' said the Sister. 'I have been here for about eighteen months now and treat everything that comes through the door. It could be a simple broken limb to cholera, malaria or septicaemia. I have to be able to diagnose and treat everything I see quickly and efficiently.'

'I can see that you can't learn everything out of a book and "hands on" practice is invaluable,' said Ellie, impressed by the dedication of the sisters.

'So, shall we begin the tour?' said Sister Margaret, rising.

They went around the surgical ward and Ellie was gloved and gowned to meet some of the islanders that had recently undergone routine surgery. It was a bright, airy ward and the nursing sisters were ministering to the wants and needs of the patients. Ellie could see that there was the best possible care for them and the all the equipment looked shiny and new. They moved onto the children's ward and there were a few sick children with their parents, and again it was a bright cheerful ward with hummingbirds and butterflies on the walls.

'We haven't painted cars and trains on the walls as many of the children have never seen a train,' explained Sister Margaret.

'Again, I'd never have thought of that,' said Ellie, doubly impressed.

'Here we have our private wing,' said the Sister and pointed through some big glass doors. 'It's not a good idea to go in there as many of the patients have paid for privacy and that should be observed.'

'Absolutely,' agreed Ellie, but she craned her neck to see if she could see anyone famous. 'I have to ask you though, what do the rich and famous come here for?'

'Sometimes they have some minor surgery to rejuvenate their faces or figures.' Sister Margaret placed her hands at the side of her face and pushed the skin upwards. 'Sometimes they have minor conditions that need treating that they don't want the world to know about, and they know that here their secrets are very safe,' said the sister. 'Who are we to judge what people feel is important to them? That is their business and theirs alone,' she said putting an end to the line of conversation.

Ellie was shown the Maternity suites that would rival anything back in England and cooed over the small new-born bundles. It made her feel quite maternal all of a sudden. The tour ended at the laboratories where all the blood work diagnoses were made. 'I'm going to leave you here for a while and please ask any questions of any of the staff. I just have a few things I must do. Someone will show you back when you're done,' said Sister Margaret, taking her leave.

Ellie had never been in a lab like this before and wandered about looking at all the high tech machinery. Some things she could recognize but others she couldn't and she asked questions she hoped were informed and didn't make her look a complete idiot. Eventually she was aware she ought to go and freshen up and use the bathroom and asked a member of staff where to go. She was directed out into the corridor and wandered down the passageway realizing that it was cut back into the rock of the mountain. The place was a lot bigger than she had previously thought and she seemed to go a long way before seeing a bathroom sign. The lighting had changed to overhead bulkheads that didn't throw the same brilliance as before and Ellie looked about her at the doors on either side. None of them had glass windows in them and she hoped she could see someone to ask where to go. The corridor ended in a set of double doors and Ellie just pushed them open.

What a sight met her eyes. There were what seemed to be cages on each side and behind the bars were people. Young girls to be specific and they were lying on thin mattresses and all silent. Their eyes were half closed and arms and legs flopped haphazardly off the makeshift beds. It looked as if they were drugged. Ellie's jaw dropped when she saw them and she moved slowly down the line of cells. The air was fetid and stale and the reek of urine was strong. All the girls were white and seemed to be young teenagers. Their hair was unwashed and their clothes rank with urine and sweat as there wasn't the hum of an air conditioning unit down here. Bits of food littered the cell floors and they were obviously being kept in a worse state than animals.

Ellie couldn't believe what she was seeing and her horror made her forget any danger she may be in. She walked openly down the middle and never even noticed a figure emerge from the other end. He stood foursquare in the middle of the passageway and Ellie almost bumped into him. He grabbed her arms and she tried to fight him off but he was too strong and powerful. She even tried to headbutt him but he was much taller than she was and obviously a trained fighter as he held her easily and securely. Ellie was dragged through the door at the end and shoved into a small cell on its own. The door was slammed and the light went off and she was left in the humid darkness alone.

'You'd better let me go as people will be looking for me,' she shouted and pounded her fists on the door.

'Shut up or I'll shut you up,' growled the male voice through the door.

Ellie subsided and her knees gave way and she sank to the floor in a heap. Her bag was still with her and she tipped it out onto the floor between her legs to see if she had anything of use with her. Out fell the bottle of water and Ellie carefully put it by her side. Besides tissues, make-up and comb there was nothing. Not even a hairgrip to pick the lock with and certainly no phone. Ellie wracked her brains and remembered the conversation she had with Claire that morning. No-one had thought this trip would be a risk so there was no tail and no backup, she hadn't even got the sat phone but it was debatable if it would work so far underground anyway. Ellie asked herself many questions in the intervening hours, how could she have let her guard down so far and been caught? Who were those poor girls kept as caged animals on the other side of the wall? and how would she ever get out of this alive? But she pushed that one to the back of her mind as it was going to make her cry. She drew hope that people would miss her and Honey would be back soon to pick her up. Whoever had taken her would have to think up a bloody good story to explain her disappearance.

That was exactly what was on the mind of Sister Margaret as she sat in her office absently pulling back the slide on her gun and letting it flick back. This was a turn up for the books and she had never expected Ellie to discover the cells and now she was incarcerated in one. She had to be got rid of but a bullet wound would cause untold problems if her body was discovered. Sister Margaret put the gun away in a leg holster under her habit and thought again. One possibility was that she could just be drugged up and shipped out with all the other girls to their new lives.

They'd get some money for Ellie as she was a pretty girl, a bit old for the majority of tastes, but she would bring in money nevertheless. Sister Margaret discarded that idea as well as Ellie could be recognized as her face was all over the internet and many people knew of her now. She would have to get onto her superiors in Russia and let them know what had happened and await instructions. She picked up the phone and put an internal call through to the cells.

'Give the prisoner some food and a bucket, she may be there some time,' was all she said.

'Da,' was the response.

Honey came back after her trip to the outlying villages and Sister Margaret was on the steps to greet her. The Sister was wringing her hands and looking upset. 'Miss Black has gone for a short walk and I'm sure she's alright but she should have been back by now. I can't see her anywhere,' the Sister said anxiously.

'I'm sure she's okay,' said Honey soothingly, 'she's probably just forgot the time. It doesn't matter as I'm not in any rush.'

They both went inside and Honey was given iced tea and settled herself comfortably to wait. The conversation was desultory about mundane matters until Honey looked at her watch. 'Exactly how long has Ellie been gone now?' she enquired.

'She must have been gone for at least an hour by now.'

'Did anyone go with her?' asked Honey, feeling alarm bells in the back of her mind.

'Not that I know of but I can check now, she passed me on the way out and said she wanted to have a quick look at the natural rain forest while she was here. I must confess I didn't pay much attention which way she went,' the Sister lied.

Honey looked out of the window at the thick verdant foliage and the alarm bells were shrieking. 'We've got to alert the Authorities now as she could just be lost or she could have fallen and hurt herself, well, anything could have happened to her.'

'Yes, yes, I'll ring them now and I'll organize a search party,' said Sister Margaret. 'I would never forgive myself if anything has happened to her. I should have been more vigilant as she doesn't know the ways of the rain forest, what have I done?' she crossed herself and reached for the phone.

'There's no need to go and get worked up about it,' said Honey. 'I'm sure Ellie is just enjoying some flowers somewhere, she's an adult and is fully aware of any risks there may be.'

A search party was organized and staff fanned out and scoured the land in a wide circle around the complex. Needless to say, they found nothing. Honey had been on the phone to the nearest Police station and they were sending some men to help look. She toyed with the phone wondering whether or not to ring Rory and tell him Ellie was missing but decided not to as she could be crying wolf and Ellie could stroll out of the jungle at any moment. Best to leave it for another hour or until the Police got there, she thought. Sister Margaret was directing the search party and doing it in a thoroughly professional manner and Honey was really glad she was in charge of the situation as with every minute that passed, she was getting more and more anxious. The Police turned up and spread out, going over old ground and beating new paths. After an hour they too had turned up nothing and the Chief began to take statements from people who had actually seen Ellie. Honey was now sure something terrible had happened and rang the resort and asked them to find Rory for her.

The dive boat bobbed gently on the swell of the incoming tide and Rory was just getting out of his gear. He had seen some amazing fish today and was now a reef diving fan of the highest order. He could even identify some of the brightly coloured inhabitants now and loved the feeling of weightlessness and the excitement of exploring a whole new world. The radio crackled and the master of the boat listened intently. He waved Rory over to his side and placed some headphones on him and showed him how to press the button to speak.

'Is that Rory?' Honey's voice came over loud and clear.

'Yes.'

'We're at the Foundation hospital we visited this morning, rather I'm here but Ellie seems to have gone missing.'

'What do you mean... missing?'

'Well, I went to do a few errands and when I got back, she'd gone,' said Honey.

'Gone where?' said Rory, still not understanding.

'That's it, Rory, we don't know where she is. The Sister here thinks she went for a short walk but she hasn't returned yet and it's going to get dark in a few hours. I've told the Police and they're here now searching,' said Honey and the anxiety in her voice came through.

'Don't move, I'm coming to you, I'll get a car and be there soon,' said Rory, agitated and beginning to rip off his wetsuit. He tore off the headphones and told the boat master they had to get to shore now, as fast as he could, as his fiancée was missing. The boatman saw the urgency written on Rory's face and called for the anchor to be raised and the dive flags lowered fast, and they took off for the shore trailing a white wake behind them.

The pontoon dock couldn't get there fast enough for Rory and as soon as the side of the boat touched it, he was off and running to the room to get some clothes. He ran up the stairs and nearly knocked Claire over as he elbowed her out of the way.

'What's the rush, Rory?' she said, pushing herself vertical off the wall.

'Ellie, Ellie's missing,' said Rory, breathlessly.

'What do you mean missing?' said Claire, not taking it in.

'I mean gone, disappeared, don't know where she is. I'm getting a car and going up there now. The Police are there and they're searching for her now,' said Rory, pulling on some clothes.

'Wait, I'm coming with you. I'll get some help organized now,' she said, pulling a phone out of her pocket.

They both raced down the stairs and skidded to a halt at the Reception desk and asked for a Land Rover now. They both waited impatiently as one was driven round and Claire got on the phone there and then to Phil and the others to get moving. The car arrived and Claire ordered the driver into the passenger seat despite his protestations and gunned the engine. She was well versed in the art of defensive driving and just needed the directions of where to go. Rory had drawn the short straw and was relegated to the back where he knelt down clutching the driver's and passenger seats in a vice like grip as they screamed round corners and drove straight over intersections without a second glance.

'We're not going to be much use if we're dead,' was all he could manage and the poor chauffeur could only manage a nod as he gripped the dashboard.

'Which way?' said Claire, totally focused on the road.

'Left, then up the first dirt track you see,' the chauffeur squeaked.

'Okay, got that, what then?'

'Keep going, then after about a mile you'll see a fork, take the right one.'

Claire handed Rory the sat phone. 'The channel's open, just give the directions and describe what we pass. It's got GPS but it's quicker and they'll see what we see. Start talking,' she ordered.

'Who are "they"?' said Rory, unclenching his fingers to take the phone.

'Doesn't matter now but Phil and the others are going to help us find Ellie so they need to know exactly where we are.' She turned and glared at Rory who took the hint and started describing what they were passing.

The Land Rover bumped and lurched over the unmade roads and Phil and the others quickly piled into their assortment of vehicles and headed off in pursuit.

CHAPTER SEVEN

Rory and Claire made it to the hospital in one piece and they stopped in a cloud of dust. It was a hive of activity with cars pulled up haphazardly and Police directing the search operation. Rory and Claire leapt out and they both ran towards the main building. Honey was waiting on the steps pacing about agitatedly. She saw them and rushed down the steps. 'I don't know what's happened to her, I was only gone for about an hour and a half and she disappeared, just disappeared. Sister Margaret is in the office and will tell you more. Come with me.'

They both followed and entered the office and Sister Margaret rose from behind her desk and held her hands out to them in welcome. 'You must be Rory, Miss Black's fiancé, welcome to our hospital and I only wish it could be under better circumstances. I left Miss Black alone when I went to sort a few things out and she seemed quite happy looking round our diagnostic labs. I did think I saw her pass the office on her way out to take a short walk or get some air. I didn't think anything of it until Honey came for her and we realized she was missing. I immediately organized a search party with some staff then called the Police as we didn't find her. All the sisters will pray for her safe return and we will keep on looking but it will be getting dark soon and more difficult.'

Claire said, 'I'm sure you've done all you can but we won't leave any stone unturned until we find her, wherever she is,' she added emphatically. 'I've organized some friends to come and help and they should be here soon, I'm going to go and have a chat with the policeman who's coordinating the search party now, coming, Rory?'

'Yep, right behind you,' said Rory, just glad to be doing something constructive and not just standing about.

'While I think about it have you got a large scale map of the area we could borrow?' said Claire, waiting expectantly.

'I've got one somewhere,' said the Sister, rummaging in some papers. 'Ah, yes, here it is. Not all of the tracks and plantations are marked on it but it gives you the general layout.' She twisted it round and pointed. 'Here's the mountain at the back and this block is the hospital. There's nothing much on it as it's nearly all virgin rainforest.' She handed it to Claire.

'Thank you, it's better than nothing at all,' said Claire, who turned on her heel and left.

In the car park was a beat up delivery van and a motorcycle that had seen better days. Phil and Robert were deep in conversation with a policeman and Jack and Nigel were unloading equipment from the delivery van. Claire went to meet them and Rory trailed behind her.

'I've got some sort of a map,' said Claire, spreading it on the bonnet of the van. 'What's the plan, Phil? How do you want to approach this?'

'I've had a chat to the local constabulary and they seem to have done a pretty thorough search here, here and here.' He marked the map with a pen. 'It's no good going over old ground but I can't see that she's wandered that far to be totally out of earshot.' Phil lowered his voice. 'We're going to have to assume that she's in some difficulties somewhere or she's been taken.'

Rory slammed his hand on the van bonnet. 'If it's that shit of a brother of hers up to no good, I swear I'll swing for him.'

Jack put his hand on Rory's arm. 'We've got to look at

motive. Why would he do that when he's got what he wanted in the first place? Ellie lives with him and he seems happy with that arrangement. All the times he took her before was only to have her near him. Now he's got that why would he engineer this?'

'Yes, I suppose so,' agreed Rory, a little deflated, 'but he could still be something to do with it.'

'We don't know if she's been taken or lost, so we've got to keep our options open,' said Jack.

'I agree,' said Phil, 'we don't know anything for certain yet so we'll assume that she's lost for now and comb this area thoroughly. Claire, go and have a chat with Honey and find out what she was wearing, her shoes, what sort? Would they stand up to jungle walking? What had she got in her bag? That sort of thing.'

'Okay,' said Claire and went to find Honey.

'Jack and Nigel will go and search this quadrant,' Phil said, drawing a search grid on the map. 'The Police are doing down this end but we'll go up the mountain a bit. I can't think why she went up there but we have to make sure. I'll take Robert and work alongside you on this area.' He pointed up the mountain and to the left of the hospital. 'Rory can work down here with the Police and Claire can do her usual snooping where she likes.' He went to the back of the van and began to divide up the kit. Everyone had a radio and the two teams working up the mountain had machetes and some ropes. They all had a backpack with essential water and some food. 'I'll give out the torches as well as it'll get dark quickly and we'll carry on as long as we can. Good luck everyone,' he said, as they grabbed their stuff and went their separate ways.

Rory was a bit miffed about being relegated to stay down but when he saw the ropes and harnesses being unloaded and handed out, he realized these guys were the professionals and he would only hinder them if he got into difficulties. He went and found Honey and Claire who were with Sister Margaret being plied with tea. Rory explained what the plan was and said he was going out to help the Police. He handed Claire a radio and she went onto the steps to call up Phil

After a few crackles Phil's voice came through loud and clear. 'I'm with Rob and we're taking the right hand side of the mountain and Jack and Nige are up and on the left. If you've got the radio then you'll know Rory is with the Police.'

'What do you want me to do?'

'Just do what you're good at and snoop,' said Phil, laughing.

'Okay, roger that, a-snooping I will go.' She laughed back. Claire glanced round her and saw that no-one was looking at her as they were all intent on their own tasks so she slid off round the side of the hospital till she found the bins and a service entrance. A quick look round made sure the coast was clear then she cracked open the door and eased in. She was in some sort of cleaning area as big buffers for the floors and maintenance carts stood around. She opened the cupboards and they were stacked with cleaning fluids, overalls and all the usual stuff she would expect. There was a main door and she opened it slowly and looked into the corridor. She saw the backs of two people in scrubs, deep in conversation, heading away from her and she closed the door. Opening all the cupboards she found what she was looking for, scrubs. She had to blend in and not be noticed so she stripped off and pulled on some blue loose-fitting scrubs that would hide her gun in its shoulder holster. Her shoes weren't right but they would have to do as there weren't any to steal and she hoped the overlong trousers would hide them. Going back to the door she opened it a crack and peered out. The coast was clear and she walked boldly out and grabbed a set of patient notes from a box by a doorway as she passed. Claire walked purposefully down corridor after corridor, past all sorts of wards and eventually found her way to the labs where Ellie had definitely been seen for the last time.

Up in the mountains Phil and Nigel definitely thought they had drawn the short straw as they had to hack through dense vegetation to gain a few yards. The one thing they hadn't got was bug repellent and every flying insect seemed to home in on them. They had begun by slapping them away but after a time just gave up and let them feast. Sweat trickled down their bodies in the high humidity and sapped their strength.

'Well, she didn't come this way, 'said Phil, pausing. 'I don't think anyone's been up here at all.'

'Let's just get a bit higher then we can look down and see if there's any track at all in this jungle,' said Rob.

'I'll radio Jack and see if he's been luckier than us while we have a breather.'

'Okay,' said Rob, sliding down a palm tree and sitting down.

Jack's radio crackled and he heard Phil. He pressed the 'receive' button. 'Jack, any luck so far?'

'Nothing we can see.' He looked at Nigel who shook his head.

'We're just going a bit higher so we can look down and see if there's any tracks or anything but we're not hopeful. Don't forget it'll be dark in an hour.'

'Okay, will do,' said Jack. He looked at Nigel. 'Onwards and upwards then,' he said, swinging his machete. 'We'll have to be quick as it'll be dark soon and we won't be able to see anything at all.' As if echoing his words, a frog began its nightly song and a hush began to creep over the rainforest as the daytime birds began to roost for the night.

The two teams hacked and struggled up the steep slope and Phil and Robert reached an overhanging rock and climbed on top. There they could see down the mountain and there was nothing but virgin forest and their own meandering path cut through it. Phil got out his radio again. 'Jack, we've got absolutely nothing here at all, how about you?'

Jack and Nigel had ploughed on and were about on the same level up the mountain as Phil. Nigel had given Jack a baleful stare as he swigged the last of his water. His one eye was half closed from a particularly ferocious bite and his face and neck was a mass of lumps and bumps from insect attack. Jack had got off fairly lightly as they seemed to prefer Nigel to himself and had homed in on all his exposed pieces of skin. Nigel was tired and tripped over an exposed tree root, landing face down in the rotting loam.

'Shit,' said Nigel with feeling as the ground smelt of rotten leaves and fruit.

'You alright?' said Jack, not really caring as he was just as tired and fed up but still anxious to find Ellie.

'Hey! Wait a minute, I landed on my arm but there seems to be a space underneath it. I can feel a hole,' said Nigel, still lying face down.

'What do you mean a "hole"?' said Jack, backtracking to where Nigel lay.

'My arm's dangling into space. It could be some sort of fissure in the rock, or the entrance to a cave or something.'

Jack joined Nigel and they both got out their flashlights and cleared away some of the undergrowth to expose a hole. It was like a pipe that led down into the mountain and they couldn't see the bottom. 'Phil, we've got a tunnel or something here,' Jack radioed.

'Do you think Ellie could have fallen down it?' replied Phil.

'Not a chance,' said Jack, 'no-one's been up here, but perhaps it's worth a look. Make your way over to us and see what you think.'

'Roger that,' said Phil, 'put your lights on so we can see where you are as we've run out of light.' As he said that the day imperceptibly changed from sun to Stygian blackness in a few minutes. Jack and Nigel got their torches and got to a higher place and signalled with them till they got an answering light and could see two glowing pinpricks wavering their way towards them. For Phil and Robert, it was a journey from a nightmare as they couldn't see their hands in front of their faces. The hospital was lit up from below but even the ambient light didn't reach that far. Jack shared the last of his water with Nigel as they waited and the lights got nearer and brighter. Eventually they all met up and stood around looking at the hole in the ground.

'I reckon it's a lava pipe,' said Robert. 'This could have been volcanic at some point in its past and this is a left over vent. Just an idea but it's so smooth and straight I can't see that it's man-made.'

'You're probably right,' said Phil, looking round at the others, ghostly in the torchlight. He looked again and his gaze lingered on Nigel. 'Your face is a mess, what have you done?'

'I've done nothing,' said Nigel, looking back at him with one eye as the other had now fully closed up and all the other bites were swelling. 'I didn't know I was allergic to the flying bugs they've got here, but I'll be fine,' he said, heroically.

'No, you're not,' said Phil, 'you've got to get those treated as soon as possible. I don't know what else we can do here tonight as we can't go down there as we don't know how deep it is.' As he fell silent and they all digested that piece of information a sibilant echo sounded from below their feet.

'What was that?' said Jack. 'That noise, what was it?'

They all stared down into the bowels of the Earth and again a small high pitched sound bounced its way up the walls of the vent and dissipated on contact with the air. They all looked at each other as if disbelieving what they had heard.

'God! Maybe that's Ellie and she's fallen down the hole,' said Jack.

'If she'd have fallen down that she'd be dead by now,' said Robert not realizing how callous it sounded. 'That goes down hundreds of feet and as we've seen, no one's been up here for many a long year,' he added.

'He's right,' said Phil, 'we're going to have to come back here tomorrow at first light with proper equipment and go down there and see what's making that noise. Nigel, you'll be in the sick bay as you're beginning to look like Quasimodo.' Everyone except Nigel sniggered. 'Let's see what we can rustle up tonight, I'll go back to Castries and get some proper gear and you can stay at the hospital,' he said, looking at Jack and Robert. 'Make that you as well, Nigel, as they'll have the right stuff to treat you with here. I'm sure they'll have a few spare beds.'

The team began their descent which was a lot quicker than the ascent as they followed Jack's path down.

In the hospital Claire had certainly been a-snooping and had even been in the wards where the rich and famous came to get their nip and tuck jobs in secret. She had just walked about as if with a purpose and glanced at her clipboard occasionally. Only once had she been asked what she was doing there and had looked at the man as if the answer was obvious. 'Health and Safety of course,' she had said while ticking an imaginary box on her clipboard. She had found her way to the labs where Ellie had been seen last and had glanced through the windows set in the doors. Again, everything was as it should have been with no undue activity or people whispering in huddles. She was about to give up and try to find the staff cafeteria where she could maybe hear snippets of conversation when a niggle touched the back of her mind and made her look again at the long corridor she was in. It went on for quite a long way and was now underneath the mountain. There were doors on either side and Claire had assumed they were for maintenance and service as the others had been. If there was one thing, she had learned a long time ago it was that to assume anything made an 'ass' out of 'u' and 'me' so she went deeper underground.

She checked a few of the doors and they were what they seemed to be, just service or maintenance, but tiny frissons were running up her bare arms and making the hairs stand up at the back of her neck. She noticed that the corridor was now only dimly lit and she came to the double doors at the end. They were painted a battleship grey to match the walls and from a distance in the dim light it looked as though the corridor ended there. They were a good camouflage to the doorway and Claire stood there wrestling with indecision. She should really go back and get some help but everyone was up the mountain or in the search parties. She couldn't stand there forever as she would just attract attention so she gently eased one of the doors open. It was heavy but swung open easily and she stood in amazement at the same sight that had greeted Ellie. The cages were ranked on either side of a long room and the girls were still in their drugged states lolling about on the filthy mattresses.

Suddenly the heavy door was slammed shut behind her and only missed chopping off her fingers by millimetres. There had been a guard behind the door and Claire had been too wrapped up processing what she was seeing that she had forgotten a basic rule, first look behind the door! She whirled round taking up a fighting stance and found herself staring down the barrel of a gun.

'Don't even think about it,' he said, gesturing with his gun for her to walk down the row of cells. He was a big man and obviously well trained as he didn't get too close to her so she could disarm him. 'I will shoot you without a second thought and don't worry about the gunshot as this place is soundproof from the hospital.'

Claire walked slowly and took in all the stench and degradation the girls were in. Their eyes followed her but no-one made a sound.

'Keep going,' he said as they came to another set of doors.

These were so deep under the mountain that there was a cool draught as she opened them. A corridor of sorts had doors on either side that looked very solid, the guard gestured to the second one and she opened it slowly. It was just a room with nothing in it except an overhead light.

'Take your clothes off,' he ordered, waving the gun at her. 'Do it now or I'll do it for you.' He leaned on the door jamb and waited. Claire turned to face him as she knew she still had her gun under her scrubs.

'Well, big boy you're just going to have to give me a hand here then,' she said, standing with her hand on her hip. She hoped it would lure him closer and she could take him down. She told herself that the bigger they are the harder they fall and she hoped she could do that in such a confined space. 'Come on then,' she taunted, 'don't you like what you see?' She stepped back as if showing herself off.

The guard had obviously dismissed Claire as a threat and

shoved his gun in his belt and took a step forward. Claire balanced on the balls of her feet while keeping eye contact with the hulk. She put both hands on her hips and wiggled them and the guard now had other things on his mind. Here was a nice clean woman, not the dirty slags out in the cells, and he could while away an hour with her quite happily.

Suddenly Claire turned herself into a writhing ball of fury and unleashed hand chops to his neck and a well aimed kick to his groin. He doubled over and gasped clutching his crotch and Claire went in for the killer blow. As he was bent double she kicked with all her strength under his chin and heard his neck snap back as his body crumpled to the floor. 'Bastard,' she hissed at him and took his gun, tucking it into the top of her scrubs.

Ellie was in the next cell along still in complete darkness. She had been given some food and the all important bucket and she sat and let despair quietly creep into the room with her. The floor was hard and unyielding and she was sitting half propped against the door when she heard the footsteps coming down the corridor. She pressed her ear closer to the door and she heard the next cell door being opened. After about a minute all hell broke loose and it sounded as if an army was doing hand to hand combat next door. Ellie stood and thought she had to take the chance and began to bang on the door and shout for all she was worth.

Then to her amazement she heard, 'Ellie? Ellie is that you in there?'

'Who's that?' asked Ellie tentatively.

'It's me, Claire,' came the answer.

'Please get me out of here,' Ellie begged.

'Wait a sec, I'll see if guard man had the keys.' It all went quiet.

The next thing Ellie heard was a key scraping in the lock.

Nothing happened. Another key was tried and this time a click sounded and the door swung open. Ellie blinked in the light and Claire hugged her to her in relief. Claire had wondered how Ellie had got on with the guard and if she'd been subjected to more than his passing attentions. It appeared at first glance that Ellie was unscathed, just very, very glad to get out of the hell hole.

'Come on, we've got to get out of here,' said Claire, urgently, and went for the door back into the room of cells. Ellie grabbed her arm to stop her.

'No, we can't go that way as there are more guards, I've heard them talking.'

'Well, I didn't see any more except for chummy here.' She pointed to the lifeless body on the floor.

'There are more, believe me. I don't know where they are right now but we can't go that way.'

They both looked down towards the centre of the mountain at the passage that curved away into darkness.

'We'd better go that way then, any idea where it goes?' Claire asked, looking at Ellie.

'None at all,' said Ellie, shrugging her shoulders, 'but it'll be a better bet than that way.'

Claire thrust the gun she was carrying into Ellie's hand. 'If it moves shoot it, okay?'

Ellie gripped the gun tightly and they ran together down the corridor and paused by the curve and Claire peered round carefully. 'Nothing ahead,' she whispered and they began to run again. Deeper and deeper they went till the corridor turned into a tunnel of solid rock.

'Where the hell are, we?' said Ellie, panting a little.

'No idea, but it's better than what those girls had up there. I think they were slaves for the sex trade and will be shipped out soon,' Claire said grimly.

'It was just awful, I've never seen people kept like animals before, and they must have been drugged or something because they never even spoke when I saw them and walked past.'

'It's all to do with money, Ellie, and I think Fortune and Honey have to be mixed up in this somehow,' said Claire.

'I can't believe that.' Ellie's disbelief was written large in her voice.

'We may never know unless we keep moving and get out of here alive.' Claire gave Ellie a shove to focus her and they began to run again. Suddenly Claire skidded to a halt. 'No-one's chasing us and you're sure there were other guards Ellie?'

'Yes, there was a shift change as I heard about five or six guys all at once.'

Claire looked about her and her shoulders sagged. She pointed at a small red dot that glowed half hidden in the rock formations. 'That's why they haven't bothered giving chase, its closed circuit television so they don't need to follow us. They're probably just sitting there drinking coffee watching us right now.' She walked past the small camera and sure enough it followed her progress. 'They must know where this goes and there can't be a way out. So, they'll just sit and wait for us.'

'Like a cat with a mouse hole,' said Ellie.

'You got it,' said Claire, thinking furiously.

'Let's just see where it goes anyway, as I'm sure as hell not going to walk back to them. They're going to have to come and drag me out kicking and screaming,' said Ellie, clutching the gun even tighter.

They started walking down the tunnel and small holes began to appear in the sides. They were too small to crawl through but sometimes there were puffs of air suggesting they led to the outside. They came to a natural cavern that was almost polished in its appearance and the walls were smooth, almost like glass. There were tunnels leading from it and they could hear sounds from deeper inside the mountain. The noises were muffled and neither Ellie nor Claire could make out what they were, it sounded almost as if machinery was running. They stood in the middle of the cave not really caring anymore if they were seen or not. The cave tapered towards the top and in the dim light they could see a chimney going upwards, seemingly forever.

'What I wouldn't give for a very long ladder and some ropes now,' said Claire, gazing upwards.

Ellie was following Claire's gaze and suddenly felt two arms clamp down pinning her arms to her sides. Her finger tightened convulsively on the trigger of her gun and it went off deafening everyone. She screamed at the top of her voice in fear and the sound echoed around the cave then the sound waves bounced their way up the chimney to the outside. Claire didn't have time to react as her arms were also tight against her sides but she did get in a well placed kick to the shin of her captor. It connected well and he yelped in pain and the sound again echoed around the chamber and up the chimney. It was a good kick but he didn't let go and she was powerless.

This is what Phil and the others had heard while they were standing round the top of the vent.

'You didn't think you could possibly get away,' said a feminine voice from out of the shadows. 'It was amusing really to watch you run, but then you realized that it was futile.' The figure of Sister Margaret emerged and looked with disdain at both of them. She was holding a gun that was level with Ellie's heart and the look on her face said she was quite capable of using it.

'But you're a nun,' spluttered Ellie, quite unable to comprehend it.

'Yep,' said Claire, 'she's even a nun with a gun. I don't think Sister Margaret has got the hang of being selfless and devoting her life to others,' she added scathingly.

'Put them in the cells with the other girls,' she ordered. 'Give them something to keep them quiet as well. It seems my passenger manifest has just gone up by two but they'll be gone by tomorrow night to a new life.' She walked round them appraising them. 'A bit old but someone will enjoy subduing them and they can fight or scream all they want to then.'

Ellie and Claire exchanged a glance of horror as they were manhandled back down the long corridor to be imprisoned.

CHAPTER EIGHT

The search party had dissipated and Honey had gone back to the resort with Rory who had chewed his nails down to the quick. Phil had left for Castries in the delivery van to get some more supplies and equipment and Nigel was being fed antihistamine and being fussed over by the nuns. He was in a sorry state and his face and arms were swollen almost beyond recognition. He lay in bed and all he could do was mumble about being sorry and he was really okay and would be all right by tomorrow. Robert and Jack had just kept nodding and agreeing with all they could make out from his swollen lips and offering him a drink through a straw at appropriate intervals. The nuns and Sister Margaret had agreed that they should stay at the hospital and could bunk down on some spare beds in the staff accommodation and they had accepted gratefully. All everyone wanted was a meal and a shower, not necessarily in that order, and regroup for tomorrow's assault on the pipe. By tacit agreement they didn't say a word of their plans to anyone and vaguely said they would be joining the search teams again at first light. Claire's absence was noted but no great alarm bells were sounding as everyone felt she was more than capable of looking after herself and would show up when she had something to report.

Rory arrived back at the resort with Honey who had disappeared immediately to find Fortune and tell him what had transpired. Rory went up to his room and felt bereft and sat with his head in his hands wondering what to do next.

A tap sounded on his door and in walked Alistair without

waiting for an invite. He drew up a chair and faced Rory. 'So tell me everything that has happened,' he demanded.

Rory fixed him with a baleful stare. 'It's all your fault, all this with Ellie going missing again. Why do you keep doing this to me?'

'I assure you, Rory, that I had nothing whatsoever to do with "this", whatever "this" is. I admit that I perhaps went a bit over the top before when I had just found my twin and wanted her to be with me, but today's occurrences had nothing to do with me. So, tell me exactly what has happened,' he demanded again.

The story came tumbling out and Rory suddenly realized he had an ally who could help him get Ellie back rather than an enemy to be kept at arm's length. 'So that's it, you know as much as I do. I'm going back up there tomorrow but I can't imagine why she should have trekked off through the jungle and if you haven't taken her, who would want to?'

Alistair looked pensive. 'Let me have a think about that one. Go and have a shower and I'll meet you for something to eat when you're done and we can take this apart piece by piece. We can't do anything in the complete dark so we'll have to wait till tomorrow but I'm sure we'll know more by then.' Alistair gave Rory a look that said he knew how he felt about losing Ellie and left him sitting in despair. Alistair went down the stairs double time and was on the phone to Karl before he reached the end. 'Ellie's gone missing after a visit to the hospital and I need you to get everyone you can for a very big search tomorrow at first light. Check out if there is anyone at this Birthday Party who could possibly want to put leverage on me for any reason. My PAs will give you any info on current business deals I have going through at the moment if you need them. See if anything ties up as no-one can believe she's just simply got lost. Also dig up what you can on this Foundation hospital place, who funds it and why? Leave Fortune to me,' he ended ominously.

'On it boss,' answered Karl, fully aware of what had gone on at the hospital and quickly thinking how he could give Alistair some, but not all, the information he desired. A bit of 'window dressing' was in order and he quickly placed a call directly to Valentin.

Valentin answered at the first ring. 'Karl, you sound bothered, what gives?'

'Alistair's going to move mountains to find Ellie. I've got to give him something by tomorrow morning and I've also got access to all his current business dealings,' Karl said, dangling a carrot in the hopes of boosting his pension fund.

'How interesting, Karl,' said Valentin, sensing a major coup. 'I'll meet you in the usual place in about an hour and we'll have a little talk about that.' Valentin now had a decision to make. He could either get rid of Ellie altogether, which would make Karl a very happy man and would probably get rid of some future unforeseen problems concerning her, or he could be the one to find her then he would be an even better friend to Alistair. Did he want the glory or did he just want her gone altogether? He mused as he paced up and down. One problem was if she was 'found' then his depot here on St. Lucia would have to close down very quickly. She wouldn't keep her mouth shut, of that he was sure. It was a very lucrative operation and girls from the poorer European countries were ferried out here with promises of jobs and good wages then drugged up and sold for the sex trade. They could end up anywhere in the world and were never seen again. They usually lasted about a year so there were always the replacements to be found and fresh flesh was always appetizing. It was perfect here on the island as it was easy access to the States as well as South America and the money was big for white girls. A dilemma faced him for sure, to take the penny now in hopes of the pounds to follow, or to keep what he already had. He had about an hour to make up his mind.

Rory met Alistair in the dining room and looked dreadful. He looked as if he had aged ten years and his eyes were feverish and bright in a pallid face. He sat down and accepted a cold beer from the waiter and waited for Alistair to speak. Not bearing the silence he said, 'I don't know if I can carry on like this, every time Ellie and I set out to do anything it always gets ballsed up by you in some way. I'm going to bet you've got something to do with this and I'm going to find out if it's the last thing I do.' Rory was an angry man and it showed in every fibre of his being.

'There's nothing I can say or do to change your mind right now, Rory, I can see that, but you must believe me when I say I haven't had anything to do with this at all. I schemed long and hard to find Ellie and literally went to Hell and back to keep her by me and I'm not going to give her up that easily. She is my twin, my other half, and I've never been so happy in my life, as when she decided to stay with me at the Castle.'

'You made it bloody difficult for her to leave you mean,' said Rory between gritted teeth.

'I admit that my tactics were a little over the top but I think she is happy with what she's got at the moment. She has spoken about you and I admit I wasn't too happy about you joining us but I can see that you mean a lot to her and believe me or not I do want her to be happy,' said Alistair, surprising himself at this revelation.

'Pity you didn't think about that when I was stuck up the North of England in a snow storm for two weeks and I didn't know if she was alive or dead. Then there wasn't even a phone call from her. Did you really know how I felt about that? Well, I felt like an "also ran", the spare part, something to be put on a shelf and taken down and dusted off occasionally,' said Rory bitterly.

Alistair sat in silence and heard all the hurt and emotion in Rory's voice and didn't quite know what to say. This was something money couldn't fix and it would be an insult to even think it could. All these emotions were new to Alistair and he had only begun to experience them when he had met Ellie, she was still the key to his future and he knew he would have to find her. Rory, with all his raw emotion that could be channelled into action, would be a definite plus and he had to get him on his side at all costs.

'There is something we could do right now,' said Alistair tentatively testing the water.

Rory perked up. 'What?' he demanded and leaned forward.

'It depends on how much you will believe of what I'm going to tell you,' Alistair said, throwing breadcrumbs down.

'Tell me now,' said Rory, looking as if he was going to hit Alistair there and then.

Alistair began to relate the events when Jack, Ellie, and himself had spent Christmas at the Chateau of the Birds. 'So we found the passageway down into the cavern below the chateau and I drew out a pentacle with the salt and the candles. We all stood in it and I managed to invoke a great big bird, a griffin, I think they're called.' He had glossed over many of the points that had led to that point.

'I know that bird as I saw it when we were in the farmhouse,' said Rory, thinking back to that cold night. 'Jack shot it but it didn't die and it knocked me out. It was the stuff of nightmares and I don't think I'll ever forget it,' said Rory with a shudder.

'Well, it didn't go completely to plan as that was where I lost my fingers on my left hand,' Alistair said, showing Rory the stumps now fully healed. It just looked as if his fingers were curled over and no-one really noticed unless it was pointed out.

'So what are you getting at?' said Rory. 'I don't quite see where this is leading.'

'What I'm going to tell you now is going to stretch your credibility to the limits, but I think I can find Ellie, and I'll need your help,' said Alistair carefully.

'Go on,' said Rory.

'I know a little bit about the occult and the Dark Arts and I think I can use that griffin to search out Ellie.' Alistair's eyes were fixed on Rory's.

'What!' Rory exclaimed, staring back at Alistair. 'You mean you were behind that griffin thing and that's how you found Ellie before?' He broke the stare and looked at the tablecloth. 'I can't believe that, not for one moment. I don't really believe in God or the Devil for that matter and I don't think Ellie would be mixed up in any sort of Satanic Cult whatever you say.'

'It's not a sort of Cult, or anything like that but I found a book when we were down in the cave and I used it. Ellie called it a Grimoire and it certainly had some sort of power I can't explain,' said Alistair, deliberately not telling Rory he had used it to bind Ellie to him and that was the reason she had almost forgotten Rory.

'So where's this book now?' said Rory, not believing anything Alistair was saying.

'Sadly it got burnt when the Chateau of the Birds was destroyed.'

'So we're stuck where we were an hour ago,' said Rory despondently.

'Not necessarily,' said Alistair. 'I can maybe recall what I did before, maybe I can use the griffin again to find Ellie, but I would need your help. We didn't have a very good meeting last time we met,' he said, putting his mangled hand on the snowy white cloth, 'but I'm willing to take the chance if you will help me?'

'I'll give it a go but I'll tell you now I don't really believe a word you've said,' said Rory sceptically, 'but if we can do something now then I'm up for it. I've got a nasty feeling time is running out and I can't stand just sitting here doing nothing.'

Alistair felt a dread at what lay ahead if he could invoke the beast, but he knew that the entity wanted them together not apart. This, he hoped, would be his ace up his sleeve and he could get the beast to search her out as before. He hadn't got the Grimoire any longer but hoped and prayed he could remember the feelings he had when he concentrated his mind. Rory would be there with him and Alistair hoped this would be enough to pull him back from the brink if things went horribly wrong.

'So, are you with me?' Alistair asked Rory.

'What will I have to do?' asked Rory, still bemused.

'We'll go up to the top of that small hill.' Alistair indicated a nearby hill, silvery in the moonlight and covered in virgin forest. 'We'll take some salt and some candles and I'll have a go at calling up the Beast. I'll explain how you can help me if I can't get back.'

'What do you mean "if you can't get back"?' said Rory still at sea.

'I don't want to do this in any of our rooms as we could get interrupted at any time. We need to be quiet and away from people as I need to concentrate my mind. If things aren't going to plan I'll need you to call me back, I don't know how but the answer will come to you if it happens. I can't do this alone Rory.

We both want the same thing and if we both want it badly enough we'll get it I'm sure.' Alistair looked at Rory intently, searching his face for any wavering on his part. 'Needless to say we can't breathe a word of this to anyone as I'll probably be certified tomorrow.'

'I'll give them a ring now if you like,' said Rory, lightening the mood. 'I didn't think you were this crazy Alistair,' he said, shaking his head.

'Ellie knows all I've said is true,' said Alistair, hammering in the last nail. 'When we find her you can ask her and she'll tell you the full story.'

'It's strange but when we were at the Castle in Italy we went looking at all the secret passages and we thought we'd found one that wasn't on any of the maps. We had to leave to get the plane but Ellie was convinced she had found the entrance to another one,' said Rory, thinking back.

'You must show me,' said Alistair, suddenly very interested. He knew this could be the entrance to another cavern full of their father's occult memorabilia. It held the key to power for Alistair and he quite forgot the promise he had made to Ellie a few months back. 'Anyway, let's get some torches and the other stuff and we'll have a short hike to the top of the hill. Let's just pray this works.'

'Yes, let's,' said Rory, wondering what he had let himself in for with a crazy man in the jungle in the dark.

Valentin had stopped pacing and began to saunter unconcernedly towards the meeting point with Karl. He ambled along as if enjoying the evening cool and the evening scents of the flowers from the beds bordering the path. He exchanged a few greetings with others enjoying the same pastime and stopped to admire the view over the bay with a few tall mast boats lit up like Christmas trees. He dodged off the path when no-one was looking to the service area by the bins. Karl was waiting impatiently for him smoking a cigarette that glowed in the dark like a red fire fly.

Karl flung the cigarette away and without a greeting said, 'So what do you want me to do then? I've got access to all Morgan's recent dealings and that info could be worth a lot to you.'

Valentin's lip curled in the darkness as he heard the naked greed in Karl's voice. It disgusted him but was a necessary evil he had to contend with at all levels in his business. Everyone was trying to cut a deal and it was 'dog eat dog' in his world, but he was top dog and he controlled the pack by force and fear. Karl was perhaps beginning to think he had a hold over him and that would never do. He would be useful in the short term but if he failed then he would be removed instantly.

'Yes, of course, Karl, you will be suitably rewarded but first we have a decision to make. Do we get rid of the Morgan twin now or do I appear to save her and use her in the future?'

'Get rid of her now,' said Karl emphatically. 'She's trouble, she killed Max, remember?'

'If I remember rightly,' said Valentin slowly, 'the feeling was a mutual one and he would have removed her if he had half a chance. Let's play this situation to our advantage. If you can get me all the latest info on what Alistair is up to his clever little neck in then I'll make it worth your while as usual. I do actually know where Ellie is right at this moment but I'm not going to tell you, Karl, not that I don't trust you,' he added hastily, 'but I think she may be useful to me in the future.'

Karl lit another cigarette and stared at his shoes. This wasn't what he wanted. He wanted the money above all but he also wanted to see that bitch squirm and beg him for mercy. That would give him untold pleasure and he would make it last as long as possible. A plan half formed in his mind and he decided to go along with Valentin and perhaps an opportunity would present itself in the very near future for his heart's desire. 'Okay, you're the boss. I'll go and see what I can dig up, but Morgan said I had a free rein for info from his PAs so I'll have no trouble. I'll go and get started.' He looked at his watch, squinting in the dim light. 'See you back here in about two hours then?'

'Good idea and I'll go and check what Alistair and Rory are planning as I saw them deep in conversation in the dining room.' Valentin turned on his heel and left. As useful as Karl was the man was repugnant to Valentin and he strode quickly away. By the time he had got back to the dining room both Alistair and Rory had disappeared. He went to Alistair's room to ostensibly enquire if he could do anything to aid the search, but it was empty as was Rory's. He was mystified as to where they could be so he enquired generally from the staff as to their whereabouts. One person said they had borrowed some torches and a map and gone that way, pointing at the small rocky promontory. Valentin was even more intrigued so he asked for a torch and a map as well and set off in pursuit. He walked up the road until he was opposite the hill and looked across and sure enough he saw the flicker of two small beams of light. There was just natural wild forest between them but he took the plunge and went into the jungle. The torches were lost to sight immediately and he felt he was on an alien planet as ferns and foliage grabbed at his clothes and threatened to trip him up. He had no control over this situation and suddenly felt very unsure as he had to rely on his wits and words had no meaning here at all. He realized he hadn't brought anyone with him to smooth his path and worst of all no-one knew where he was if he had an accident. That thought nearly made him turn back. Mentally he shook himself and resolved to find out what Alistair and Rory were up to. Eventually he saw the two lights between the trees and stealthily crept towards them. He positioned himself where he would have a good view but would be well hidden and he put his torch off as he crawled the last fifty metres.

For Claire and Ellie the walk back to the cells couldn't have lasted long enough. Ellie's arms had been pinned behind her and they were now quite numb and Claire was furiously making plan after plan and discarding them all just as fast. The man she had kicked hard was holding her in a vice-like grip and as much as she wriggled he wouldn't loosen his hold. His fingers dug into her arms and she winced with pain at every jab. The end of the passageway loomed closer and the double doors were open invitingly. Claire could even see the corner of the row of cells but she couldn't think of what to do to get them out. Sister Margaret had padded along behind and kept her gun levelly pointed at them and Claire knew she would have no hesitation in pulling the trigger.

'Wait,' said the Sister and the procession stopped. 'Give them something to drink first.' She went and got two glasses of what appeared to be milk. 'Her first.' She indicated Ellie and gave the glass to a guard. He offered the glass to Ellie's lips but she turned her head away. The guard held her face in a meaty paw and put the glass to her lips again. Ellie jerked and nearly knocked the glass out of his hand. Sister Margaret watched all this ineptitude and came forward taking the glass from the guard. 'This is how to do it,' she said. She pinched Ellie's nose hard so she couldn't jerk her head then as she opened her mouth to breathe she poured some of the liquid in. Ellie tried to spit it out but she had to breathe as well and swallowed some of the drink, gasping. 'Just repeat that,' said Sister Margaret, giving the glass back to the guard, and wiped her hands on her habit.

'Cow,' gasped Ellie, struggling to breathe as the guard repeated the procedure and Ellie felt a strange lassitude gradually sweep over her and she drank the rest unresisting. She could walk after a fashion and she followed the guard to the cell and sank gratefully onto the thin mattress. Claire must have suffered the same force feeding as she was led to the next cell and collapsed onto the bed. They lay next to each other but with no more energy or strength than a new-born kitten. Ellie did register before she fell asleep that the cells were now empty of girls and the place was silent.

Maria had watched as Claire had left in the wake of Ellie's disappearance and had wrung her hands and alternatively cursed the name of Morgan and worried herself sick about Ellie. She was all ready to rush off and join in the search but thought she could probably be more use here. There were things going on that she had caught undercurrents of from the other personal staff and she waited and watched. She couldn't resist calling Robert and had found out that they were bunked in the hospital for the night as they had drawn a blank in the foot search. Robert had agreed with her that she would be useful to keep a watch on the other guests. They hadn't got anyone there who could do that and any information could prove useful to the team. Maria suddenly felt she had a role to play and wouldn't let Robert down so she changed from her maid's clothes and took some black leggings and a black T-shirt from Ellie's wardrobe. She waited until the coast was clear and slid down the stairs and hid herself in the gardens away from the lighting. She saw Valentin pacing up and down and then head off to the long path that snaked round the edge of the resort. She followed him and it all seemed innocuous at first till he suddenly left the path and headed for the service area. She crept, wraith like, till she could see and hear him in conversation with Karl. She was shocked at what she heard and stored it all up word for word to report it back to Robert. She saw Valentin go and get some things and resolved to follow him as he set off down the road. There was something big going on here and she was scared as he headed off into the rainforest. She had to follow him now that she had come this far, but she hadn't got a torch and couldn't have risked using one if she had. She ended up flat on her face on more than one occasion but didn't even squeak when she felt things slither past or clutch at her clothes. She began to get the hang of moving carefully and almost silently as she followed his torch beam and saw him conceal himself in some thick foliage where he could watch what was going on. She gradually eased herself round about fifty yards to his left so she could have a good view of what he was watching and keep her eye on him at the same time.

Rory and Alistair had found a flat expanse of ground at the top of the hill that had been swept bare of soil from the wind. It was a big area of exposed rock and perfect for what Alistair was planning to do. He got the salt and the candles and began to lay out a pentacle with a candle at each corner. He was muttering words as he did so, and all Rory could do was watch and wonder what the Hell he was up to. When it was all to Alistair's satisfaction he held out his hand and invited Rory inside the pentacle with him. They both switched off their torches and the candles made tiny pinpricks of light that made no impression on the fitful moonlight.

Rory stepped into the pentacle and held his breath. 'What's supposed to happen now?'

'Nothing till I've invoked the Beast,' said Alistair grimly.

'Beast! You never said anything about a Beast,' said Rory, exhaling loudly.

'I've got to call this thing up then I can become one with it, and I can go anywhere I like and find Ellie,' Alistair explained, 'but I need you with me so you can bring me back if it all goes haywire.'

'I still don't know what I have to do,' said Rory, getting scared at what might happen.

'For now, just don't let go of my hands whatever happens,' answered Alistair, staring at Rory in the half darkness. 'Promise me that, please,' he almost begged. 'You have to be my anchor to the Earth and if you let go I'll probably be carted off to Hell.'

'Are you serious?'

'I've probably never been more serious in my life,' said Alistair earnestly.

'Okay,' said Rory, holding out his hands and Alistair clasped them firmly. Rory felt the stubs of Alistair's fingers digging into his palm and felt slightly repulsed by it. He didn't really know what Alistair was going to do but he recognized the fear in the other man's voice and he held on tightly.

Alistair began to say words under his breath that made no sense to Rory at all but the constant repetition gradually drew him in and he found himself repeating and keeping time with Alistair. It must have been about five minutes and Alistair's eyes had taken on a dead stare. He seemed to be looking at something a million miles away and had an odd glazed look. Rory held his hands even tighter and the darkness about them became more opaque. The moon seemed to disappear and the frogs and cicadas fell silent. Rory still chanted but he was getting really scared and wished he was anywhere but here. The dark closed in on them even more and stray gusts began to make the candles flicker but there was no answering rustle from the trees or foliage. The sky disappeared and all that was left was an inky void with no stars and the darkness was almost palpable. Rory felt that the air had turned to treacle and was thick to breathe. He felt the hairs at the back of his neck stand up and an all pervading sense of dread enveloped him. All he wanted to do was to let go of Alistair's hands and run, as far and as long as he could.

At the edge of the circle Valentin and Maria watched and waited. They saw the moon's light and the stars snuff out one by one. The two people in the pentacle were shrouded in a gauzy vortex that seemed to spin faster and faster, but didn't disturb the plants where they were hiding. There wasn't a breath of a breeze but the air was definitely moving causing a whirlwind round the pentacle. It got thicker and more tangible and Maria crouched in terror as something seemed to coalesce out of the dark. It grew big and seemed to shroud the pair in the pentacle with wings that were real and solid. Maria and Valentin watched as a beast emerged and stood waiting on the outside of the pentacle. It had taken the shape of a huge griffin and they both recognized it from heraldic coats of arms but this one was now stalking about on its clawed feet seeming to find some way in to Rory and Alistair.

It ruffled its feathers and the sound was like dried leaves of parchment rubbing together then it tilted its head to one side and they could see the hole in its head where its eye should have been. Creatures with slimy carapaces crawled and slithered in and out of its head. It had been in the French Chateau that Ellie had flung the cross at the creature and it seared a hole that hadn't healed

'So you have bought a new friend for me to meet, Alistair Morgan. I am pleased to make your acquaintance,' the thing said as it paced round the pentacle. 'Tell me your name.'

Alistair spoke loud and clear, 'His name is of no interest to you but I do need your help.'

'Help?' The beast laughed loud and long. 'You are asking me for help after what you did to one of my sacred homes?'

'Yes,' said Alistair, 'that which was two is now only one as Ellie has been taken and I need her back with me. Will you help to restore the two parts together?'

The beast ceased its pacing and fixed a blood red eye on Alistair. 'I told you what I wanted before. One of you must come with me as the contract decreed, but it wasn't fulfilled last time was it?'

Rory was totally aghast and horrified at what had been invoked but he didn't understand any of the conversation at all. He felt Alistair holding onto his hands like a drowning man and he looked into his dead eyes and saw nothing at all, there was no spark of life, nothing there to say Alistair was even alive. His breathing had almost stopped and his body was as if rigor mortis had already set in. Rory didn't know what made him say it but he shouted, 'I'll go with you if that's what you want, but we need to find Ellie now!'

The beast pondered. 'I'll accept the payment offered and you can find Ellie Black, but I need to know your name first.' It then looked at Alistair. 'This doesn't release you from the contract but I'll make whole what is separate.'

'My name is Rory,' he said in a whisper.

'Thank you.' The beast rustled its wings. 'I will take Alistair now where he wants to go. Don't think that stupid little pentacle can save you as it won't, but you can sit in there until we return.'

Alistair suddenly slumped forward and Rory found he was cradling an almost lifeless body in his arms. He decided that it was probably best to stay exactly where he was as the night was far from over. He needed guidance from Alistair as to what to do next and could only wait and see what happened.

The beast rose up and flapped lazily away and Rory clung onto Alistair for dear life. He said every prayer that came into his mind and shut his eyes tight but the images of what he had seen were burned into his brain.

Valentin had seen enough to know this wasn't anything of this earth and all his nerve endings tingled with the flight response. He couldn't take any more and shuffled quickly back out of his hiding place and ran as quickly as he could towards the lights of the resort. He missed the road completely and slipped and slithered down the rocky hillside catching at vines and tree trunks on the way to slow his fall. He ran and fell till he could run no more and felt a blessed relief when he could see the buildings and the guests strolling about with drinks in their hands by the pool. He slid down the last bank and landed in a heap near the bins where he had met Karl earlier. He lay panting and relished the warm earth beneath him and the muffled sounds of conversation and normality wafting towards him.He had never been so glad to reach people in his life but he realized he looked a complete mess with his clothes tattered and dirty. He gathered the remains of his dignity and slunk off in the shadows to get a shower and make sense of what he had witnessed.

Back in her hiding place, Maria had curled into a ball and couldn't look at the beast any longer. She held onto the cross around her neck till her palm bled. Back in her home village she had listened to many tales told on dark nights of mythical creatures that had roamed the mountains and waged war on the human race. They had always been defeated by a hero who possessed a magical sword or used some cunning to get the better of them, either by trickery or help from some angel or other.

Maria wished with all her heart for an angel now but none was forthcoming. She screwed up enough courage to open her eyes and look at Rory and Alistair who seemed to be frozen in stone. The huge bird had gone and she wished she had enough faith to go to them, but she didn't. She wasn't a coward by any means, but this was all the horror stories from her childhood come to life and she didn't have a magical sword. So she lay, curled in a ball, and watched and waited.

Alistair went into the body of the beast and felt a weightlessness as it took wing and soared over the dark forest. It was as before and he could see what it saw in blinding clarity. It was as if night had turned to day and he could see every roosting bird and every small mammal as it scurried about its night time business. They went over the hills and Alistair revelled in the freedom of flight. He felt energized and free of all earthly restraints, it touched his soul and he felt power coursing through his veins. They soared together and saw the lights of a cluster of buildings below them. There were Police vehicles dotted about and it seemed to be a hive of activity.

'Where are we?' Alistair asked subconsciously.

'This is the hospital that Ellie Black was visiting when she went missing,' came the answer in his mind.

'Where is she now?'

They soared upwards until they were halfway up the hill then went into a heart stopping dive that Alistair was sure would kill them both. They plunged through the canopy and down into the mouth of a hole that yawned on the forest floor. The beast folded its wings and they shot with the speed of a bullet down the lava pipe into the cavern below.

CHAPTER NINE

The girls had been hauled to their feet and moved to small cells and packed in like animals waiting to be transported to the abattoir. They slumped and slouched in the two small cells where Ellie and Claire had been kept. Sister Margaret had arranged that a couple of ambulances would bring new patients to the small Emergency Department and then drive round the side of the building away from prying eyes. It was risky to move the girls now but she didn't have a choice. They could be packed into the two ambulances and driven to the small airfield where a plane was waiting to take them to their new lives. Usually she would have cleaned them up a bit and given them some clothes that didn't stink so much but there wasn't time for that now. She tried to put a call to Valentin but his phone wasn't on, so she had to consider the possibilities and make a decision now. Also there was the small problem of Claire and Ellie; she also didn't know what to do with those two. They were full of GHB, gamma hydroxybutyrate, which was essentially the 'date rape drug' and rendered them incapacitated and pliant. They were locked in the cells and were basically asleep. She didn't know what Valentin had in mind for them but they couldn't stay there. One of the ambulances was coming down the drive and she had to use this time productively and get some of the girls out. It drew up in front of the emergency department doors and a stretcher was unloaded holding a man who clutched his stomach and moaned piteously. It was a good performance and he would be paid well for his time and his quiet mouth. The ambulance moved away from the doors and drove slowly out of sight round the side to the door that Claire had used to get in. The girls had to get from their cells to the ambulance and this was down corridors with night staff in attendance. The only way to do this was to do it herself. No-one would question her ministering to a sick, bandaged person in a wheel chair, so she went off post haste with her habit billowing out behind her like a large black crow.

Jack lay with his arms behind his head in the small room kept for overnight staff and stray travellers that came upon the convent. It was air conditioned and comfortable but he couldn't sleep. Nigel was now out of immediate danger and was being pumped full of anti-histamines and the swellings had begun to go down but he would be out of action tomorrow. Jack kept thinking about the lava pipe and where it would lead, he wasn't a fan of enclosed spaces and if the truth was told he hid his fear in a macho bravado in front of the others but he was a bit scared of going down there. It was making him restless and sleep was a long way away so he decided to turn his mind to other things to push his fears into the background. He decided to go outside and have a short walk to clear his head and he pulled on his clothes and crept past the other rooms. The clock in his head told him it was about midnight and all was quiet in the hospital. A few staff were walking purposefully, pushing drug carts or clutching clipboards but no-one paid him much attention.

Outside the air was full of the sounds of the forest animals and there was a whisper of a breeze rustling the leaves. Jack strolled until he found a small bench and sat just soaking in the sounds of the night. An ambulance drew up and the medics unloaded a man clutching his stomach and moaning. They wheeled him into the Emergency Department and it all went quiet again. The medics came out and loaded the gurney onto the vehicle and slowly drove round the side of the building. They were obviously waiting for their next call but Jack thought he would have a stroll round and maybe have a conversation with them to pass the time. There wasn't anything more boring than a night shift with nothing to do except listen to the radio, play cards and read. He knew from his past experience on the beat back in England. After about five minutes he rose and ambled around the corner but there wasn't anyone there and he was just about to amble back when he saw one of the medics hold open the ambulance door to receive a patient in a wheelchair. Jack slid into the shadows and waited. The patient was hauled unceremoniously from the chair and dragged up the step into the ambulance and Jack heard the thump as they hit the floor.

 He got down on his hands and knees and crawled into a large fern that had enormous leaves and covered him well. Another wheelchair came into view and another person swaddled in a blanket was treated the same way. This went on for nearly half an hour until six people were crammed into the ambulance and the crew, laughing and joking, slammed the doors on their cargo and drove away. Jack just sat there and tried to make sense of what he had just seen. They couldn't be the rich people in the hospital for the minor plastic surgery as they paid for a lot better treatment than that. They would have certainly used the front door, not a service door, and they would have been secreted into air conditioned luxury cars to make their way home. The local islanders would soon have had something to say if they had been treated like that and Jack didn't think for an instant that Honey would allow them to be treated like animals. So, Jack asked himself, who were these people. There seemed to be a lot more going on at this hospital than met the eye and Jack decided to tell Phil all about it right there and then. He began to back out of the fern and noticed that he was staring at a highly polished man's shoe. His gaze travelled from the shoe up a sharply-creased trouser leg to the business end of a gun pointed at him.

'Couldn't sleep sir?'

Jack didn't answer.

'Please stand up?' Jack complied with the request. 'Walk this way.' He felt the gun barrel firmly in his ribs as he went back to the hospital and Sister Margaret was waiting on the steps to greet him.

'Take him back to his room,' she ordered and followed them back to Jack's room.

Jack considered trying to overpower the man with the gun but he was a big guy and looked as if he could handle himself in a fight. Sister Margaret was the surprise card in the pack as she was also holding a gun and looked as if she would use it without hesitation. The entourage got to Jack's room and he was shoved inside and the big guy grabbed his arms and Jack saw Sister Margaret coming towards him with a needle in her hand. Jack struggled wildly but to no avail and he felt a stab in his arm and the world receded. The last thing he heard was, 'night night' as he slipped into oblivion.

Sister Margaret holstered her gun and said, 'Well he won't be a problem anymore as he'll just wake up tomorrow with a thick head and won't remember anything at all. It will just seem to have been a dream to him. Put him in bed and make the room normal,' she ordered and swept out. The night was just throwing up problem after problem for her and she was using all her ingenuity to cope. The sister decided to get the rest of the girls gone as soon as possible and that would be one problem done and sorted. She still needed to get hold of Valentin and find out what he wanted to do with Ellie and Claire or else she would take matters into her own hands and just ship them off with the next cargo of girls.

The bird had arrested its heart stopping dive and alighted in the cavern and Alistair managed a mental 'phew'. It pushed off again with its claws and swooped down the corridor towards the cells. The dim lights went out one by one behind them as they silently drifted down the passageway.

Alistair had to ask subconsciously, 'How do you know where you're going?'

The bird clacked its beak and fed back that the question was nothing whatsoever to do with Alistair and that it knew where everything was on Earth and in Hell.

'So, what if we come to a door?' Alistair asked. 'Can we just go through it as if we were invisible or something?'

'Sadly no, as you are with me, but if I was alone, I can go anywhere I choose, but we are getting close and I can feel the vibrations from her soul and yours beginning to mesh. Then it's up to you, as you asked the question how to restore the two parts and make them whole again. I have answered that question as she is on the other side of that door.' The beast had banked its wings and settled noiselessly onto the floor by a set of double doors which led to the cells where Ellie and Claire were incarcerated. 'I have shown you where she is, now you have to get her back. We will return to your friend Rory and hope he is where we left him,' the bird said ominously, as it lifted into flight again and swooped back up the corridor.

Alistair began to understand the implications of what he had done by invoking the beast again and tried to make his mind a blank as they reached the cavern and the bird circled a few times before picking up momentum and flying straight back up the lava pipe. Alistair didn't revel in the freedom of the flight back towards the pentacle but he was filled with dread at what might happen if Rory had left it and perhaps taken his body with him. He would be forever bound to this creature and destined to be a sentient being within a monstrous form and wander the Earth for Eternity.

'Stop the futile prayers, they just give me a headache,' the bird sneered. 'It's a pointless exercise and I can read your mind as my own. I've done what you asked me and you can now find her. Rory will have to pay me in due course, but not today. So nice he told me his name,' the beast added conversationally. They were wheeling above the rain forest and as the bird cocked its head Alistair could see Rory still within the pentacle clutching a lifeless body. They alighted just outside the pentacle and the beast spread its wings and opened its beak. A gust of fetid air was expelled and the candle stubs guttered. Rory's face was a mask of horror and his eyes were riveted to the being. The air smelled of sulphur and the stench of decay and Rory recoiled and let Alistair's body fall to the ground as he covered his face with his hands. He heard the words inside his head, 'I'll bid you farewell, Rory, until the next time we meet.' He was numb with terror.

Alistair's body gave a convulsive twitch and he coughed. Rory heard this and quickly scrambled to Alistair's side and supported his shoulders as he struggled for air. Alistair coughed again and began to breathe in ragged gasps and Rory held him tightly even though he still reeked of stench and decay.

They hadn't seen the beast dematerialize into thin air and didn't notice the silvery moonlight bathe everything in a pearly glaze. The stars had come out again and night creatures began their scurrying and hunting again. Maria had seen all this and felt a great weight lift from her soul and, as she released the crucifix, she had to pull it out of her palm. She wadded up a corner of her blouse and held it tightly to stop the bleeding and ran over to Rory and Alistair.

Alistair's breathing had become normal now and his eyelids fluttered. Rory was nearly in a panic and was shaking Alistair. 'Come on, come on, talk to me,' he repeated. He started as Maria came running over and knelt down beside Alistair. 'Where did you come from?' he asked, amazed.

'I was here all along and saw everything but we'll talk later, how is he?'

'Don't know,' said Rory, who was nearly close to tears. 'That thing took him somewhere and he seemed to be dead. He's breathing now but I can't get him back.'

Maria knelt closer. 'Don't let go of him, just keep holding him and I'll have a look.' She reached out for Alistair's torch and shone it on him. He was definitely breathing regularly and she noticed the small flicker of his eyelids. 'I think he's coming round, just keep talking to him.' As she said that Alistair's eyes opened and he gazed at them both.

'Can you hear me?' said Rory urgently. 'Talk to me. We're here and you're safe now, come on, talk to me.'

A few grunts came out of Alistair's mouth and he started to move his arms and legs as if to sit up. Maria shoved him back down and said, 'Just lie still for a minute and you'll be fine.' She wasn't convinced about this but it was all that sprung to mind. 'Do you know where you are?'

Alistair had collapsed back down to earth and lay looking at the stars. 'I think I'm on the top of a hill in a pentacle,' he said, sardonically, and everyone exhaled a sigh of relief. He pushed himself up on one elbow and looked at them both. 'But I do know where Ellie is.'

'My God, Alistair, you have given me the scare of my life,'

said Rory, settling back on his heels. His voice conveyed the relief he felt. 'Are you okay, I mean really okay?' he asked, concerned.

'I'm as weak as a kitten right now but I know where she is. We've got to get down back to the resort right now and organize some help.' He looked quizzically at Maria. 'What are you doing here?'

'It's a long story, Mr. Morgan. And I'll go through it with you later but we've got to get you down from here. Do you think you can walk?' Maria put her hand under Alistair's arm and he tried to stand up. His legs buckled and he ended up on his knees. 'Sorry, Mr. Morgan, but I don't think Rory and I can carry you, but with an arm round each shoulder we might just be able to do it.' Alistair tried again and stood upright wobbling precariously. Maria was silently saying every prayer she knew as she shuffled herself under one shoulder and Rory did the same the other side. With Alistair draped between them they began the laborious walk back to sanity and reality.

Sister Margaret had never been a woman of indecision and as the second ambulance rolled up to the Emergency Department she embarked on her plan. Valentin was still off the radar and the next load of girls was ready for shipment. As the ambulance went round to the service entrance she ordered that Claire and Ellie be loaded on as well. They were dragged from the cells and strapped onto gurneys, covered with blankets, and rolled down the hospital corridors with fake drips as if they had been to surgery. They were propped up in the ambulance and the other six girls were piled in like sardines in a tin. The ambulance rumbled away to the airfield. Sister Margaret swung into action and ordered the cells cleaned and hosed out, and all traces of the last shipment obliterated. It was, after all, just a defunct part of the hospital where they used to house mental patients before the new Psychiatric Facility was built in Castries.

Rory and Maria struggled with Alistair through the thick undergrowth and his strength began to return slowly. Maria was glad as her muscles were screaming for respite and they often had to shuffle crabwise down non-existent animal tracks to make any headway at all. She went first and had the torch between her teeth and her jaw ached. It made conversation impossible but Maria was glad as with Alistair's returning strength there was a barrage of questions. She was exhausted and took the torch from her mouth and said, 'That's it, I've got to have a rest.' As she let go of Alistair and she sank to the ground.

'Me as well,' said Rory, lowering Alistair down. 'Just give us five minutes and we'll carry on.' The physical and emotional roller coaster had drained Rory totally and the gauge was nearly on empty. He sank to the floor in relief. They were like the sole survivors of a shipwreck, ragged and tattered. Maria's blouse was bloody as she had tried to staunch her hand, Rory was dirty and emotionally spent and Alistair looked as though he had a terrible disease as his eyes were sunk into his head and his face was deathly pale. His clothes still reeked of death and decay and that smell had permeated all three of them. Even the night animals fell silent as they passed.

Rory broke the silence. 'So where is Ellie?'

'I know she's in the hospital. The bird took me there, I couldn't see her but I felt her on the other side of some doors.'

'What do you mean, you "felt" her?' said Rory, peering at Alistair in the dark.

'The bird took me there and we went down a sort of hole in the ground into a part of the hospital that's under the mountain. Because I was with it we couldn't go through the doors but it was as if a magnet was in me and I felt her there. I can't explain the feeling but I'm sure she's there.' Alistair had a sudden flash of the feeling he had when he was soaring through the air, weightless and powerful, and it felt good. He had been mastering of the earth and hadn't been subject to earthly constraints of gravity, time and space. He wished with all his heart he could feel like that for ever. 'We've got to get her out,' he said with a sudden urgency. 'I'm getting stronger by the minute and we'll be back down there within the hour,' he said, looking far below at the lights of the resort.

They all stood up again and Maria went to shoulder Alistair but he shook her off and began to shuffle down the path unaided. Maria looked at Rory through the gloom. 'Be thankful for small mercies, at least we haven't got to carry him all the way,' she said wryly.

Alistair had been right and they did reach civilization within the hour and they all paused at the edge of the compound still hidden in the dense foliage. In the ambient light they looked at each other. 'Well,' said Maria, 'we can't just wander in looking like this. We look like a train wreck and forgive me, but Mr. Morgan you smell like a sewer.' A half smile played on Rory's mouth as her humour began to dissipate the emotional desert that had settled on him.

'You don't miss, much do you? I agree we do all pong a bit,' Rory said, delicately sniffing an armpit. 'I suggest we all split up now and meet in Alistair's room in about half an hour after getting cleaned up then we can have a plan and raise the alarm. One thing though.' He paused. 'How are we going to convince people you've not gone stark staring mad, Alistair? I mean, what's the storyline going to be on this one?' He looked directly at Alistair. 'So, man gets taken by big supernatural bird and is shown, no sorry, not shown but feels he knows where his sister is. This needs some thought.'

'See your point Rory,' said Maria. 'It's hardly a story that hangs together well is it?'

'We can't sit here forever,' said Alistair impatiently. 'We'll go and get cleaned up and meet in my room and have a think how to play it.'

They all went one by one through the undergrowth and made it back to their rooms unseen. Alistair went to the mini bar and grabbed the first bottle that came to hand and poured it down in one. He wiped the back of his hand across his mouth and stared at himself in the mirror. He looked like a man on the brink of death. The flight with the Beast had taken its toll and it was as if the life force within him had been diminished. His eyes were sunken pools and the skin was pulled taut over his cheekbones giving him a cadaverous look. There were black smudges, almost as dark as bruises, under his eyes and even his shoulders sagged as if he had aged twenty years. He stood up and stretched, but even that was an effort, time was ticking away and the others would be here soon so he shambled into the shower and binned all his clothes.

Rory and Maria met on the stairs to Alistair's suite and besides scratches and bruises they didn't look much the worse for wear. Rory knocked then, as the door opened, he stepped back a pace as Alistair opened it. He looked dreadful and Rory and Maria exchanged a glance.

'At least we all smell a bit better,' said Rory, entering, trying not to stare at Alistair.

'Sit down please,' said Alistair, motioning to some chairs. 'First I have to thank you both for doing what you did and literally saving my life. I can't imagine what you were doing there, Maria, but thank you for virtually carrying me down that mountain. Rory couldn't have done that by himself. I'm sure that story will keep for another day, but now to business. What story can we come up with to mobilize everyone and get inside the hospital?'

Everyone looked at each other and Maria that coughed tentatively and said, 'I've had one thought. I get on quite well with Robert and we've been in contact since they went with the search parties. The team up there is quite good at plans that work and they seem to able to get hold of kit and things. Remember when they helped Miss Ellie and me in Morocco? Well I'm sure if I tell Robert all about it they can do what we can't.'

Rory sat forward. 'I haven't got any plan at all as I don't think anyone would believe me anyway. Also, it's now one o'clock in the morning and I don't think the local police are going to get everyone out of bed on my say so. I say, let Maria give Robert a ring and see what he says.'

Alistair didn't say a word but just nodded. Rory looked expectantly at Maria and she fished out the sat phone from her pocket and speed dialled Robert.

The phone rang a few times then Robert's sleepy voice said, 'Hi.'

'Robert, it's Maria and I've got some news.'

'What news? What's happened? Are you allright?' Robert's voice carried with it concern and Maria was secretly pleased he should ask about her first.

'It's a long story but Alistair linked up with a big bird thing and he knows where Ellie is now.'

Robert was alert now and said, 'So, where is she?'

'She's somewhere in the hospital. Alistair said…' she got no further as Alistair snatched the phone out of Maria's hand and began telling the story quickly.

'...So we came to a set of double doors and we couldn't get any further but we were heading back into the main hospital complex.' Alistair finished breathlessly.

'So, the lava pipe goes down into some sort of cave and then there's a corridor that leads back out of the mountain to the hospital. We're in the traveller guest rooms attached to the Convent now so I'll go and wake everyone and get them moving.' Robert finished the conversation abruptly then and a dial tone buzzed in Alistair's ear.

'Well, he didn't think we'd gone completely mad,' said Rory.

'I think we should go up there now,' said Alistair and they all nodded.

'How?' said Maria.

'I'll ring the night concierge and get a Land Rover from the car pool; can you remember where to go?' Alistair looked at Rory who suddenly looked confused.

'It was daylight and I think I can remember the way, but I'm not sure,' he added hesitantly.

'Maria, ten minutes only, but go and see if you can find a map with the hospital marked on it.' Alistair said as an order not a request. 'Then meet us at the front.'

Maria jumped up and slammed the door as she ran out and Alistair winced. He picked up the house phone and spun some story to the night concierge and was assured that a Land Rover would be waiting for them in five minutes. Alistair stood and held out his hand to Rory. 'I haven't thanked you properly but I'm eternally grateful for what you did and I did need you and you were there for me. I'll admit to having reservations about you and my sister and I apologize if I was less than welcoming when you came to Italy, but you stepped up to the plate and I welcome you into the family.'

Rory took the proffered hand but couldn't help thinking about what he and Ellie had discussed when they were at the Castle. Would he always be just another hanger-on to the coat tails of Morgan & Co? This wasn't what he wanted but he took the hand and shook it with a firm grasp, mumbled, 'Anytime,' and left it at that.

Maria was already waiting with a map and some torches and waved the keys to the Land Rover at them. 'I got rid of the driver as I thought we'd be better off alone. I did tell him where we were going though as he was most insistent, we didn't do anything stupid in the dark. He seemed to understand we were anxious to find Miss Ellie and wanted to be there at first light.'

Alistair began to climb in the back but Rory looked at him and said, 'But I don't drive, I've never had to learn as I've lived in London all my life.' He looked at Maria who shrugged.

Alistair got down from the footplate and looked at Maria. 'Sorry but I don't drive either,' she said and Alistair grabbed the keys with a grunt.

'Maria get in the front with me as you've got a map and a torch. Rory just hang over the back and tell us where to go if you remember,' Alistair added acerbically.

The Land Rover set off with Alistair at the wheel and if the truth be told it had been many a long year since Alistair had driven anything so there was much gear crunching and fitful starts till he got the hang of it again. Thankfully traffic was non-existent and they weren't a real threat to any other road user. It took about twenty minutes before they saw the turn off onto the unmade road and Rory pointed emphatically at it jabbing his finger. 'Up there, I'm sure, as I remember that huge rock and a palm tree leaning over. Then we get to a fork in the road and I think we go left.'

'I certainly hope so,' said Alistair, drawing on reserves he never thought he possessed as he tiredly fought with the car on the unmade road. 'Why they put a hospital up here beats me.' They bounced over yet another pothole.

'Probably to keep what goes on up their secret,' said Maria absently. 'I mean it's a good place to hide things from plain sight. I know a lot of very rich people go there to have surgery done on the quiet and there'll be no cameras and press when they step out with their new faces. The other staff told me that one or two of their bosses have been there already and they do a good job.'

Alistair and Rory digested this information. Suddenly the fork in the track was upon them and Alistair slowed and Rory pointed to his left. Maria interjected, 'No the map says go right.'

The Land Rover ground to a halt and everyone pored over the map in the torchlight. It wasn't clear at all and only showed meandering tracks between the banana plantations. 'Okay,' said Rory, 'get the phone out and see which way is east, that's supposing you can get an app on it.'

Maria got the phone and fiddled with it and an app came up which pinpointed their position. She turned the phone round until north was pointing to the top and the direction, they had to go was the right fork to go east but that didn't match up with the map she had.

'Oh God, please let's get on with this,' said Alistair, nearly at the end of his tether.

'So, you make a decision then,' said Rory tetchily.

'Okay, Rory remembers, maybe, that he went up the left fork so we'll go that way and see where that takes us. Maria, see if the phone will do a larger scale map to show the hospital or any contour map as we know it's by a big hill.' Alistair reversed a few yards and they jolted down the track to the left. They set off again through the plantations and everyone's tempers were wearing thin with fatigue.

By this time Robert had alerted everyone and they went to Jack's room to rouse him for the search. They knocked but got no answer and eventually just walked in to find him tucked up in bed snoring. Phil said, 'Come on Jack, you must have heard us.' He gave the bed frame a kick. Jack continued to snore.

Robert leaned over Jack and shook him but there wasn't a response, he still snored. 'He's out for the count,' Robert observed and looked at Phil. 'He wasn't drinking last night and everything seems to be as it should be.' He glanced round the room.

'My bet is he's been drugged but I don't know why,' said Phil. 'We'll have to leave him for now and come back later. Leave him a note to say where we've gone, better still send him a text as a note will be easily visible and we don't want it seen. Nothing we can do as I don't think he'd be any good even if we bought him round. He'll have to sleep whatever it was off in his own time. There's something nasty going on here and I want to find out what it is.' He beckoned to Robert and they both left Jack, intent on finding Ellie and uncovering the secrets of the hospital.

Sister Margaret had heaved a great sigh of relief as the last of the girls were loaded onto the ambulance with the two extras. She knew in her heart of hearts that the operation here was going to have to close down, and soon. It was a pity as they had successfully duped Honey and Fortune out of a lot of money for the seemingly 'good' cause. 'It had been a good cause,' she said aloud to convince herself. A lot of islanders had been treated quickly and efficiently and money had come in from the plastic surgery unit, she just had to massage the patient numbers a little to allow for the other staff such as the guards. She liked being a nun as it gave her a perfect disguise to hide behind. She'd even read up on the nuns and their Order to give herself credibility but this quiet life wasn't really for her. She was beginning to crave the nightlife and the designer clothes again and a bit of her was secretly pleased she would have to close the trafficking down. She picked up the phone and put a call through to the guard station and ordered them to abandon ship and disperse now. They were to only take what they could carry and also take their uniforms with them. Before they went, they were to destroy all the close circuit television and any records that may have been kept. She told them they had half an hour maximum and she would personally shoot anyone left behind.

The guards set about the job with a will and everything was trashed seemingly beyond repair. They left the hospital and quickly got into three cars hidden round the side. The lead car revved up and sped off down the track hotly pursued by the other two. Phil and Robert heard this and went running to the main hospital door just in time to see the tail lights of the last car disappear round the bend.

'What was all that about?' said Robert.

'Rats,' said Phil succinctly.

'Rats?' queried Robert.

'You know, the sinking ship variety, the ones that leave for safety when trouble threatens, they also will eat each other to survive. I think we're the trouble and they're out of here. We won't find them again but we must have rattled the cage a bit,' said Phil, turning away.

Alistair was still driving carefully down the unmade road when he suddenly saw some headlights coming towards him. He looked for a passing place and cursed what he thought was an ambulance on a mercy mission. It was a straight piece of road and the headlights kept on coming. Alistair wrestled with the wheel and looked frantically for a place to pull over. On the right side was a banana plantation with thickly planted trees and on the left was a drainage ditch. The headlights were nearly upon them and Alistair tried pressing every knob and switch to find the horn but all he could do at the last second was wrench the wheel to his left to avoid the certain collision. The Land Rover left the road and hit the bottom of the ditch and they stopped dead. Rory had tried to brace himself but was flung over the front seats and ended up between Alistair and Maria upside down. Alistair had a vice-like grip on the wheel but it had been wrenched out of his grasp and he was lying with the steering wheel pressed into his chest. Maria had put her hands up and they had hit the windscreen and smashed it. She was lying over the front fascia with her arms on the bonnet. It was silent except for the ticking of cooling metal.

CHAPTER TEN

Sister Margaret hurried down the corridors to the holding facility to check that everyone had left. She wasn't a woman to leave anything to chance and she wanted to make sure that all the surveillance data had been either erased or destroyed. That was the one incriminating piece of evidence that could send them all to Hell in a handcart. She smiled at this thought as her robes flapped as she walked quickly. The hospital labs along the corridor were empty and quiet and as she progressed deeper the low light barely threw her a shadow.

Phil and Robert were looking again at a map of the hospital pinned to a notice board.

'There must be a way along here,' said Robert, tracing his finger along a corridor towards the labs. 'It's the only one that goes east.'

'That's where Ellie was last seen as well. I also don't like the fact we haven't heard from Claire. She should have reported in by now. I know she can look after herself very well but it's been a long time since she went looking for clues. We know Jack has been given something to knock him out and I can only think he saw something he shouldn't.'

'Lucky he wasn't killed straight away,' said Robert, 'but he's out of it now. Just me and you then.' He looked at Phil. 'You can bet that Nigel is out of it as well, God only knows what they've put in his drip but he was asleep when I looked in last.'

'We'll start there then and see what we can turn up. I don't like the way this is turning out at all, too many variables and unknowns at the moment to make sense of it. Come on we'd better hurry up as I feel that time is racing ahead of us.'

They began to jog down the corridors and were just passing the labs when they caught a glimpse of a billowing black habit seemingly disappearing into a solid wall. The dim light was playing tricks with their eyes and they both looked at each other to verify what they had just seen. Proceeding cautiously, they crept forwards and just made out the carefully concealed doors set into the end of the wall. Phil waved Robert to one side and opened one of the doors a crack. He peered round and listened carefully, it was as quiet as a tomb. He was faced with a long room with cells like cattle pens arranged down each side. He slid through the door and motioned Robert to follow him. They stood in the shadows on each side of the doors and willed their breathing rate to a steady rate. Phil put his finger to his lips and motioned Robert down one side and he took the other. It made sense not to provide a big target if anyone wanted to take a pot shot at them. Phil drew his gun and Robert did the same, holding it in front of him as he looked around. The floor was wet and he was aware his shoes squeaked on the tiles so he quickly took them off and shoved them in his waistband.

The room stank of bleach but under that there was a smell of a blocked sewer. Phil wrinkled his nose and was aware that Robert was holding his hand in front of his nose and mouth. They crept along to the end and were faced with another set of doors. Phil again motioned Robert to one side as he peered through a crack in the door. There didn't seem to be anyone there and Phil eased the door open wider. The door jerked in his hand and a splinter of wood struck him on the forehead immediately followed by a loud report.

Phil fell back and hit the floor, rolling away to his right.

Robert followed suit almost as quickly, rolling away to his left. The door slammed shut.

'Seems we're not alone,' said Phil, feeling for damage to his head.

'No cover in here,' said Robert, glancing round.

'Got any ideas on how to get us out of this mess?' Phil queried.

'Nope,' said Robert.

They both lay on the wet tiles and it was Robert who said, 'We've got to flush them out so we know where they are. How about if I get one of those metal frame beds and prop it up by the one door. I'll climb up it and you open the door from ground level. Chances are they'll fire again at head height and maybe I can see the muzzle flash and give us a clue.'

'Better than nothing, we'll give it a go,' said Phil, as Robert got a bed frame and propped it up like a ladder by the door. Luckily the left hand door was secured to the floor by a drop bolt and it didn't swing open when the bed was placed there. Robert climbed up and hung sideways, ready to have a look when the door opened.

'Three, two, one,' said Phil, counting down, and gave the door a hefty push from ground level. Two bullets thwacked into it and would have killed Phil if he had been standing there. Robert opened fire as the door began to close and nearly overbalanced on his precarious ladder.

'There's one gunman hiding behind a door to your right. They haven't got the best line of sight but enough to pin us down,' said Robert, breathlessly clambering down. 'The door seems solid enough to stop a bullet, maybe it's got a steel lining?'

'Then maybe the others down that end have as well,' said Phil, pointing to the first two they had come through. They looked at each other and a plan began to form simultaneously in their minds. Leaving their posts, they ran back down the line of cells and opened one of the doors. Phil looked at the hinges and breathed a sigh of relief when he saw they were the pin variety and could be lifted off. They both grasped the door the best way they could and heaved it off its fastening. They nearly dropped it as it was heavier than they thought. 'It must have a steel lining to be this heavy,' grunted Phil as they manhandled it back to the other end.

'A bulletproof shield ready for use,' grinned Robert.

They propped the shield up ready for use and cracked the door open attracting a hail of bullets. They slid the shield through the door and both got behind it as bullets thwacked harmlessly into it. Robert dodged out momentarily as Phil was giving him covering fire and got one shot into a door frame and was rewarded with a yelp as splinters flew in all directions.

'You might as well give up now and surrender as you can't get away,' shouted Phil during a lull.

Surprisingly a female voice answered, 'Never, go stuff yourselves.'

'Charming,' Robert said as he looked at Phil and raised his eyebrows questioningly. 'How about we just run Bonnie here out of ammo?'

'Sounds good to me,' Phil answered, letting off another salvo and getting one back in reply. He continued until he was nearly out of bullets then signalled Robert to take up the fusillade. After a minute they both heard the tell-tale click of an empty magazine and dropped the door and confronted their assailant. Sister Margaret was working the slide chamber of her gun furiously but to no avail.

'Now just be a good nun and put the gun down,' Phil said,

keeping her in the gun sight at all times. He was astounded to find out it was the head of the Convent that was trying to kill them. Robert went forward and took the gun away from the sister and motioned her to put her hands above her head.

There was nothing saintly about her face as she complied. It was fixed in a scowl of hatred and she spat out venomously, 'You've got no chance of finding your little lady friends as they've gone. Gone for good and I'll never tell you where. I'm sure they'll have lots of fun and I'm sure they'll enjoy every minute.'

Phil raised his hand to smack her across the mouth and shut her up but he stopped as hitting a woman who could possibly be a bona fide nun was beyond him. Instead he forced down the contempt he felt and said, 'Bring her with us and we'll explore this place while we have a chance. I think she's the boss of this and there could be more people deeper in the tunnels.'

Sister Margaret didn't resist, as her hands were tied behind her back with a piece of flex, but her face said it all as a contemptuous sneer curved the corner of her mouth. She was made to walk first as they went in procession down deeper into the mountain.

Rory was the first to regain consciousness as he lay draped over the back rests of the Land Rover. He had a pounding headache and his ribs felt as if they'd been repeatedly kicked as he hauled himself back upright. The Land Rover was head first in a ditch and tilted at nearly one hundred and eighty degrees and he had to climb laboriously up to the back door. It was very heavy to open and took nearly all his strength but he eventually flopped out onto the ditch bank. He lay wheezing and painfully gasping for air and began to crawl towards the front of the Land Rover to see what had happened to Maria and Alistair. He went to Maria's side first and managed to get the door open and the torch was still shining in the foot well. He got the torch and played its light over Maria's body half in and half out across the bonnet. Her arms were outstretched and he held her wrist and could feel a pulse, a bit weak but a pulse nevertheless. He held her round her waist and as gently as he could pulled her out of the car. She was heavier than he thought and his ribs protested violently and he dropped her into the ditch. It was a relatively soft landing as there was about a foot of wet sludge in the bottom. As she landed, he heard her cry out with pain. Telling himself not to panic he leaned over her and tried to remember the First Aid training he had to endure last year at the college. He checked she was breathing and could hear her making incoherent mumbling sounds so that was a good sign. As best as he could he laid her out so she could breathe easily and played the torch over her. There wasn't any blood to be seen but if she felt anything like he did then her ribs could be broken. She was breathing more easily now and he left her to look at Alistair. He doubted he could lift Alistair up and get him out of the car but he could at least make him more comfortable while he fetched help. The torch light showed Alistair slumped over the wheel and Rory eased him back and Alistair flopped over towards the passenger side. Rory went around the other side of the car as quickly as he could and leaned in to see if Alistair was breathing. He thanked every God he knew as he felt his breath on his cheek. He couldn't do any more and after a cursory look again at Maria he set off down the road. Every step was a torture. His steps wavered from side to side and he stopped once or twice convinced he was going to pass out.

  They had been nearer to the hospital than they had thought and it was only after about fifteen minutes that Rory saw the lights glimmering through the trees. He quickened his pace and promptly fell over and lay in agony, hardly able to breathe. He got onto all fours and began to crawl the final hundred yards and had never been so glad to see habitation. He tried to call out but he hadn't got the breath and got to the doors of the Emergency Department and collapsed by the big glass doors. All he could do was to knock with his torch on the door to attract attention. The doors swung back and he fell into the light and suddenly there were doctors and nurses rushing to his aid. Someone clamped an oxygen mask over his mouth and nose and he felt the life-giving gas course through his body. He weakly raised his hand and tore it off. 'Car crash, down the road,' was all he could manage before he lapsed into unconsciousness.

The staff mobilized quickly on what was a Code Red alert as they didn't know what they might find. An ambulance was dispatched and staff grabbed emergency kit bags and began to run down the track. They got there before the ambulance and began to give emergency aid in what was a disaster situation. Maria was stabilized as the ambulance drew up and quickly placed on a spinal board and loaded into it to be rushed to A&E. Everyone held onto Alistair and slowly began to ease him onto a board to begin the same journey. He hadn't regained consciousness and a drip was set up to stabilize his blood pressure and staff began to carry him down the track instead of waiting for the ambulance to return.

It was a scene of controlled haste as the day nurses were dragged from their beds to assist with the emergency and Rory, Alistair and Maria were laid out in adjoining cubicles in the Emergency Department which was now buzzing with activity. Blood samples were taken from all three as it was suspected that they would have internal injuries and the lab staff rushed them off to their own department for analysis. As the first technicians arrived at the labs, they saw a gaping hole in the wall at the end of the corridor and looked askance at each other. One of them picked up a phone and called Security before getting on with the job in hand.

Rory seemed to have fared better than the other two as he was fully conscious and, if he lay very still, he could breathe with very shallow breaths and suffered minimal pain. The doctor bent over him. 'Do you know your name?' he asked as he removed the oxygen mask and shone a light into each of Rory's eyes.

'Yes, it's Rory,' he wheezed. 'There was a car crash, someone ran us off the road. How are Maria and Alistair?'

'They're okay,' said the doctor, placating. 'It seems as if you've got some broken ribs and we're going to run a few more tests to see if there are any other internal injuries. There may be some bruising to some other organs but your blood pressure is stable so I don't think you're having internal bleeding. Please lie very still and we'll continue to check you over.'

All Rory could do was to lie very still and he wished he could be given some mega pain killer very soon. The attention seemed to be focused on the next cubicle and he heard Maria give a low moan. He was glad he heard that as at least she was still alive and he shouted her name and heard another moan. A nurse came in at that point and administered the painkiller and Rory lapsed into a happy haze.

Phil was shoving the nun, none too gently, in front of them as they walked down the corridor. He wasn't sure what they were going to do with her but they would cross that bridge later. The corridor wound round until they came to the cavern that tapered up to a lava pipe in the roof. Robert looked about him. 'I know where we are, remember the pipe we found half way up the mountain? Well, I think this is it.'

'So, what are those other tunnels?' Phil pointed to the other entrances. 'Talk.' He jabbed his gun in the nun's back. She was silent and Phil wondered how far he could push it. 'So. we'll just go for a walk then.' He frogs marched her ahead of him to the first tunnel. It wasn't far to the next natural cavern and in it was lots of machinery and wooden crates stacked round the sides. Robert went to the machines and looked at them but shrugged his shoulders, then turned his attention to the crates. He pried the lid off one and stood back in amazement.

'Phew, look at this.' He held up a wrapped block of American hundred dollar bills.

Phil's attention was on the banknotes that Robert was holding and he took a step forwards to look more closely in the dim light. As he did so, Sister Margaret spied her chance and spun round with a kick that would have put a mule to shame and caught Phil on the side of his chin. He went down as if poleaxed. Robert couldn't react quickly enough and all he registered was the nuns billowing habit disappearing round the corner back down the tunnel.

He ran over to Phil who was still on the floor. 'Are you okay,' was all he could manage and was glad when Phil gingerly opened his eyes and began to feel his jaw.

'What hit me?' he slurred.

'Looks like the sister has got a few more tricks up her habit and she laid one on you, mate,' said Robert, helping Phil to sit up. 'She's gone, it was all too fast, but I don't know if I could have shot her anyway,' he said ruefully. He was still clutching the banknotes. 'But there must be millions of dollars here if all the crates are the same. Those machines must be printing presses. Our friends in the USA will love to hear about this.'

Robert helped Phil to his feet and he was still feeling about in his mouth checking his teeth as they went into the next cave. There, they found vats of some sort of chemical and piles of one dollar bills and deduced that what had happened was that small denomination bills were collected then bleached and reprinted as hundred dollar notes. The paper would have been correct and would have passed any scanner. All the gang would have to do was redistribute the notes throughout America and Robert was somebody's uncle.

'I've got to admit that it's neat,' said Robert. 'Money laundering on a massive scale but I think we'll be friends with our American counterparts for a long time when we show them this.'

'Yeah, but it still doesn't explain where Claire and Ellie are hidden,' said Phil. 'Sister Bitch said they'd gone for good but I don't think she meant they were dead. Chances are they aren't even on the island anymore and I'll bet they were kept in those cells we passed. I don't think there's anything else we can do here as there's no-one to interrogate anyway as it's deserted. The place will be crawling with the local constabulary anyway at first light to begin the search again, but that's pointless now. Let's go back and see if we can tie up a few loose ends and I really need to get a few hours shut eye as I won't be functioning tomorrow.'

Robert concurred and they shoved their guns in their waistbands and began to amble back down the corridor. They got to the scene of the gun battle and heard the unmistakable sound of guns being cocked and voices shouting, 'Put your hands in the air and stand still.' It seemed as though the local constabulary had turned up in force and were arranged in a semi-circle with guns trained on them both.

'Okay,' said Phil, now weary. He raised his hands and Robert did the same. 'We are English policemen and we seem to have uncovered a big money laundering operation down there,' he jerked his head. 'Please just check us out and let us get to bed,' he requested.

'No, you're coming with us and we will check you out down the station,' said the Chief.

'Whatever,' replied Robert, too tired to care as he was frisked and his gun was removed. 'I just hope you've got a bed in the cell as I'm bushed.' He didn't resist as he and Phil were each handcuffed to an officer and led away.

Valentin was now a bit more composed as he mingled with the other guests and, besides a few scratches that he put down to a particularly challenging rock climb, felt he was holding his own. He looked everywhere for Alistair but couldn't find him and was loath to go up to the pentacle again in the dark to see if he was there. He couldn't find Maria or Rory either and resolved to set Karl on the trail and uncover what was going on. His phone was a dead duck and by the time he had got a replacement, Sister Margaret wasn't answering. He hated anyone being off the radar and as the night was now very late he decided to go to bed and see what he could salvage in the morning. He would be up at the hospital at first light, which wasn't many hours away now, and offer his help with search parties. Hopefully then he could get more information first hand and question Sister Margaret as to what was going on. He drained his drink and sauntered nonchalantly back to his room, but inside he was being eaten up with indecision and not knowing the facts and that wasn't a comfortable feeling for him.

First light saw Nigel now fully recovered and sitting up in bed. The swellings had subsided and besides a few red itchy patches he was feeling fine. He was drinking a cup of water like a drowning man and shovelling toast down his throat like he hadn't eaten for a week. He spied his clothes neatly folded on a chair and decided to get dressed and see if he could find the others. He waited until there was a lull in the nurse's activity and quickly shrugged on his trousers and shirt and slid out of the ward. He made his way to the guest rooms and tapped on the first door he came to but there was no answer. He tried another two but got no response. On the fourth attempt he was rewarded by a grunt and he cracked open the door to see Jack sitting up in bed holding his head in his hands.

'What's up mate?' Nigel asked as he sat alongside Jack. 'You look as if you've had one too many. What happened while I was out of it and sleeping like a baby?'

'I don't know,' Jack groaned. 'I've got the worst headache in the world and I can't even see straight. I've had some very weird dreams, I mean seriously weird. Have you spoken to the others yet?'

'No-one's about. What say we go and get you some painkillers for your headache, after all it is a hospital?' Nigel helped Jack get out of bed and realized that Jack wasn't just sporting a hangover as he was still uncoordinated in his movements and he didn't smell of alcohol at all. He helped him dress and gently led him to the main hospital. 'Do you remember anything about your dreams?' Nigel asked as they weaved their way down the corridors.

'Only a man's shoe and some ambulances. Then there was a nun that was waving a gun at me. Like I said before, seriously weird.'

They reached the Emergency Department and found a nurse who asked them to sit down and she would find someone to give them some help. She took their names and looked at Nigel.

'You're already a patient here, what are you doing up and about? The doctor has to discharge you, you know.'

'Well, I haven't left yet, but my friend here was in a guest room and he's come down with something nasty and needs a few painkillers for a headache, any chance?' he added with a winning smile.

'I'll see what I can do but we're a bit busy at the moment as there was a car crash and we've got three casualties. They all seem stable at the moment but one's just gone down for surgery.'

'Anyone we know?' asked Nigel offhandedly, not for one moment dreaming he would know them.

'Actually, they're all from the resort and were guests of Honey and Fortune. It seems they were forced off the road but they all have quite serious injuries.'

Nigel sat up straight. 'Any chance we could know who they are as they could be friends of ours?' It was worth a question even if the answer was a 'no'.

'I'm not really supposed to tell you but the one that was talking was called Rory and he was with another man and a young woman.'

Nigel leapt to his feet and totally forgot Jack sitting there. 'He's a good friend and we came on holiday together, is he going to be okay? Where is he as I've got to talk to him?'

The nurse looked at Jack and said, 'You don't seem to be having a lot of luck with your friends at the moment, do you? I'll tell you he's on a ward now but he isn't going anywhere soon as he's got broken ribs and we're monitoring him for internal injuries. Promise me you won't say I told you?' She looked at Nigel. 'My job could be on the line here.'

'I promise,' said Nigel hurriedly and gave her a quick hug. 'Please look after my friend here as I'm sure he just needs a couple of painkillers. Where did you say Rory was?'

'I didn't,' she replied, stepping back a pace, 'but I'm sure you'll find out anyway. He's on the minor surgery recovery ward as that's where he'll get the monitoring he needs right now. Don't you go disturbing him as he needs all the rest he can get,' she added sternly.

'I think I've just fallen in love with you,' Nigel said as he hugged her again and left.

'What about your other friend?' the nurse called to his retreating back.

'Just shove a paracetamol down him and he'll be okay,' shouted Nigel as he ran out of the room.

Nigel found out where Rory was and begged for a few minutes with him and Rory's face brightened when he saw Nigel.

'What happened to you then?' said Nigel, making himself inconspicuous behind a half-drawn curtain.

'We were coming up to the hospital because Alistair said he knew where Ellie was and we got forced off the road by some cars tear arsing down the track. Alistair's not much of a driver but neither me nor Maria can drive at all, it was the best we could do.' Rory reached for the oxygen mask and took a few gulps. 'I'm not much good now, but I've got to find her.' He reached for Nigel's arm. 'You'll find her for me won't you? You and Phil and the others, you'll find her?' Rory looked at Nigel pleadingly as a nurse bustled up ready to eject Nigel from the ward.

Nigel put his hand over Rory's. 'Yes, mate, I'll find her for you, I promise. We're all here ready to go and I'll be back soon with some news,' he added, as Rory sank back into his pillows looking more relaxed. Nigel hadn't the faintest idea where the rest of his team was. All he knew was that Jack was being ministered to by a nurse in the A&E and Rory, plus Alistair and

Maria, were somewhere else in the hospital being put together again. He squeezed Rory's hand and was led out of the ward by the nurse then stood there indecisively. He made his mind up to find them and raced back to the guest rooms and flung open the doors searching for Phil and the others but the rooms were bleak and bare. His phone warbled. 'Yes,' he almost shouted.

'It's Phil, calm down.'

'What do you mean calm down? Rory's in a ward and can't breathe; God knows what's happened to Alistair and Maria, Jack's in A&E mumbling on about weird dreams and can't even walk straight, so where are you?'

'In a Police Station with Robert, but.' He paused. 'We'll be back with you within the hour. We were picked up last night after uncovering a huge money laundering scheme. Just a case of mistaken identity but we'll be back there pronto and I think Honey and Fortune will be there as well with some explaining to do. Have you seen anything of Sister Margaret?'

'No,' said Nigel, bemused. 'Why should I?'

'Well, she's got a lot of explaining to do as well. If you do run into her be careful as she's a gun-toting nun.' Phil rang off before more questions came.

Nigel decided to go and find Jack as he had abandoned him rather hastily and he wandered down to the A&E carefully scrutinizing all the nuns he passed. Jack was sitting where he had left him holding a glass of water and looking much better. 'I've found Rory and it seems as if he and Alistair with Maria were on their way up here and got forced off the road. They're all in the hospital now and I don't think they'll be going anywhere soon. As far as I can tell they're not on the critical lists but I'll find out more about Alistair and Maria soon. Phil and Robert will be here within the hour,' Nigel said, glossing over the state of Alistair and

Maria. 'Don't worry, I'm sure all will be clear as soon as they get here. You look much better,' he said, changing the subject.

'I certainly feel it. I don't know what they gave me but it's worked and I can see straight now. I still get flashes of the dreams,' said Jack pensively. He sat there staring at his water. 'I think I saw something I shouldn't have and I was drugged. I certainly didn't have anything to drink last night and what I've got isn't food poisoning, but it's only all in snatches and I can't make sense of it yet.' Jack touched his arm. 'I've got a sore spot here.' He rolled up his sleeve.

Nigel peered at the arm. 'It looks like a puncture wound to me, maybe from a syringe, but I'm no expert.' He helped Jack to his feet. 'Let's get you back to your room.' And Jack managed to walk unaided but flopped down on the bed with relief.

Nigel went to the entrance and watched as a squad of Police cars drew up disgorging a platoon of policemen. Phil and Robert were among them as were Fortune and Honey. The Chief led the way and everyone gathered in Sister Margaret's office. The chief took the power position behind the desk and motioned everyone to sit down. Phil leaned negligently on the door frame.

'So what we have here is a massive money laundering operation that you say you know nothing about,' the Chief said to Honey. 'The nun has disappeared and we have all ports and airports on alert but if she gets rid of the habit we don't even know what colour hair she has. We still have two missing persons, and I have since found out that we have a suspicious car crash that has injured another three of your friends. Would anyone like to fill me in with any more details?' he added sardonically.

Honey jumped to her feet. 'You can't possibly think that either Fortune or I had anything to do with all this? The

Foundation I support makes some serious donations to the hospital but I don't have anything to do with the day to day running of the place. I do sometimes volunteer for jobs but all the staff are appointed by the Trustees. Who was injured?' she added quietly, sitting down again.

'As far as I know the injured were Alistair Morgan, Rory, who is the fiancée of one of the missing women, and Maria who is the missing woman's maid,' the Chief said, looking at his notes.

Nigel said, 'You can add another one to that list as I think Jack was drugged last night and can't remember anything about yesterday.'

Phil stepped forward. 'Well I think we can safely say that Ellie, Claire and the erstwhile nun are no longer on the island, so there's no need for any search parties now. If you'll allow us I'd like another look at the cells under the mountain.'

'Cells? What cells?' asked Honey, looking at Phil, puzzled.

'If the Chief will let us I'd like to take you and Fortune to see exactly what was going on at your hospital.' Phil glanced at the Chief who nodded. 'We'll collect Jack on the way as he needs to see this as well.'

Nigel went to collect Jack who was sound asleep again but roused up when Nigel told him what had happened and where they were going. The party went to the gaping hole where the door had been removed by Phil but now had two armed policemen standing guard on either side. Honey was horrified when she saw the cells and clutched Fortune's arm. 'Whatever went on down here?' she asked. The smell of bleach was still underlaid with urine stench and the rows of cells looked bleak and forbidding.

'It appears to have been a human trafficking operation,'

explained the Chief and Honey blanched. 'The girls were collected here until there were enough to make a shipment and then sent God knows where. All the records seem to have been destroyed. It seems everything was kept on computer in the next room.' Nigel and Robert looked at each other.

'Maybe we can help you there,' said Robert as his fingers itched to get hold of the computers. 'Sometimes even fragments of data can be retrieved from the hard drives, and we'll have a go if you want?'

'Be my guest,' said the Chief, motioning them to the next room where the trashed remains were strewn about.

'At least there are two happy people now,' Phil said wryly as Nigel and Robert almost danced their way into the computer room talking animatedly. He turned to the Chief. 'If anyone can find anything on those computers they can. I'd like to do a search in these cells; if Claire and Ellie have been held here then I believe Claire would have left a sign of some sort. I've already seen the Bank of America down there so if that's okay?' The Chief acquiesced and the party continued under the mountain.

Phil went into the first cell and lifted the wet mattress and wrinkled his nose. He wished he had some gloves but he fingertip searched the cell from top to bottom and found nothing. Moving on to the next one he also drew a blank. It was in the fifth cell he tried, when the party was coming back from seeing printing presses and loads of cash that he made a discovery. Caught in the bedsprings was a fine gold chain and a small pendant shaped like a curly cross. He lifted it out gently and went to Jack. 'Does this look familiar to you?'

'That's Ellie's, she always wore it. It'll probably match to one that Alistair has in his pocket. It never leaves either of them,' said Jack, thinking back to the Christmas in France.

'So I think we can safely say that Ellie was held here and I'd lay a very big bet that Claire was here as well. The next job is finding out where they were taken. Let's just hope our two wizards next door can deliver the goods.'

CHAPTER ELEVEN

Valentin was pacing up and down talking into his phone. The news he was receiving wasn't good. Karl had done his homework and had gleaned much valuable information from Alistair's PAs but that was secondary now as he learned that Alistair was in hospital and Ellie and Claire had vanished. The news on the street was that human trafficking had been going on and the cargo had got shipped out. Also, the nun in charge had done a runner and there had been shed loads of cash discovered. Valentin cursed the day he had invited his cousin into his web and had her impersonate a nun. She had initially been a very safe pair of hands and the operation had run smoothly under her command. They had phoned each other but never met as the family resemblance may have been noted but it was always difficult to hide body language. They had virtually been bought up together and bore the shared scars of childhood but now she had disappeared. He could hazard a guess that she had hightailed it back to Russia but he would have to sort that one out when he got home. It was, in fact, the last day of his holiday and his staff were packing as he spoke.

'Well done, Karl, I'll make the usual payment to your Pension Fund,' he said, keeping his cool. Karl didn't know that all the information he was giving Valentin was causing him great consternation as it appeared his operation in the Caribbean was now in tatters and a very lucrative tentacle had been chopped off. Valentin wanted to go to the hospital and find out more but his instinct for survival was overriding that and he decided to go as soon as possible after bidding his hosts farewell. He spotted Fortune walking by the pool and made his way over to him with his hands outstretched.

'Fortune, my man, what a wonderful party. I don't think I've been to a better one,' he said, clasping Fortune's hands.

Fortune looked distracted as he spoke. 'Yes, yes, it was good to see you again but I don't know if you've heard that there's been a car crash and some people are in hospital.'

Valentin's ears pricked up at this as he sensed a fount of information at hand. 'Come and sit down and tell me all about it. Who's been injured? It wasn't that nice couple from Germany was it? I did wonder if he should be driving as he didn't seem to be quite with it sometimes,' Valentin said ingenuously.

'No, man, it was your friend Alistair and Ellie Black, his sister, she is still missing. Her boyfriend apparently went to find her and they got run off the road. There have been some strange things going on at the hospital that Honey funds from the Foundation. We saw mountains of cash, American dollars, all in crates. Someone's been printing the stuff and shipping it out. The Police think Honey's involved and she's down the station now making a statement. I don't know what to do,' said Fortune, putting his head in his hands.

Valentin sat back feigning disbelief. 'I can't believe that. You've got a good legal man here? If not, I'll get one flown in from the States immediately.'

Fortune looked at him and grasped his hand. 'Thanks for that but I'm sure it'll all be sorted out soon. Thanks again for being a good friend. I'll let you know how Alistair gets on and if, I mean when, they find Ellie. It looks as if the gang trashed all the computers they used when they left.'

Valentin held Fortune's hand and thanked his lucky stars that

Valentina hadn't left a trail for the authorities to follow. She was thorough if nothing else. A great weight seemed lifted from his shoulders but came crashing down again with Fortune's next words. 'Some of Ellie's friends were here as well, but they stayed in the village, and there are a couple of computer blokes there that think they can get some information from the hard drives.'

'Well just let's hope that's the case,' said Valentin, even surer he should leave right now. He'd get Karl on the case as he was a member of Alistair's staff and could probably gain access to the computer room as Alistair's Head of Security. He would most likely be staying on the island for the duration.

'Another thing is that there's a load of American Agents coming over today to have a look at the money and the presses, and I suppose I'll be interviewed again,' said Fortune morosely.

'Get your lawyers on the case now, please don't wait,' said Valentin solicitously. 'I've got to go back today but I mean it, if there's anything I can do just give me a call.' Just then his phone warbled again and he glanced at the screen. 'I'm so sorry that it's all turned out this way and don't forget I'll help if I can. I have to take this,' he apologized as the warble came again. He gave Fortune's hand a reassuring grasp and walked away round the corner. He said to one of his PAs on the phone before he could speak, 'Get the jet ready now as we're leaving as soon as possible. I mean now, not this afternoon. Within the hour or you'll all be out of a job.' He rang off. Valentin knew he had to get off the island before the Americans turned up.

Fortune came hurrying round the corner and spotted Valentin. 'There was one other thing I've just remembered. There were questions asked about a book that you donated to the Library in Castries. It was a medieval manuscript and the Police wanted to know where it had come from. I told them that you had donated it to the Foundation and they maybe want to ask you some questions about it. Sorry I forgot earlier,' said Fortune, searching Valentin's face.

'That book, I just thought it would be a useful addition to your collection,' said Valentin dismissively. 'No problems as I will be pleased to answer any questions the Police want.' He felt the net tightening by the minute and wanted to shove Fortune out of the way and run. 'I should be here for a while yet,' he lied, 'just point them in my direction.' He smiled. Valentin shook Fortune's hand again and sauntered away. When he got round the corner of the building he broke into a jog and got his phone out and began issuing orders thick and fast. His staff were scurrying backwards and forwards complying as they knew if he wasn't out of the resort pronto, they would be dead meat. A car was waiting at Reception as he reached it and he leapt into the air-conditioned cocoon and sped away.

In the computer room, Nigel and Robert surveyed the remains of the hardware and sighed.

'Don't think this is going to be an easy one,' said Robert, surveying the trash.

'Never say die,' replied Nigel, arching his eyebrows and set to trying to mentally put back which piece fitted like a messy jigsaw made of wires, cables and bent pieces of plastic. 'You take that side and I'll do this.' He began tracing feeds to the various components. 'I think we have some surveillance cameras set up and they all led here. I'll do that and see if I can get some images. Have we got our own laptops and gear in the kit here with us?'

'Yep,' said Robert, 'I'll nip and get it and we can download what we've got. Looks like I've got the records and transactions side of the operation. Anything would be useful now.' He left at a jog to get their high-powered gear from the kit store in Phil's room.

Nigel walked about the facility and looked at where the cameras were placed and built up a mental map of the operation. He looked at the monitors and assigned them to different locations and began to see where and what they oversaw. He traced cables and fed them into the mental map and looked at all the electronics lying on the floor and began carrying pieces back to their original locations. Robert came back with all their own electronic kit and Nigel began to plug leads into sockets and pray.

They worked without respite for a couple of hours until Nigel suddenly said, 'Bingo, and you, Robert, are my relative first removed. 'The first blurry image took shape on his lap top. 'Guess what?' he said and motioned Robert to come and look.

Robert peered closely and said, 'I think that's Claire.' As he watched about twenty seconds of replay of a female being forced to drink something out of a cup. Her head was being tilted towards the camera by a guard and as her jaw was grasped, he could see her mouth some obscenity before being made to drink. 'Replay it again,' he said and the images were rewound. 'I'm sure that's Claire and if I'm not mistaken that's Ellie in the background partly out of shot.' They replayed the section of tape again and again until they were sure, then Robert put in a call to Phil.

'I think we've got Claire and Ellie on the tapes down here so that'll prove they were held here before being shipped out,' Robert said definitively.

'Great,' Phil replied, 'I've got our American counterparts here now and we'll be coming down to see you soon. Anything on where they could have been taken?'

'Not yet,' Robert replied. 'Nigel's dragging his feet as usual, can't seem to get it together today, maybe those things that bit him took more than a chunk of flesh.' Robert laughed as Nigel just flipped him a finger. 'I'll give him a hand in a mo.' Nigel shot him a murderous glance.

Phil was sitting in Sister Margaret's office being grilled by two American agents who seemed impervious to heat. They were trussed up in collars and ties and sat like all American quarterbacks, hunks of muscle with gleaming white teeth. Phil was finding this hard going and looked to the Chief of Police for help who sat there stoically watching him squirm.

Now, sir, you allege you are with the Secret Services in the U.K but you don't carry any identification?'

'No, sir, but a call to this number will verify our authenticity.' Phil proffered a piece of paper with a number written on it.

'Excuse me, sir.' The American was all manners. 'That number could be a call centre in Indonesia for all I know, I need a name.'

Phil sighed and wrote down a very high profile UK name on the paper and pushed it across the desk. 'That should satisfy you, well I hope it does.' he added under his breath.

'We'll verify that shortly. First we need to see the American currency that you say is in a vault under a mountain.' The agent was oozing disbelief with every word. He obviously believed the whole thing was a wild goose chase and wanted to go home on the next available plane.

'Walk this way, gentlemen, and I'll fulfil your every wish,' said Phil, with a flourish. The local Chief of Police shot Phil a small smile as they filed out. The Americans had given him hell with their requests and demands, and he was pleased to see an ally standing up to them. They all trooped out and they stopped off momentarily to see what Nigel and Robert had uncovered.

The tape was replayed and the entire American contingent swapped glances at the abuse of Claire.

'We know that's another member of the U.K Security Squad and she's disappeared. Nigel and Robert are trying to glean data from these computers to see where they've been taken. This is just the tip of the iceberg and we'd appreciate any co-operation from you and we think that millions of US dollars, albeit counterfeit, buy us that,' Phil added succinctly.

'Sure,' said one of the Americans slowly. He looked at the others. 'Lead on.' He motioned.

They went down the tunnels and reached the presses and the crates of cash. 'Wow!' was all the agents could manage as they held up bricks of hundred dollar bills. 'This could bring down America,' said one.

'I thought it was already broke,' said Phil under his breath.

'I'm sure we could broker some deal but I need to speak to my bosses in the States,' said the lead guy, as he fingered the cash, and Phil was sure his mind was wandering to what he could do with all the lucre.

'The Chief of Police here will make sure it's all removed to a secure facility and then you can personally see it all destroyed,' said Phil, putting an end to any daydreaming.

'Absolutely,' agreed the Chief. 'Please feel free to do any forensics you wish. You have until'– he glanced at his watch– 'two hours from now. As this is a British Protectorate then British law will prevail and I'm the lead person in this investigation. I will have the final say in the jurisdiction of this case and I say that this cash will be destroyed on the island and will not leave it.'

Phil mentally applauded the Chief for this show of authority and agreed wholeheartedly with his decision.

'Yeah, sure,' said the lead agent and reluctantly let the money fall back into the crate.

'Well, gentlemen, if you've seen all that you need to, I suggest we start reviewing all the interviews,' the Chief said decisively and led the way back.

Robert and Nigel were still lost in a maze of electronics and Robert had made the most headway by beginning to piece together snippets of footage that confirmed that both Ellie and Claire had been held in the cells. He could confirm that they had both been given something to drink and had been held until they had joined a group of young females being moved out. All hinged on Nigel to say where they had been taken and he was aware that this information was crucial. While he was lost in his own world Robert said, 'I think I'll just nip off and see if there's any CCTV footage of the outside of the grounds, you never know, but I'll bet our American friends have got there first.' He listened for Nigel's mumbled reply then ambled off to find the security booth for the main hospital. It was tucked away and took Robert a good fifteen minutes to find it. It wasn't a manned station and was deserted so he began playing with the footage and managed to find Jack going outside in the dead of night. He watched as Jack walked round the corner then backtracked and hid in a bush. He couldn't see what was happening as Jack watched but then saw a murky figure standing guard over Jack and waited for him to notice him. It appeared that the figure was holding a gun and Jack slowly backed out of the bush and was taken prisoner. 'Well, there's your missing night,' said Robert to himself as he burnt a copy onto a disc. He went back to Nigel clutching the disc as a prize and was all set to tell him when he saw the American contingent interviewing Nigel. Robert slipped the disc into his pocket and decided to say nothing.

'Sir, could you please give me an account of your movements last night?' one of the big guys said.

'Yep, no probs, just check on Ward Five and they'll tell you I was out of it on a drip. See.' He lifted his shirtsleeve and there were still big welts left from the bites he had attracted in the jungle. 'It seems I'm a very tasty individual and I also react badly to what they've got flying round here, so I spent the night in hospital, in a bed, in a ward.'

'Certainly, sir, we'll check that out, thank you for your co-operation,' the big guy said as he left with not an iota more information than he came in with.

Robert had slipped into the shadows and watched as they left. 'Give you a hard time did they?' he asked, with a grimace. 'Well, guess what I've got? No, bet you can't,' he said waving the disc under Nigel's nose. 'It proves Jack was ambushed and I'll bet they jabbed him with something to make him sleep.'

Nigel twisted round on his stool. 'Well guess what I've found then? No? Bet you can't,' he said returning the friendly jibe.

'Bet I can, let me see.' Robert held his hands to the side of his head as if in a trance. 'It's a programme that logs movements, no, not movements, cargoes. Am I right so far?' He swayed as if in tune with mystic forces. 'I'm seeing a programme with names and destinations, there may also be dates involved.' He swayed again. 'Could there also be some e-mail addresses to see where the information was sent?'

'Cut the crap,' said Nigel frowning at Robert who was openly laughing at him by now. 'I might have magic fingers but I haven't got a magic wand. But what I have got is this,' and he tapped a few keys on his laptop. He twisted it round so that Robert could see it better. There were certainly dates and some three letter codes that Nigel had divined were airport codes. Many of the cargoes had been sent to South America but the most recent ones were for destinations in the US. There wasn't one for the date they most wanted. It was possible the information had never been uploaded as the operation had been blown apart in a few hours. 'Working on what we've got so far, I would hazard a guess that Ellie and Claire were on the last plane out and if we go by the last few destinations, then I would surmise they went to the States. What do you think?'

Robert mused, 'If we can go on the last information then there was a big contract or something that they were fulfilling. There's been nothing to South America for a few months so we'll have to discount that. My bet is that all the girls were shipped out to San Francisco as this code crops up the most. It's not an absolute definitive route, but it's a "best bet" scenario. Shall I tell Phil?'

'Let's see if there's anything else first as we can't really say where they went and I don't want us all high tailing it off to SF without more proof,' Nigel said, as he bent back to work. 'Tell you what, you plug into this lot as well and we'll make more headway. It's not all as trashed as we think. It was a hasty, sloppy job and there aren't any codes left to break.'

'Told you that you would need some help eventually!' Robert laughed.

It was a small plane and it sliced through the sky enroute to America. There wasn't any turbulence and the girls were strapped in their seats sleeping peacefully. It was almost a flight of the dead and no cabin staff wandered the aisles and the silence was omnipresent except for the droning of the engines. In the cockpit the pilot and co-pilot were chatting amicably and expected to land in a few hours. 'This is delta yankee three four hotel alpha requesting a new beacon and course change,' the pilot said, as he scheduled his course to take them to their destination.

'Roger that,' came back the air traffic controller and reeled off the co-ordinates for a new heading. 'Good to go.'

'Thanks Atlanta, new heading is…' and he repeated back the references and set the plane on a new course. They both relaxed and the pilot took out a sandwich and began to eat. 'You think they would give us better food than this,' he said, surveying the sandwich that had started to have curly corners. 'Maybe it's cheese, maybe it isn't,' he said, chewing slowly. 'What do you think?' He looked across at his counterpart.

'I think I'll leave mine till I land unless it makes a break for freedom in the meantime.' He laughed.

Inside the cabin, Claire had begun to stir. She felt a slow tingling sensation in her hands and feet that intruded in her dreams. She twitched and her lips began to move in sync with her dream. She was on another planet far away from Earth and she was saving the population of Earth from an invasion of gross mutants. They were grouping for battle and she hefted her huge phaser gun to take them out. An alien spacecraft hovered overhead and bathed everything in a blinding light. The chips were down and only she stood between life on Earth and total annihilation. In truth the light from the plane window was directly in her eyes with the course change and she was reliving a scene from a DVD game that was her secret obsession. The sun got stronger and she woke up just as she was about to blast the first onslaught and blinked, then squinted in the fierce light. She sat silent and her first thought was, *Damn, I was going to have them this time*, then relaxed for five minutes, half awake and half still asleep. *I must have dozed off*, was her next thought and she opened her eyes again. The brilliant sunlight shining straight into her eyes finally jerked her into full wakefulness. She lurched forward and was caught in the seat belt. 'Where the hell am I?' She let her eyes rove round the cabin to rest on Ellie snoring peacefully beside her. Her head lolled to one side and a small trail of spittle was snaking down her chin. Claire tried to make sense of her situation but it was all just a blur. A mishmash of fragments fired haphazardly into her brain. This wasn't a DVD game she was reliving; it seemed to be in real time. The idea that she should pinch herself to see if it really was a dream came into her mind but she almost laughed at the idea. She raised her hands and looked at them, then flexed her fingers, yes; she was really awake now and had no idea why she was on a plane. All her training kicked in and a swift analysis of her situation told her that it wasn't a good one. She quietly unbuckled her belt and after a quick scan round to see if she was alone she climbed over Ellie to stand in the gangway. She noted the empty seats which she could dodge into and play dead if she heard anyone coming. She crept down the plane towards the cockpit and paused by the galley at the end. She was desperately thirsty and a drink of water would do a lot to revive her. She grabbed a bottle of water and went into the toilet at the end of the seats. She didn't know but a light flashed in the cockpit when the toilet door opened.

'Hey, Luke, we seem to have got a wanderer. Is it your turn or mine?' The pilot looked at his friend.

'I'll do it as you seem to be still chewing,' he said, as he indicated the half-eaten sandwich lying on the console.

The co-pilot climbed over and went to the door sectioning off the flight deck from the cabin. It should have been locked but there were no cabin staff and it was just a formality anyway. He opened the door inwards expecting to see a half-drugged girl lurching uncertainly down the gangway but instead met a flurry of fists and feet. This took him completely by surprise and he fell back into the cabin poleaxed by a vicious chop to the neck. Claire wasn't feeling really up to it but she had summoned some reserves and made it count when she delivered the blow. It only took one and this was it, the co-pilot was out cold.

Claire fought down a wave of nausea that suddenly threatened to engulf her and she thought that the water hadn't been a good idea as she strode into the flight deck.

'This seems to be a flight where I haven't bought a ticket. Care to tell me where I'm going?' she asked evenly. The pilot's sandwich dropped from his lips into his lap and he just stared at Claire who was dirty and smelly from her incarceration but oozed confidence. She didn't have a weapon and the pilot's thoughts went to the gun under his seat. 'Don't even think about it,' said Claire as if reading his thoughts. 'One drop kick from where I'm standing and you'll be toast,' she added, with more confidence than she was feeling.

'But who'll fly the plane?' the pilot asked with a show of bravado he was far from feeling.

'Me, stupid,' said Claire, 'if it's got wings I can make it fly. I suggest you get out of that seat now,' she ordered. The nausea suddenly got the better of her and bile rose to her throat and she bent and retched over the co-pilot's inert body.

The pilot saw his chance and reached for the gun under his seat and he was halfway there when a stream of projectile vomit hit him. Claire had seen his movement from the corner of her eye and thought that if she was going to be sick she might as well do it over him. *Well, that's a first*, thought Claire as the pilot reeled back into his seat covered with the contents of Claire's stomach.

'Out!' She gagged again and wiped the back of her hand across her mouth. The pilot was horrified as he climbed out from his seat covered in an evil smelling gastric event.

'What about Luke?' The pilot gestured to his comatose friend trying to wipe himself down at the same time.

'What about him?' Claire prodded him with her foot. 'He's breathing. Let's get this straight; I care about you as much as you cared about me, which is basically zero. So move to this seat and sit down now.'

The pilot frantically thought through his options which weren't many and decided that discretion was probably the better part of valour and he wasn't cut out to be a fighter anyway. He edged past Claire and sat down. Claire was now in a quandary and had two prisoners she needed to disable. She couldn't really turn her back on the pilot as, although he wasn't a fighting man, he could overpower her in the cramped space. His friend was breathing heavily but regularly and could come round at any second. She quickly looked about and spied a life jacket in its container. Life jackets had tapes and she could at least tie them up. She reached it down and opened it and sure enough there were tapes to secure the jacket in place. Claire thanked her lucky stars she had paid attention in the past to the safety talks by cabin crew. She got the pilot to lean forward and tied his hands behind his back then, for good measure, she got him to lean back and put his seat belt on. He glowered at her. 'You don't think you're going to get away with hijacking this plane do you?' Claire ignored him and trussed his friend up who was lying in the gangway. She climbed into the pilot seat and felt underneath and found the gun. She held it up and waved it at the pilot.

'Yes, actually I will get away with it, this says I will. So shut up and keep quiet or I'll use it.' She didn't have any intention of using it on the plane but it didn't hurt to let him think that. She read the instruments and found they were locked onto a beacon and there were no apparent problems. She had done some fixed wing training but was more conversant with helicopters. She pushed a few buttons and twiddled a few knobs and got air traffic control. 'Air control this is private flight...' Then she realized she didn't know the number. Claire looked at the pilot who sat back and looked smug. No help there then. 'Air traffic we have a medical emergency and need clearance to land at the nearest strip. It's a Gulfstream or Lear jet. I'm a passenger who has control of the plane. I have flying experience but don't know exactly where we are. I will need assistance to land.'

'Roger that. Do you know controls of plane?'

'Yes, but unfamiliar with this layout.'

'Okay, we have you now on radar and nearest field is Atlanta, can you circle back and lock onto beacon?' and he reeled off a string of co-ordinates.

'Roger that, tower.' Claire disabled the auto pilot and felt the plane respond in her hands. Her hands began to sweat. She looked over her shoulder at the pilot. 'You can either help me with this or be the first at the crash scene.'

The pilot had gone white and realized she was serious in her intentions and he could either help her or mentally die a thousand deaths while she wrestled with the controls. 'Okay, I'll help you but I want my assistance noted when we land. I was only following orders,' he added lamely.

'Noted,' said Claire, as she flicked the auto pilot back on and clambered out and set him free. She held the gun on him for good measure as he climbed into the co-pilot seat.

'Tower, the pilot is feeling a bit better and I have his assistance now. Please give us headings for Atlanta.'

'Roger, good to go,' answered the controller, who had breathed a sigh of relief at this. The plane smoothly banked on its new course.

CHAPTER TWELVE

The flight back to Atlanta was uneventful as the pilot didn't put a foot wrong and landed with scarcely a bump. The plane was directed round the back, away from the main passenger terminals, and came to rest outside a hanger where some ambulances and Police cars were awaiting them. Claire motioned the pilot to drop the door and a stairway was waiting to be shunted into place. He opened the door and as the stairs were nearly locked into position he leaped from the plane onto the stairs and tumbled down yelling, 'It's a hijack and she's got a gun!' Suddenly from nowhere an armed response team appeared and surrounded the plane. A chief with a loudhailer requested that the hijackers show themselves. Claire almost laughed out loud until she saw the red dots trained on her and wavering over her body and the window. She slowly raised her hands.

'Okay, let's take this nice and slow,' said the voice. 'Move from the cockpit to the stairs with your hands on your head.'

Claire put her hands on her head but couldn't restrain a grin as she thought of the cargo behind her. She signalled that she was coming out and let the gun slide from her lap onto the floor. The co-pilot was grunting and straining at his bonds as he watched her leave. Claire got to the stairway and made sure her arms and hands were the first thing the gunmen would see round the edge of the door. She yelled, 'I'm coming out, hold your fire,' and edged into full view. She heard the sounds of the guns being locked and loaded. Her hands were firmly on her head as she walked slowly down the steps and onto the asphalt.

'Hit the deck,' ordered the voice again and Claire complied. About six heavily armed men in black uniforms and bullet proof vests surrounded her and she was tightly cuffed with her arms behind her back. As she was yanked to her feet she said, 'You will need the ambulances for the people on the plane as I think they've been drugged.' This was ignored.

'Are you alone?' asked the voice.

'I am alone,' Claire replied and nodded her head. She was frogmarched towards the hanger and a waiting armoured vehicle. 'You need to look at the people on the plane,' she said more urgently. 'I think they are all drugged and are probably getting dehydrated by now.' She was ignored. 'Look, don't ignore me,' she yelled. 'I'm a member of the British Security Services and I took control of that plane because it's full of girls for slave trafficking.' She was ignored as she was bundled into the back of the vehicle.

Claire sat down on the hard seat and looked at the two hefty guys flanking her and by the set of their faces she knew they wouldn't answer any questions. She shrugged and thought that it would all be sorted out very quickly when she reached their base. The journey was about two hours and Claire got more and more conscious of how difficult her situation had become. She hoped she would be given the one phone call that could sort all this out. Quite how she would explain it all to Phil in a minute was another matter.

In the hospital, Rory was wincing his way round the ward pushing a stand and a drip. He was very sore but realized he was the hero of the moment and managed to get to see Alistair and Maria. She had come off worse and was still in an induced coma while she healed after surgery to remove her spleen. Alistair was in a bit better shape and was sitting up in bed nursing a fractured sternum and numerous ribs, one of which had punctured a lung He was still breathing in short gasps and the drain from his chest was still bloody. An oxygen mask lay within easy reach and he frequently applied it. 'Alistair, you look awful,' was all Rory could say as he gazed on the gaunt figure.

'Thanks,' gasped Alistair and took a couple of drags of oxygen. 'Any news?'

'Nothing yet but I'll be seeing Phil soon. Are you ready to have visitors as I'll bring them all down here if you like?'

'I don't think Sister Psycho would let them in.' He glanced toward the Sister, who was stemming down the ward like a black ship in full sail.

'I'll be back soon,' Rory assured Alistair as he collected his paraphernalia and shuffled off. Rory also spent a few minutes with Maria and sat by her bed talking to her. He didn't really know what to say and kept up a stream of banal drivel until he was ushered out. As he wasn't a relative he couldn't get any information on how she was but had told the nurses on the station that he was in the car with her and his fiancée was her employer. That had gained him a few minutes, nothing more. Try as he might he couldn't get information about the goings on at the hospital from the nun's point of view. All the sisters had obviously been told to say nothing and there was a Sister Bertha flying out from Russia to take control of the day to day running of the Order. She would be arriving the next morning and everything would be back to normal.

Phil had received reports from Robert and Nigel that they had managed to piece together what had happened to Jack the night before. He had been ambushed and been taken back into the hospital. They had no knowledge of what he had been drugged with, but he seemed to have made a reasonable recovery although his memory was still missing big chunks of the night. Dreams had faded and he was left with a sense of disorientation and unease. Phil had assured him that it was normal that his brain should try to fill in the gaps in his memory but Jack felt he wasn't being any help at all. He walked around muttering to himself until Phil told him to shut up and get a grip. Jack duly shut up and tried to be of some help with the American agents who were still trying to make sense of what had gone on.

They were all sequestered in Sister Margaret's old office and the local Chief of Police sat there with a smug look. He addressed the assembly, 'The American dollars have been removed and their destruction is due in about two hours time if you would like to witness that and film it?' He looked at the Americans.

Robert and Nigel said in unison, 'Yeah! We would.' The thought of millions of dollars going up in smoke appealed to their anarchic tendencies.

Agent Tavares looked at his counterpart and said, 'I suppose we should be there.' He glanced at his watch. 'Let's get this over with.' They had both been harbouring thoughts of how to get the shipment back to the good old US of A and doing some fancy footwork with the paperwork when it got there. It was more than their job was worth; it was their lives at stake if it didn't get back to America. Their job for their department was done when the counterfeiting operation was closed. They had no interest in the slave shipments even though there was speculation the last plane load had gone via Atlanta. It was only speculation and both agents didn't deal in speculation. They rose and the Chief smiled at Phil as he went out followed by Nigel and Robert, keen to see a conflagration of cash.

Phil looked at Jack when they were alone. 'This doesn't solve our problem of where Claire and Ellie are though. We've got them probably going to America but we can't prove it. St. Lucia air traffic has got lots of private planes leaving and many flight plans, and I'll bet many don't match up with where they're actually going. The people at this party don't want to be seen or be known for whatever reason, so we'll have to discount a lot of the information. All we can go on is the past movements gleaned by Rob and Nigel and hope they form a pattern. Are you up for it to have another look at the data? Maybe, with your maths brain you can see something we've missed?'

'Give me another coffee and I'll give it a go,' said Jack, realizing that he better step up to the plate quickly if Claire and Ellie would even have a chance. 'You've no idea then what happened to Sister Margaret?'

'Nothing,' said Phil despondently. 'She was certainly not what we expected.' He felt his jaw. 'She was a nun, or maybe she wasn't, we don't know, but she could have hopped on any flight out of here and escaped. I'd really like to interview her but that's not going to happen. I did notice she had a very slight Russian accent and maybe she was linked to our friend Valentin at the resort, but it seems that bird has flown also. He took wings earlier and cleared out pronto. It may be that he's the link, anyway let's see what you can make of this recovered data. A coffee is on the way,' he added.

Valentin sat on his luxury jet and wondered how everything could have gone so bad in such a short time. A lucrative cargo of girls had disappeared off the radar totally and all his cowering aides sitting at the back couldn't give him any information. His cousin had gone AWOL and he didn't know where she was. Undoubtedly, she would turn up eventually but she wasn't available now, and that was when he wanted her. Now! Karl was doing his best but no intelligence was forthcoming as he was stuck in the resort and all the action seemed to be taking place at the hospital. Valentin was metaphorically sweating. Millions of US dollars had gone and his operation in the Caribbean was at a standstill, it could take years to rebuild. But he wasn't one to dwell on failures and disasters that to his mind weren't of his making so he ordered a glass of champagne with a flick of his hand and began to plan his next move. It was like a game of chess to him; he weighed up the opposition and tried to seek out their weaknesses. The world was a big place and there were plenty of small communities that would like a bit of extra cash. Many small islands, perhaps in Indonesia, could benefit from the influx of cash. A few palms greased here and there would enable a smooth passage and blindness towards his dealings. Valentin sipped his drink. If all had gone to plan the agents from America that would have undoubtedly been summoned to St. Lucia would have transferred the cash to the USA. and everything would be hunky-dory. They had already received a large backhander to ensure that it was done and it was to a traceable bank account so they would be seriously in the mire if they failed. He sat back and considered what to do next. Karl had already given him a great deal of information about Alistair's current business dealings so he thought he would peruse those in greater depth and see if there was an opening for himself. Valentin summoned an aide and dictated an e-mail to go to the hospital to show that he was thinking of his old friend. Then as an afterthought he arranged for some flowers to be delivered to all three of the injured. At least it would make it seem as if he was concerned about his erstwhile friends. He settled back with the business papers and began to plan.

Claire's journey came to an end and she was unloaded from the van and saw she was in a compound in the desert somewhere. There were high fences topped with razor wire and armed guards everywhere. To all intents and proposes it looked like a prison. She was shepherded to one of the main buildings and despite her protestations she was shoved in a cell still handcuffed.

'Get these things off me,' she shouted and decided to keep on shouting it till someone took notice. She sat on the floor and also began banging the cell door with her feet and kept the racket up for nearly an hour till the slide in the door was pushed back.

'What's your problem, lady,' a disembodied voice enquired.

'A girl's got to go to the bathroom sometime,' Claire answered.

'Shut up and I'll go and get someone.'

'What if I don't shut up? You'll only forget me again.'

'We won't forget you. If you don't keep quiet I promise we'll forget you for a very long time.'

'Okay, got the picture. I'll shut up and you'll let me use the bathroom.'

'Got it in one, lady,' said the guard as he slid the letterbox opening shut with a clang.

Claire realized that she was being slowly broken down by being denied small basic human needs. She might get a bathroom trip, but she might not. She may get some food, but again that might be denied. So, when she was even dirtier and smellier than she was now, plus being ravenously hungry and thirsty, she would be interviewed. She would probably sell her soul for a drink and a crust. Her cell was probably wired for sound so she decided to make up some songs and sing them out loud just to let the guards know she knew what they were doing. She gritted her teeth and mentally told herself they wouldn't cause her any hardships, only minor inconveniences. So, what was the problem with being dirty and smelly, a hot shower cured all! A few days without food would be just the start of a detox diet she had always promised herself. She settled herself into a corner of the bare cell, closed her eyes and began to hum.

A few hours later, it may have been more or less, but Claire couldn't see her watch and there wasn't a window in her cell, she heard a key turn in her lock. She kept her eyes shut and was still singing when she was hauled to her feet. She was definitely smellier than when she had been first incarcerated as she couldn't wait for the bathroom break any longer. She had just shrugged her shoulders and did what she had to. The guard wrinkled his nose but Claire kept on humming to herself. She kept singing as she was led to an interview room with her head downcast. She looked up and saw a man in army fatigues behind a desk with a file in front of him. She was plonked unceremoniously down in a chair in front of him and the guard took up a position by the door.

She decided to make the opening gambit. 'My name is Claire Frances Helen Agnes, but don't tell anyone about that one…'

'We know exactly who you are.'

'Well, why are you holding me here?'

'We know you are a rogue agent from British Security Services and you hijacked a plane. We don't like hijackers here.'

'I only hijacked it because it was carrying a cargo of girls for sex slave trafficking.'

'You held the pilot at gunpoint and disabled the co-pilot, thereby endangering the passengers.'

'There was no endangerment about it. I can fly a plane and we landed without incident. Just ring London and they'll tell you who I am and why I was in St. Lucia.'

'We did,' the army interviewer replied. He let a moment's silence prevail then said, 'You were sent to St. Lucia to reclaim a stolen book and take it back to England. Instead you ended up hijacking a passenger flight, albeit a private one, and forcing the pilot to land at gunpoint.'

'There's much more to the story than that. I can corroborate all I say if you let me have one phone call?'

'Phone call denied.'

'What did the pilot tell you?'

'That information is denied.'

'What about the supposed passengers? They were all young girls and were drugged up to their eyeballs. In fact, my friend Ellie Black was abducted and put on that flight. She can tell you everything I say is true.'

The interrogator looked at the papers in front of him and perused a list with his finger. 'There is no Ellie Black noted on this flight.'

Claire fell silent at this and looked at the man. She realized then what a mess she was in. She couldn't phone Phil. No-one had any idea where she was. London had her pegged as a 'rogue' agent and Ellie had disappeared again. She decided to try again for the basics. 'Please take the cuffs off as my arms are going numb.' She leaned forwards. The interrogator gestured to the guard by the door and he moved forward and undid them. Claire was eternally grateful for that as she massaged her wrists. 'Thank you.' She made eye contact with the main man. No harm in being polite she thought. 'Where am I?' she tried.

'Information denied,' was all the answer she got.

'So what's going to happen to me?'

'Information denied.'

'This is all getting a bit repetitive and pointless then isn't it?

I can't phone anyone, I don't know where I am, I don't know what's going to happen to me. I was denied a bathroom break, food and water as well, and it looks likely that I'm not going to get the chance to clean myself up, am I?' Claire stared hard into the interrogator's eyes.

He momentarily looked down and Claire mentally scored a hit. *Yes*, she thought, *I'm going to get something now*. He would seek to appease her if her psychological take was right.

'You can have a cell with a bed and facilities but we'll be continuing our discussion soon,' he said as he closed his file and rose.

'So what do you really want to know?' Claire followed him with her head as he moved round the table. 'Let me know and I'll tell you everything,' she said provocatively. 'On second thoughts,' she pondered, 'could you tell me exactly what my bosses in London actually said?'

'Yes, ma'am,' he said with obvious relish. 'They said that you were not doing the job you had been sent to do and not following the protocols in the red book. I hope that makes some sense to you?'

'Yes. Thank you. It makes perfect sense now.' Claire breathed a sigh of relief. She would have to put up with the bad behaviour on the part of the Americans but the reference to the 'red book' was a code word that told her she was expected to work undercover. Quite what she was supposed to uncover was another matter but she thought it would have something to do with the trafficking. Also, how she was going to that whilst incarcerated in a compound in the middle of a desert defeated her.

CHAPTER THIRTEEN

Phil and Jack sat back and looked again at all the recovered data. They had managed to print everything out on spread sheets and Jack had applied his reasoning to it and was making some headway. He stabbed at an entry with his index finger. 'This is the flight we can't account for. I am going to say that this is the one the girls were taken to America on. The flight plan says San Francisco but we've already checked and nothing has landed or even making an approach. We haven't got a flight number yet but maybe you can give London a ring and see if they can get any info we can't.' Jack looked at Phil and Phil nodded and got out his phone.

Phil dialed and was rewarded with an instant response. He began nodding and he furrowed his brow. 'So she's in a prison, being held on hijacking charges and will be moved to a more secure facility soon. What the hell is going on?' Phil had a look of utter disbelief written large on his face. Jack leaned closer to try and get some idea of the conversation. 'I've had half my team disabled and Claire hasn't got any backup at all and no idea of what she's supposed to do. Excuse me for saying this but this operation stinks to high heaven. What about Ellie Black? She was on that flight as well as Claire.' Phil listened again and Jack saw a muscle begin to twitch at the side of his face as Phil clenched his teeth. 'Well, let's give thanks for small mercies,' he said sarcastically, and mouthed, 'Ellie's okay,' to Jack who was now on the edge of his seat. 'What did you say again about the US Agent, Tavares, and his sidekick? Sorry, I didn't quite catch that.

I got it as they're dirty agents and could possibly be in the pay of a crime boss?' Phil sat back in utter disbelief. 'Got to go as the Agents are now looking at millions of dollars going up in smoke, or supposed to be. Will report again later,' he said tersely, and rung off. 'Jack, we've got to get to the cash disposal site quickly. It seems that the two US guys are not all they appear to be and London has done a bit of digging and there are some funny transactions in their bank accounts. You ring Nigel and Robert now and get them to hold off the bonfire till we get there.' Phil sprang up and they both ran to Phil's room to get a firearm each.

Outside they looked at the cars and ran over to a Police car that was standing with the door open. Phil jumped in and the key was in the ignition and he fired it up and put it in gear as Jack was half in the passenger seat still with his phone glued to his ear. The passenger door swung shut as Phil sped away and two local Policemen came haring down the steps and stood and watched their transport disappear in a cloud of dust. Jack hung on for dear life as he relayed the destination point to Phil and began giving him directions. The money was going to be incinerated in a small factory that had the facilities to burn fuel in a closed environment. They were just about to start shovelling the cash into the incinerator when Jack's call had come through. Robert had stopped the proceedings and the two US Agents had begun to look decidedly uneasy. Robert relayed that information but then the phone went dead. Phil drove even faster and they screamed to a halt outside the factory. It was all too quiet.

Phil put a restraining arm on Jack and put his finger to his lips. After their noisy approach it seemed a bit of a waste of time to be quiet now but Jack sat still. Phil motioned him to go round one side of the building while he went round the other. They would enter where least expected and hopefully take people by surprise. Jack slid off his seat and opened his car door but didn't let it close properly. He crouched and ran round the side of the building looking for another door or a window. Phil ran round the other side and spotted a window high in the wall. There was a large bin underneath it and Phil climbed on it and peered in. The glass was very dirty and he rubbed a small spy hole with his finger and saw the two agents with their guns out and everyone else lined up against the opposite wall. The cash was still in its crates and two factory workers were lined up with the others. The Chief of Police who was overseeing the disposal of the notes was obviously trying to talk the gunmen down as Phil could see his mouth working, but he couldn't hear what was being said. Robert usually had a gun tucked down the waistband of his jeans but Phil didn't know if he had been disarmed or not.

Across the factory, Phil saw Jack's face appear at the opposite window and a shadow was cast on the floor by the gunmen. One of them looked up and caught sight of Jack and he fired his gun as Jack ducked down just in time. Phil drew his gun and fired twice in quick succession and both gunmen dropped to the floor. He hadn't aimed to kill, just immobilize. Nigel and Robert leaped forward and disarmed both the gunmen before they could fire and the two factory workers slumped to the floor in shock.

Jack had heard the two shots and guessed what Phil had done and ran round the building and came in the door with his gun held out before him, just in case. He put the safety on as he saw Nigel and Robert tying the hands of the men behind their backs. Blood was pooling beneath them as Phil had hit them both in the lower leg and they were lying down moaning and groaning in pain. The Chief of Police ambled over to the two. 'I think this case is now closed. As I explained previously St. Lucia is a British

Protectorate and you have held British subjects at gunpoint and tried to steal counterfeit currency. You will be charged with those offenses and tried on the island. If the United States wishes to extradite you, they can try but it will be a very long and drawn out procedure. Good day gentlemen.' He turned to Jack and Phil. 'Many thanks to you both for your forethought, planning and marksmanship. Who would have thought that this'– he kicked a crate –'could cause so much trouble?' He reached into the crate and pulled out four hundred-dollar bills and gave one to each of them. 'Just a small memento of your day. Don't bother trying to spend them as I've made a note of the serial numbers.' He laughed and got out his phone. 'I'll get an ambulance for these people and then we'll burn some cash.' Robert and Nigel nodded enthusiastically and the factory workers gingerly helped each other up.

The furnace door was opened and a rush of heat came out and everyone stepped back a pace or two. The workers donned their protective aprons and facemasks and began shovelling the wads of money into the conflagration. It burned well and the Chief sat on the side of the crate and smiled beatifically. His job was done and he totally ignored the ambulances that turned up for the miscreants, except to direct that the injured should be kept in a secure unit. Robert and Nigel were like two kids at a fair and began throwing bundles of bills into the flames. Overarm and underarm they vied with each other as to who could get the most spectacular shot. Phil just shook his head at their release of tension. He said to the Chief, 'I'm sorry about the Police car.'

'What car?'

'The one we hijacked to get here and drove through every red light. We must have a string of traffic infringements to answer.'

The Chief smiled. 'Like I said, what car? As long as it gets back to where it is supposed to be I don't know anything about a car.'

Phil reached over and shook his hand. 'I'll take Jack and these children away now and leave you in peace.' He walked over to Robert and Nigel who were whooping with delight as more and more cash was burning. 'Got to go home now, sorry boys.' As he took the arm of each and led them away with a wry grin at the Chief.

Ellie was lying quite comfortably in a hospital bed only dimly aware of her surroundings. Her eyelids felt as if they had been glued shut and her mouth felt like cotton wool. She moved her head to the side and strong sunlight filtered through her closed eyes. She turned her head back away from the light. She desperately wanted a drink and opened her mouth and a croak was all she could manage. Sensation began to flood back into her limbs and she raised her arm, but abruptly stopped as she felt a sharp pain that jerked her back into wakefulness. She was conscious of someone holding her arm and saying, 'Lie still, you're all right, you're in a hospital.'

'Where am I?' It came out thickly.

'You're in Atlanta General Hospital, and you'll feel better soon. Nice to have you back with us.'

Ellie struggled and managed to open her eyes and everything swam fuzzily backwards and forwards as she tried to focus. It made her feel nauseous. 'I need a drink, water.'

'Here, have a few sips of this.' Her head was raised and some water made its way down her throat. Ellie nodded her head and a few more drops went the same way as the first and she felt much better. She lay back into the soft pillows and began to take stock of her surroundings. She was in a small hospital room on her own and she could now see the nurse hovering by a drip bag at her side. That explained the sharp pain in her arm as she looked down and saw the needle.

'How long have I been here? The last time I saw daylight I was on St. Lucia. How did I get here?'

'Sorry but I don't know,' said the nurse. 'There are a couple of investigation agents who want to speak to you but we won't let them in till you're ready. How do you feel now? We can hold them off for as long as you like. You were full of some drug or other and we're just waiting for the blood results to see what it was. Your blood pressure and all other vital signs are good now but your memory of what happened might not be so good, so just have a rest for now. I'll be back in half an hour.'

'I'm feeling better by the minute, if you can leave the water within reach I would be grateful. Hold off those guys for a bit longer and I'll gather myself together.' Ellie closed her eyes again and drifted into a half sleep and tried to remember the events that had led her to being in America. It was all disjointed and all Ellie could really remember was a place with bars, a bit like lion cages, but she wasn't sure if it was a dream or not. Everything seemed out of sequence and viewed through a fog. The half an hour must have gone by as she sensed the nurse coming in again. Ellie managed to semi-sit up and had another drink. 'Do you know who I am?' sheen quired.

'Yep, we have you down as Jane Doe,' the nurse replied glancing at her chart. 'Believe it or not I once looked after someone who was really called Jane Doe. It caused a lot of confusion for the poor woman.'

'I know, that must have been terrible for her. I heard of someone who was called Dot Comm once, can you imagine that?

Trying to get an e-mail address must have been hell.' Ellie laughed. 'Seriously though, my name is Eleanor Black, if you want to write that down instead of Jane Doe.' The nurse duly wrote it down.

'Can you remember anything else?'

'Yes, absolutely! It's all fuzzy for the past day or so but I'll fill you in with all the other details.' Ellie reeled off her date of birth, nationality, address and all the other relevant bits and pieces the nurse wanted to complete her forms.

'That's really good, thank you. There will be a doctor to see you shortly, now you are back with us and the blood results are through, but he'll talk you through them when he comes.'

'Any chance of a phone call as I'd like to tell my family I'm okay?' It felt weird to Ellie to say the word 'family' as it had been a long time since she had used it. Now it meant blood relatives, a twin brother no less, and she wanted to make a connection with him again. There was also Rory included in that as he was now her fiancé and soon to part of that family. The urge to speak to them was suddenly overwhelming.

'Sorry, I can't as the detectives want to speak to you first. They're still waiting and don't look as if they're going away anytime soon.'

'Best get it over with then, wheel them in but I'd like you to stay if that's all right with you.' Ellie felt a need for a bit of support as she didn't know what to expect.

The nurse ushered in two detectives that smiled and showed off two sets of perfect teeth. Ellie didn't know why but they reminded her of polished fangs and the smiles never reached the eyes.

'We'd just like to get a few details from you as you have turned up on our doorstep unannounced.' The speaker wore a jacket that was a bit crumpled and Ellie could smell the cigarette smoke and coffee on his breath. 'We wouldn't want you to be an illegal trying to get into the country, now would we?'

'I'm not an immigrant.' Ellie was surprised they would think this. 'My name is Eleanor Black and I was with my twin brother in St. Lucia attending a party hosted by Fortune and Honey with my fiancé. As far as I know my brother Alistair Morgan is still there and is probably worried sick by now.'

'So you were at the resort owned by Fortune?'

'Yes, I've just told you that.'

'So you were there when that place got busted wide open?'

'What do you mean?'

'So you're saying you know nothing about the counterfeit dollar bills found on you?'

'What dollar bills?'

'Your pockets were stuffed with them.'

'I haven't got a clue what you're talking about. All I know is that I was drugged with something or other and ended up here. I haven't any idea how I got here but I'll give you every help I can. I am not a money smuggler and I'm not saying any more till I can speak to my brother.' Ellie deliberately didn't say anything about the reasons why she had gone to the party and her connection with the British Security Services. She didn't like these men at all and thought that the less she said the better it would be. 'Also, you can find me a lawyer if I'm going to be charged. I am going to be charged with something aren't I? If not, goodbye as I'm beginning to feel a bit sick.' She lay back and closed her eyes. Ellie was not aware that the nurse sitting quietly up in the corner had shrugged her shoulders and ushered the detectives out of the room closing the door firmly behind them.

'You're okay now, you can open your eyes,' the nurse said,

smiling.

'So that went well, didn't it,' said Ellie, sarcastically.

'One good thing was they didn't say that you couldn't have a phone call, so I'll get you a line now.'

You're a pal…Ruth.' Ellie peered at her name tag.

Ruth fiddled with the phone and handed it to Ellie. 'You have got an outside line now, I'll leave you to make your call and make sure the goonies don't wander back in. I would be quick if I were you though as they could raise the roof if they find out.'

Ellie held the phone for a moment then decided she would ring Phil rather than Alistair. She had memorized Phil's number and secretly put more faith in his abilities to get things moving rather than her brother's. It only rang twice before Phil answered. 'Hi Phil, its Ellie. Got to be really quick. Am in Atlanta General and I'm okay. I'm on my own and two detectives are hounding me regarding some stolen cash or something. I've got to get out of here quickly. Tell Rory I'm okay.' She rung off as the door handle rattled expecting the detectives back again but in strolled a doctor with a sheaf of notes in his hand. The nurse was with him and came to Ellie and sat her up a bit more and plumped her pillows whilst discreetly moving the phone.

'Well, Miss Black,' he began, 'you were out cold when you were bought in but it's nice to see you have made a speedy recovery. All your vital signs are as we expect them and you are now apparently fighting fit. That is to say, you will probably experience nausea but that will fade away over the next twenty-four hours. Just think of it as having a prolonged deep sleep.' He motioned to the drip in Ellie's arm. 'I think we can dispense with that now as she appears to be fully hydrated. You may experience some memory loss about the last day or so, this may come back, or it may not, we're not sure. We've done all the blood works we can but can't find anything. This could be a drug that is broken down by the body very quickly, it could be one of the "date rape" drugs that show no trace, but I can safely say it's gone now. Have you got any questions?'

Ellie had a raft of questions but none were pertaining to her medical condition, so she said nothing except to thank the doctor for all his attentions and to send the bill to Castle Ucello in Italy and it would be dealt with immediately. The doctor gave her a few papers to sign concerning this; he seemed to have come prepared.

'So, if you would sign this, I can discharge you in the morning.' He proffered yet another piece of paper. 'I would like you to stay here for another eighteen hours or so just to make sure, but otherwise you are good to go.' The doctor smiled as Ellie scribbled her signature on the forms. 'I'll leave you now to catch up on your beauty sleep and just ask the nurse for anything you want to eat or drink. Don't overdo it at first though; the nausea could come back with a vengeance.'

When he said that, Ellie realized she was actually quite peckish and smiled at the doctor as he went out. She looked at the nurse. 'He's mentioned food and I'm actually quite hungry. Do you think you could find me something light to have a go at, maybe some toast or cereals at first?'

'Yep, coming right up.'

As the nurse left the phone purred and Ellie snatched it up. It was Phil again and she breathed a sigh as he quickly explained that she would be picked up from the hospital at twenty hundred hours that night. 'One thing,' she said, 'I haven't got any clothes, they've taken them all.'

'No worries, we'll get you fixed up with something. Just be ready to leave.'

'What about the detectives? I think they're sitting outside the door now,'

'Don't worry about them, just go. It may be a back door exit but you'll be out of the USA by nightfall.'

Ellie began to ask about Rory but the phone went dead in her hand and she stared at the receiver willing it back to life. She replaced it slowly and began to guess and plan what might happen in four hours time.

CHAPTER FOURTEEN

Phil felt as if he was running round in circles getting nowhere. He was glad Ellie had turned up and he quickly made a plan to get her out of America. He made notes as he thought it through, a wheelchair would take her to X-Ray or some other department where the detectives couldn't follow her in. The chair would be manhandled by one of their American friends. Into the department she would go and out would come an old lady courtesy of a wig, blanket, and a different orderly. Then the detectives would be sitting there for a very long time and Ellie would be on a plane back to St. Lucia before they noticed something was wrong. Simple sleight of hand should be enough to fool them, particularly as they would least expect it at the hospital. He put the plan in motion and wandered up to see how Rory was getting on. As predicted, Rory was over the moon that Ellie had been found and he managed to clap Phil on the shoulder as a 'man hug' would have been just too painful. They went down to see Alistair and got another few minutes with him and told him the good news.

Alistair was sitting up in bed and looked a bit more comfortable than before, but the oxygen mask was still within easy reach. 'I was going to get a transfer to Castries Private Hospital but I decided to stay here,' he wheezed. 'I need to be where I can get news fast.' Alistair coughed and winced at the same time.

'Just hang in there Alistair; we'll bring you every bit of news as soon as it happens,' said Rory as he rearranged his drip stand.

'Maria is still out of it but I'll go down to see her again this evening and I'll report straight back, promise.' Alistair managed a weak smile as a nun bustled in to shoo them out. She was carrying a huge bouquet of flowers and Rory looked at them, saying, 'Someone loves you, mate. 'Phil grinned. There was a card attached and Phil took off the bouquet and offered it to Alistair. He shook his head and motioned for Phil to read it.

'It says the usual, hope you get better soon. It's from Valentin. He was at the party at the resort,' said Phil.

'Yes, we've known each other a long time,' said Alistair. 'We were actually at prep school together, but I wouldn't trust him. The only thing he cares about is Valentin.' He subsided back into his pillows after such a long sentence.

The nun began flapping her hands and, as they rose, Phil pointed at Alistair and said, 'I'll be back,' in his best Arnold Schwarzenegger impression. This raised a smile and Alistair weakly raised a hand in reply.

As Phil walked back to the ward with Rory he said, 'Alistair is going to take a fair while to mend but I'll pay a quick visit to Maria while I'm here. You go back and get some more rest and I'll come and tell you when Ellie is here, no matter what time it is, okay?'

'Yep, I'm feeling a bit bushed right now, a few minutes' walk and I'm all in. I've never felt so tired in my life but I would like it if you could wake me when Ellie's back safe and sound.'

'It's probably all the drugs they're shoving into you,' said Phil, reassuringly. 'Don't worry I will come and tell you, or even better I'll bring her with me, depending on what state she's in? That girl of yours certainly knows how to attract trouble.'

'She certainly does,' said Rory as they reached the ward. 'Sorry but forget to ask, will Claire be on the same flight?'

'No, she won't, it seems she's got her own problems to solve and at the moment she's in deep cover and I can't help her.' Phil frowned as he said this and recalled a conversation he had with London and was told to leave Claire alone for a few days to see how she got on and not go in with all guns blazing. He didn't like it at all but could only trust Claire not to make any bad decisions in the next forty-eight hours.

Karl was lounging by the pool as he waited for further instructions. This was allowed now as the guests had left and gone on to the next party or were checking out how many millions they had made while they were sunning themselves. His lip curled in disgust as he compared their privileged lifestyle to his own. He had to stay in the shadows, not that he really minded that, but he had to follow in Alistair's wake and shovel up any crap he left behind. He thought back to when Max was his boss and how they had been in tune with each other. It wasn't a matter of shovelling up crap, it was being included in the decision making process. Max would always back him to the hilt and ran his own operation differently to Alistair. They used to joke it was called Operation Exocet, silent but deadly, and Karl could use all his skills to the full. Now he was working for Alistair and things were anything but deadly. Alistair was a rabbit compared to Max's wolf, and now the long lost twin had turned up he seemed to be swayed by what she said. Max had always had a plan to get rid of her from the first moment but the bitch had kicked him out of the helicopter and he had fallen to his death. From that moment, Karl had sworn vengeance and his fists clenched involuntarily. While the rage was bubbling up inside him his phone rang and he looked at the caller ID. It was unlikely to be Alistair as he was still banged up in hospital. Karl didn't really care if he lived or died but he was still paid by the man, but the caller was Valentin.

'Karl?'

'Yes, boss,' Karl answered. 'I've had a look through the business info of Alistair's and there are a few little gems in here. A bonus will be heading your way.' Karl sat up straighter. 'I need you to get yourself back to Italy if you can and call me when you're there. I assume most of his PAs have already left but I need you at the hub as soon as possible. Do you think you can do this?'

'I'll try. I'll go and see him tomorrow at the hospital.'

'Just think of a few good reasons why you should go home, dream up a security leak or something. I'll ring again tomorrow evening.' The call ended before Karl could respond.

That suited him fine as he was bored and wanted a mission, a job. Lying in the sun was all right but he couldn't see how to let Ellie have her accident here and one palm tree was beginning to look the same as another. No time like the present, he thought, so he dialled the number of the hospital and told them who he was. He enquired about the health of all those involved in the car crash and requested a visiting time to see Mr. Morgan. He was told that Mr. Morgan was off the critical list and was now in a stable condition and he could see him for a few minutes tomorrow morning. Karl gave his thanks and relaxed back and reached for his drink. Soon he would have enough money to disappear for good and live his own life and indulge his whims and fantasies to his heart's content.

The new Sister who was to be in charge of the hospital had arrived. She was from the mother house and had flown in directly from Russia. A big woman who had a stern gaze and her eagle eyes seemed to miss nothing. There was no jet lag for her and she swept through the hospital with another nun toting a clip board.

She issued orders, not requests, in a stentorian tone and they rattled off like machine gun fire. Her English was reasonable but not that good and the young acolyte was having trouble keeping up. She had asked once for Sister Bertha to repeat something and had been immediately branded as stupid, so she didn't ask again. She just hoped that the new head didn't have a wonderful memory as well and wouldn't pick up on her omissions as she scribbled away. Bertha was a nurse but was also of the Salnikov bloodline and a close relative of Valentin's. She was over here for a mission and she intended to do it, not like that silly young girl Valentina they had sent before. She was good but Bertha was better and she would soon have this hospital running like clockwork and in a few months Valentin would see the error of his ways in not sending her sooner. Valentina may have been her niece but it was she, Bertha, who would restore the cash flow in the Caribbean. The local police would be going soon and also those British people who were poking and prying into every nook and cranny. She would personally reassure them that it would be fine now, hunky-dory, didn't they say? Then they would leave as well. But for now she would be the very soul of efficiency and get this place up and running quickly.

Ellie had been wheeled into X-Ray then out again, swathed in a different blanket and with a different orderly. A grey wig had been jammed on her head and she kept her head bowed and her hands beneath the blanket clutching a pair of jeans and a T-shirt. Her hands would have been a giveaway as they weren't gnarled and arthritic but smooth and manicured, so she kept them well hidden. She had been whisked away to a car and had got on a private plane and was now landing in St. Lucia. She had held her breath throughout the change about routine in the hospital and only let the adrenaline slide when she was in the air. She was soon at the hospital and couldn't wait to see Rory again, and, after a few enquiries, managed to find his ward. He was sleeping peacefully and she was loath to wake him, but sat by his bed holding his hand. This was where Phil found her as soon as he heard she had landed.

'Wake him up. He was waiting for you to get back.'

'No, I think I'll just let him sleep,' Ellie whispered. 'He looks so peaceful. What happened to him and how are Alistair and Maria?'

Phil drew up a chair and began to fill Ellie in on all the events. 'Maria's not so good at the moment but Alistair seems to be getting better every day. Valentin's hightailed it back to Russia, we think, and the sister in charge here was certainly not all we thought she was. That girl could wield a gun and kick like a mule, but she's disappeared as well. The good news is that we found a huge counterfeiting operation as well and Nigel and Robert took great delight in burning all the cash, so it looks as if the pipeline of girls is now closed down.'

'I don't know how I got shuffled out of St. Lucia but I'm so sorry everyone got injured trying to rescue me and Claire. Maria's really poorly and I haven't seen her yet and Rory seems to be the best one of the bunch but he looks all battered and bruised.' A tear slid down Ellie's cheek. 'I've messed everything up really badly and it's all my fault. I don't know if I'm cut out for this, perhaps I should just wear pretty dresses and swan around to parties. I'm useless.' The tears began to flow faster and Phil was at a bit of a loss what to do.

He reached out and took Ellie's hand. 'Look at me,' he ordered. 'Jack got ambushed and drugged. Nigel got laid up in hospital with an adverse reaction to insect bites. Fortune and Honey got duped, so all these things are not your fault. Bad luck can happen to anyone, you just had a big dollop of it but you did well.'

'I suppose so.' Ellie sniffed, only half believing Phil's pep talk. 'I suppose I should really wake Rory and show him I'm back in one piece then I'll have to go and see Alistair as well.' Ellie leaned over Rory and rubbed his arm and his eyes flickered open. Ellie smiled at him and leaned over and planted a kiss. Phil decided that this was the moment to leave and he quietly went outside the ward to wait in the corridor.

He found Jack hovering there from one foot to the other. He asked Phil anxiously, 'Is she all right, I mean really alright?' Phil looked at the concern and consternation written large on Jack's face.

'Yes, mate, she's fine. I've always said that she's a girl that can look after herself but trouble does seem to search her out. She's going to see Alistair in a few minutes and you can tag along while we fill him in. That's if Sister Hatchet will let us,' he added.

Ellie came out at that moment and smiled when she saw Jack. 'I didn't expect to see you here?'

'I heard through the grapevine that you'd been sprung from the States and thought I'd pop along and say hello,' he ended nonchalantly.

'Well I'm glad you're upright as most of the team seem to have suffered mishaps galore. No doubt you've had your own adventures and I'll sit tomorrow with a quiet cup of coffee and you can tell me all.'

Jack looked mightily pleased at this. 'Will do. You going to see Alistair now? Mind if I tag along?'

'No problem. I have to go and see him as he'll raise the roof off the hospital if I don't. You know what he's like.' Ellie smiled as she waited for the others to lead the way.

They got to Alistair's room and he was, even at this late hour, half propped up in bed reading some papers. The nun strode over ready to wave them away but Alistair spoke quickly, 'Let them in. It'll be for only five minutes. This is my sister, my twin, in fact, so she's as near as you can get relative wise.' The nun acquiesced and pointedly looked at her watch pinned on the front of her coverall.

'Seems you have got her trained,' said Phil, ushering Ellie to the forefront. 'I must say you look a lot better than the last time I saw you.' Some of the deathly pallor had left Alistair's face and a healthier colour had begun to suffuse his skin. Phil glanced down at the drain bottle half hidden at the side of the bed and noted that the fluid it contained was now clear and not like bloody goo as it had been before. Even the oxygen mask was discarded, half hanging off the bed, now forgotten.

'I certainly feel a lot better and I can talk for longer now without running out of breath. Ellie, Ellie, I can't tell you how glad I am to see you again. I've been here tortured by thoughts of what could have happened to you.'

'Don't lie, Alistair,' said Ellie, moving forward and taking his hands. 'You're being melodramatic as usual. The real truth is that you didn't know what was going on and you weren't in control. But I have to thank you for trying to mount a rescue mission and riding into battle with all guns blazing trying to rescue me. It's most unlike you to be at the forefront of the charge.'

Alistair saw his chance. 'Sister, anything for you, you know that.'

'Pity you're driving wasn't up to much though,' Ellie added with a grin. 'Don't lie 'cos I've heard all about it from Rory.'

'We were forced off the road,' said Alistair indignantly.

'Absolutely,' agreed Ellie, 'but, seriously, Alistair, thank you very much for doing what you did. I really mean it.'

Alistair lay back more comfortably and basked for a few moments in the approbation of his sister. He decided not to tell Ellie how he had come by the information of how he had found out where she was. Ellie would blow a fuse if she ever found out he had used the occult again to his own ends. Particularly that he didn't need the Grimoire anymore and could summon the beast at will. He sent up a silent prayer that Maria and Rory could keep their mouths shut. Maria was still comatose and he hoped that Rory had forgotten all about their night on the top of the hill in all the excitement of the past few days.

Ellie was talking to him and he focused his thoughts back to her. 'I'm going to leave you now and hope that you'll feel a bit better in the morning and I thank you again, Alistair, for your efforts. I'll come and see you again first thing, promise.' Ellie rose to leave and Jack and Phil sketched a goodbye wave just as the Sister came in to usher them out. Alistair did feel much better but he felt he had been to Hell and back in a few days. He had been totally drained both physically and mentally and all that had been left was a husk. The fluids being pumped into his body had restored him physically but Alistair wondered if they also acted on mental scars and wounds. He resolved to put the last few days behind him and do what he was good at. If he totally immersed himself in his work again he could perhaps find some of the former peace. Karl was coming to see him in the morning and there were a few things to go over with him, and it was on this thought that the papers slid out of Alistair's hand and he finally fell asleep. The Sister gathered them up and switched off the light and left him to his rest.

Ellie was also bushed and she let Phil and Jack lead her back to a room in the guest accommodation and fell into bed in her T-shirt to a sleep unpunctuated by dreams.

CHAPTER FIFTEEN

In the staff cafeteria it was eight a.m. and everyone was slowly gathering to discuss what was to happen next. They were all a bit at sea as to where to go next. Ellie sat down with her tray of coffee and croissants and was greeted enthusiastically by Nigel and Robert who quickly launched into a tale of how they had burnt millions of US Dollars. 'I've got this,' said Nigel pulling out a hundred dollar bill from his pocket. 'You can't tell it from the real thing. Chief says we can't spend it though.'

'You guys get paid very well and, no doubt, have millions stashed away somewhere so don't go upsetting the local Chief as I assure you your extradition will be done in record time,' Phil said with mock severity. 'Anyway, while we're all gathered here, I'll fill everyone in on where we are at the moment.'

'Where's Claire?' said Ellie, gazing about. 'She's not up yet, that's a bit strange for her. She's usually the early bird, is she alright?'

'I'll come to that,' said Phil. 'I'd like to say how glad we are to have Ellie back with us safe and sound. Rory seems to be on the mend now and I saw the Doctor who is in charge of Maria and they are going to reduce her medication today and gradually bring her out of her induced coma. By tonight we should all be celebrating. Alistair is now okay and should be allowed up and sitting in a chair today as well. If we can all remember this all began with a book. This manuscript had been stolen from England, courtesy of Alistair, and eventually found its way into the safekeeping of Fortune and Honey. The book has now been placed officially on loan from England to St. Lucia for six months and there will be various exhibitions finding their way over to enhance the cultural and historical education on the island. So, we can all give ourselves a quick pat on the back for that one. Fortune and Honey have been exonerated from all charges on that count.'

'What charges?' asked Ellie.

'Well.' Phil paused. 'They could have been done for handling stolen goods for one.'

'You're not serious?' Ellie sat back in her chair.

'Sure am. The law doesn't, or shouldn't exclude anyone. Remember Magna Carta.'

Ellie subsided into silence and reduced the remains of her croissant to crumbs.

'But all's well that ends well on that score and I think we resolved that amicably. Basically, everyone gets what they wanted. We also uncovered a major money farm and millions of US dollars were being filtered into their economy from here. We uncovered printing presses and a clever plan to bleach the ink out of existing one dollar bills and reprint them as hundred dollars. We don't know how long that's been going on for but we suspect for quite a while.'

'Yep, and we burned the lot,' chimed in Robert and Nigel high fiving, still on a high from the experience.

Phil pointedly ignored them and continued, 'We did have two American agents come over to oversee the operation but it appears that our American counterparts were not all they appeared to be. Needless to say, they were removed from the operation and are now in hospital and will be tried according to the laws of St. Lucia.'

'When I was in hospital in Atlanta, I did have two guys come and try to interview me, supposedly as an illegal immigrant. I didn't like them at all and didn't tell them anything. I felt they were fishing for more as they knew I was drugged up and on a plane against my will. Also they never told me where any of the others were. I think there must have been a plane load of girls as I remember bits and pieces but can't seem to put it back together in my mind.' Ellie stopped at that point and looked confused.

'Too right, Ellie. We did recover some CCTV footage of you and Claire, thanks to Nigel and Robert and their wizardry on computers. You were given a dose of something like a "date rape" drug that would impair your memory. Jack also got a dose of it and was out of it for a day or so. We don't know exactly, at this point, where Claire and the other girls are. Rest assured we will find out, and soon. The party at the resort has now ended and it seems that your friend, Valentin, got off the island as fast as he could. Also, Sister Margaret has disappeared as well, so maybe the two are linked in some way.'

Ellie bristled. 'He's not my friend. Valentin is definitely not my friend. I only tried to befriend Mr. Salnikov because you asked me to.'

'Okay, Ellie, point taken, but did he say anything or give us any clues.'

'Only that he seemed to be a good friend of Alistair's and they go back a long way.'

'We figured that one out, but all we have to go on is that the girls went to America and it seems that our nun with a gun had a very faint trace of a Russian accent. Salnikov is also very Russian and the two could be linked. But that's just surmise at the moment as the nun's mother house is in Russia and our new Sister in charge, Bertha, is also very Russian. So, as a plan, I suggest that we try and find out where Claire is. I've had intel from London that's she in deep cover for the next twenty four hours and we can't mess with that so we'll be cooling our heels here till tomorrow night at the earliest. Has anyone else anything to add?'

Mutters and shrugs went round the table and everyone shook their heads. 'I would like to see how Maria is,' said Ellie. 'I still feel very bad as she's been injured and it was all on my account.'

'The news this morning is that she will be gradually brought round and then we may be allowed a few minutes with her. They may allow Ellie that time as she had the closest links with her, maybe that could be your job for today?' Phil nodded at Ellie who nodded back. 'So, guys, take a break, enjoy what's on offer and tomorrow we may be asked to rock and roll again.' Phil pushed his chair back signifying the meeting was at an end.

Ellie decided to go and see Alistair first and found him sitting in a chair dictating a missive to a PA on his phone. He finished as Ellie dragged up another chair. 'Well, you certainly look better now you're up and about,' said Ellie brightly, still a little shocked at his gaunt appearance.

'So, sister, give me the news. You seem to have come through unscathed yet again and I take my hat off to you but I must admit that we were all a bit worried by your disappearance.'

'Be honest, Alistair, you were more than a bit worried as you drove a Land Rover up here to come and try to find me. I've never seen you drive before and I didn't think you could. What made you set off in the dead of night with Rory and Maria all of a sudden?'

Alistair thought through this question at lightning speed. He had to be very careful with his answer as Ellie would smell a very big rodent very quickly. 'I don't really know, it was just one of those feelings you get. We are twins after all and I know that there is a bond between us.'

'Bullshit!' said Ellie decisively. 'I've always maintained that's a load of it, a very big load, and you know it.'

Alistair tried to take the high ground and sat up straighter. 'I know you don't believe it but I felt I just had to get here and quickly. It seems that I was just a bit too late and you got shipped out, but you're back here safe and sound now.' He took her hand and gazed into her eyes. 'You are my sister and also my twin and we make a very good team. You may discount the "twin thing" but I did what I thought I had to.' Alistair tried to make every word true and sincere so the matter would be closed. He couldn't chance Ellie finding out about the information he had from the Beast and his use of the Occult again.

'Okay,' said Ellie slowly and withdrew her hands. 'I believe you but please don't try and drive again. You're not safe behind the wheel!'

'I only did it because Rory and Maria can't drive at all, but it has been a very long while since I learned. Also, I was forced off the road, so it wasn't totally my fault. Maybe I should take a brush up course and have a go at racing driving?' he mused.

'Put that idea straight out of your head now, Alistair. Forget it now, this instant. You don't drive, now or ever again; let's just leave it at that.'

Alistair was pleased the conversation had turned and he agreed that perhaps the world would be a safer place if he left the driving to others. Ellie left him making yet another phone call and walked down to see Rory. She passed Karl in the corridor and a frown momentarily crossed her face before she collected her emotions and smiled a passing greeting. She hadn't known he was here and still didn't like the man at all, but, she shrugged, that was Alistair's problem, not hers, and she quickened her step to Rory.

Rory was drip free and looking forward to being discharged that afternoon and he and Ellie made some plans to enjoy what the resort had to offer in a low key way. Thoughts of Maria kept intruding and Ellie eventually kept the meeting short and promised to be back later after she had checked in on her maid.

Maria's ward was a quiet place except for the hum and click of machinery keeping the most serious patients stable. Ellie explained who she was and was allowed a few minutes at Maria's bedside. She was being slowly brought out of the induced coma and had mumbled some words and her eyes had followed the nuns round the room. The signs looked good but Ellie approached the bedside with trepidation of what she might find. Maria was hooked up to all manner of gizmos and contraptions with pipes and tubes leading everywhere but her eyes were open.

'Can you hear me, Maria?' said Ellie, gently taking Maria's hand. 'It's Ellie and you are in hospital. It was my stupid brother that put you here with his atrocious driving. They said you will be feeling much better soon and we'll soon be back saving the world as usual.' Ellie tailed off not knowing what to say next.

Maria's eyes were open and fixed on Ellie and she blinked three times in rapid succession.

'You can hear me,' said Ellie thankfully and Maria blinked again. 'Do you want anything? Is there anything I can get or do for you?' Ellie held onto Maria's hand and felt the fingers curl round returning her clasp. 'I'm so sorry this had to happen to you and I'd do anything to put it right. You're my friend and, God knows, I need one. You've always been there for me. You saved my life once and were on your way to try and do it again. I thank you from the bottom of my heart, Maria.' Ellie felt a tear slide down her cheek but didn't lose Maria's hand to wipe it away.

Maria's mouth moved and Ellie bent closer to try and make

out the words. All she could make out was, 'it's nothing'. Ellie bowed her head and wept with her hands clasped round Maria's wishing with all her heart she could have a magic wand and make the whole sorry situation right again.

Claire sat alone in her cell and went back over her memories, both real and perceived, of the events leading up to her incarceration. Most of them had a dreamlike quality and were disjointed but the recent ones she could view with the utmost clarity. At least now she had a very small wash basin, toilet and a bed of sorts. It was a concrete pad that jutted out of the wall and a thin mattress was laid on top. There was a pillow and a blanket, and she sat with the blanket round her shoulders as it was chill in the concrete box. She had drunk her fill of water and managed to clean herself up a bit but she desperately wanted a shower and some clean clothes, but kept pushing that thought out of her mind. The worse she smelled the further away the guards would stand. Serves them right, she smiled. One meal had arrived, pushed through a slat in the base of the door. It had been a burger and some fries, so no imagination there. She would have eaten a 16oz rib-eye steak with all the trimmings all by herself if it had appeared. Needless to say, the burger had filled a gap and she kept telling herself she was full up and couldn't eat another morsel. There was no chance of keeping track of time in the cell, so it could have been midnight for all she knew. If the next meal was pancakes she would be spot on. There was also a dim light on, enough for her to see by but not enough to stop her sleeping and Claire was thankful for this. It didn't seem that they were going to use sleep deprivation as a weapon against her.

The code 'red book' kept coming into her mind. That was a code for 'you're on your own' and 'you're in deep cover', deep shit more like. There was no way out of this at the moment as Man in Charge was not telling her anything, plus she hadn't been charged with any crime. She didn't even know where she was and what branch of the Security Services had her incarcerated. She just had to sit it out as she couldn't escape from here. Claire suspected they would just gun her down without a thought and cover their tracks as no-one knew where she was. 'That's comforting,' she said aloud. So she whiled away an hour doing some exercises and press-ups to warm her up. It must be night as this seemed to tire her out and she felt sleepy. So, curled up on her mattress with the blanket round her, she drifted off.

In the middle of a particularly ferocious battle with the Zygon king who was falling back under the onslaught of her double-bladed battle sword, she felt a hand on her shoulder. Immediately she went to attack the King but it was one of the guards shaking her awake. He jumped back as Claire lashed out shouting her battle cry.

'Steady, lady, time to get up now. Don't go attacking me again as we've got you covered.' He pointed to his partner standing in the doorway holding a machine pistol.

Claire apologized to the man, 'Sorry, buddy, I was in the middle of a dream.' It didn't hurt to get the guards on her side. She rolled over and sat up with the blanket clutched round her shoulders. 'Is it morning? Do I get anything to eat?' She asked, aware of the rumblings in her stomach.

'You've got to put this on.' The guard gave her a blue jumpsuit.

'I'd like to shower first please,' she asked politely. 'Also can I have something to eat?'

The guard stood immobile.

'I'm not going to put that on till I shower, and I'm not going to put it on with you standing there watching me,' Claire stated, emphatically, kicking the plastic-wrapped jumpsuit to the other end of the cell. 'Please yourself.'

'Now listen lady.' The guard started forward. 'You'll do it now. Those are my orders.'

'Well, you listen, buddy, and listen good, fuck you. I want a shower and I want something to eat. Now! Am I making myself clear? You just trot back to whoever it is in charge and you tell him that. Okay?'

The guard turned to his friend in the doorway and they had a whispered conversation and then they both left, locking her in again. *Well that went well*, thought Claire, *nothing like a bit of 'détente'*. She didn't have to wait long before the slat in the door was opened and pancakes and bacon were pushed in on a cardboard fibre tray. Best of all there was a cup of coffee. It was steaming hot and smelled better than the most expensive perfume. Claire savoured every mouthful and chewed every morsel with relish, and mentally gave herself a high five for scoring another point. She must be worth something to them if they had caved in on that point.

The door opened again and the guard appeared again with a pair of handcuffs clutched in his meaty paw. 'Let me put these on without a fight and you can have a shower.' His buddy still had her covered with the machine pistol.

'Okay. No fight if I can get a shower. I'll also put the suit on.' She held her hands out in front of her. Another high five was ticked off in Claire's brain. *This is a 'win-win' situation now*, she thought. She was walked down an austere corridor to a shower block and motioned inside a cubicle still with her clothes and the cuffs on. 'So what am I supposed to do now?' she asked, waving her cuffed hands under the guard's nose. 'I can't take my clothes off, and I can't get the suit on, now can I?'

He breathed a sigh. 'Just don't try any funny business.' He unlocked the cuffs.

'I ain't laughing,' said Claire. The shower was glorious and she revelled in the hot water and the suds. It was all male-type shower gels but she didn't care a jot that she smelled of Adidas when she came out. The jumpsuit fitted her when she rolled up the arms and legs a bit and she felt a new woman when she emerged. The guard gave her a pair of flip flops and then cuffed her again. 'Off to see someone important are we?'

Silence from the guards.

Claire was feeling a bit cocky now after being allowed to shower and having eaten so she kept up a meaningless stream of questions as she was taken another way away from her cell. The guards wouldn't answer any of them but it made her feel good having a little bit of control over her surroundings. They marched down to an interview room identical to the first one she had seen but this one was pale blue décor rather than battleship grey and there were padded seats instead of the functional metal ones. The same chief sat behind the desk with an even thicker folder in front of him. There were two men in suits sitting alongside him and they were staring into space.

Claire felt quite chirpy now and sat up straight with her hands in her lap and a smile plastered on her face. 'Hiya, Mr… Sorry don't know your name, but that's probably classified anyway. Thanks for the food but I must say your chef is a bit unimaginative, you should fire him. Get that guy from the Ritz; he'd cook you up a storm.'

'Shut up.'

'No. You're not saying anything so I'll fill in the gaps till you have something interesting to say. Like I said before one of my middle names is Agnes.' Claire leaned forward and said in a whisper, 'Bit of a bummer now the name's gone out of fashion but it was all the rage in the '20s. I had a great aunt called…'

'Shut up and listen. These are agents with the Homeland Security force and they are to take over from us with your' –he searched for a word– 'care.'

'I'm so sorry I'll have to check out early, I was just beginning to enjoy my stay here now the plumbing has been sorted out.'

'If you don't shut up I'll have you gagged.'

Claire looked at him out of the corner of her eye. 'Sorry I don't do those sorts of games.'

Man in Charge totally ignored her. 'I'm signing your release papers now and you will leave immediately with the agents.' He closed his folder and even permitted himself to join in the game. 'Glad you enjoyed your stay, please recommend us to your friends.' There was a half smile playing at the corners of his mouth as he left.

'Okay, boys, so where are we going next?'

'We're going for a drive in the country, you'll enjoy it.'

Claire doubted very much that she would enjoy the drive at all, but the chances of escape were far greater on the outside than on the inside and she couldn't wait to get out of this place. 'Lead on,' she said as she stood.

Flanked by the agents she went out into blinding sunshine and into a car and they cleared the inner and outer perimeter fences and gates, and then the road stretched out over the horizon. Claire was in the back of the car and there was a wire grille separating her from the driver and his partner, also, there weren't any handles or latches on the inside of the doors. She could move about though and stretched out and dozed off. When she woke up they had left the desert behind and were in a wooded wilderness. Just the sort of place people drove to in camper vans to enjoy the solitude and the trees. They passed a campsite and Claire was suddenly aware she needed a bathroom break.

'Hey, guys, any chance of a bathroom break and something to eat and drink?' Claire shouted at them through the grille.

'Okay, next rest stop we'll get you something.

'Thanks, guys, you do want your prisoner alive not a dehydrated skeleton don't you?' Claire said, still feeling a lot better about her situation. She did notice the look that passed between the agents when she had said about being alive that suddenly wiped that all away. There wasn't going to be a Claire standing trial on a trumped up charge, there was going to be a Claire that was stiff and cold in a hastily dug shallow grave in the woods.

'Hey, make the bathroom break snappy as I'm busting in here. You must have cast-iron bladders.'

'Okay, okay, about another five miles. You just hang in there.'

Claire rapidly began to plan what she was going to do and run through it in slow motion in her mind. She began to breath evenly in and out and slowing her heart rate so that she would get the huge burst of adrenaline when she needed it, not now by getting jumpy. 'You're going to have to uncuff me as this suit isn't lady friendly. Don't worry I'm not going anywhere I'm just glad to be out of that prison.' Claire was trying to lull the agents into believing she wasn't a threat. 'Anyway, I can't run very fast as I've got my beach flip flops on.' To make the point she slid her foot out of the sandal and raised her foot wiggling her small toes so the agents could see. They looked at each other and smiled.

Sure, enough a rest stop came into view. It looked unkempt

and run-down with weeds growing out of the tarmac on the forecourt. An old man was sitting on a chair tilted back on two legs leaning against the wall. He appeared to be asleep with his hat pulled forward shading his face but dropped his chair forward and sat up straight as they pulled in.

The driver wound his window down as the man sauntered over. 'What can I do for you, folks?'

'Lady wants to use the bathroom and we'll have some food. Whaddya got?'

Claire piped up from the back, 'I'll have a load of carbs please, burger, sandwiches, anything to fill me up. I'm starving!'

'Bathroom's round the back. I'll do you some takeaway bags as cook's off today. Do you want gas?'

'No thanks, we're good. I'll park up for a moment and come and collect the food.'

The agents decided that the driver would go and get the food while the passenger would take Claire round the back to the bathroom. *Bad move*, thought Claire as the easiest way to conquer was to divide.

'Come on, guys, stop chatting. I really gotta go, now.'

As the passenger got out of the car Claire noticed his sidearm was just that. Not a shoulder holster but on his belt, best of all the top of the holster flap was snapped shut. That would give her another five or six seconds. That was a lifetime when the chips were down.

Claire walked sedately by the agent making sure she was on the same side as his gun. She walked close to him and tried to distract him by chatting. 'I'll bet the short order cook hasn't been here for a long time, just look at this place. At least he seems to have some bread so I'll get something.' She reached the door to the Ladies and turned holding out her hands in front of her. The agent fumbled in his pocket and came out with the key and Claire looked sideways at something over in the trees. The agent was holding both her hands with both of his as he inserted the key in the lock but his gaze followed Claire's.

CHAPTER SIXTEEN

As Claire felt the key snick in the handcuffs she held onto both of the agent's hands tightly, then bought her cuffed wrists up with all the strength she could muster. It was a perfect move executed with grace of a sledgehammer. The metal cuffs connected with the agent's chin and she heard his teeth smash together. She knew that the shockwave would travel up through his skull and would render him momentarily unconscious. That was all she needed and she delivered the knockout blow sideways as he fell. He fell, poleaxed, and even better hadn't uttered a sound. One cuff was dangling off but she ignored that and got the agent's gun and set off at a run into the trees. She headed for the higher ground as she would be able to see where her pursuer would come. It would only be a minute or two but she could cover a lot of ground in that time and the driver hadn't looked as if he had spent much time in the gym recently.

She paused and took a few deep breaths then began running again through the undergrowth. Branches lashed out at her and she quickly lost both her shoes but the adrenaline stopped her feeling any pain from her cut and bruised feet. After about a minute and a half she looked back and made out the driver carrying some white takeout bags back to the car. *Sloppy procedure*, she thought, *rookie mistake, they need to go back to training school. Never underestimate the opposition.* She took another deep breath and began to run again and the slope was much steeper now and the going was tougher but she ploughed on. She mentally counted off another sixty seconds as she ran, then stopped and looked back again.

Driver had deposited the bags and had obviously spotted his partner on the floor and he was running about with his gun unholstered. He paused and scanned the densely wooded slopes and Claire sank down into the undergrowth. She counted to thirty and allowed herself a peek at what was happening. The agent was standing with a mobile phone to his ear and the old man was standing by him, wiping the sweat from the brim of his hat, obviously enjoying the drama.

She had to stay put for a short while as any movement might be spotted and the old man would probably be woodcraft wise and see her in an instant. Like she had thought before, never underestimate the opposition. She fiddled with the handcuffs and got them off and stowed them in her pocket. They might come in useful at a later date. The gun was loaded and had six bullets, that was a bonus as she wouldn't have hesitated to wing the agents if she had to. One small problem was that she hadn't got any shoes and her feet were already a mess and she hadn't got a clue where she was other than she was somewhere in America. Deal with one problem at a time, the gun went into the other pocket and Claire surveyed her feet, messy. Bright ideas were in short supply right now and although she looked around, the flip flops were long gone. Claire sat and pondered the problem.

The agent, whose name was Tavares, had virtually cleaned out the old man's shop and had got various sandwiches and chocolate bars. It was sometimes good to be on the road instead of driving a desk, and be able to eat chocolate and doughnuts without his wife nagging at him all the time. He looked at his watch and thought it was nearly time to check in with that Russian. The money was safely in his bank account and the other half would be there when they sent photos of the woman in her grave. No problems there as it was only a few more miles and they would be at the place where they had dug a small pit for her. He was carrying her last meal and he hoped she'd enjoy it as it cost him twenty bucks. The old man was a robber in disguise but he hadn't argued, as what was twenty bucks when he would get another twenty thousand. He opened the car and put the food inside and left the door open as it was getting hot in there. He thought he'd better go see how the bathroom stop was going and he sauntered round the corner of the building.

Agent Tavares's mind went a complete blank when he saw his partner lying on the floor with blood dribbling out of the corner of his mouth. He bent down and felt a pulse but when he opened the bathroom door it was empty. Nothing. He caught sight of his face in the fly-spotted mirror and realized his mouth was hanging open. He shut it with a snap and drew his gun as he ran out. The only thoughts running through his mind were 'shit' and 'bitch' as he scanned the woods that ran for as far as the eye could see.

The old man wandered over and Agent Tavares pointed his gun at him. 'Did you see the lady?'

'Well now, I sure saw her when she got out of the car,' the old timer said slowly, enjoying every minute of winding the city boy up. 'What's wrong there boy?'

'She's gone. Took out my partner and gone.'

'Gone where?' The old guy removed his hat and carefully wiped the sweat from the inside band. He knew exactly where she had run as his keen eyes could see the trail she had left like it was a four lane highway. 'Well now, there ain't many places to go round here.'

'I know that, stupid old fool,' Agent Tavares added under his breath.

'She could have gone thataway,' the oldster said, pointing to the left, 'or thataway,' he added, pointing to his right not liking to be called stupid. 'Anyway she couldn't go far as it's all woods and bears up there.'

At the mention of the bears Agent Tavares blanched. He was no woodsman and didn't like nature in the raw at all. He thought for a moment. 'I'll get my partner in the car and get him some medical attention and we'll organize a search party. She's a dangerous criminal and if she comes back get the State Police straight away. Better still give me a call direct.' He fished a card out of his pocket.

'Sure will.' He pocketed the card to be lost later. 'Your best bet for a doctor is old Doc Willis and he lives about ten miles back there, the way you've just come. Go back and hang a left and you'll see his shingle. I'll give you a hand with your friend.' The old man smiled as he knew 'old Doc Willis' had probably been dead for many a long year but something didn't smell right with the two agents. He trusted his nose and his gut and it got him through thirty years of military service without a scratch. He wasn't as old as he looked as he was just chilling for a few months looking after his friends place. So he had let his beard grow and let his hair grow long. It was just to try the other side of life without the military precision and the buzz cuts he had all his life. He hadn't made his mind up yet but it was just an experiment. 'I'll give you a hand with your friend if you like?'

The offer was gratefully received and the agent went round the back with the old man hanging a few steps behind him. His partner was now sitting up and holding his jaw and his eyes still had a glazed look. They took an arm each and hauled him to his feet and they shuffled him to the car where he collapsed in the passenger seat. 'Don't you forget now, hang a left,' said the man, and raised his hat in salute as they drove off.

Claire sat with her back to a tree and was still trying to decide what to do about her feet. She thought she had all the time in the world as she had seen the agents drive off. It was time to plan her next move when she heard the unmistakable click of a gun and a bullet being put in the chamber. It was behind her and she raised her arms out sideways.

'Now you get up nice and slow,' said a young male voice and Claire couldn't imagine who it was. She carefully got up still facing away from the man. 'Now turn round,' the command came.

Claire turned round and was face to face with the old man from the garage. He was holding a massive rifle that looked as if it could bring down an elk, or at least cause it some serious damage from half a mile away. The voice didn't fit the persona at all and all Claire could think of to say was, 'A few minutes ago I saw you down by the garage. How did you get here so quickly?'

'You left a trail like a highway, so I just skirted round and come up behind you. You must be one dangerous lady to floor that agent then get away so quick. They told me you were bad news.'

'They have it all wrong. I'm no security threat but I work with the Security Forces from England. I've been in a prison somewhere but I've not been charged with any crime. I think those agents were out to kill me, you must believe me. I need to make just one phone call and it'll prove I'm who I say I am.' Claire was pleading with the man now.

'Okay,' he said slowly, 'but I'm going to ask you to turn out your pockets as they seem to be hanging rather heavy there.' He gestured with the rifle.

'In this pocket I have a pair of handcuffs.' Claire inserted two fingers into her pocket and bought them out. 'In this one I have a gun with six bullets in it, the safety is on. I took that from our friend when I got away.' She pointed to her pocket.

'Just pull it out real slow, barrel first. I'll shoot first and ask questions later.'

Claire did as she was bid and the gun ended up on the floor.

'Now you and me are going down to the garage and I'll check out your story. Start walking.'

Every step was a nightmare for Claire and her feet were a bloody mess when she reached the asphalt which was baking hot by this time. She looked at her captor. 'I don't think I can do this.' She showed him her feet by pulling up her trouser legs which were now sagging onto the floor.

'Well, you ain't going to run very far with feet like that,' he said shouldering the rifle. 'What if I trust you?'

'What do you mean?'

'Will you try to overpower me if I carry you? You could still be a very nasty lady, I don't know?'

Claire sank to her knees, every vestige of dignity gone. 'Please don't make me walk across that.' She gestured to the acres of tarmac. 'I promise, I really do, that I'll be good if you just let me make one phone call.'

'I always was a sucker for a pair of pretty eyes, come on then.' He got her to her feet and picked her up as if she weighed nothing. He strode to the house and deposited her inside the door. 'Through the back.' He gestured to the door to the living quarters.

Claire hobbled through and sank gratefully into a chair. She looked around and it was totally different to the unkempt appearance of the outside. Everything was neat and orderly and there was a coffee pot bubbling away on the stove. Books were lined up precisely and towels folded and the bed was made to hotel standards. 'Just who are you?'

He sat down and removed his hat and Claire could see that there weren't that many lines on his face and his hairline hadn't receded. He placed the rifle within easy reach and said, 'Suppose you tell me the whole story, right from the beginning. We'll have a cup of coffee to help it go down. Now mind, I'm very good at telling when people are lying, so be sure and tell me the truth.'

'I'll go with the coffee and I'll tell you the whole tale, right from the beginning if you've got time to listen,' she quizzed.

He put the rifle under one arm and got two mugs and the coffee pot and poured her one and pushed it over. He sat at the other end of the table taking no chances he might get a face full of scalding coffee. 'Start talking.'

Claire sipped the brew and felt it make its way down and revive her. She started from the very beginning and related the whole saga right up to her incarceration without charge and the two dodgy agents. 'So you see all I need is one phone call and I'm out of here. Simple.'

'I actually believe you,' he said. 'I must be mad but I do. I didn't like those agents one bit and I'm usually a good judge of character. There was something about them that didn't ring true. Don't ask me what it was but it was there. In answer to your question, no, I'm not really the old guy running a gas station. I've just come out of military service and I'm just chillin' for a bit to see where I want to go next. Thirty years is a long time, a lifetime really and I just wanted to walk on the wild side for a bit. So I pass as an "old guy" and I'm just looking after the gas station for a few months. I was in the Military Police so I've interrogated loads of people and I can tell if they're lying and I don't think you are, so you can have your phone call. I'll also get some things to make your feet a bit easier.' He put the rifle back in the hooks over the door and poured Claire another cup of coffee. 'I'll get you something to eat out of the shop and you can use the phone.' He gestured to the phone by the bed.

'I thought you must be military or something like that,' said Claire, hobbling to the phone. 'A bed made like that and everything in its place just shouts training and order.'

'Some habits just die hard, some don't,' he said, fingering the beard.

Claire quickly dialled Phil's number and got straight through. 'I'm okay,' she said, breathlessly, as she had never been so glad to hear his voice. 'It's a long story but I've got to get out of here now, I think there's going to be a search party organized soon and they're going to be coming after me with all guns blazing. They just want me dead.' She listened to Phil switch to leader mode as her rescuer came back through the door with a hot boxed burger and fries. 'I'm going to hand you over to… What's your name?'

'Matt.'

'I'm going to hand you over to Matt and he'll tell you exactly where I am 'cos I haven't got a bloody clue and he's just turned up with food.' Claire swapped the phone for the food and began to eat ravenously. The coffee had given an edge to her appetite and she realized she was starving.

'So that's eighteen hundred hours and we'll meet you at the airstrip.' Matt nodded to Claire and she shrugged as the extraction plan was relayed to Matt. 'We'll be there.' He looked at Claire. 'Anything else you want to say?' Claire thought of a million things that she wanted to say but decided to save them till later. She shook her head with a mouthful of food. Matt hung up. 'Seems you were telling the truth, we've got to get you out of here fast as those agents will be back soon with a posse. Eat up and I'll just put a quick bandage round your feet and you can have a few painkillers to tide you over and we'll go. There'll be a chopper waiting for you at the nearest airstrip but we've got to move now.'

As Claire gulped the food down her, Matt quickly bound up her feet after giving them an antiseptic spray which stung and made tears blur Claire's vision. 'I can't thank you enough, you've saved my life,' she said, as she stood upright. 'I'll make sure you're paid back somehow, I don't know how but I'll do it.' She planted a kiss on the hairy cheek.

Supported by Matt she gingerly walked outside and he led her to an outhouse and threw the door open and revealed a Harley Davidson motor bike. It gleamed as the sun caught it and Claire just gasped. 'I've only seen these, never ridden one, wow!'

'Put this on.' Matt handed her an old coat that buried her and a crash helmet. 'Get on.' She did, as he gunned the bike and they roared off. It was the biggest thrill in the world for Claire and she held on with her arms round Matt's waist as they burned rubber round the winding mountain roads as if the beasts from Hell were on their tail. As they crested a hill, Claire saw a small airstrip laid out below with tiny toy planes set in neat rows glinting white in the sun. A helicopter was circling in preparation to land and Matt went even faster down the hill towards it. They drew up by the chain-link fence and Claire eased the helmet from her head. 'I thought you were going to deliver a body the rate you were going,' she said, as she drew a deep breath of relief.

'Not to worry, I'd have been at the crash scene first.' He grinned back at her and they proceeded at a sedate pace towards the chopper idling on the tarmac. Phil jumped out as they drew close and Claire got off the bike. She was engulfed in a bear hug that took her a bit by surprise but she enjoyed it nevertheless and returned it with change.

Phil extricated himself and extended his hand to Matt. 'Can't thank you enough mate, you've done the UK a real service. Thanks again for getting one of our best operatives out of the clutches of Homeland Security.'

'I'm not sure they were agents, or if they were, they were dirty. It just didn't seem right somehow and the lady's story checks out, so that makes me surer there's something going on. There's going to be a big search party soon and I've got to get back as I don't want them thinking an oldster rides a Harley. I've got to get this baby under cover again.' He lovingly patted the petrol tank. 'They did give me this though.' He fished in his pocket and bought out the card the driver had given him. 'Don't know if it'll be of any use but you never know.'

Phil took the card and put it away carefully. 'If you want a short break we'll fly you over to St. Lucia for a day or so and you can update us on the rings you run round the search party. I'd like to get to know you better as I know you're out of the military now but a useful pair of hands in the US of A. could always come in for the future if you're interested?'

Matt pondered for a moment then said, 'I'll think about it as I'm still chillin' but you never know, I might get bored.' He smiled and sketched a salute before putting on his helmet and with a throaty roar he disappeared.

CHAPTER SEVENTEEN

Phil took Claire's arm and helped her into the chopper passenger seat. 'I'm driving, as you and airborne objects don't seem to get on to well. You either hijack them or trash them so just sit back and enjoy the ride.'

Phil climbed in and went through the take-off procedure and they were soon wheeling away through the impossibly blue sky to St. Lucia.

Everyone was overjoyed to see Claire back safe and sound and Phil immediately put a call in to London and bought them up to speed. He thought that behind the measured tones on the phone he sensed an overwhelming relief that she was back. London's hands had been virtually tied behind their backs as Claire had technically committed a crime on US soil by hijacking a plane, even though she had been drugged and abducted by what appeared to be a crime network operating in America. Memos must have been flying backwards and forwards in their droves but the US had stonewalled the entreaties. So Phil had extracted a criminal that the US didn't recognize officially was in their jurisdiction. So be it, but Claire wasn't going to set foot on American soil for a long time to come.

Robert gave Claire a hug. 'Like the new style but not much on the couture,' he said. 'The colour is okay but the fit, what can one say!' Nigel laughed as Claire hitched up her sleeves again.

'Don't get sassy, I've had enough for one day.' Claire plumped herself down on a chair and took a long drink of some very good coffee. 'I won't be getting my dancing pumps on yet though.' She pushed her bandaged feet out in front of her. Phil bent down and gently unwrapped the bloody bandages and sucked air in through his teeth. Claire winced as the dressings stuck to the cuts. 'I had to run through the forest with flip flops on and I lost them. Matt gave them an antiseptic spray and put the bandages on, but it was all we could do in such a short time. They'll heal up okay but they need a doctor to have a look and I'd like a few painkillers right now.' Claire squeezed her eyes shut as a few of the lacerations opened up.

Jack jumped to his feet. 'I'll go and get a wheelchair and we'll take you to A & E to see a doc.'

Claire nodded gratefully and settled back. 'You'll have to fill me in on what's been going on and what the next plan is, I'm a bit out of touch.' She laughed.

'Plenty of time for that, one job at a time,' Phil said, as Jack came in pushing a chair.

'Hop in,' said Jack, wheeling the chair closer and Claire duly hopped. He set off at a jog to A&E and Claire was clutching the sides of the chair and laughing at him making motorbike noises round the corners. The Department was virtually empty and they took their place in the short queue. Jack wheeled her into the cubicle that came free and waited for the doctor to arrive. The curtain was pushed back and Sister Bertha came in carrying a clipboard. She stopped as she saw Claire and Jack but quickly recovered and flicked over some papers.

'You have wounds to your feet, yes?' Her English wasn't the best. 'You are worker?' she said, eyeing the jump suit. 'We clean up your feet and you go straight home, yes?'

'They hurt a lot but I don't know if there is anything in the cuts,' said Claire. 'So perhaps a quick clean up and I'll be gone. You must be the new Sister in Charge, pleased to meet you.'

Claire extended her hand.

Sister Bertha shook it with a very limp grasp and Claire stifled the impulse to wipe her hand after the contact. 'Please to get on the bed and I'll have a look.'

Claire dutifully hopped on the bed and her feet stuck out from the ragged ends of the jump suit like they had been attacked by an army of rats. They were torn and bloody and Sister Bertha said, 'How you do this? You walk on blades?'

'It's a very long story but I won't bore you with it now, but please just check for thorns and give them a spray of something and we'll be gone,' Claire said, liking Sister Bertha less and less with each passing minute. Sister Bertha swung a large light over Claire's feet and began poking and prodding and Claire reached for Jack's hand as the probing went on.

'I don't see any problem for you at all. I will spray then wrap them up then you go.'

Claire looked at Jack and they exchanged glances as the Sister seemed to want them gone at the earliest opportunity. 'Okay, fine, just do that,' said Claire, now wanting out as soon as possible. The spray stung again as Claire's feet were turned bright yellow with the stain and dressings were applied that made shoes an impossibility.

'You not get them wet. Keep bandage on for two days then change. Doctor at home will do that,' said Sister Bertha with finality as she abruptly turned and went.

'Okay, I not get them wet,' said Claire in a parody of the Sister. 'What do you make of that then?' she asked Jack. 'She wasn't exactly the soul of humanity and compassion was she?'

'I don't think she likes us at all, but she's new to the job and has been flung in the deep end a bit. Another Russian from the Sister House but I'll admit she wasn't very welcoming or very delicate with what she did. Your feet must hurt like hell.'

'They do a bit,' said Claire ruefully, 'but she never even offered me a prescription for any painkillers or anything. Bitch,' muttered Claire under her breath. 'Do you think she was anything to do with the slave trafficking? I wouldn't put it past her as I didn't like the woman one bit. But then again you can't like everyone can you?' Claire swung her legs off the bed and gingerly made it to the wheelchair. 'I suppose a shower is out of the question now as I can't even dip my toe. I'll have to have a bath with my legs in the air. Don't even go there Jack,' Claire said, as she read a smile on Jack's face that mirrored lewd thoughts.

They made their way back to the cafeteria but everyone had gone. 'I suppose I'd better get myself a bed and some clothes sorted out,' said Claire, 'I can't keep looking like a "worker" after all, now can I?' They trundled off again to the guest rooms and found that the team was crammed into Phil's room and a muted buzz was coming through the door. With difficulty, Claire was manhandled through the door and deposited in the place of honour on the bed where she sank with a sigh of relief. 'So what gives guys?' she said when there was a lull.

Phil took the floor. 'Nigel and Robert say that they think this place is bugged up to the hilt but they can't find anything in here so we're having this as our centre at the moment. We've solved the initial task with the rare manuscript and it's all sorted that it's officially on loan now, so everybody's happyish with that. The latest problem is that we uncovered the sex trade trafficking and we seem to have stalled on that one.'

Claire piped up, 'When I was a guest of the President I did get one phone call relayed to me from England telling me in code that I was in deep cover but that all went pear shaped as I was taken by two supposed agents from Homeland Security. I thought for one moment I was a goner as I'm sure they were going to bury me, literally. I still don't know what the deep cover was supposed to be as I was imprisoned and had no contact with anyone, so I just had to sit it out. It's thanks to Matt that I'm here now, he was one of the good guys, but I don't think I'm going to be welcome in the States anytime soon.'

'No you're not,' said Phil, 'the deep cover was to do with the sex slaves but that trail seems to have gone cold for the moment. If those two agents were dirty then we don't know how many more are as well so we can't go pressing buttons with them in America. Anybody got any ideas?' Silence reigned.

Agent Tavares raised a dust storm as he drove his injured partner to the Doc's. He found the turning and soon came upon a small town. It was a very small town indeed and the Main Street was less than half a mile long. He pulled over and asked a passer-by where Doc Willis lived and the passer-by just smiled and said that he had been misinformed as the 'old Doc' had been gone these last nine years. Tavares hit his hand hard on the steering wheel and fought to control his temper. Was everyone in this neck of the woods retarded! Politely he said, 'Please could you tell me where the nearest doctor's is as my friend has had an accident?'

The passer-by leaned down to look at the passenger who was conscious but had blood all down the side of his face staining his shirt front and livid bruises were just beginning to make their appearance. 'Looks like you need Doc O'Brian, go back the way you come and hang a right, it's just down there 'bout half a mile. Can't miss it.' The passer-by strolled off after imparting the information.

Tavares swung the car in a U-turn ignoring the honking from

a truck making its way sedately up the road. He gunned off and swerved round the right turn and found the doctor's with no problems. Under his breath he was cursing the 'old timer' from the gas station as he heaved his friend onto his feet and into the surgery. The doctor was in and saw Tavares and his partner immediately.

'Now what have we here,' the doc said, assuming a professional demeanour. 'Sit him down there and tell me all about it.'

Agent Tavares fished his badge out of his pocket and thrust it in the doctor's face. 'This guy needs medical attention now and I'm on the trail of an escaped criminal so I can't sit with him and hold his hand. Just do what you can and I'll be back in a few hours to pick him up. He got into a fight and got bashed up bad, I'll get him to a hospital as soon as I get back, just keep him alive till then.'

'No fear of that, it looks as if he's got concussion,' the doctor said, shining a light into his partner's eyes to check for pupil contraction. 'I'll patch him up and he can lie down for a bit and I'll monitor him, but he should really go to a hospital right now. I can call an ambulance if you like?' The doctor put his hand out to his desk phone.

Agent Tavares put his hand over the doctor's. 'No need, he's had worse and survived. Like I said, just keep him here and I'll be back in a few hours. The case shouldn't take more than that to wrap up,' he added confidently. 'I'll be back soon,' he stressed as he exited, leaving the doctor staring after him.

On the way back up to the gas station, Tavares was formulating a plan. He hoped that the old guy hadn't called the local Sheriff's office and reported an escaped criminal in the vicinity. What he wanted was to get the job done, dusted, and the body buried as soon as possible. He'd deal with the old timer in his own time as for some reason he'd led him on a wild goose chase. He drove fast and screeched to a halt by the gas station that seemed to be deserted. The weeds looked even more unkempt than before and the whole place had an air of desertion and desolation. He suddenly got a prickle at the back of his neck and the hairs on his arms stood up. Something wasn't right somehow, but he couldn't put his finger on it but his gut was telling him likewise. Very carefully he got out of the car and looked around then made his way to the shop. His hand went to his gun and made sure the flap on the holster was undone and the butt rested on his palm. His hands had started to sweat for some reason.

'Hello,' he shouted, but the sound echoed back to him. 'Anybody there,' he shouted again as he reached the shop door and pushed it open. The bell jingled and he heard a shuffling sound and the old guy appeared rubbing sleep out of his eyes underneath the brim of his hat. Tavares wondered if the guy bathed in it.

'What can I get yer?' His rheumy eyes squinted at Tavares. 'Oh it's you agin' I ain't seen nothin' of that gel you lost.' He rubbed his eyes again. 'Appears I must have dropped off after all that excitement earlier. You got a posse with you this time?' The old guy peered out of the grimy window.

'You led me on a wild goose chase to "Old Doc Willis's" place. Seems he's been dead and gone for years. Why did you do that?'

'Mighty sorry 'bout that, my memory ain't what it used to be. Thought he was still up and runnin'. Your friend okay?'

'Yes, and no thanks to you,' said Tavares acidly. He didn't deal too well with old timers in the grip of dementia. Suddenly he thought better of it and decided this guy could maybe be of some use after all as he didn't want to go ploughing through the forest on his own. 'Looks like I need a bit of help after all. You look like the kinda man who knows these woods like the back of your hand.'

'Sure do.'

'What say me and you go on a little hunting trip. You can be my tracker. Would you like that? I'll pay you.'

The old man appeared to think it over and then said, 'You'll be needin' another gun as there's bears in them woods.'

'Have you got one? I mean a rifle that'll stop a bear.'

'Sure do.'

'Well would you like to go and get it then,' said Tavares thinking that the conversation was a bit like pulling teeth.

'Sure will.'

Tavares turned away looking at the fly-spotted adverts on the wall, thinking they would do well in a museum, while the man shuffled off again into the back room. He was suddenly on full alert as he heard a bullet snick into a chamber of a rifle. He stood for a moment then turned slowly to see a big well-oiled carbine pointing unwavering at his chest. The hat was gone and a pair of steely blue eyes was fixing him with a stare.

'I wouldn't go for that little pop gun you got there. How about just easing it out with your finger then drop it on the floor?'

Tavares was stunned and he just stood and stared. True, the man facing him with an easy stance had the same clothes on and the same long hair and beard but he now noted the muscular forearms and the physique of a man forty years younger. His hand shook as he did as he was asked and the gun fell to the floor.

'Just give it a kick over here.' He complied with the request. 'Now how's about you and me having a little conversation, nice and calm, maybe then you can tell me the full story?'

Tavares wasn't a hero, particularly when he had a very big rifle pointing at him, but he began to bluster, 'Now look here, I'm with Homeland Security and I'm on the trail of that woman that escaped this morning. You'd better just lower that gun and then we can get on with trailing her. I'll show you my badge.' He made to move his hand to his jacket.

'Stop right there.' The gun lifted slightly and Tavares could see right down the barrel.

'I know who you are as you gave me your card and I don't doubt the lady in question has caused you a whole lot of problems, but,' Matt paused, 'it seems you were taking her somewhere. Where were you taking her? I don't recall any facilities round here and you were going the wrong way for the airfield. So where were you going?'

Tavares couldn't think of a good answer to that one. A shallow grave in the middle of the woods didn't seem the right thing to say so he stayed silent.

'Like I said, I think you and me should have an in depth conversation about what you were doing and where you were going, don't you?' Matt moved round the counter and pulled a chair out with his foot from a Formica table and gestured Tavares to sit down. His eyes never left the other man. Tavares sat down heavily. 'So to start again, just where were you taking the lady?'

'Who are you anyway? I thought you were some old timer.'

'Bit of a mistake to make, wasn't it? You're like a lot of people, you only see what you want to. If you had really looked and seen then you wouldn't have gone by your first impression. So back to the first question, where were you taking the lady? This is going to get boring very quickly and I don't do "bored" very well so you'd better start talking now.' Matt leaned on the counter, still with the gun pointed at Tavares.

Tavares still didn't answer as his mind was racing trying to concoct a plausible story.

'Oh and don't try to lie as I can spot that a mile away,' said Matt, watching Tavares's eyes dart from side to side. 'I'm beginning to get bored now. I shall begin counting down from five. Five…four…'

Tavares was now in a panic. 'You're going to kill me aren't you? Just get it over with now.' He squeezed his eyes tightly shut.

'No, I've never killed a man in my life and I'm not going to start that now. When I've finished with you may wish that I had. You may even beg me to, but I won't. Three.'

The threat percolated through to the agent's brain and he believed the man implicitly. He wouldn't kill him but what state he would be in at the end would be anybody's guess.

'Two…'

'Okay, okay, I'll talk, but you've signed my death warrant if I do,' Tavares said all this in a rush and he shuddered.

'Got yourself in a bit of a mess then, but I'll tell you that I've already heard one side of the story from the lady and yours had better match up.'

Tavares sat up straight. 'You found her. Where is she?'

'Nothing to do with you, so start talking and I'll just listen.'

The agent began to talk and the whole sorry story of ineptitude unfolded. He hadn't said who was his paymaster and had glossed over that part describing receiving his orders from just a voice on the phone. Matt didn't believe him but thought he had a good part of the tale so he decided to probe a bit deeper. 'So you were going to take out this lady and bury her body in the woods and you were doing this for money.'

'No, my family will be hurt if I don't do as they say. I did one job for money then they had me and I can't get out now.'

'Who's "'they'"?'

'Some Russian. It seems this lady had caused him a lot of grief and he wanted her gone. She had endangered some operation or other and he wanted her removed. It was just lucky she was on American soil and I was the nearest.'

'So there's more of you?'

'I suppose so, don't know.' Tavares had relaxed a bit and sat with his hands loosely clasped in his lap. He was between a rock and a very hard place and couldn't mentally deal with it, so he just talked.

'Do you know what this "operation" was?'

'Don't know, maybe something to do with drugs.' Tavares shrugged and Matt believed him.

'Could it have been something to do with sex trade workers?'

'Possibly.'

'How about you and me do a deal?' Matt lowered the gun barrel about an inch. Tavares jumped at the chance to save his skin. A pissed off Russian didn't even come close to iron man here pointing a gun at him. 'How about we tell your Russian friend that with my help we tracked down the lady and you finished the job, but, and it's a big but, you find out where the girls were taken? Which city will do, that's all.'

Tavares thought about it. He could get some information from the network and find out where the drugs or girls had been taken. It seemed a small price to pay for his life. If it ever came to light that he had lied to the Russian, he was a dead man but he'd be one anyway if he didn't do the trade. His life for information, or at least the rest of his life in a wheelchair. He was in no doubt this guy would hunt him down and he wouldn't have to look very far. 'Okay,' he said slowly. 'So I get you the information on where the last shipment of drugs or girls went and you'll leave me alone?'

'Let's just make that the last shipment of girls and I'll leave you alone.' The gun barrel went down another inch. 'Oh, there is a time limit on this, you've got thirty-six hours, not a minute more. You understand?'

'That's not much time.'

'So start looking over your shoulder.'

'Okay,' said Tavares, thinking furiously on how he could weasel out of this.

'I'll ring you once in thirty-six hours' time. I've got your number anyway. I can fix your phone to anywhere you are so don't try to run. Rest assured I'll find you. Don't bother coming back here, I'll be gone, long gone, and you'll never find me. Don't try and give me false info either as I'll come back and haunt you. Deal?'

Tavares was roped and branded and could only nod. 'Thirty-six hours then and I'll do my best to find out.'

'No trying, just do it. Now go before I get really bored.' Matt lowered the gun and the agent stood shakily to his feet and edged out the door then ran to his car and fumbled with his keys then drove off.

Matt smiled as that had been easier than he thought. The agent wasn't a hard man at all and a few threats had reduced him to jelly. He must have had a very active imagination thought Matt as he collected his gear and went to his beloved bike. He may come up with the goods or he may not, it was a wild card but worth playing and he would lay a bet now the agent would get the information he wanted. Matt got his phone and placed a call to Phil to tell him of the turn of events and, as he suspected, Phil was over the moon as suddenly they had a lead on where the girls had been taken. He said that he had also thought over Phil's offer of coming over to St. Lucia for a few days and taking in a little sun and sea. It was perhaps better he disappeared altogether for a short while in case Tavares got any big ideas. So, Matt gunned the engine and made his way down the winding mountain roads again to the air field.

CHAPTER EIGHTEEN

Matt's call came through when the team was still all crammed into Phil's room at the guest house. 'Well that's certainly interesting,' he said, as he killed the call. 'Matt's coming over to see us for a few days, anybody got a razor he could borrow? You'll see why when he lands. He says he ran into one of the agents that tried to take Claire and thinks he's persuaded him to help us find out where the girls have been taken. He's given the guy thirty-six hours to come up with the goods and thinks it's better if he has a short holiday in case it all gets messy. So we have got a break now and we need to follow this up with all we've got.'

Everyone looked pleased at this bit of information but Jack said, 'I'm continually getting bad vibes about this place, I don't know if anyone else feels the same but I think we've outstayed our welcome. Maybe we should go back down to the resort. Alistair and Rory will be out of here in a day or so and Maria is now on the mend. I don't know, but I know I'd feel happier.'

Phil looked round the group and everyone nodded. 'I'll go and see Sister Bertha today and we'll decamp down to Fortune's place again if he's got the room. Start gathering your gear, and Nigel, can you get Matt shipped in to wherever we are? One thought for everyone to ponder over the next few hours is that "the Russian" seems to be cropping up all over the place and I'm pretty sure now it's our old friend Valentin Salnikov. It's good that we can close down the operation here and hopefully get the girls back but he'll just open up shop somewhere else. We'll go all out to prove the links, but it won't be easy. Just everyone have a think about it and we'll have another chat soon.' Phil stood and pulled out his phone to make the call to Fortune.

As if on cue there was a tap on the door and a sister stood there hovering from one foot to the other. 'Sister Bertha says to give you this.' She proffered a folded piece of paper. Phil took it and looked at it. It was an invoice for their stay in the guest house and it appeared the rooms were now needed for the next guests. Phil nodded at the sister and told her that everything was in order and he would be down to pay the bill directly and she left looking very relieved.

'She certainly wants us out pronto,' said Phil dialling Fortune's number. It was answered on the first ring and Phil explained that they had to leave and asked if Fortune had any space.

'Your rooms are still as you left them, my friend, and you're welcome back to stay with Fortune and Honey. We'll have another party now you come back to us.'

Phil smiled at the irrepressible Fortune and agreed that it would be worth a party when all this was over. He assured him they would be down within the day and could he put up another man who was flying over from the States as he spoke?

'Sure thing, my friend, sure thing. He may have to share but it'll be a good room, a big one.'

'I'm sure it will be fine and thank you, Fortune, once again for all your help. You've certainly had an eventful birthday.' Phil rang off and said they could all move back as soon as they wanted to. Ellie shot off to tell the news to Rory and Alistair and was thankful to be leaving the hospital. She was sure that they would both be glad to be back in civilization. Jack helped Claire back into her wheelchair and they trundled off to collect her stuff and see if she could manage a bath and change before they left. Jack had already decided they he would hijack a wheelchair for a few days to make Claire's life easier. As Robert and Nigel were heading for the door, Phil called them back. 'I think you should go over to the States and keep an eye on Agent Tavares. Just try and listen in on his conversations and check his bank balance, things like that. Maybe give him a friendly wave just to focus his thoughts if he seems to be going off track. Nothing too overt, just be like his shadow for a few days then disappear. If we get the information we want then you'll be in place to fly wherever he says and you can get the girls out, but be careful there seems to be a lot of money flying about and your lives won't be worth jack shit if you mess up. Also be careful if you do locate the girls as you'll need help from the proper authorities over there and they'll need to be repatriated or at least given a chance of a new identity if they want it. There seems to be a lot of dirty money and dirty agents, just be careful.'

Robert and Nigel looked at each other and Robert said, 'We'll leave right away as tourists and put the willies up Tavares. We'll pick him clean then spit out the bones and to be honest we'll enjoy that. Promise we'll never lay a finger on him but we'll get that information if he doesn't come through. Before I leave, though, I've got to go and see Maria, she's talking a bit now and I've been visiting her.'

Nigel and Phil exchanged a glance and Nigel wrapped his arms round himself and gave himself a hug. It was lucky Robert didn't see him as he went out the door and he hadn't said anything to anyone how he was beginning to feel about Maria but everyone had guessed already. He'd been spotted sitting by her bed and holding her hand and had gently kissed her brow when she had been comatose. Robert was due for some serious ribbing but that could wait until they had completed their mission.

There was one thing Phil had decided to do before he left the guest house and he put another call to the Chief of Police and nodded satisfied that the Chief agreed. A team of welders would be dispatched to the caves behind the hospital and all the steel doors would be welded shut, forever. The cage doors would be welded shut and the printing presses disabled beyond repair. The place would be sealed off. No-one at any time in the future would be able to access the hell hole, it would be gone. He would also order the lava pipe sealed up so that no-one could get in that way. Hopefully the place would pass from memory and all the misery would be buried deep in the mountain to stay there forever.

Valentin relaxed as soon as he had cleared Caribbean airspace and gave orders not to refuel as usual in Great Britain but to fly to Madrid and refuel there. Best keep away from England for the moment, he thought, as he went back to perusing the paperwork that had been purloined from Alistair's PAs and computers. Karl had done a good job and there was a lot to keep him amused throughout the eight hour flight. He noted with interest that Alistair had been investing heavily in stem cell research. He didn't understand a lot about the science behind the concept but he knew many breakthroughs had been made recently and it could possibly be the 'magic bullet' that could cure many ills including cancer. This tied in neatly with Alistair's pharmaceutical companies and it would seem that he was about to steal a march on competitors within the next few years if the research kept heading down the same path. Alistair was already a very rich man but he would be a phenomenally rich one if this gamble paid off. He would be able to have royalties from virtually every tablet, capsule and treatment sold and he also owned major shares in many private hospital groups so his holdings could be gold bricks. *Clever man*, thought Valentin as he perused the papers further.

Valentin's own portfolio veered more towards the sex trade, nightclubs and drugs. He also dabbled in small arms for war-torn countries and did a fair trade in conflict diamonds. He hired out small mercenary armies for a good price and was getting to be a bigger fish in oil trading. He maintained his position mainly through having a lot of information on various people at the top and they knew he wasn't afraid to use it. This was hard work as with the fall of the Iron Curtain and trading with Europe a lot of people had been replaced fairly quickly. He had to keep his eye on the ball and be aware of who were the rising stars in the Russian firmament. But, he paused for thought, if Alistair had built a big portfolio that was outwardly legitimate then he could use this information and perhaps set up his own competition. He would be well ahead with all this information and it would be an easy matter to call in a few favours and start now.

There was already a shipment of girls that were destined to be used in his brothels and clubs but they could be side tracked to be used in some dubious clinic as human guinea pigs for the research. They would probably fetch as much there and he would be able to tie some of the clinics to his portfolio with ropes of steel. Valentin beckoned a PA forward to begin to do some research into who was doing what to whom in the stem cell world.

In Atlanta the girls sat on the edges of their beds in a dormitory. They were still in the same clothes as they had been incarcerated in. They sat talking in hushed tones as they surveyed the bars up the windows and the single naked electric light bulb that shone day and night. They had a blanket and a pillow each and there was a partition at the end of the room with a toilet and wash basin, but that was all. Security cameras were placed high on the walls and the blinking red lights told them that they were functioning and all their movements were being watched.

'I don't want to be here,' sobbed a younger girl about fourteen years of age. Her hair was lank and fell over her face and a little pink hair slide of a cat was hung loosely tangled in the back. 'I want to go home, pleeeease.' She subsided into wailing sobs until one of the older girls put her arm round her and held her close. The youngster collapsed against her and clung on for dear life.

'Well, you should have thought of that before you signed up for the "job" in France then', said the oldest girl of sixteen. 'We all thought it was legit and we would be waitresses or something. Looks like we're not going to be serving coffees after all.'

The young girl sniffled. 'What do you mean?'

'I mean that we're going to be used in clubs and things as prostitutes.'

The young girl sat up straight and looked at the oldest girl who probably wasn't more than a few years older than herself but her heavily smeared make up and cheap tarty clothes told of a different former existence. 'We've got to go with men?' The question made the older girl smile. 'I've never been with a man before, but I did kiss Grego on the lips. The man said he would let me get a good job then I could help my family, we haven't got much.'

'All you've got to do is think about something else while it's happening and then it's not so bad.'

'I still want to go home now. Where are we anyway?'

'No idea, princess, but I don't think you'll be going home

soon.' At these words the girls exchanged glances and a few tears began to flow.

There were heavy footsteps along the corridor outside and the door was unlocked and a tray of food was put on the floor just inside the room. A large woman stood there and surveyed her charges with her meaty hands on her hips. Her gaze rested on the young girl who had pushed her hair from her face and was eyeing the food. 'You.' She pointed with a fat finger and the girl looked around at her companions but they all looked away. 'Come here,' she ordered. There was a language barrier but the young girl knew exactly what she wanted. She stood and pulled her skirt down over her scrawny legs and walked hesitantly towards the woman.

'Go', said the eldest girl, 'remember, don't think of what is happening, just think of something else.'

The fat woman waited by the door then got the young girl by the arm and pulled her into the corridor, locking the door behind her. 'Come on, we're going to make you pretty now,' she said, raking her eyes up and down the girl's body assessing her. The girl cringed under her gaze and tried to make herself as small as possible, but she was dragged to another room with a shower and a bath. *Such luxury*, the young girl thought as she surveyed the plumbing. There were even some towels and some of the luxurious shower and bath products she'd only seen in adverts. 'Wash,' the woman said, and mimed showering or bathing. She pushed a towel into the girl's hands and mimed taking her clothes off. 'Now.' The woman nodded and smiled as if it was okay and she wasn't a threat. The girl sighed with relief as all they wanted her to do was to be clean so she peeled off the rank garments as the woman switched on the shower and the hot water filled the bathroom with steam. The shower was glorious and the girl revelled in the seemingly limitless heated water which was in itself unheard of. She tried all the different products and felt the grime and filth wash away. The woman had gone but the girl hadn't even noticed until she came back with some new clothes. The woman swung the shower curtain back and switched the shower off and handed the towel to the girl who tried to cover up her nakedness. The woman gestured to the clothes and the girl looked at them in surprise. They were schoolgirl's clothes with a short pleated skirt and hair ribbons. There was a blazer with a logo on the breast pocket and some frilly knickers. The woman plumped herself down on a stool that creaked under her weight and sat silent. On top of the pile of clothes sat the pink cat hair slide.

 The woman dried her hair with a hairdryer and put it in two ponytails with the ribbons and the hair slide was pinned at the front. The girl tried to say that she didn't want to wear the childish clothes but the torrent of Russian went unheeded and her arm was bruised by the strong fingers that yanked her this way and that. Eventually she complied as it was easier and she was surveyed by the woman who squinted her piggy eyes and made her turn round to look at her back. When she was satisfied with a few tweaks to her hair, the girl was led to another room containing a bed and a chair. She was pushed down onto the chair and a school satchel was placed on her lap.

 The girl clutched the satchel and launched into another Russian tirade but was stopped by the woman putting her finger to her lips and making a slicing motion across her neck. This left the girl in no doubt that she would be hurt, and hurt badly if she tried to make a fuss. Two tears started at the corner of the girl's eyes and left two trails down her cheeks but the woman only smiled as this was the picture she wanted to create.

A man came into the room and he was a stout man who wore a suit. He nodded when he saw the girl and licked his flabby lips. He reminded the girl of a former headmaster and she sat silent with her eyes wide as the woman sidled out of the door leaving them together. The man extended his hand and the girl put her satchel down and went hesitantly towards him.

The fat woman crossed her arms and leaned against the wall outside of the room and waited. It was very quiet and she stood up straighter and nervously fingered the wad of American dollars in her pocket. Then the screams began and she smiled as she walked away.

In America Robert and Nigel sat drinking a coffee and playing the latest game on a laptop. They looked for all the world like a couple of nerdy dropouts from college and they had their backpacks stuffed under their chairs. The door opened and in came Agent Tavares who motioned to the waitress called Mel for a coffee and some pancakes. He enjoyed his breakfast every day and grabbed the newspaper from the stand and sat down to enjoy a break.

Nigel leaned across to Robert and whispered, 'That's him isn't it?'

Robert pulled up a photo of the agent on the laptop and they covertly compared the picture with the man. 'Looks like one and the same,' he agreed. 'Shall I go and make his acquaintance?'

'No, let me do it. I look scruffier than you and while he's stuffing his face he's off guard.' Nigel got up and made his way back down the diner to the booth where Agent Tavares was reading and eating. Nigel slid in opposite the agent who looked up bemused.

'It is isn't it? It's Emilio Tavares; well I haven't seen you for years. How's that lovely wife of yours and your little girl? Well I'll bet she isn't so little anymore.' Nigel let all this rattle off so that Tavares couldn't get a word in edgeways. He saw a myriad of thoughts go through the man's mind as his brow furrowed as he dug deep into his memory. He obviously didn't want to look as if he had forgotten an old acquaintance. 'You would probably remember me better when I had my hair short and wore a suit and tie,' Nigel started off again, 'but never mind. So, how's life treating you then? Still living at the same place?' Nigel paused. 'No I seem to remember that you moved to that new house on the ridge, about two years ago wasn't it?'

In a few short sentences Nigel had let Tavares know that he knew all about his family and where he lived. Tavares answered, 'I'm sorry but I can't seem to remember you.'

'Not to worry, it was when we did Russian together.'

Suddenly it all fell into place for Tavares and he dropped his fork with a clatter. But he still wasn't sure which side this man was on, he could have been an operative for the Russian voice he heard on the phone. He gulped.

'Well I won't keep you today but don't forget it's only eighteen hours left on the clock. Now don't go roughing up any old timers and keep out of the woods, there may be bears!' Nigel said this and slapped him on the shoulder as if they were sharing an old joke and slid out of the booth again and re-joined Robert. Tavares left within the next thirty seconds and hurried past them both.

Robert said, 'Now there's a man in a hurry, what say we do a little surveillance and see what he does? I've got some gear in the back packs so we can listen in on any phone calls, should be fun.' Nigel nodded as he drank the dregs of his coffee and they wandered out into the sun. It was a fun day for the two drop outs, as every time Tavares left the office, he caught a glimpse of either one or the other of them, but they were always polite and smiled and waved a greeting. Tavares felt as if his world was coming apart at the seams and he knew he would have to come up with the goods, and soon, so he began to make a few phone calls.

At the end of the day Robert and Nigel sat again in a diner and high fived each other. Robert said, 'Well that went well. I actually got the numbers he called and he should be making the call to Matt, right about now.' He glanced at his watch. 'We've just got to sit tight for tonight and we should be able to move in tomorrow.'

'We're going to need some help with this and don't forget to take on board what Phil said about not knowing who's dirty and who's not.'

'How about we just go and have a look at where they are when we get the address then we'll make a plan?'

'Since when have you ever made a plan?'

'Well it usually turns out all right, doesn't it?' Robert feigned indignation.

'Granted, but we may have to be a bit more careful as Tavares could set us up with an ambush. Let's go and listen in to his calls tonight at home.'

'Okay, Nige, you win. Let's go and have a listen and we can have a catch up on the numbers he's already called and get them run through the computer. See if there are any surprises there.' The two left for the agent's home to begin their stakeout.

The team had eventually decamped to the resort and all were glad to be back there and been made welcome again by Fortune and Honey who seemed to have regained their former spirits. Sadly, Maria would have to stay in hospital for a few more days but she was getting stronger by the minute and hoped to join them within the week.

Matt had landed and had met them over drinks and Claire was pushed forward by Jack to perform the introductions. 'Well, guys, I'd like to introduce Matt, who literally saved my life.' She smiled round at everyone who looked in askance at the unkempt figure lounging with a beer. 'Don't be rude, you lot,' she admonished, 'underneath that rather woodsy exterior is a man who is a fighting machine with a heart of gold, and.' She paused. 'Also he's a sucker for a pair of pretty eyes!'

Matt smiled and his blue eyes twinkled. 'Sure am glad to be sharing a beer with you folks,' he drawled.

'Stop it, Matt.' Claire leaned over from her wheelchair and punched him on the arm. 'You can drop the backwoods act right now.'

Matt rubbed his arm. 'Okay, point taken, but I'm still glad to be here. I'll introduce myself. I'm Matthew Devereaux, late of the Special Services and Military Police, but I'm finished with the army now and just wandering about letting myself drift for a bit till I sort out what I want to do or be. Hence the hair and the beard, but it sure came in useful as a disguise a few days ago,' he drawled again.

Phil leaned forward to shake Matt's hand. 'We all owe you a debt and we're sure glad you could come along.' He matched the drawl and everyone laughed. 'You did us a great service and I don't know how we can repay you as we're sure Claire wouldn't be here now if you hadn't been there.'

Ellie, Rory and Alistair sat a little way back from the group and Ellie was still concerned about Alistair as he still looked gaunt and pale under his tan. Ellie spoke, 'It seems as if all we've been doing is rescuing each other with varying degrees of success. I seem to have a penchant for getting abducted and drugged but I'd like to take this time to thank everyone who helped me escape or rode to my rescue. I think I'm a bit of a weak link in the team but my name's Ellie Black and this here is Alistair my brother and twin. There's a long story about all that which you will probably find very boring so I won't start it now but thanks for bring Claire back safe and sound.'

'Don't think that, Ellie, as you've been the one to uncover a lot of leads and put us on the right trail many a time. You're our ticket to the inside of a lot of places we couldn't get, besides that we like working with a celebrity!' Ellie blushed at Claire's words.

'You mean you're that Ellie Black?' said Matt.

'How can you have heard of me?' Ellie looked surprised.

'You were all over the news some months ago and I think every dress you have worn has been on Twitter and Facebook. You're a very well known lady, Ellie,' said Matt.

Claire looked at him. 'So how would you know about Ellie's clothes on Facebook?'

Matt tapped the side of his nose, 'Secret,' he whispered.

'Well if that's your thing,' said Claire meaningfully.

'In reality we were given a list of people to monitor and Ellie's name was on my list as a newly-emerged celeb. All very low key as she wasn't perceived as a threat to the US. But,' he added, 'some of the people she came into contact with could be.'

Jack said, 'I've come in contact with some of the info that can be got from phone conversations in the Met. Usually it's been to do with terrorists and suchlike but it goes on all the time.'

Ellie bristled. 'You mean you were listening in to my phone calls and things?'

'Only a couple, then you weren't highlighted as a threat so it was discontinued.' Matt shrugged. 'Orders were orders and I had to do what I was told, like it or not.'

'Does that mean I was as well?' asked Rory.

Matt held up his hands. 'Whoa, no you weren't monitored. You are not being monitored now at all. Ellie's name has gone off the list and unless you've got a plan to nuke New York you will never be on the list again.'

'That's comforting to know,' said Ellie sarcastically.

'I'm sorry if I've upset everyone now, just as I was beginning to enjoy a beer, but I've got no reason to tell lies and if you'd rather I wasn't here then so be it, I'll leave.'

Phil intervened. 'No reason to do that, Matt. It was just a bit of a shock for Ellie, that's all. If you can do covert work like that, to that degree of sophistication, we could certainly use someone to help Robert and Nigel.'

Ellie was still indignant. 'It wasn't a "bit" of a shock,' she said with emphasis, 'that bit of information was a "hell" of a shock. I a) didn't think I'd gone global, and b) don't know if I like the idea that anyone can poke and pry into my life without me knowing.'

Jack seeking to diffuse the situation said, 'Remember when we were stranded in the middle of nowhere in the middle of winter? We had to use the secure phones in case anyone traced us via the signal, so it works both ways, and, yes, you've gone global. Enjoy.'

Phil turned his chair to look directly at Ellie. 'Unfortunately, that's the case today. Anyone can get information about you whether you like it or not. Think of the phone hacking sagas in the newspapers, it only really came to light when there was a whistle blower. It went on for years without people knowing. We've put in place firewalls and safeguards so that our phones can't be listened in on and they're secure.' Phil looked at Matt.

'Yep, they sure are, we haven't got any way of hacking those yet. We know about your team but that's in conjunction between London and Washington and information sharing. So, rest assured you're safe in the team. On your own, I'm not so sure.' Matt looked at Ellie.

Ellie felt her ruffled feathers lie down a bit. 'You're all absolutely positive about that?'

Phil, Jack and Matt nodded.

'Looks like we're stuck with each other for the duration then. Sorry I was a bit shocked by your revelation but I'd never really given it much thought, but I will be more careful in the future,' said Ellie, half-mollified.

'Well, on that little bombshell, I'll introduce myself,' said Alistair. 'To my right is Rory, Ellie's affianced, date to be set, and I'm Alistair, Ellie's twin, and just recovering from a car crash. So, pleased to meet you but I will be retiring very soon as this is my first real day out of bed and I'm not completely the ticket at the moment. In fact, I think I'll take my leave now but would be pleased if Rory would walk with me back to my room. I hope to join you for dinner.' Alistair rose and Rory rose with him. Alistair was perfectly capable of walking back alone but wanted a short stroll with Rory to see what he remembered about the night on top of the hill that led up to the car crash. Ellie must never know about that as she would surely have no mercy. He had evoked the Beast partly out of concern and as a way of finding out where Ellie was, but the deep part of his soul knew he could do this again if he wanted to. It was as if he had a conduit to untold power and information and this was like an aphrodisiac to him. He wanted more.

Ellie sat and watched as the desultory conversation ebbed and flowed around her. She was slowly digesting what Matt had said about her being on some sort of 'watch list'. It made sense when she analysed it but it didn't make it any more palatable. Alistair had been remarkably quiet and she sensed he was brooding about something as well as in recovery mode. It could be his work or it could be anything, no doubt she would find out soon enough. He kept on with the crap about twins being linked in some way and she had dismissed it out of hand but she could definitely sense some sort of undercurrent. Matt was talking about his time in the military and sharing some anecdotes and he seemed to be an amusing raconteur and Ellie had to admit that it was opportune he was there at the right moment for Claire. As she sat cradling her swiftly warming drink, Phil's phone went off with a chirrup.

'Hi, Nige, how's it going?' Phil listened for about a minute then the furrows in his brow eased out and he smiled. 'Well done, so the girls are still in Atlanta. That makes sense. What's the plan?' He listened for a few more moments then said, 'Give me five and I'll get back to you.' Looking round, he relayed that the mild harassment of Agent Tavares had paid off and Robert and Nigel had found the girls in Atlanta in some brothel. It seemed to be in a very poor part of town and they didn't have very high hopes of storming the place and staging a rescue. They had called in for any ideas. They had done a preliminary surveillance but it was guarded and seemed to be run by one of the major gangs operating in the area. Even the cops didn't go in there so local back-up wasn't going to work.

They were sitting tight in a motel that overlooked the site armed with sandwiches and drinks and a good pair of binoculars but that was all. Phil looked round at the assembled remnants of the team. 'Any ideas?'

Maria, who could have posed as a service worker, was still

recovering in hospital, Ellie wasn't able to carry out this sort of operation. Claire couldn't walk yet so that left Nigel and Robert already over there and himself, Jack, and Matt who looked as if he could handle himself in a fight. 'Houston we have a slight problem,' he said. 'Looks like it's going to be me, Jack and you.' He looked pointedly at Matt. 'I don't know what your plans are for the next few days but I'll let you into my secret. I've already got your security clearance from London and I've done a bit of digging into your record and you seem to be just the guy we need right now. We've broken a ring of bad guys selling East European girls for the sex trade and stopped it from this end but we weren't quick enough to stop the last shipment going over to the USA. They've been located in Atlanta and we would like to get them out in one piece. It's not stopped the trade but maybe a few girls will get home again safe and sound. Sadly, we've uncovered a few "dirty" agents along the route so we don't know who is good or bad within the local forces. It'll be covert to the extreme but we've got good resources at our disposal. We're going to need a bit of help on this one.' Phil looked at Matt.

Matt sat with his beer half raised to his lips. 'Looks like I'm gonna need a razor.'

Back in the girls' hostel the young girl with the cat slide was now forcibly dragged from the bedroom and shoved back into the dormitory where she collapsed onto the floor. She was almost catatonic and lay there whimpering and holding the satchel as if her life depended on it. Tears streaked her face and there were bruises beginning to show round her neck and on her face. Her one eye was beginning to close and her lip was split, making a bloody trail down her chin mixed with saliva. The oldest girl looked in horror at the youngster and rushed over and gathered her up and put her on her bed with the filthy mattress. The girl curled into a ball and began the whimpering again.

'Get me a wet cloth and a towel and we'll clean her up.' She galvanized the others into action. 'Let's get you changed.' She began to prise the satchel from the clamped fingers. 'Get me some clothes and let's get rid of these.' She said, gesturing to the ripped school uniform. Another girl bought a pair of jogging bottoms and another bought a t-shirt and they began to undress and clean up the young girl. The older girl whose name was Marika was horrified at the state of the child and realized she didn't even know her name. She had given the advice of putting your mind in another place and distancing yourself from the act but that was obviously too much for the young girl to take in and apply. The youngster was a tattered wreck mentally and she couldn't imagine what the girl had been forced to endure. Marika had thought that it was a normal 'pay as you go' brothel but the state of the girl spoke of untold depravity and abuse beyond her comprehension. She was horrified and scared.

CHAPTER NINETEEN

The fat woman was lounging in a room that passed for an office and looked at two men from behind her desk. 'That was good.' She peeled off a few bills and passed them over. They were pocketed with alacrity and the young men resumed their studies of inactivity. One was smoking and flicked the ash onto the floor. 'Stop that, what do you think this is?' The fat woman slammed her hand on the desk causing them both to jump. 'It may be a shit hole but it's where the shit comes from, don't forget that. I've bought you up better than that.' The two took up more attentive postures. 'I've had a call from the Russian and some of the girls are going to a "clinic" soon. Maybe it'll be today or tonight. It's worth a lot so don't mess up. You'll ride shotgun on the van and collect the payment.' She paused. 'I want it all. No fancy footwork with the bag, you got that? We got ten girls in that last shipment so we'll send six and keep four for us.'

Both of her sons nodded as they knew that Ma would have no trouble in causing them untold grief and misery if her orders weren't carried out to the letter, they were processing those thoughts and letting their imaginations run away with them when the phone on the desk dinged. 'Yes.' The fat woman answered it immediately. 'Okay, nightfall then. Delivery will be on time.' She addressed her sons and took in the bling and slightly unkempt appearance of both of them. In a place a long time ago she had thought they would grow up to be lawyers or doctors or other upstanding members of the community but, try as she might, they had ended up as street rats of the first order. Both their fathers had been no good SOBs so what could you expect? She turned her mind to the task in hand. The Russian had just sent orders that five girls, the youngest ones, were to go to a clinic of some description and there would be a payment waiting. All of the money would be split 80:20 and she would get the 20%. Not a lot but it was worth it to be trouble free from the other gangs that always wanted to muscle in on the action. Her sons never seemed to understand that you had to pay for protection and saw money to burn, but she knew that if she reneged on a deal she would soon be at the bottom of a river and there was always someone to take her place. 'Go get the van and I'll go and get the girls, get ready you pieces of shit.' She pointed a finger. 'Don't mess this one up.'

Phil, Jack and Matt were already boarding a plane to go to Atlanta and Matt looked a totally different guy as he had located a razor and the beard had disappeared. The long hair was tied back as he didn't have time to get to a barber and he was wearing a blue shirt and chinos. He moved with an easy grace and Phil was even more sure that this guy had the attributes he needed right now. He seemed to understand the mission and the implications right away and had asked all the right questions whilst professionally preparing his gear. Phil had let Nigel and Robert know that they were on their way and set Ellie and Claire up as a communications hub for their sortie. Rory and Alistair hadn't shown up before they left but Phil was sure Ellie would fill them in when they reappeared. Phil wasn't sure how much Alistair would care but he was sure Rory would be glad Ellie wasn't placed in any more danger than necessary. As they sat on the plane and they taxied for take-off Phil said, 'So we'll rendezvous with Nige and Rob then take it from there. Try and memorize the numbers for the sat phones as we don't want any written evidence. I've arranged a chopper to pick us up and the girls will go on a private plane straight to London. I don't know what state they'll be in and I don't want them here on St. Lucia in case anyone gets any fancy ideas.' Matt nodded and stared down at the list of numbers then after a few minutes crumpled it up and handed it to Phil. Phil looked surprised. 'You've got them all?'

'Yep,' said Matt, 'I have one of those memories for numbers. Don't ask me how but I can see them in patterns and remember them. Ma always wanted me to do math at school but I wanted some action,' he said laconically.

'Lord preserve us, not another one,' said Phil, rolling his eyes. 'Matt meet Jack. 'They both looked at each other, puzzled. 'Jack is also a math brain and has done some very good analytical work using various theories and the like that I can't begin to understand, let alone explain. He cracked this case right at the beginning and sees things from a slightly different way to the rest of us. Nige and Rob have superb computer skills and it all gels together well from my point of view. They can be a little strange at times, all of them, but I suggest we change seats while we can and you two can get together.' Phil smiled and unbuckled as the others looked set to have a maths conflab that would seem like a different language to him.

The flight to Atlanta was uneventful and on landing they hired a car and set out for the motel room where Nigel and Robert were holed up. They pulled into the forecourt of the seedy motel and didn't even look at the bored girl sitting behind the desk examining her nails but went up to the second floor room.

They entered the room and took in the tired carpet and fittings and breathed in the stale air redolent with spent cigarettes and sweat. 'You really do bring us to the best places,' said Jack.

'Welcome to Hotel Riviera,' answered Nigel, waving an expansive hand. 'Not the best place to park as the wheels will be gone by tomorrow but nothing seems to be happening right now.'

Robert was feeding his face with a sandwich and looked up at the entrance. 'Who's that?' he asked, waving a crust at Matt.

'Meet Matt, he's a new addition for this operation. He's the guy who rescued Claire and he's agreed to help us with this one,' Phil said, as he sat on the bed and felt the springs groan.

'Okay, no probs. Just to bring you up to speed. We don't know how many are in there but there has been a steady stream of punters through the front door. We haven't seen any of the girls but we don't know what they look like anyway and I don't think they're likely to let them out to take a stroll. Two guys have recently bought a van round to a side entrance and parked it up so some action could be on soon,' said Robert.

Phil sat and had a look through the binoculars and took in the rubbish-strewn side entrance. 'I think you're right but there's not much chance of local backup on this one. We've got a plane waiting on the tarmac at Hartsfield-Jackson and whoever we can get out will go straight to London. There'll be a chopper waiting for us as well so we can fly out under the radar, so to speak. Any noise from the palace of delights?'

Robert said, 'We've tried to set up a bit of surveillance with this but nothing meaningful has come out yet.' He gestured to a small parabolic antenna pointing to the brothel. 'You never know but it only has a small range and we obviously haven't pointed it at the right place yet.' He grimaced. 'We have heard some screams and shouts but nothing that could be of use to us or make sense of.'

Phil tensed. 'I think something's going down as two guys are opening the side door of the van, looks like they're going to move something.'

Robert was fiddling about with the antenna and said, 'Yep got 'em. Looks like they're planning to move whatever it is out at dusk.' He twiddled with his laptop and concentrated again on the scene below. 'Hold it, I can hear them.' Robert held up his hand then reeled an address off and repeated it. 'Someone get that as it looks like that's where they're going to take some of the girls within the next hour.' He looked round. 'So is this a divide and conquer situation?'

'Looks like it,' said Phil, 'as you said they're going to take "some" of the girls so we'll divide up and stage an ambush where they're going. Their van will be useful to move them straight to the airport. Let's just hope they move a lot as we've only got the car for the getaway. I suggest Jack, Matt and me will take out the van and you two will cause this place some serious hassle.' Everyone nodded. 'I suggest we get to it quickly as they'll be on the move very soon.'

Matt, Phil and Jack grabbed their things and exited the room with alacrity, leaving Robert and Nigel packing up their stuff. They heard the sound of the engine of the hire car being gunned as they raced to the clinic to intercept the van.

Nigel looked at Robert. 'So what's the plan then?'

'Don't have one right now,' he answered.

'We're gonna need some wheels as the cavalry has just shot off in the only ones we had.'

'Okay, first things first, let's go get ourselves a big car, preferably not a drug dealer's car as we'll be toast right away,' said Robert. 'There was a mall down the road where we got the sandwiches from so let's have a look on the car park.' He glanced out of the window and the van was still there but the two guys were opening up the doors and glancing about to make sure no-one was watching. 'Don't think we're going to have time for that as things seem to be on the move down there.' He let the curtain fall back over the window in case they were spotted. 'Looks like there are a few punters in there anyway and they've parked in the street. What do you say to hiking one of their cars, leaving it unlocked and ready for a quick move, and getting the girls out while everyone is otherwise engaged?'

Nigel looked at Robert. 'That's the best plan you've had for years, couldn't have done better myself.' Robert didn't even bother responding to that one but raised a finger as he crammed the last of his stuff into his bag. They left the room and ambled down to the reception desk and paid the girl who was still examining her nails with dollar bills which she stuffed into her pocket and murmured a 'have a nice day' as they left.

'She never even looked at us,' Robert said.

'I never saw her lips move either, maybe she's a robot programmed for nail care or something,' Nigel said as they started across the street.

As they were crossing the road a big car pulled up and an overweight man got out and straightened his tie and tucked his shirt back into his sagging trousers. Robert and Nigel saw him pocket his keys into his right hand jacket pocket before checking his appearance again in the wing mirror. They were deep in conversation as they approached the man and Robert bumped him with his backpack and caught him as he almost fell. 'Sorry man, so sorry, you okay?' Robert asked solicitously.

'Look where you're going next time.' The man dusted himself off and turned on his heel and walked into the brothel.

Robert and Nigel kept on walking but Nigel was playing with a set of car keys as they chatted.

'Not lost your touch I see,' said Robert.

'Well, it saved a walk to the mall didn't it?' Nigel grinned as they continued round the block. They soon made it round to opposite the back door and there was an alley full of rubbish but it led straight to the back of the brothel. They wormed their way in so they could see what was happening and crouched down. Nigel said, 'I've got no idea of the layout of the place but there are bars on that window up there so I will assume that's where they keep things they don't want to run away.'

'If that's a fire door those guys have opened then when it swings shut, we can't get in. Do you want to flip for who gets to put a wedge in it?'

Nigel looked at Robert. 'Well, I got the keys so it's your turn really, unless you're scared of two thugs with guns and probably knives and you've got nothing.'

''Cause I'm scared it's what keeps me alive,' said Robert, 'but I suppose it is my turn so cover my back if it all goes pear-shaped,' and he shrugged off his backpack and started to climb over the rubbish.

The two guys had gone inside the building and Robert sprinted and hid behind a small alcove on the back wall. He picked up a small piece of wood and held up his thumb. Nigel replied by holding up his own thumb, meaning that the coast was clear, and Robert wasted no time in edging round the building and jamming the piece of wood in the locking mechanism of the door. He just managed to get back round the building when some girls were being led out and pushed into the van. Robert flattened himself against the wall and watched as Nigel held his thumb down signalling that there was activity. He crossed his fingers behind his back and prayed that the door would appear to close properly behind them. He heard the van engine start up and Nigel held his thumb up again as the van pulled out. Nigel joined him and they peered round the building and Robert edged forward and gave the door a gentle push, it moved, and he heaved a huge sigh of relief. He gave the thumbs up to Nigel and they both went into the building. It was very dark and their seemed to be a staircase going up but it hadn't been used in a long time and it was covered with trash. They stepped very lightly on the stairs making sure they didn't rustle any of the papers or kick the soda cans till they reached a landing with rooms branching off to the right. There was a fly-spotted light bulb burning, throwing out a dim yellow haze, and Robert flattened himself against the wall. 'Don't know which room had the bars up. Where are we in relation to the back of the building?' he whispered.

'It's probably going to be that room at the end,' said Nigel sibilantly.

'Can't you do better than a probably?' asked Robert in mock annoyance.

'Okay, I get it, it's my turn now.' He sidled past Robert. 'Just be ready for a quick move if I'm wrong and I walk in on someone – well you know what.' Nigel walked quickly to the end room hugging the shadows as he went and tried the door. It was locked and he could just hear a noise filtering through. He gave the thumbs up to Robert who took up position and began to fiddle with the lock.

'Five, four, three, two.' The lock slicked open and Robert held onto the doorknob and looked at Nigel. 'Ready when you are.' He opened the door and they both went in. They both quickly put their fingers to their lips to signify silence as the four girls looked up in terror at their entrance. 'Shush, please,' Robert pleaded and held up both hands to show they meant no harm.

A girl who was sitting on the edge of her bed said, 'Who are you?' taking in their scruffy appearance.

'Thank God you speak English,' said Nigel, 'we weren't sure. Listen, we're friends and we've come to take you home.'

'No understand.' The girl shook her head and clutched the

edge of the mattress tighter.

'Home, we go now,' said Robert trying again. 'Come on but shush.' He put his finger to his lips again.

'Oooohhh.' The girl seemed to cotton on and rattled off in a foreign language to the three others who began to nod.

Nigel and Robert wanted to hurry this along as fast as possible and Robert began waving his hands towards the door. 'Now, we go now.' He mimed the finger on the lips and made car noises with his hands on an imaginary steering wheel. 'Now, go!'

With Nigel in the lead and Robert checking the back, they got to the stairs and mimed going down very carefully. Besides a few rustles from discarded packets they made it to the fire door. Robert edged his way forward and Nigel said, 'I'll go and get the wheels and reverse up here but be ready to move in a parsec.' Nigel nodded. He turned to the first girl and mimed again putting his finger on his lips and pointed back up the line. She duly passed on the message.

The door opened easily, Robert was gone and within a few minutes there was a tap on the door. Nigel hustled the girls out into the back of the car. He sprinted round to the front and the car was in motion before he had slammed his door. The last girl in wasn't quick enough to slam her door and it ricocheted off the building with a clang before slamming shut. As Robert screeched out of the driveway into the road, he caught sight of a fat woman waving her arms and shouting at them. He ignored her and fishtailed up the road till he turned a corner then settled down to a more sedate pace. Robert and Nigel high-fived each other and the girls in the back began to jabber away to each other. It wasn't far to the airport and they drove straight round to the terminal for private passengers and Robert had a quick chat with the guard on the gate and showed him his credentials and was waved through to a jet idling on the tarmac. The stairs were already lowered and a woman was awaiting them. They screeched to a halt and got out.

'Phew,' said Robert. 'That was enough adrenaline to keep me going for months.' They opened the back door and ushered the girls out. They were dirty and very smelly but the woman on the plane greeted them in their own language and they visibly relaxed. The one girl who had got some English turned and ran back down the steps and kissed both Robert and Nigel with a big hug and they both were a bit taken aback but waved her onto the plane with, 'It's nothing, nada, no problem,' and 'Anytime.'

'Let's go and park up this slightly dented car,' said Robert. 'I know, let's leave it in the "long stay", they'll find it sometime.'

'Good plan, you're full of them today, but I suggest we wipe it down first, you never know,' he added sagely.

'Too right, bro, then we'll have a little trip in a helicopter and we'll be back in our island Paradise for breakfast.'

CHAPTER TWENTY

Phil, Matt and Jack had located the clinic which appeared to be a plush, well-funded, enterprise with lawns and gardens and a big flashy sign plastered across the building. 'There must be a service entrance,' said Jack, surveying the edifice.

'Go up a block and see what's round the back,' said Matt, and Phil put the car in gear and complied.

It was some sort of Business Park and all the lots were for science and related services but they came to a small road that seemed to serve the business on that lot. Phil drove in carefully and positioned the car by some dumpsters and killed the engine. 'What about we go and have a look and see if there's an entrance round here?' They all got out of the car and began to walk towards the back of the chrome and steel designer building when Matt suddenly started to wave his arms and he jumped in front of the other two, shouting.

Jack and Phil stopped dead. 'Play as if we're lost,' Matt said quietly, then began to berate Phil for bringing them the wrong way at the top of his voice. 'You stupid ass, I told you this wasn't the way' he shouted and shoved Phil back towards the car. Phil and Jack quickly joined in and they began to walk back to the car. 'I saw a security camera,' said Matt as they reached the car. He reached in and pulled a map out of the glove pocket and spread it out on the bonnet and began jabbing at it with his finger. With much arm -waving and arguing they piled back in and reversed till they could turn round.

'What now?' Jack asked.

'We've got about a quarter of an hour and the van will be here,' said Phil, 'we've got to get it before it gets here.' Matt was driving and he screeched off to the left and went round the block again.

'I think they'll come in from that way and there was a mall down there,' said Matt, 'maybe we could just force them off the road and hijack the van, but we haven't got much time.'

'Better that plan than no plan at all,' acquiesced Phil, 'drive on.'

They found the mall and parked up near the entrance with the engine running. 'I'm going to drive out in front of them but the timing's going to have to be good. Brace yourselves as there may be an impact but hopefully, they'll swerve round into the mall entrance and then we take them.'

I'll go with that,' said Jack, and Phil nodded.

It was quiet on the road but the van soon hove into view as it rounded the corner and Matt made the engine growl as he revved to pull in front just at the right moment. Jack and Phil hung onto anything they could find as the car wheels spun and left a trail of burnt rubber. Matt held his line and pulled in front of the van when it was about ten yards away. Phil saw the driver's look of horror as he wrenched the wheel to the right trying to get the van into the mall entrance. Matt spun his own steering wheel and the car did a 360 and ended up facing the van and he accelerated back behind it.

Everyone jumped out and ran round to the driver and passenger doors and yanked them open. Jack got the passenger by the collar and pulled him sideways. He was held in by his seatbelt but Jack got hold of a thick gold chain round his neck and began choking him. He managed to reach across, as the guy was clawing at his throat, and release the belt and Jack deposited him on the floor gasping for air. With a sudden mental flash Jack bent down and found a gun tucked into the waistband of the guy's trousers and relieved him of it.

On the other side, the driver's attention was taken by Phil and Matt who were grappling with him to get him out of the van but he was proving to be a harder nut to crack as he fought with his fists and feet. In a split second, Jack had jumped into the passenger seat and poked the guy in the ribs with the gun. 'Out, now,' Jack growled, and the guy went, still feeling the gun boring a hole in his torso. As he turned to get out, Jack relieved him of his gun which was also stored in his waistband.

The guy's feet hit the floor and Phil gave him a roundhouse punch to the jaw and he slumped forwards into Matt's arms. Matt deposited him none too gently next to his friend and Phil jumped into the driver's seat. 'Get in.' He motioned to Matt.

'No, get going. I'm going to stay here and find out what's really going on at that clinic. Go now. Catch you later.' He turned and ran to the car.

Phil looked at Jack. 'Got to do as the man says.' He revved the engine and the van peeled off back onto the highway to the airport. Jack looked down at the two guns, he had got one in each hand and he checked the safeties were on then carefully placed them in the footwell.

'I should have given these to Matt. What do you think he's going to do?' Jack looked at Phil who was intent on the road.

'I'll have a chat with him later but I think he's right, there's a lot more going on at that clinic than meets the eye. Now we're on the freeway, just have look through that little hatch and make sure we have actually got the girls. It was a bit rushed back there and we don't want to have hijacked an empty van.'

Jack looked at Phil in horror and scrambled over the seat and pushed back the little sliding hatch. The smell hit him first and he saw the girls bouncing around sitting on the van floor holding onto what they could. Their hands were tied behind them and their faces turned towards him. Suddenly Jack didn't know what to say to them and he slammed the hatch shut.

'Oh God, Phil, they look terrible and they stink.'

'What do you mean "look terrible"?'

'Well they've got their hands tied behind them and it seems as if one has been beaten up. A little girl and she looks a mess.'

'We're nearly at the airport now,' said Phil, indicating right and following the signs. 'They'll be safe in about ten minutes. Just try and reassure them a bit, they may think we're their next owners and they've been sold. Tell them they're going home.'

Jack opened the hatch again and smiled at the girls, he was met with blank faces. 'My name's Jack and we've taken you away from the bad men and we're going to get you home.' The girls looked at each other and one of the eldest repeated the word 'home'. Jack nodded then realized they could only see a bit of his face through the hatch. 'Yes, you're going home,' he repeated. 'We take you home now.' The biggest one repeated the word home again like a mantra and began to talk to the others. They appeared to get quite excited and began firing questions at Jack but all he could say was, 'No comprende,' and smile a lot.

Jack shut the hatch again and looked at Phil who was smiling. He said, 'I don't think Spanish is their first language but I think you got the message across.' They could both hear the girls now in the van and the odd peal of laughter rang out. Phil smiled again. 'It was worth it all just for that.' He turned into the airport and found his way to the private section.

The guard on the gate waved them through and Phil pulled the van up to the jet and the same woman came down the steps to greet them. 'You might want to see if you can clean them up a bit before they sit down as they're not in too good a shape.'

'No problem.' She smiled as if it was all in a day's work.

'My friend tells me that one looks as if she's been beaten up and may need a bit of TLC.'

'Again, no problem, I'm also a trained nurse and will patch her up but I think the mental scars will be longer healing than the physical ones.'

'Right, let's get them gone now – also they've been going on in some language I don't recognize so I hope your East European or Russian is up to it.'

The stewardess walked to the back of the van and opened the door; she recoiled slightly but soon found her professional face and fixed a smile. She greeted the girls in some language they obviously understood and they began to climb out. Phil and Jack cut their bonds and then helped the youngest girl out onto the tarmac. She could barely stand and they helped her up the steps into the plane. Her face was a mass of bruises and her lip had swollen. One eye was closed shut and a livid bruise spread half down her face. The stewardess took the girl from them and carefully sat her down to begin her ministrations.

'We got to go now,' said Phil, 'we've got our ride waiting for us. Just tell the girls "best of luck" and a safe journey to London then home.'

The stewardess nodded. 'I'll be sure to do that, I'll keep them safe.' She sketched a wave and moved to draw in the steps and close the door. 'Goodbye, whoever you are, no don't tell me as I don't want to know, but you did a grand job and I'll make sure they know in London.'

Jack and Phil shouted their thanks as they skipped down the steps. 'Okay, let's rid of the wheels,' said Phil as they climbed in.

'What about these?' said Jack, kicking the guns that were still lying on the floor.

'Tell you what; let's have them as a souvenir. You can have it stuffed and mounted if you like.'

'Ha ha, very funny,' said Jack, tucking one into his waistband and giving the other one to Phil.

'I spy a chopper park,' said Phil as he swung the van round in a tight circle, 'and if I'm not mistaken that's our ride.' He pointed to a helicopter with two scruffs lounging by the skids.

They parked up and all four met with high fives and back slapping. Robert said, 'Well our end went well and by the look on your faces yours did too.' He looked round. 'Where's Matt? I thought he was coming back with us.'

Jack looked at Phil and said, 'He decided to stay and have a closer look at the clinic these girls were to be taken to. It was a big plushy job that covered a whole lot on a science park. Lots of money washing around that place. They'd got security as well so we couldn't get in. I don't know why they would want those girls in that place.'

'You got the name of it?' asked Nigel. 'We'll have a little look and see what we can find out, then we'll relay any info to Matt and it might help him. Least we can do.'

'Yep, got it stored all up here,' said Jack, tapping his forehead. 'I'll work with you on this when we get back.'

The pilot was making 'come on' gestures with his arm as he began to fire up the rotors. They all got in and strapped themselves in and put on headsets to cut out the noise and settled back for the flight. No-one would admit it to the others but they were totally exhausted but happy and relieved it had been a successful mission. The drone of the engine soon lulled them all to sleep and they woke when the chopper dropped with a bump that Phil thought the pilot had done deliberately. A car was waiting for them and they got in still half asleep to go back to the resort.

'Well, that's the end of a lovely holiday,' said Phil.

'What do you mean?' said Robert and Nigel in unison.

'Time to go home now boys, job done. You had a great time burning all that dosh, which was probably the highlight for you pair.'

Nigel said, 'Yep, sure was, but I can't wait to get away from all these flying things they have out here. They're like B52 bombers with one end that bites and the other end that stings. Give me a simple bad guy any day. At least you can usually see them coming and you can fight them off.'

Robert looked at the back of Phil's head. 'So what about Maria, she's not going to stay here alone is she?'

Nigel wrapped his arms around himself and began rocking with a beatific smile on his face.

'Stop that,' said Phil, but Nigel only carried on. 'No, Robert, she's going to the resort soon and will be with Alistair and Ellie and I presume she'll travel back with them. You'll be able to see her tomorrow to put your mind at rest before we leave. We'll probably have a short time in London to regroup and make sure Claire's fully fit, then we'll meet up with everyone, probably in Italy, to discuss the next job.'

Jack said, 'There's a next job?'

Phil turned his head. 'There's always a next job! We were told to get those books and manuscripts back to where they should be and there's still a fair few to go. Some we can simply steal back but some need Ellie and Alistair to get us into the inner sanctums. Also, we've met that "shit" Valentin, who I don't like at all, and I'm going to do some serious digging about him. I'm not bothered if he's Alistair's friend or not but I'm sure he's mixed up in a lot of this and I'm going to take him down. Remember when Matt was talking about Ellie being on a "watch list"? Well I've made sure that Alistair and Valentin are on one now. I want to know if they talk to each other, what they say, even what they have for breakfast, but that's strictly between us, got it?'

They all nodded.

When they arrived at the resort, they wandered into the beach bar and were met with the sight of Maria sitting on a cane lounger propped up with pillows. She seemed very pale and frail but they were really glad to see her. Robert took up position at her side and took command of her drink and couldn't do enough for her. Ellie and Claire drew back to let the others welcome her but Ellie said, 'She's out of hospital but she's on a strict regime of bed rest and short walks but she's on the mend.'

'Looks like Claire's on the mend too,' said Phil, as he watched Claire carefully hobble to her chair. The wheelchair had gone and she was obviously in pain but she looked adamant that she was going to walk and not be pushed about like an invalid.

'Couldn't be doing with that thing anymore,' said Claire. 'I got the local doc to have a look and they're mending well. As long as I don't get the wounds wet, they'll be all gone in about a week. So, it'll be back to dancing the two step for me! I'm okay now and it'll only get better so you'll just have to wait a short while and I'll be back in action.'

Phil knew Claire was a trooper and wouldn't give in easily and he admired her immensely so he sat down by her and said, 'We're pulling out tomorrow and going back to London so I'll give you a few weeks sick leave when we're back, and you can be fully recovered and join us wherever that may be.'

'No way, you can shove that idea. I'm not mouldering round London while you lot go off somewhere. I'm going with you. If I'm not fully fit I can always do logistics or comms but I'm not staying there.'

'Okay, I get the picture,' said Phil, 'but we'll have a medic look at your feet when we get back to England and we'll abide by what he says. Okay?'

'Okay,' said Claire slowly, 'I'll do that as long as I can pick the doc.'

Phil smelt a rat immediately but didn't argue as he knew it would be pointless. He just nodded and said, 'We'll see.' He left it at that. 'Your friend Matt decided to stay in the USA and check out an establishment that looked shady to us.'

Claire's face fell a bit and Phil wondered if Claire didn't have some deeper feelings for her rescuer. He had told himself many times over the last few days that he didn't mind but deep down he knew he did, a lot. He settled back and began to tell the whole story of the rescue of the girls and how they were probably still on a plane to England. What would happen to them when they were there would be up to the mandarins of Whitehall but they would probably be repatriated if that was what they wanted.

'I'd have loved to have been there,' said Claire, imagining the rescue. 'They might have felt safer if there was a woman there and I do know some Russian, well, a bit anyway.'

'I've no notion what language they spoke or where they originally came from but where they were being delivered is going to get some serious investigation. You couldn't have been there anyway as you're seriously *persona non grata* in the USA. They'd have probably locked you up and thrown away the key by now.' Phil smiled.

'True,' said Claire. 'I'd probably have been in the bowels of some high level security jail by now being interrogated. I still wonder who was being difficult about that as I think London were trying to get me out but were being stonewalled all the time. Someone over there doesn't like me. Come to think of it, I don't think I like them very much either as I nearly got executed and dumped in the woods.' Claire furrowed her brow. 'That had some sort of Russian angle to it as well. We'll have to let all the ideas stew a bit and have a big meeting when we get back to London and pool all our bits of knowledge. Get Jack to do his wizardry again and see what his computer makes of all the threads. You never know, all roads may lead to Moscow,' she said, misquoting. 'Anyway, I'd better go and pack my stuff up and say goodbye to Fortune and Honey if we're leaving tomorrow.'

Phil stood as she stood and offered his arm but Claire shook him off and winced as she hobbled out. Phil sat back down and smiled as he shook his head at her stubbornness.

As she went slowly out, Alistair and Rory came in deep in conversation. Alistair sat down and Rory ordered the drinks. It was almost as if he was a PA now and they seemed to be the best of friends. Ellie had noticed this and was glad that Alistair seemed to have put his previous animosity behind him. She was happier than she had been for a long time and in the dead of night she had asked Rory what had changed Alistair's mind about him. All she had got were a few incoherent mumblings but she had gleaned that Alistair was seeing Rory more as a business partner and they had been working on a few angles for negotiations together. Rory seemed happy enough and apparently had even handed in his notice in London. Ellie had been surprised at this as he was the one who had been vehement about not 'hanging onto the coattails' of the Morgan clan. But whatever had gone on was obviously a 'man' thing and honour on both sides had seemingly been satisfied.

Fortune came in and Phil offered him Claire's vacant chair. 'We've got some news for you,' he said. 'We're leaving this island paradise tomorrow.'

Fortune looked aghast. 'You can't leave me now, and we've been through so much together, how am I going to cope?'

Phil looked sideways at Fortune. 'You'll cope. The bad men have all gone now and Honey is back doing her charity work and all you've got to do is sit and admire the view.' Fortune was an innocent abroad and Phil could see how easy it was to take advantage of him. Honey kept him on the straight and narrow path and basically told him what to do to run the place. He did it admirably and the guests wanted for nothing. 'All you've got to do is work out the bill and e-mail it to London and it'll be paid by return so no worries there. We've got to go as we're on the trail of some more bad people and you know it's our job to catch them, but I'll certainly be back to St. Lucia as it's a paradise and I love the place and the people.'

Fortune's face brightened when Phil said that. 'I know, we'll have a party tonight and I'll get the steel band in and we'll have some dancing and lots of food on the boardwalk by the beach.'

'That'd be great Fortune as I'll take some pictures and then it'll seem like we've been on holiday rather than getting shot at, drugged and abducted.'

'The last memory will be the one you carry,' said Fortune sagely, 'but I'll get the party all organized and let everyone know. Is Miss Ellie going as well?'

'No, they're staying a few more days so that Maria can get a bit stronger before the flight back, but they'll be heading out this week as I know Alistair is champing at the bit to get his hands on the steering wheel of his companies. Apparently, there's only so much you can do by e-mail,' said Phil not wishing to trade places with Alistair at all.

Fortune left with alacrity and made his way round the guests, informing them of the party, and scurried off to get it organized.

Day turned into night and the fireflies came out and the cicadas lent their own special music to the steel band. It was a bitter sweet night as suddenly everyone was sorry to leave St. Lucia and as Fortune and Honey played mine hosts to perfection, Phil kept his word and had many photos of people he knew and loved, smiling, and for once just being themselves.

CHAPTER TWENTY-ONE

The next day dawned and everyone was lethargic and some had thick heads and sat nursing tonic waters. Robert was still hovering attendance on Maria who seemed to be lapping up all the attention. He had asked Phil if he could stay a few more days to ostensibly keep in contact with Matt in America, as they had been digging up information on Slate Corporations which was the parent company of the huge edifice in Atlanta. Phil had said a resounding no to that one as they could easily keep in contact from London and it was plain to see what Robert's real motive was. As Phil watched Robert's face fall, he had reassured him that they would all be meeting up soon when Alistair and his entourage were safely ensconced back in Italy. Robert had gone to relay this information back to Maria who was now taking little walks up and down the garden. Phil had watched them wander hand in hand and wondered why life couldn't be that simple for himself. Maybe he should just bite the bullet and tell Claire of his feelings for her. He would, but he was afraid of what might happen. Here he was, the leader of one of the best task forces on the planet, and he was scared. Frightened that Claire would trample all over his ego and blow him away. She might ridicule him and tell him to grow up and that would make working together in the future well nigh impossible. He thought about it some more and decided to err on the side of caution and leave well alone. He could live with just being close to her and feeling the frisson of excitement when she was nearby. He knew he couldn't let the guard slip as he would be risking all. Phil nursed his drink and let his mind wander back to the few hobbles Claire had managed on the dance floor with him and he treasured those moments and stored them away.

The day passed in a desultory way and the time came after lunch for them to leave. The gear was packed and the cars were waiting and everyone came to the reception drive to wave them goodbye. Honey was openly crying and kept thanking Phil for organizing all the cultural exchanges that were going to take place, Fortune looked bereft, and Ellie kept going round and hugging everyone. Robert and Maria stood a little to one side, holding hands and were deeply engrossed in each other. Only Alistair was missing but he appeared at the last moment and waved them off. The cars drove away and Ellie looked at Alistair. 'I suppose it's our turn next?'

'Yep, can't wait to get off this godforsaken island and back to real activity again.'

Ellie looked surprised and said, 'You can't mean that Alistair? It's been an eventful time I know but everything turned out all right in the end.'

Alistair held onto Ellie's arms. 'Look at me, I'm a bloody wreck. I nearly lost you for good and I went to Hell and back to try and save you.'

Ellie looked at Alistair and took in the sunken eyes and the skin stretched paper-thin over the high cheekbones. 'What do you mean? You said you went to Hell and back. As far as I know you only tried to drive a car when you couldn't. Sorry,' she apologized, 'were forced off the road and nearly got everyone killed.'

Alistair backpedalled swiftly. 'I tried to keep you safe and failed and that weighs heavy on me.' He released her arms and stood back a pace. 'I just want to go home and get back to what

I know the best. I'll be okay when we get back to Italy and it's only a few more days so just ignore me.' He suddenly stood up straighter. 'In fact, I think I'll go back tomorrow and leave you to your own devices for a few days then you can fly back with Maria and Rory.'

Ellie looked puzzled. 'First you say you want to look after me and keep me safe, then in the next breath you're going home and leaving me alone here. You'd better make your mind up, Alistair, what you really do want. Just let me know.' Ellie turned to go, then waited and said, 'You know I'm really grateful that you tried to rescue me and all that you've done but I'm sensing that there's something wrong. I'm sure you'll tell me when you feel the time is right, but don't leave it too long, Alistair, please.' Ellie put her hand on his arm and gave it a squeeze. 'Just let me know what you want to do.'

That was a question Alistair was wrestling with and had been for many nights. He really didn't know what he really wanted. Ellie had arrived in his life and shaken him to the core. Suddenly his well ordered life was turned upside down. He used to have a huge empire and the tentacles stretched all over the world. Granted, not all of it was legitimate, but that had just added to the excitement of it. His God had been money. That had not strictly been true as the making of money had been his motivation. It was just numbers on a page, a game to be played, win some or lose some. When he looked back he could see that it was a somewhat sterile existence. There had been Max to play the game with and he said he missed his half brother, but if he was honest, he didn't miss him that much.

Ellie had strolled in and it was like looking at a mirror. They were two sides of the same coin and Alistair felt something he hadn't even felt for his parents. He would move Heaven and

Earth to keep her safe and he couldn't understand why. He could have lived his life never knowing he had a twin, but there had always been a part of him that felt that something was missing. Totally unexplainable, but there it was. Alistair pulled out his phone and began to make arrangements to go back to Italy.

Maria, Rory and Ellie went to sit by the pool and they all felt calm and peaceful just listening to the surf and watching the humming birds flit among the flowers.

'It all seems a bit quiet now everyone has gone, doesn't it,' said Rory, slouching even further down in his chair.

'I can't say I'm craving any more excitement,' said Ellie, looking at Maria, 'and I'll bet you'll be glad to get back to the Castle and get back to normal.'

'Yes, I suppose I shall,' said Maria pensively. 'I'll miss Robert though. I should be able to leave in a few days after the doctor's signed me off then I'll be back to work in a moment. I think you miss me for your hair is looking a mess.' Maria eyed up the sun-bleached mop and raised her eyebrows.

Ellie laughed. 'Yes, you're right as usual, I've missed all the wardrobe help and the beauty treatments but you must be well enough to work again before you start. Don't try and do too much too quickly.'

Maria looked at Rory and his gaze was bland. 'I think I should say something about Mr. Alistair and the night he went to save you.'

Both Rory and Ellie sat up straighter. 'What do you mean?' said Ellie.

Maria looked again at Rory and he shook his head slightly. 'I mean he tried his best and you shouldn't be too hard on him. His driving is awful but he tried to get there and we were forced off the road, so it wasn't totally his fault.'

Rory relaxed internally. If Ellie knew what had happened on the hilltop with him and Maria, Ellie would probably kill both of them. It was Alistair's choice to tell her or not and Rory decided not to muddy the waters by spilling the beans.

Maria was still rambling on and it was making matters worse as Ellie had got a look on her face of total disbelief. Rory jumped in and cut Maria off. 'I think what Maria is trying to say is that Alistair has been under a tremendous strain. You know how he dotes on you with all that "twin" thing? Well I think it hit him harder than he admitted when you disappeared. Don't get me wrong, it hit me just as hard and we were trying to be the cavalry and ride to the rescue, it just didn't go as planned.' Rory tried playing the emotional card to try and deflect Ellie from probing deeper.

Ellie looked slightly mollified and sat back in her chair. 'He does look terrible, and in a way I'm glad he's scooted back to Italy. He does have a lot on his plate as we were only supposed to be here four days max. All his businesses will be crumbling round the edges if he hasn't got his hand on the tiller. Whatever he is, he's a worker, I'll give him that.' Ellie sat back in her chair and Rory and Maria exchanged a glance and ordered some more drinks as Fortune and Honey strolled round to join them.

'So, you're here on your own now and we can really show you what our Paradise Island is really like,' said Fortune dragging two chairs to the table. 'We'll go and see the street market and I'll take you to see the Pitons, they're on the flag you know.'

Honey looked at Fortune. 'You're a mad man. Can't you see these good people only want to sit a while and enjoy the sun and the sea? They've had enough excitement for a lifetime. In fact, I'd like you all to come for a little dinner at our house tonight. Nothing special, but I'll cook you up a few little local delicacies and we'll just sit and enjoy the night. Don't bother getting dressed up as it will be very relaxed. Early to eat then you can go and get your rest. That's the best thing,' said Honey sagely.

Fortune leaned over and gave Honey a quick peck on the cheek. 'She's always right you know, I go in stormin' like a hurricane but she knows what people really want. I've got things to do right now but we'll see you all about six o'clock?' He pushed back his chair and wandered off.

'That man of mine, his heart is gold but sometimes he just doesn't see what's in front of his nose.' Honey shook her head and sighed.

'We'd love to come and have a meal with you,' said Ellie. 'I'm glad it'll be informal as I just haven't got the energy any more. I think I've totally switched off.' Rory nodded. 'Do you know any of the folklore of the island as I'd love to know some of the stories about this place?' Ellie asked Honey.

'Yes, I do actually,' said Honey. 'I'll give you a potted version of the history of the place but it gets a bit boring as it switched from the French to the English and back again lots of times. There is a strong Caribbean background as well but I have a few stories of pirates and local customs you might find interesting.'

'I'm sure we will and you can regale us with your best tonight,' said Ellie, 'we'll all look forward to it.'

'Sadly, I've got to go now as well,' said Honey, pushing back her chair, 'but see you at six o'clock.'

Maria had stayed silent throughout the conversation and she looked at Ellie. 'Did that mean me as well? I don't usually eat with you and I'm not sure if I'm invited. It's no problem if I'm not.'

Ellie reached and took Maria's hand. 'Don't be silly, of

course you're invited and I'll personally push you into the house.'

Maria looked horrified. 'No! I can't let you do that. Imagine what would happen if Mr. Alistair found out that you had been waiting on me?'

'Okay then, Rory can push you if that makes you feel better,' said Ellie.

'It's still not right I should eat with you,' said Maria.

'Maria, you've been my only friend on lots of occasions and you're only in this mess because of me. You have helped me lots of times and so what if we eat together sometimes?'

Maria withdrew her hands from Ellie's grasp and felt a pang as she thought about what secret she was keeping from her. 'Okay, just this once I eat with you,' she said, 'but you don't push me.'

'Okay,' said Ellie, laughing, 'I don't push you.'

They all met up again as the sun was sinking over the sea making the sky glow with fantastical colours imprinted on the white boats bobbing in the bay. The birds flapped lazily to their roosts and the frogs and cicadas began their nightly chorus. Dusk was short and they made their way through the gardens lit by hidden lamps that made the foliage glisten after the evening watering. Honey was waiting for them at the door and Maria left the wheelchair and hobbled on Rory's arm to a place on the balcony. The table had been set so that it jutted out onto the balcony and everyone had a magnificent view of the bay.

Ellie could only draw breath as she sat down. 'Honey, I have to ask you, do you actually see the beauty of this place as you live here all the time? I mean, when we have something beautiful we sometimes fail to see the true beauty after a few weeks. We just accept it.'

Honey sat down and poured Ellie some wine. 'I know what you mean but I do see it and I marvel at it. It doesn't stay the same so that keeps my eyes looking at it again and again. Sometimes there's a new flower, or there's a storm and the lightning strikes the sea. The surf is always different and nature is always reshaping what we have here. I mean, we don't actually have it, more that we are allowed a short time in this Paradise and it's up to us to do what we can to help it along.'

Ellie sipped her wine. 'I see what you mean. We are only custodians of the Earth for a short time and it's up to us to make it better if we can.'

'What are the two most beautiful ladies on the island talking about?' said Fortune sitting down and reaching for the wine bottle.

'Trust my husband to break the moment!' said Honey laughing. 'We were having a deep philosophical discussion about the beauties of nature.'

'Don't let me stop you, carry on,' he said expansively, waving the bottle.

'We were just discussing how beautiful this place was and how we have to keep it as it is or try and make it better. Also does the beauty become mundane after a while?' said Ellie.

'You've lost me there,' said Fortune, taking a drink and furrowing his brow.

'My husband, you are an out and out liar,' said Honey punching his arm. 'You know exactly what we mean and you've often said you feel the same.'

Fortune ruefully rubbed his arm. 'You know I only say those things to keep you happy, precious,' he said, looking sideways at Honey.

'This man knows how to wind me up good. If I thought for

one moment he really thought that I'd divorce him in an instant.' Honey drew back her tiny fist to hit the solid muscle mass of her husband's shoulder again.

'Hey, woman, you stop beating me up. I got witnesses.' Fortune looked at the others who were grinning. 'You got to help me here; this woman is a she-devil in disguise.'

As Fortune cowered away from the diminutive Honey and the laughter died down, Rory shot a quick glance at Maria and saw that the laughter hadn't reached her eyes and knew she was thinking of the words, 'she-devil'.

'Anyway, now I have subdued my man,' said Honey as she stood, 'I'll just go and finish in the kitchen. I'm sure he'll regale you with stories of my combat skills whilst I'm gone.' She planted a quick kiss on Fortune's brow as she sidled past.

'Yep, she sure can fight mean when she wants to.' Fortune smiled up at her as she slid past. He looked across at Rory. 'Have you two set a date yet?'

Rory and Ellie looked at each other and Rory answered, 'No we haven't yet, there just seems to have been so much going on.'

Fortune looked at Ellie. 'That ain't an answer. I mean has he even asked you properly. Down on one knee and all the flowers and things you ladies like?'

Ellie nodded. 'Yes he did ask me properly and yes, I did accept.' She held up her hand. 'See, I wear my engagement ring. He's right though, there doesn't seem to have been a moment when we could sit down and really plan out what we want.' She looked at Rory. 'Maybe when we get back to Italy, we'll make that priority number one.'

Maria clapped her hands. 'Yes, yes, then I can plan the dress and the make-up, and there'll be lots of bridesmaids and…'

'Whoa there!' said Ellie. 'Don't worry, Maria, I'm sure we'll plan it all down to the last detail and you'll be there every step of the way, but just let's get back to the castle and take a bit of time out first. I'm sure Rory will agree with that?' Rory nodded. 'Anyway it might be your turn next what with Robert and you two spending so much time together.' Ellie smiled archly.

Maria suddenly looked flustered. 'I don't know what you mean, Miss Ellie,' she said, suddenly finding the cutlery very interesting.

Honey came in at that point and the attention turned away from Maria who was grateful. Everyone was overwhelmed at all the Caribbean delicacies put out for them to enjoy. There were many fruits and vegetables that no-one had even seen before and the party was a hit and everyone finally relaxed with the food and wine. Honey was as good as her word and regaled them with stories of pirates and hidden treasure but when she got onto the old beliefs of the pre-Christian era and how they still lingered on today the guests felt a little uncomfortable. They had all been witness to things beyond their ken and knew first hand how powerful evil could be.

'Not to worry about that though,' said Honey, attuned to their discomfort. 'Just think of it like when the Romans came to Britain. They bought lots of their own Gods and then melded them in with the local Gods and Goddesses. No-one became upset then. One example is Easter, we all celebrate it in the Christian way but then there are Easter bunnies and eggs for the children. That's part of the pagan belief of Oestra who was a goddess of fertility. Her symbol was a hare as the Romans bought rabbits to England, so it all became mixed in. Same here, we have our own Goddess of love, same as you celebrate St. Valentine's day, it just all mixed in.'

Rory reached for the last morsel of christophine and said,

'It's just the Black Magic bits I'm not so sure about.'

'Think of it the same as when you read your horoscope or go to a séance. People will always hang onto the old beliefs even if they don't work or they are being tricked or duped into believing they will.'

'So, you don't believe all that voodoo stuff,' said Rory, probing deeper.

'No, sorry I don't,' said Honey. 'I'm a Christian and my belief is firm and I've seen all that "voodoo stuff", as you call it, but to me it's just for the tourists and people who want to believe it. It's quite a show; I can take you to one if you want?'

'No thanks,' said Rory emphatically. 'We've all had quite enough excitement for one holiday.' Everyone nodded.

The chat was desultory after that and Rory steered the subject away from the dark side quite adroitly. Ellie was pleased and Maria had breathed a sigh of relief. The 'dark side' wasn't somewhere they wanted to revisit in a hurry.

After the party had broken up, as Maria was looking very tired, and they wound their way back through the gardens, Ellie said, 'I think we ought to set a date, Rory. I mean we can't keep chasing round the world forever. We have to settle down sometime. Where that might be I've no idea at the moment but we have to think about it.'

'I agree that we can't keep getting into these sorts of scrapes all the time. I was worried sick about you and I don't want that to happen again. In fact, I've been worried sick about you lots of times; you do seem to attract trouble, Ellie.'

'I know but it's not my fault, it really isn't. I'm always the one getting shot at or kidnapped and I'm not equipped for all this James Bond type stuff. Claire is, she revels in it, but she can fly planes and shoot straight and things like that, I can't.'

Rory pondered this for a moment then said, 'It all started when you met your brother and it seems like you're going to be tied to him for the rest of your life. Well, both our lives really. I can't see a way out. I mean, you even killed your half-brother.'

'Don't!' said Ellie shuddering. 'He was a sociopath and if I hadn't killed him he would have killed me.'

Maria who was being slowly pushed back to her room by Rory piped up, 'Yes, I agree. Mr. Max was a bad man and he would have killed Miss Ellie if he had half a chance. He thought you were going to take his half of Mr. Alistair's fortune and he wanted you out of the way.'

'That doesn't change the fact that I actually killed someone, a relative, a very close relative.'

'So, all the murdering was about money?' asked Rory.

'It seems that way,' replied Ellie, 'but that doesn't really change anything. I shouldn't have done what I did.'

Rory squeezed Ellie's arm. 'Don't beat yourself up over it, as you say, he would probably have killed you if he had the chance.'

'I know that but I've still committed fratricide, I think that's the right word for killing a brother.'

Maria said, 'Yes, but he was only a half-brother so maybe that doesn't count so badly.'

Ellie laughed. 'Maria, you've bought me down to earth again. There's nothing I can do about it now and, as you say, he would have killed me by now if he could. Here am I laughing about murder, it just seems so surreal. I was a librarian and had a simple life a few months ago and now everything's stood on its head. Will we ever be "normal" again Rory?'

Rory looked at her through the half light cast by the lamps that up-lit the flowers. 'You'll always be my Ellie and you're just as "normal" as you've ever been to me.'

'I think I am home now,' said Maria quite loudly, breaking through the reverie of two people in love.

'Oh, sorry,' said Rory, blustering. 'I'll help you in.' He parked the chair outside the door.

'No need,' said Maria, smiling. 'I'm just a bit tired now but I feel better every day, I can manage quite well,' she said, as she eased herself out of the chair and went into her room.

Rory and Ellie walked back to their rooms and the moon and the stars lit their way and the cicadas sang for them.

CHAPTER TWENTY TWO

Back in London, Phil, Jack and Claire sat at one end of a large conference table. Claire's wheelchair sat snugly under the overhang. She didn't want to be in it and sat drumming her fingers on the arms.

'I can walk now, I'm not an invalid you know,' she said testily.

'Look', said Phil, 'you know why. When we got to the security check they started spouting off about Health and Safety and what would happen in case of fire. You could be evacuated quicker in your chair than trying to walk.' He added, 'at the moment,' to placate her.

Claire snorted. 'We're five floors underground in the highest security building in the nation. When is there going to be a fire?'

Jack and Phil stayed silent as they both knew it was hopeless trying to get her to follow rules if she didn't want to.

The door opened silently and in padded three men in suits, noiseless on the thick carpet. They each took their places flanking the trio and placed substantial files of paper on the polished surface before them.

A well-groomed, perfectly-manicured man in his mid fifties cleared his throat. 'It's nice to see you back again safe and sound. Your other team members aren't here but are being debriefed by the computer section as we speak. They are certainly able personnel and I may say that we are going to have to give them a higher security clearance as they can run rings round some of the staff we have here. You have certainly been through the mill recently and have come away relatively unscathed. We apologize for the wheelchair but we think you know the reasons.' He nodded in Claire's direction. 'No doubt you will be up and running soon and back to your old form of hijacking aircraft and the like.' He smiled and Claire bristled, ready to tell him the circumstances of that episode. Phil laid his hand on Claire's arm and she steadied. He continued, 'We all know the circumstances surrounding that, so no worries that there will be any reprimands or notes on files.' He patted the file marked with a big red diagonal cross that lay in front of him.

'However, you do seem to have uncovered a rather nasty trade concerning young girls.'

Jack broke in and leaned forwards. 'The girls that were rescued and put on the plane, what happened to them? They were scared stiff and had been through a lot. Where are they now?'

'Rest assured, Jack, they have all been taken good care of.'

Jack wasn't happy with this response. 'What do you mean "taken good care of"? It sounds like they've been...' He searched for a word. 'Killed.'

The fifties grey-suited man threw up his hands in horror. 'No, no, Jack, not at all. The ones that want to will be repatriated and the ones that don't are having their identities changed and are being placed with families who have the same ethnic backgrounds. They're learning English as we speak and will go back to school or college to do what they wish.'

Jack sat back with a sigh. 'That's all right then. For a moment then I thought you had just *removed* the problem.'

The fifties man sat forward. 'Maybe, Jack, you have experienced things and seen things you only thought existed in cheap novels and your worst dreams. That can cause stresses on your mind you may not be aware of. Perhaps you need to be put in touch with one of our counsellors to talk this through?'

Jack sat stunned then gathered his wits. 'I don't think so on both counts. I know perfectly well the depths to which the human race can sink to, and no I don't have any dreams about what I've seen or experienced. My psych and ego are well intact and I won't be going to see any counsellors either now or in the future. Thank you for the offer though,' he added, making a mental note to be very careful about what he said within these walls.

'That's all right then, just so that we're clear.' The fifties man smiled as he scribbled a note on the pad in front of him.

A discreet tap sounded on the door and a lady came in pushing a little trolley with coffee and biscuits. She was an oldster and had grey permed hair and that's all they could really see of her as she busied herself with the trolley.

'Thank you,' said fifties man and he indicated where she could put the refreshments. 'Is Gladys not in today, I hope she's not poorly?'

The old lady suddenly straightened up and in her hand was a gun that she pointed at the fifties man. Without wavering she pulled the trigger and all anyone could hear was a loud pop. A red flower bloomed on the fifties man's chest and he slumped back in his chair with his arms hanging limply by his sides. Jack had taken all this in and in a split second he fell off his chair under the table. Phil was a nanosecond behind him and he yanked Claire's chair hard so that she fell sideways onto the floor with him.

Above the table was silence and the other two men just watched in horror, frozen to the spot.

Below the table, all Jack could see were the two legs covered in thick beige stockings ending in sensible flat shoes. His brain registered that the legs didn't particularly look like they belonged to a woman in her sixties. They were far too muscular and as he reached out to grab them his thoughts were confirmed. His hand grasped a taut ankle and he pulled with all his strength and the leg shot forward unbalancing the gunman. Phil lunged for the other one and they heard another loud pop as another shot was fired. The gunman fell on his back and was dragged under the table. He was well trained and bought his gun arm up to fire another shot along his body towards his assailants. Suddenly he went limp and the gun fell to his side. Jack grabbed it and flung it out of reach. With the gunman out of commission they unceremoniously pulled him from under the table and he lay with his head lolling and the pretty floral apron at odds with his intent.

Jack and Phil sat each side of the gunman watching him for any movement and Claire crawled out from under the table on her hands and knees. She was holding an old-fashioned walking stick with a silver head. The head was shaped like a horse's head and was a solid piece of metal attached to the cherry wood shaft. 'Just enough weight to get a bit of a swing on it,' she said, hefting it in her hand. 'Grandma would have been pleased.'

Alarms had begun to sound and the door burst open and a tactical force came in with full body armour clutching machine pistols. Jack stood up slowly and noted the steely eyes behind the face masks and half raised his hands to show he had no weapon. Phil was helping Claire back into her chair and Jack's gaze fell onto the fifties man still slumped back at the table. The other two men were now standing and one had his fingers pressed to the fifties man's neck feeling for a pulse. He slowly shook his head as he confirmed he was dead.

Jack said, 'He's down here; we think he's still alive. I mean the guy with the gun. The gun's over there, I haven't made it safe yet.' He motioned with his hand and the leader of the tactical force edged round the table to where the erstwhile woman was lying spread-eagled.

One of the suits said, 'You three come with us now.' He led his partner and the others from the room. The suits carefully collected all the paper work up with them as they went and led the way into the corridor.

Phil was pushing Claire and said as they followed, 'What the hell went on in there?'

The suits bustled along walking quickly. One of them answered, 'We've never had a security breach at level five before. Unheard of.'

'Who was the guy who got killed, and what for?' said Phil, hurrying to keep up.

'Matthison was the section leader, as to why, I've no idea yet? We'll interrogate the gunman and learn all we can. Best advice at the moment is to forget what you've seen altogether. We'll debrief you of course but just forget it.'

Jack and Phil exchanged glances and Jack shrugged with a puzzled frown.

The suits led them into another conference room and a member of the tactical force stood outside the door on high alert. They all sat down again and Claire said, 'Pity, I was looking forward to a cup of coffee.'

Jack and Phil looked at her with surprised looks at her mundane attitude at what she had just seen and done.

She shrugged her shoulders. 'Well, it could have been me he was after but it wasn't. I'm sorry for the other guy but it comes with the job. I mean, how many times have we been shot at and blown up. I'm still here right now and I sure would like a cup of coffee. It may be my last, but I want to enjoy one right now.' Claire looked at the suits and one of them gave in and reached for the phone and ordered refreshments again. 'Just an idea,' she began, 'but you better check on the real Gladys as the poor dear may be lying somewhere trussed up.' The suit reached for the phone again. Claire smiled.

Both Jack and Phil suddenly understood what Claire had done. The power shift had been imperceptible but it was there. They had ostensibly saved both men's lives and overpowered a gunman who had got past all the security checks and fail-safes in place at the highest security building in England. This probably hadn't been just a debriefing but an assessment of them all as no doubt there had been complaints flying back and forth across the pond from the USA. There had also been questions from the French Authorities and Interpol was pulling its hair out. The last thing they wanted was to be labelled 'rogue' and be disbanded but they had to act as the circumstances dictated and sometimes, they upset people on the way.

'So back to business,' said a man who wore a label with a hologram that reflected in the light and was unreadable. He was also perfectly groomed and not a hair was out of place considering he had just been threatened and seen his boss killed. He carefully sorted the files and spread them on the table. 'Thank you for acting so promptly, Jack, and Claire's timely intervention with her walking stick saved us from further embarrassment.' The other suit nodded as if suddenly realizing he had been a hair's breadth from meeting his maker.

'We will be revising the files in the light of what has happened today and I feel safe in saying that Her Majesty's Government is quite happy for you to continue with your current lines of investigation. As Phil has noted in his reports there seems to be a strong Russian connection with the trade in the girls and you seem to have recruited a Matt.' He glanced at his file.

'Devereaux along the way. Matt has passed all our security clearances and we are happy to allow him to continue. In fact our cousins over the water are more than happy for this to continue as it is their own soil after all. We will be forwarding all the reports to them simultaneously of course.'

There was one knock on the door and the Tactical force hulk came in bearing a tray of coffee and Claire smiled. 'Oh, good, I was as dry as a ...' She lapsed into silence as Phil shook his head. She grinned again and began to be 'mother' and pour.

The suit accepted his coffee and continued, 'It appears Mr. Devereaux is currently looking into a conglomerate called Slate Corporations. They do lots of research into stem cell rejuvenation and have clinics and research facilities all over the world. We are digging into their paper trails with the help of Nigel and Robert as we speak but it appears, they are well versed in the art of computer smokescreens. We have only found one tenuous link to our Russian friend so far but that's enough to start with. It's a solid piece of evidence for you to follow.'

There was another discreet tap on the door and tactical man came in with a piece of folded paper. The suit took it and smiled. 'It appears Gladys is safe and sound, she was found in a broom cupboard. She apparently wants to interview the gunman herself and refuses to take time off.'

'Good for her,' said Claire appreciatively, 'she sounds like our kind of gal.'

'From what I know of Gladys she was one of the old war horses and was behind the Iron Curtain for a long time and was one of our best agents for many years. Salt of the earth and she's as incorruptible as they come.' The suit smiled to himself.

'Maybe we should have a quick chat with Gladys as she could give us some useful pointers,' said Claire, thinking aloud.

'Yes,' agreed Phil, 'people like that are a rare and dying breed and their hands-on knowledge is unsurpassed. Could we have some time with her?'

'I think that could be arranged. As it stands now, I'm going to say that you have two weeks to prepare for a trip to Russia. Use the time to gather any info you can and all our services will be at your disposal including Gladys. Claire,' he said, half turning towards her, 'the note on your file to say that you have been "released" from flying duties are to be expunged and your pilot's license will be reinstated.'

'I didn't know it had been revoked,' said Claire, spluttering her coffee.

'Sadly, it was, as every aircraft you seemed to come in contact with, either fixed wing or helicopter, ended up on the scrapheap. The accounts department had decided you were a bit expensive.'

Claire sat silent as she knew it was true and someone would have to pick up the tab sooner or later. She decided to change the subject. 'What about our original remit of finding the priceless books and artifacts that were stolen? We also have two other members who are probably on their way back to Italy as we speak. Ellie and Alistair are our ticket to their world which includes all the high flyers who probably dabble on the wrong side of the law. I suppose Alistair is still not welcome back in England?'

'Sadly no, it's best if he stays put for the moment. We can cover up and change many things but to radically alter the process of the law is even beyond us. He was too well connected and has upset too many people high up, so that's a no for the moment. They're safe enough in Italy and we've done a deal with the Italians and they won't bother him. He's our big link with the

Russian we're interested in. This Valentin Salnikov has been tagged for many years but we can't link him firmly to anything. There is a link again to the rare books as some of them may have made their way into his possession. Books are like stamps in that they can be easily moved about and are worth a great deal of money. Paintings are the same but a little more difficult to launder but there's still a huge trade in them. The stolen books were worth millions on the black market and your friend Ellie seems to be very knowledgeable about them. Worth having an expert on the spot, so to speak.'

Phil absently twirled his pen. 'So, just to be clear, we can have time with Gladys. We've got a fortnight to regroup and learn everything we can about the Russians. We can use Ellie and Alistair again to help gain entrance into the Russian high society as Alistair and Valentin are friends and go back a long way. Then it's off to the land of the sickle and hammer to see what we can dig up. Matt will still be in the USA digging around in Slate Corporations to find some link but may join up with us or not as the case may be?'

The suit closed his file and placed his hands on the table to stand. 'You've got it in a nutshell. Best of luck and we'll keep you up to date through all the usual channels.' Everyone except Claire stood as the suits made their way out taking all the papers with them.

Jack sat back down. 'Well, what do you make of all that then?'

Phil motioned with his eyes and hand to say their conversation was probably being monitored. 'Par for the course, I'd say. All the usual stuff, reprimands, budgetary constraints, further orders etc.'

Claire wheeled herself to where the suits had been sitting and ostensibly was looking out of the windows at the panorama of London, hazy through the bulletproof glass. She fiddled with her walking stick. 'I think I may have loosened the head of this when I cracked that guy over the head. Can you pass me some tape from over there by the pads and pencils?'

'Yeah, sure, you should have that lethal weapon stuffed and mounted,' said Phil as he fetched the tape.

When they both got to where Claire had moved to she motioned with her eyes to the polished table top and there were a perfect set of prints left by the suit as he had stood. 'It's good to know who your friends are in this game.' She peeled off some tape and fumbled it and it lay right across a thumb print.

'Idiot!' said Phil laughing and peeled off some more and went to stick it on the walking stick but Jack nudged it out of the way and the tape went over the index finger. They carried on until they had lifted thumb, index and middle finger prints and laid them carefully along the polished shaft of the walking stick.

'There, that should do it,' said Claire, and began to propel herself towards the door. It opened immediately and that confirmed their suspicions that they had been watched. They were escorted to where Nigel and Robert were still playing with large banks of computers and the guys looked up momentarily.

'Come on now, we've just got you two a two week window to play all you like with your toys, but now we've got to go and meet a lady called Gladys.'

CHAPTER TWENTY-THREE

With his twin still in St. Lucia, Alistair decided to use his time productively. Not that he was planning to do nefarious deeds but to use a few days working out his strategies for the future. He knew Karl was awaiting him with full reports but he was also aware that Ellie detested the man and Alistair knew the feeling was mutual. Alistair was beginning to like living in Italy and in some ways it was easier than England. The Castle was well appointed and the staff he had retained seemed to have adapted to their new life quite happily. His father had obviously enjoyed living there, and there were still some of his old friends like Mr. Salieri who could reminisce and fill in some of the gaps of his knowledge. He hadn't seemed to have been excluded from any of the white card invitations he was used to and the Police seem to be leaving him alone. So, on the whole, life was good and he could continue playing with his fortune to his heart's content.

There was one cloud on the horizon however. It took the shape of a very big bird and it haunted his dreams. As he tossed and turned at night he could see the gimlet eye fixed on him and he heard shadow voices whispering in the darkness. They were indistinct but they scared him. He thought they were the lost souls that had been claimed by the entity when they had made their own pacts with the Devil. He hadn't made a pact but his father had and had taken great pains to cover his tracks. It could have been fate that bought the twins back together but now Alistair had got suspicions that it had been his half brother Max who had engineered it in some way. Max was dead but as Alistair pondered his past life with his half brother he grew more certain that Max and his actions had been the crux of the matter. Ellie was as white as the driven snow in Alistair's eyes and she was a good person, she was more than that to him, she was a force for good and subtly acted as his conscience. He hadn't had one before and now he realized that he was thankful that she had been found. Alistair himself was a deeper shade of grey and his half brother had been definitely murky. With Max as his compatriot, Alistair had been led down paths he shouldn't have ventured down and he knew that now. Ellie had turned his life in a different direction and with all his heart he wished that Rory and Maria hadn't been on that hilltop with him in St. Lucia. He knew there was a price to pay, an old debt to settle, and blood was thicker than water and that debt had been passed down from father to son.

A knock sounded at the door of the study and Alistair made a show of shuffling some papers together. Karl came in at his call clutching even more papers.

'So, what's the report, Karl, any major breeches in security that need to be dammed?'

'Nothing major I can see but there's been a little trickle of info which I've found came from one of the computer guys and I have taken the liberty of firing him in your absence. I hope that meets with your approval, sir?'

Alistair was pleased that Karl had taken to calling him sir rather than boss and he seemed to taking on board the corporate image as his suit seemed to fit him better and his shoes were shined. 'So, what was the breech and where did it go?'

'Not absolutely sure as yet, but it seems to have stopped.' Karl was covering his own back as it was himself that had given the Russian the information on the dealings and mergers soon to take place.

'Good job, Karl. Keep me updated on anything else that may be significant,' said Alistair.

Karl stood. 'I'll leave you these reports to go through when you have a moment.' He placed them on the desk. He left the office and closed the door behind him. That was too easy, he thought. Alistair had absolute trust in him and believed anything he was told. The computer guy had just disappeared one day and never showed up for work. It had been easy to blame him and Karl's tracks were now well covered. A nice fat pay check was waiting for him in a Swiss bank account and was untraceable. The Russian was pleased with the information and Karl now had unlimited access to the computers that ran the empire. He also had all the passwords so he could blame anyone for anything as he saw fit. Life was good and definitely going to get better. He didn't want Alistair's empire to crash as why should he want to kill the golden goose when it had just started to lay golden eggs? He whistled softly to himself as he walked back to his security hub.

Back in America, Matt wandered from the diner and hefted his backpack more firmly onto his shoulder. He had watched Agent Tavares wolf down his cholesterol-laden breakfast and Matt was torn between watching the agent and checking out the Slate Corporation facility again. He knew that Robert and Nigel were moleing through the company accounts in London trying to find links between them and the Russian. He had browsed their website and seen the glossy blurb and all the 'before and after' photos of the rejuvenation clinic side of their enterprise. No doubt that was all legitimate but it didn't answer the question of why the high security? Or why a van load of young girls were being taken there. Matt decided that Agent Tavares could wait and he would have a go at getting into Slate Corporations facility and having a nose round. Quite how he was going to pull that off was another matter. He took a bus that was heading in the vague direction of the Science Park and decided just to look, listen and see what he could learn.

It was nearly midday when he got there after innumerable stops and he walked the last half mile. Matt realized he stuck out like a sore thumb with his backpack and scruffy clothes so he booked himself into a motel nearby and went shopping. He had decided on the interminable bus ride that the best way in was probably through the front door. He would spruce himself up and try and be a rep for some other company that dealt with Slate Corporations. Nigel and Robert could provide him with the identity he needed and all the portfolios to tuck under his arm. Today though, he would shop and put some calls into London to clear the plan. It felt strange to Matt to have his long hair cut short and to ease himself into a suit again. The shoes were particularly constraining after wearing trainers for so long. A new briefcase completed the picture and he stepped out a different man. He was a clear-eyed corporate wolf intent on catching his prey. He thought of the quote, 'clothes maketh the man' as he went back to his motel and began to prepare. Even the girl on the desk said 'Good morning sir' as he strode past whereas before she had hardly given him a second glance.

Matt spent the rest of the day on his laptop and phone and by the end he sat back satisfied he could get past the door and into the building. He had an appointment set up with the head of research at 4.45 p.m. It was intentionally that late so that the head knew he would only be there a few minutes before home time. It was Matt's plan to get there late so that the man was just leaving and he would say he would just leave everything with his secretary so that the head wasn't inconvenienced. Hopefully the secretary was in another room, or even another part of the building, so that would be Matt's chance to slip away. As plans went it wasn't the best but was all he could come up with. To break in seemed a near impossibility as there were cameras and security everywhere.

He gazed at the blue prints of the building and it appeared that the back part was of the most interest. This was devoid of windows and screened by trees and there wasn't even a service entrance. Whatever was going on was going on in there. His laptop chimed and Robert's face popped up signalling a call. Matt sat down and relaxed.

'Who are you and what have you done with Matt?' Robert laughed.

'What you see is the real me, or is it? I'm not sure at the moment.' Matt laughed with him, still not entirely comfortable with his new identity.

'Anyway, you were right,' said Robert, 'the back part of the building is the one to aim for. The office for the Head of Research is near that but as for a quick exit point your best bet is the service entrance we saw on the side by the bins. I've hacked into a company called Pharmlive. They did a bit of business with Slate a few years ago but nothing in the past two years. They've dropped off the Slate radar a while ago. I'll send you all their info but they are into stem cell research stuff. The usual nuts and bolts of the operation with the machinery and liquids used in lab processes. They don't seem to have any interests in the end product.'

'That's good,' said Matt, 'as I haven't got a clue about where stem cell research is these days. I remember that it was big a couple of years ago and was touted as a "magic bullet" for all sorts of ills but I can't say I've read much about it since.'

'That's probably because it's undergoing trials and all the companies involved are keeping a very low profile as there will be megabucks involved in the next few years.' Robert tapped a few keys on his computer. 'I'll send you some light reading about what trials have been authorized by the USA and at least you can sound a bit more knowledgeable if the question comes up.'

'Are Slate Corporations involved in any of the trials?'

'No, strangely enough they're not listed as a company progressing with trials at the moment. That's not to say they're not doing any though. Trials involving humans aren't happening at the moment except for a few very specialized ones in some of the huge teaching hospitals. It's a very costly branch of research and few venture capitalists are going to commit that sort of money to it without some concrete results.'

'So why,' Matt pondered, 'are there girls being taken there?'

'Don't know, mate,' Robert shrugged his shoulders, 'unless it's just to keep the staff happy.'

'Whatever the reason, they shouldn't be there and are being kept against their will. I'll give it a go and see what I can find out. It may be something or nothing but one sniff of something and I'll call the cavalry.'

'Oh, and another point,' said Robert, reading from some notes, 'I'll send you a list of agents who are best to avoid. We've been in a big pow wow with your security heads in Washington and they're on a dirt digging campaign. They know you're there and they know what you're trying to do and you have their full backing. There is a list of numbers I'm sending through now. They are all safe and the top three are all in your vicinity now or will be by tomorrow morning. You won't even have to talk to them so just put them in the speed dial of your phone and if shit hits fan then just punch a speed dial and they'll come running. No questions asked.'

'Whew,' exhaled Matt, 'that makes me feel a whole lot better as I wasn't sure that I wouldn't end up in a dumpster somewhere.'

'Best of luck, break a leg, or whatever they say, and enjoy the light reading I've sent. I'll be in touch tomorrow morning and we'll go over the fine details,' said Robert, signing off.

Matt slowly pushed the laptop shut and leaned back in his chair. He would go out and get a coffee and find a print shop to pull off the reams of info that Robert had sent.

In the Slate Corporation facility the Head of Research was hunched over his desk. He was scanning pages of complex figures looking for the one anomaly that would set his pulse racing. The trials were looking good but he hadn't yet had the one concrete area of proof that he needed. The trials with mice, rats and chimps had looked good and he had been funded by Slate to take his work forward to humans. It had to be clandestine as the human trials would never get past the research authorities in America. They needed the human stem cells and they were best harvested from embryos, human embryos. He had worked in South America and had to assume a new identity to get back into the USA to get access to this facility. To say he had left America the last time under a cloud was a bit of a downplaying of the actual events. He had been marched to a plane in handcuffs and the words, '...and don't even think about coming back,' still rang in his ears. He was tied to this facility and rarely saw the light of day but when his work became published and irrefutably worked then all would be forgiven. All the traits of inhibitions could be enhanced or downplayed. The masses could be controlled and the fighting forces would be legendary. The process could be eventually tailored to each individual and a race of superhumans that knew no fear would be at the beck and call of the masters. There had been promising drug trials along the same lines but they had ended up giving the recipients psychosis, but his engineering would induce a simple personality change. Gone would be the rabbits armed with guns relying on training to shoot to kill. In their place would be fighting men that wouldn't hesitate and would know no fear. That was a good analogy he thought, the human race would be the rabbits and the masters would be the wolves with their packs. It would be a simple solution to the problems inherent today. Everyone was striving to be top dog and make money so they were like rats trying to get up a ladder. In his world the king rats would be at the top and the others would be content scratching about on the floor.

He pushed back his chair and wandered out to the corridor. Facing him was a set of double doors and he swiped his key card and placed his palm on the pad and a green light signified he was clear to go in. Rows of doors were on each side and a glass panel allowed him to look in at the young girls lying on hospital beds. They were all half asleep hooked up to drips. He glanced at the notes in a niche outside each room. Patient 0246/45 was doing well after donating one of her kidneys. The next one along was nearly at the end of the second trimester of her pregnancy and in a few days they could harvest the embryo and begin some more trials. She was down to have her uterus and ovaries removed within the next month as well, all was going well. There was a constant flow of important organs to go to the labs and when the girls had nothing more to give they could be replaced. Dr Saviddes, or more rather Dr Samson as he was now, felt a lightening in his step as he was sure they were on the brink of something big, so big it would be earth-shaking.

The hours crawled for Matt as he read and re-read all the information Robert had sent and he also memorized the brochure package he had put together for lab machinery. He was a company rep and was supposed to know the products. His scientific knowledge was limited but he absorbed all the facts he could in the short space of time. The time came and he checked his watch and his phone for the numbers he had programmed in and began the half mile walk to the facility. He did wonder if he should arrive by car but decided to say that his doctor had suggested a walk every day and this was an ideal opportunity to do that.

Matt timed it to perfection and pushed open the glass door at exactly 4.55 p.m. The guard looked up and Matt gave his name for Dr Samson. He was checked off on a list and his briefcase was rifled through. Eventually a tag was pinned to his lapel and he was ushered to a lift and taken to the second floor. There was also a guard in the lift who didn't speak but stared stonily ahead during the short ride. The lift door swooshed open and there was a knot of people waiting to get in, obviously it was home time and the guard pressed the hold button and Matt was directed to the second door on the left. It seemed that everyone was escorted in and out of the building at all times and guard man had to go down with the workers. Matt smiled and nodded his thanks and turned left as he was supposed to. There were only three doors on the corridor and Matt stood to the side as workers went past and surreptitiously tried the door handle on the first one. It was locked and he had to move away and he walked down to the third door but that was also locked. There was nothing for it but to go to where he was supposed to be. He raised his hand to knock but the door opened before he could tap on the door. A small man opened it and looked him up and down. Matt decided the best thing was to steamroller the guy.

Matt stuck out his hand. 'Dr Samson, sure am glad I caught you, the traffic was bad tonight and I was held up. So sorry.' Matt pumped the man's hand and slightly pushed him back into his office. 'I'm not going to keep you, in fact I'm just going to leave you all the information you will require to have a look through. Pharmlive has come a long way in the past few years and I'm sure there'll be something there to interest you.' Matt perched his briefcase on the edge of the desk and began to pull papers out and made sure some spilled over a block of computer printouts neatly stacked on the edge of the desk. He nudged them and they all slid across the desk. 'Look at me, I sure am clumsy today, my ma always said never to hurry as you always made more work for yourself.' Matt began to gather the papers up.

Dr Samson literally threw up his hands in horror and rushed round the desk to try and save his precious work. Matt managed to shuffle some of the Doctor's papers in with his own and neatly piled up the others with the top sheet still in place. 'See there you are. I've put our brochure right where you can see it.' Matt straightened the papers again and put out his hand. 'I won't keep you any longer, Dr Samson, but I will give you my card.' He made to open his briefcase again.

'No, no, please go. I have all your company information and I'll be in touch if I need anything.' Dr Samson held onto Matt's elbow and steered him away from the desk.

'You do have a nice office here,' said Matt, gazing around. 'I sure would like to see the labs sometime. In fact I'll be back this way next month and maybe we can have a bit more time together. I'll give you a call,' said Matt as he was firmly ushered back into the corridor. The door was shut behind him and Matt smiled as he joined a few straggler workers as they went back to the elevator. He couldn't see a way of getting around the building as it was all key pads and guards but he did have some papers to go through when he got back to his motel room.

He got to the lobby and returned his badge and bade the guard farewell and walked out and immediately mingled with the walkers enjoying the evening stroll home on the sidewalk. It was a fine evening and Matt decided to get a coffee to go and stopped at a little shop where the aroma of the fresh roasted coffee was wafting out luring him in. He got his black coffee and was edging out of the door when it was held open for him. 'You could use another hand,' a female voice said. Matt turned and saw a petite blonde lady smiling at him. 'Let me help you there,' she said, and held the door, then began to walk alongside Matt up the sidewalk. 'I trust you had a good day,' she enquired brightly.

'Sure did,' said Matt, not knowing really how to respond.

'You been at Slate Corporations long?' The blonde continued to walk alongside Matt.

'No, I don't work there, I am only a lowly rep,' Matt said guardedly.

'Let me introduce myself, I'm Tasha, and I work for the speed dial company.'

Suddenly everything fell into place for Matt and he realized she was one of the agents put in place to be his back-up if things went horribly wrong. 'Look, here's a small park and a bench just waiting for us,' Matt said, and he turned onto the patch of grass and a bench under a tree. 'Let's sit a while and just watch the world go by.'

'Okay by me,' Tasha said as she perched on the edge of the bench. She was wearing a loose-fitting top and as she sat, Matt could see she had a gun in a holster on her hip. Her eyes never left the crowd and she was scanning for any trouble that could crop up. 'So, as I said, how did your day go?'

'Just the usual, I made a mess of the last visit and all my papers got mixed up with poor Dr Samson's and I just hope I sorted them out right. I'll have to go back to my motel and see if I've got everything I should have. We didn't have time to visit any of the labs but I don't think he would have let me anyway as the security is real tight in there. I mean, there aren't even any windows in the back part and any fire escapes or service doors.' Matt sipped his coffee and it tasted as good as it smelled.

Tasha leaned across to Matt. 'What do you say if I came back to your motel with you.' She nodded imperceptibly.

'Sure thing, it's not very far and maybe dinner as well?' Matt hoped the agent would play along and he raised one eyebrow.

'I'll give it some thought,' she said, and deliberately kicked his ankle as she stood.

They got back to the motel and Matt took the back route so they wouldn't have to go past the Reception desk. In the room he emptied his briefcase onto his desk and set up his laptop. 'I've got to run this past London as they want to be in on the action as well.'

Tasha pulled another chair up to the desk and almost immediately Phil's face filled the screen. 'Hi Matt,' he said, 'who's the blonde?'

Matt said, 'Meet Tasha who is one of the security force operatives keeping me company.'

'Let's just check that shall we,' said Phil. 'Tasha, what's the weather like today over there?'

'Sunny, but with a chance of meatballs,' Tasha said laughing. 'Who dreams these things up?'

'Okay, Tasha, you're good,' said Phil, smiling.

Matt leaned forward. 'I didn't know there was a password.'

'Just a precaution from our end,' said Phil. 'Anyway what did you get?'

'Maybe something, maybe nothing as that place is shut down tight, and I mean tight. I couldn't get farther than Dr Samson's office but I did get some of the paperwork lying on his desk.' Matt retrieved the papers from the pile. 'They've got a bit mixed up but I'll scan them and send them to you. It's just pages covered with test results of some sort.' Matt began to put the pages through the scanner.

'We've got some experts standing about doing nothing so they may be able to sort this out. Tasha, do you want to keep the hard copies?' Phil asked.

'Yes please, I'll get them sent to HQ as soon as possible. We're all interested now as to what goes on within the walls of Slate Corporations.'

Matt finished feeding the paper into the machine and began to look at them. 'It seems to be trials results of some kind. Some of the written notations refer to patients with numbers at the side of them. Maybe they're testing some new drug on the girls?'

'They're coming through now,' said Phil, glancing to one side. 'I'll get these sorted now. Perhaps you should stay this last night in the motel then hightail it out of there. You're welcome to come and see us in London if you want to?' Phil let the question hang there.

'Sorry, not on my agenda at the moment as I'd like to go to the west coast for a time and catch the surf. Snap decision, but that's the way I work right now.' Matt saluted Phil. 'You've got my numbers, anytime I can be of service just let me know, I've never had so much fun in years.' The screen went blank as Phil signed off.

Tasha slumped back in the chair with the papers in her hand.

'So Matt, I've got to get this information to the correct people then I think I would like dinner as I've been walking up and down that street nearly all afternoon. I'm starving and a girl's got to eat sometime.'

Let me get changed,' said Matt, 'it's been a long while since I've been trussed up in a suit.' He collected some of his clothes that were on the bed and disappeared into the bathroom.

'Better hurry up,' shouted Tasha, 'as I think we've got company. There are two men pulled up outside and are scanning the room numbers. They don't look like good guys to me.'

Matt hurriedly dressed and came out of the bathroom to find Tasha peeking round a corner of the drapes with her gun in her hand. Matt grabbed his laptop and the papers lying about and shoved them in his rucksack. 'Let's get out of here now,' he said, grabbing Tasha by the arm and propelling her to the door. 'We can talk later when we're safe. Dr Samson must have thought those papers mighty important if those guys are from Slate Corporation. He must have checked them and raised the alarm straight away. I don't know how they traced me to here as I used a different name again.' Matt opened the door a crack and peered out. The men were not in the car park any longer and Matt suspected they were on their way up to their second floor room. The door opened onto a walkway that ran the length of the building and Matt pulled Tasha after him as he ran the wrong way leading away from reception. He tried all the doors as he ran and the very last one was loose in its frame. It was obvious that the lock was worn and he gave it a good shove and they both fell into the room and shut the door to.

'My guess is that one of them is going via the reception desk and the other one is covering the fire escape round the corner,' said Tasha.

'We don't know if they're coming for me, I mean we can't be sure,' said Matt.

'Let's not take that chance shall we,' said Tasha, now all business. 'They probably don't know about me so I'll go and see what they're doing.' Tasha gave the gun to Matt. 'Use the speed dial as we could use some back-up right now.'

Matt hefted the gun and said, 'I'm going to hold you to that dinner.'

Tasha smiled and began to muss her hair up and opened a few more buttons on her blouse. She stepped outside as one of the men was approaching Matt's room. 'Hey honey you sure you got the right room?' she called, and began to walk towards him. 'My last one didn't turn up and I'm here all alone right now.' Right then her phone rang and she fished in the pocket of her jeans. 'Dang it, just look at that, he only went to the wrong motel. Hey honey,' she shouted into the phone, 'you're supposed to be at the Riviera motel not the Revere. Okay,' she added slowly, 'well you just hurry along and I'll wait for you. About ten minutes you say, I'll try and hang on that long.' Tasha turned to the man. 'Sorry, sweetheart, I'm sure we would have had some fun but I'm all booked up right now.' The man was knocking on the door of Matt's room. 'Don't waste your time there as I saw him go out not five minutes ago.' Tasha smiled and patted her hair. 'Well I'd better be getting back now, nice to have met you.' She turned away, not before she'd seen the look of disgust that played over the man's face. She sauntered back to the end room sashaying her hips. She got to the door, turned and gave the man a little wave and saw him talking on his mobile and he turned his back on her.

Tasha opened the door and practically fell into Matt's arms. Her heart was hammering and she blew out a sigh. 'Well, he didn't like working girls much.' Then added a heartfelt 'Thank goodness.'

'Let's just hope it bought us a little time,' said Matt, not wanting to release the petite figure in his arms.

Tasha pushed herself upright and began to button up her blouse and finger-comb her hair back down. 'Should be about six more minutes till the cavalry arrives.' She looked at her watch.

'Tasha,' Matt began tentatively, 'thank you for that, I mean what you just did. It saved me climbing over rooftops and things and probably getting shot at. I would like to take you out to dinner, properly, a real dinner not just some diner. That's if you would let me.' He paused. 'If there's not a significant other that would object.'

All was riding on her answer and Matt held his breath.

Tasha cocked her head a little to one side and coolly looked him in the eye. 'No, Matt, there isn't a significant other at the moment.' She smiled and Matt smiled back totally relieved. He wasn't much good at the pick-up lines and he hadn't had a significant other for a long while. As they gazed into each other's eyes a tap sounded on the door and they both tensed. Matt went to one side of the door and Tasha took up her position on the other holding the gun. She nodded and Matt opened the door slowly back onto himself to give Tasha a clear line of fire.

'Well, you took your time,' she said, and Matt peered round the door to see two men who came in and faced them both.

'Get your stuff we're out of here now,' one said. 'They have gone now but I don't think they're going to stop hunting. We're going to just walk right down to the car and get in and go. We'll go via the fire escape.' He gestured Matt to walk between them both as they made a human shield. 'The car is the black Lexus and it's open, get straight in the back and get down low.'

The two agents edged carefully out of the door and Matt got his backpack which was very light as he had only managed to pick up his laptop when they had left his room. He slung it over his shoulder and they walked out onto the balcony in Indian file and down the fire escape to a large black SUV with tinted windows.

'Get into the back and keep your heads down.'

Matt and Tasha complied without demur and the car eased into the flow of traffic and disappeared.

The driver turned round to Matt who was crouched down in the back foot well with his nose pressed up by the other agent's knees. 'Okay, you can get up now, we don't seem to have a tail, but they sure knew you.'

'I don't know how they did but I didn't look like this when I came to town. I don't think suits are lucky for me,' Matt said as he tried to extricate himself with difficulty. Tasha was openly laughing at him trying to uncurl and get on the seat.

Tasha smiled but looked a little sad. 'Doesn't look like we're going to get that dinner after all.'

The driver glanced in his mirror and shrugged. 'Best if you disappeared for a while. Have you got anywhere to go?'

'My only plan was to go west and catch some surf, but it was just a thought and right now it sounds good.'

Tasha thought about it for a minute. 'We could put you in some sort of safe house but it's only staving off the inevitable that you're going to leave one day and you can't live your life that way.'

'No,' agreed Matt. 'We'll just take a rain check on the dinner but I'll hold you to it,' he said emphatically.

The other agent, who had sat mute throughout, leaned across and tapped the driver. 'We'll drop Matt off at the airport right away and he can catch an internal to wherever he wants. Go with him and arrange it.'

Tasha suddenly looked concerned. 'But Matt hasn't got any money and no clothes or anything. We only just got out of there with his laptop.'

'We'll organize some cash for you to be waiting when you get off the plane. Don't go drawing off your bank for a while and certainly not your credit card as that'll be traced in an instant. We'll keep in touch and maybe do a bit of a name change and identity massage so you can lie low for a few months.'

Matt could see the airport on the signs and they were getting close now. 'I can't thank you guys enough. You don't have to do all that for me as I really didn't do anything.'

'You did more than you know. Sometimes a little information can go a very long way. You've flagged Slate Corporation as somewhere we'd like to have a much closer look at.'

Matt looked at Tasha a bit sadly. 'You're right, I don't really know where to go or what to do from here. I don't think I can get into the Slate facility and have a nose around, it's just too well guarded.'

'I agree, Matt, you can't go in there on your own, and you'd be dead meat before you even got up one level. We need to look for a weak link in the chain. What was the guy's name who ran the place, the man you met? Can you describe and we'll check him out thoroughly?'

'I don't think he actually ran the place but his name was Samson and he was Head of Research. Don't know much more than that but his pic wasn't on the web at all. Seems he likes to keep a low profile.'

Tasha mused, 'So you reckon this guy has something to do

with the girls who have gone missing?'

'Seems like it,' said Matt, 'half the girls were rescued from a brothel, not even an up market one at that. The other half were rescued in transit from the brothel to Slate. Lord alone knows what they were going to do with them there.'

The driver half turned. 'We think you're right, Matt, you can't go in there alone and what Tasha said about a weak link is about right. Does anyone you've been in contact with not smell quite right?'

Matt pondered awhile then said, 'The only person I can come up with is an agent like you. I won't give his name as I could be wrong but I think he's worth a closer look. 'He paused. 'You could be friends.'

The two agents looked at each other and nodded. Tasha voiced what everyone was thinking, 'You're right, can't be too sure who your friends are these days, 'adding swiftly, 'Not that we don't trust you guys, it's just that the less you know at the moment the better.'

'Sounds good to us, we just follow orders. When you want us in the loop, we're on the speed dial anyway. That's our job right now, just making sure you have back-up when the time comes. Pleasure to be of service.'

Agent Tavares leaned back and enjoyed the view.

CHAPTER TWENTY-FOUR

Phil and Claire were ensconced in a minute room being plied with tea and cakes from Gladys, while Jack lounged on the door post with a mug in his hand.

'Now don't be put off because there's snow on the roof.' She smiled. 'Just because us old ones are getting a bit doddery doesn't mean to say we don't have all the faculties up here.' She tapped her forehead.

Phil and Claire were captivated and could only nod.

'I mean I was doing "dead letter" drops when you were in primary school. There wasn't any of all this new-fangled communication then. All we had was a radio tucked up in an attic somewhere and certain when the wind was in the right direction, we could use it.' Gladys laughed.

Phil smiled. 'It was a lot different then and a lot more dangerous as there wasn't the détente there is now and you would have had to pass for a Russian all the time. Now we can stroll about as tourists.'

Gladys laughed and said, 'The food's probably still the same. Still can't stand cabbage.'

'Anyway,' Phil said, and bought the conversation back on track, 'what we really want to know is have you any thoughts or memories about the Salnikov family.'

Gladys looked at the ceiling and marshalled her thoughts. 'There's a great big file on that lot in the archives. There wasn't a good one amongst them but I think all the old order has died off now. Are there some new branches from the old tree?'

'We seem to have run into a Valentin Salnikov,' said Claire, 'he's an "A" lister and seems to be rich and holds a lot of power.'

'A pretty blond boy?'

'Yes, he's blond and excruciatingly rich, with an eye for the ladies,' said Jack sourly.

Gladys thought a bit. 'I think that must be Gregori's son. He was sent to England for his education and then went and inherited all the old man's wealth. If he's anything like his father he'll run all the drugs and nightclubs in Russia. He's never known anything different so why should he be on the side of the angels,' said Gladys sagely.

Phil put down his cup and rose. 'We can't keep you any longer but thanks for your time Gladys and we'll certainly dig out the file on them and have a look.'

'You watch that family carefully as they will stamp you out like a bug.' Gladys stood up. She rolled up her sleeve and her forearm were a mass of scars and puckered flesh. 'That's what old man Gregori Salnikov did to me to try and get information out of me. He held my arm over a simple candle and watched me burn. He smiled as he did it as well. So if you can take that Devil's spawn down, do it, with my blessing.'

Claire was aghast at the sight of all the mangled flesh and she gasped and her hand flew to her mouth. 'Oh my God, Gladys, what have you been through?'

Gladys rolled down her sleeve and smiled. 'Bastard never got the time of day out of me!'

Phil grasped her hand. 'You sure are one tough lady, Gladys, and I take my hat off to you. I'll make you my Intelligence Officer for the Russian sortie and we'll report back as soon as we know what and how we are going to do.'

'Glad to help, you'd be surprised what tea ladies know! I'll show you out as I've got top security clearance. Bet you didn't know that?'

Phil grinned at her. 'Gladys, I love you already.' They followed her out.

In St. Lucia the sun beat down and Maria was reading a book parked on a sun lounger under a palm tree. Rory and Ellie ambled past hand in hand, and settled themselves either side of her.

Ellie looked glum. 'We have to go back tomorrow you know.'

Maria carefully marked her page. 'I know, and I feel better every day. Stronger and fitter so I will be able to look after you again.' She cast a despairing eye over Ellie. 'You have let yourself go on this island, how you say a beach bum?'

Ellie laughed and punched Rory on the shoulder. 'He's the beach bum if there ever was one. Diving on the reef, having sundowners, fishing with the locals, he's got this place taped.'

Rory rubbed his shoulder. 'You can talk, having your massages every day and iced Bellini's at seven o'clock sharp every evening. But seriously though, I know it's Paradise but we have to go back to reality soon. It's woven its magic on us and the last week now seems a long time ago but Maria is still not a well girl and we can't stay here forever.'

'Why not?' said Ellie.

Rory looked at Ellie and sighed. 'Firstly, we don't live here and Fortune and Honey don't run a retirement home for escapees from the rat race. Secondly, you can't just disappear from public life now, you're supposed to be famous, albeit as Alistair's sister, and thirdly, I thought we had a job to do?'

Ellie nodded slowly. 'I suppose I can't leave Alistair to his own devices for too long as Lord alone knows what he'll get up to and he looked a shadow when he went back to Italy.'

Rory looked at Maria and by tacit agreement they admired the ocean view. Maria broke the silence. 'I was wondering if you two had even begun to set a date yet for the wedding. I will have lots to do and it could take months to plan properly. Mr. Alistair will want the wedding of the century and there will be hundreds of guests and at least four outfits for you Ellie, not least the gown.' Maria clasped her hands and gazed heavenwards.

'Whoa!' Ellie stood with her hands on her hips. 'Whoa there for just a minute. Did I get the gist of that right? This wedding, date to be set, it's going to be what Mr. Alistair wants?' Ellie gave Maria a hard stare.

Rory intervened. 'I think what Maria was saying is that she'll enjoy every last minute of the primping and preening that's going to take place, but it's a big job and needs a lot of planning. Am I right, Maria?'

'Of course, Mr Rory. You seem to understand my job is the details that make perfection. The world will be watching,' she added to no-one in particular.

Ellie sat down and watched the waves lap the shore, her mind racing. Her beach bag was at her side and her phone jangled but she was in half a mind to ignore it. The insistent tone caused all eyes to turn to her and she quickly got it out, mindful of the peace it was disturbing. It was Phil and he spent no time in pleasantries except for enquiring after Maria's health.

'We've got a lot of info on this Valentin and it seems he's the nasty big boy at the top of the Russian tree. We're going to be in London a few more days but wondered if we could all meet up in Italy and get some sort of plan together. That's if,' he added hastily, 'Alistair agrees.'

There was a pause. 'Trouble is that Alistair and Valentin are something of big buddies and I don't really want him to get wind of this and tip him off or something.'

Ellie thought for a moment. 'You are welcome to stay in my

home. I don't think I need Alistair's permission as it's half mine anyway,' she added acerbically. 'He works his socks off most of the time and besides dinners you probably wouldn't see him.'

'That's a done deal then, many thanks. We'll meet you there when you get back. By the way it may be a Russian trip is in the offing, so sort out your furry leggings.'

Ellie smiled as she put the phone away. 'Well, we're not going back to relax at the Castle. Phil and everyone are coming over when we get back,' she related. 'Looks like you'll see Robert soon.' Ellie glanced at Maria who stared fixedly at the ocean but had a blush creeping up her tan.

'The wedding may have to be postponed for a short while as we may be going to Russia soon, so we'll think of it as another pre-honeymoon honeymoon.' Ellie said this to Rory to sugar coat the pill and glanced in his direction to see if he swallowed it.

Rory's brows knit together, 'I don't like that Valentin fellow one bit.'

'We'll just be going for the usual round of parties and jet setting so don't get all the "keep my wife in purdah" routine going. I can't stay in seclusion the rest of my life.'

'It's not that, Ellie. It's just we always seem to be getting shot at or something and it gets scary and I don't really know what I'm doing or supposed to do. I'm not like Phil and that crew.'

'Tell you what,' said Ellie, brightening up with a brilliant idea, 'you can stay at home if Alistair doesn't want to come along. You seem to be his right hand man of the moment, so you can keep him company.'

'Not on your life,' said Rory emphatically. 'Where you go, I go. Forever.'